Thank you for purchasing this book from Lia Jaye!

Please sign up to periodically receive:

Free eBooks

Updates

New Releases

Bonus Chapters

& Announcements on Giveaways, Book Signings,

Or Speaking Engagements

At: liajayebooks@gmail.com

And visit our website at: liajayebooks.com

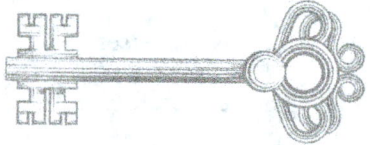

Slivers of Light

Light

~Unlocked~

LIA JAYE

Copyright © 2022 Lia Jaye
ISBN 979-8-9854382-3-9 (paperback)
ISBN 979-8-9854382-4-6 (hardback)
ISBN 979-8-9854382-5-3 (eBook)

Unless otherwise noted *

Scripture taken from the New King James Version®. Copyright © 1982 by Thomas Nelson. Used by permission. All rights reserved.

Scripture quotations are from The ESV® Bible (The Holy Bible, English Standard Version®), copyright © 2001 by Crossway, a publishing ministry of Good News Publishers. Used by permission. All rights reserved.

*The following verses are from The ESV® Bible:

Lamentations 3:22 The steadfast love of the LORD never ceases; his mercies never come to and end; they are new every morning; great is Your faithfulness.

Mark 15:45-46 And when he learned from the centurion that he was dead, he granted the corpse to Joseph. And Joseph[a] bought a linen shroud, and taking him down, wrapped him in the linen shroud and laid him in a tomb that had been cut out of the rock. And he rolled a stone against the entrance of the tomb. And they went out and preached everywhere, while the Lord worked with them and confirmed the message by accompanying signs.

All Scripture quotations, unless otherwise indicated, are taken from the Holy Bible, New International Version®, NIV®. Copyright ©1973, 1978, 1984, 2011 by Biblica, Inc.™ Used by permission of Zondervan. All rights reserved worldwide.

*The following verses are from the New International Version:

1 Corinthians 13:4-8 Love is patient, love is kind. It does not envy, it does not boast, it is not proud. It does not dishonor others, it is not self-seeking, it is not easily angered, it keeps no record of wrongs. Love does not delight in evil but rejoices with the truth. It always protects, always trusts, always hopes, always perseveres. Love never fails. But where there are prophecies, they will cease; where there are tongues, they will be stilled; where there is knowledge, it will pass away.

Colossians 1:21-23 Once you were alienated from God and were enemies in your minds because of[a] your evil behavior. But now he has reconciled you by Christ's physical body through death to present you holy in his sight, without blemish and free from accusation—if you continue in your faith, established and firm, and do not move from the hope held out in the gospel. This is the gospel that you heard and that has been proclaimed to every creature under heaven, and of which I, Paul, have become a servant.

Ephesians 3:12 In him and through faith in him we may approach God with freedom and confidence.

Dedication

This Unlocked Book Series is dedicated to my parents, George, and Gloria.

Since your passing, I have experienced the painful and ever-changing ebb and flow of grief. I hope through my books and the lessons I have learned from my loss, that I can encourage others to press on.

Thank you for being incredible parents and some of the most amazing people God ever made. Your shining example of faithful service to others has been a bright light in this world. So many people who had the privilege of meeting you, love you still. I don't blame them.

Because of your example while serving Him daily for the sake of the gospel, you have changed the world and shaped mine into what it is today. Thank you for leading me to Him. I will never forget you.

Rest in peace, knowing that one day, at the sound of the trumpet when the dead in Christ shall rise, or in Heaven, I will see you again. Save a seat for me in the garden next to Jesus on the white bench by the pink roses and white lilies. I will love you forever... because love never dies.

From the Author

Thank you for purchasing this book. I am so grateful. I pray it will bless you richly. Please see the *About the Author* page and our *Acknowledgements* page toward the back to see if your name is inside. You just might see a personal note from me. -Warmest Aloha!

Warning: Although this book may help those struggling through difficult times, it might trigger some readers. Note that it is purely fictional and is intended for entertainment purposes only. It is very suspenseful at times and touches on topics that deal with illness, accidents, loss of a child, siblings, grandparents, parents or spouse, injury, sexual abuse, mental illness, addiction, suicidal ideations, and depression, which may cause fear or flashbacks, depending on the reader's sensitivity or past experiences.

Be advised: The author is not licensed in psychiatry, nor is she a pastor. The advice contained herein is fictional and is not meant to take the place of your doctor, therapist, psychiatrist, pastor, teacher, priest, parent, coach, or licensed counselor.

Charitable Contributions

Thank you for your support. Please visit us at liajayebooks.com for details about the various charities and foundations Lia Jaye and her team will be donating a percentage of profits to each month. Follow the provided links to join our email list to receive our newsletter, learn about our potential upcoming podcasts, interviews, speaking engagements, bonus chapters, new releases, audiobook announcements, events, giveaways, or to connect with us on social media.

One of our missions here at Lia Jaye Books is to end human trafficking. But we can't do it without you. Please visit: A21.org to join the fight and volunteer, or donate whenever possible. Any amount to help the victims caught in the pain that is slavery will help!

E-mail

Join our email list at liajayebooks@gmail.com to connect and share your story with us on how our books may have touched your life. We'd love to hear from you!

Unlocked Series Book Reviews

"I read most books rather quickly but found myself wanting to take my time with this one. I was able to feel the characters' heartbreak and emotions, as well as visualize every detail in the unique locations throughout the mansion grounds. There was so much insight on every page, also humor, beauty, just enough unexpected twists to keep my nerves on edge, coming of age, and of course - romance. I can just imagine an actor like Robert Downey Jr. playing the part of Master Nathan if this becomes a movie. Hopefully it does, and I also look forward to the audiobook release. I learned so much and thoroughly enjoyed this series." -Crystal

"Wow! This book (series) is the perfect blend of romance, intrigue, and God's wisdom. I enjoy romance books and was looking for a clean approach to romance but with an interesting storyline and lessons learned. This book checked all of my boxes. The characters are well defined, and I enjoyed how she brought about the characters' strengths and their weaknesses and the forgiveness that was given. Great story with marvelous twists and turns! Pace was intriguing, layers of details in the plot, excellent, and perfect tension. I highly recommend both books! I can't wait to see what this author writes next!" -Nicole Hickey

"I absolutely loved this book, as it is very creative and unique. While reading, I grew to love all the characters and share their feelings of grief and joy. I found a lot of inspiration and wisdom throughout that I could apply to my own life. I really connected to this book series, and I highly recommend it to everyone. You'll love it." -G. Azariah

"An incredible read. The perfect blend of faith, and love in all its forms, this tale of second chances and brave choices swept me away. It also put light on a new chapter of faith for me. It was beautifully written. Rachel is simply amazing and has so much courage you can't stop reading." -Heather P.

"Both books in this series dealt with grief and loss in such a beautiful way. As a mother who lost her 21-year-old son, I found comfort in the hope and support that this story provided. I also found myself encouraged to get closer to God. What a wonderful mix of spirituality, grief, and romance that took place in the Victorian Era. And I thought the second book was better than the first!" -Maribeth

"I was immediately drawn to this story. I normally do not read much due to my busy schedule, but these books have been exciting from start to finish. Echo of the Soul's Cry Unlocked is powerful and amazing! Spiritual lessons, descriptive writing, romance, heartache, fairy tale story, suspense... it has it all! I highly recommend this book and its second book, Slivers of Light, to all ages and genders. They will not disappoint!" -L. Delgado

"The writer has spent many years empowering women of all ages to find their identity and purpose. I am one of them. This was such a lovely story. The teachings were deep in this novel, yet it was also a fun read." -G. Fisher

"I love this book series! It deserves my highest recommendation. I laughed and cried so much, I could not put it down and honestly forgot to drink water! It keeps you in suspense, is full of surprises and is truly inspiring. The incredible detail transports you to another place. It's so vivid in your mind that it's like you are watching a movie and it's a movie and I really want to be able to see at some point! This is an outstanding series. I'm totally blown away by these books. I have both happy & sad cried so much I feel like they should come with a box of tissues and a bottle of electrolytes! These books are far from stories. There is something powerful going on and I actually feel like I'm a better person from having read them. It is weird for sequels to be as great as the original, but this book did not disappoint. Life can be really hard, and these books are filled with hope. I can hardly wait for more books to be released in this series!" -Loralai Rigot

"Such a great story! I am not one for reading, but this book was so descriptive that I could close my eyes and picture the scene! It has so many amazing life lessons too. Well done." -F. Thompson

"Having always been a voracious reader, I devoured these books. Even though I was raised in the church, I've not been a regular church goer for several years. This series has reached me in ways I would not have expected. It is fun to read, amusing, and intriguing. I have been reminded of many interesting teachings that I had long forgotten. It has taught me different ways of looking at some of the things I did not care for in the churches I attended in the past. Thanks to the author, I have learned good things about God, and see Him in a different light now. Since reading this, I better understand some of the tough questions in life that all of us struggle with. I think it's time to find a new church." -L. Garcia

"I read this book (series) in three days and could not put it down. I loved it. Although I've been a Christian all my life, it helped me with my grief after losing

Wayne, my husband and best friend of forty-six years! It brought me comfort and made me feel closer to God. I would highly recommend these books as I know they will help anyone facing the loss of a loved one." -J. Hassinger

"This story is an easy way to retreat into an alluring and mysterious world filled with adventure and delight. At the same time, it captures the heart and draws the reader into an intimate awareness of the heart of God, and His deep, tender closeness to those broken in heart and spirit. I could not put this book down, and I felt myself heal from deep loss in my own life. Thank you, Lia Jaye, for this beautiful creation!" -C. Adelmann

"Life at times can get incredibly difficult. I am not much of a reader, but this book filled a need I had this year. I found myself wanting to be teleported into the world this author created. I could easily picture everything in my head since it was so visual. I can see this becoming a movie. I know we all have a lot to learn about God, but this book (series) teaches of His kindness, undying love, and sacrifice, which is a message we all need to hear." -Anonymous

"A surprisingly easy read! I don't normally go for romance novels, but this book captured my interest right from the start! I'm glad that I purchased this book at the same time as book 2 (Slivers of Light), because the ending of the first left you desiring to see how it would all end! I'm glad I didn't have to wait! Ms. Jaye has a talent for making everything so colorful. From the lush gardens, rooms, walls, and even the ceilings, to every single detail, you are left with the visual imprint that I don't often see. I thoroughly enjoyed the experience of being transported!" -Chris Perez

"As a man, I have never read a book like this. However, I found that this book really drew me in, and the things I learned while reading it applied to my own life in ways I never expected. Having known the Lord for over thirty years, I was surprised by how much I got out of these teachings. This story covers heavy topics, yet its' fun characters made me laugh out more than once. I only wish I could go visit this incredible place in person. If I could vacation there, I would in a heartbeat. Truth be told, I couldn't wait to start book two, because of how book one ends. I'm already thinking I might just read both books through a second time in case I missed something. Plus, it has been really engaging and a great way to relax after work." -Anonymous

"I got so into this entertaining, clean Christian romance, I completely forgot to drink for hours. For over twenty years now, I have read at least three romance novels every week, and sadly, they all seem the same. This story was different than anything I've ever read. It is my favorite story so far. As an avid gardener, I could not get enough of this Heavenly place. With Biblical teachings throughout, I learned a great deal and it has helped me to grow my faith. Due to how descriptive it is, I could easily imagine it all. The last few chapters of book two were my favorite part, yet I did not want this series to end. I hope this author writes more." -Gloria P.

"Author Lia Jaye certainly has a way with words. Her ability to make a story come to life plays out beautifully before your eyes with her dynamic and colorful descriptions. This story is engaging and keeps you wanting to know what comes next for the cast of characters who desire to heal and live a life wrapped in the goodness of their Father in Heaven." -M. Goodroad

"Reading a Christian romance? I was a little apprehensive, but from the very beginning I was very impressed by the skill of the writer and was intrigued by the storyline. However, as I read further into the book it was something else that deeply impressed me more. I am a retired pastor after more than fifty years of pastoral ministry. I am also a bereaved parent having experienced the death of our 36-year-old daughter, Crystal, seventeen years ago. She died from leukemia seven weeks after diagnosis. She was an incredible person who had left a great Christian legacy. For several years I also directed a ministry for bereaved parents. So, what impressed me first, was the deep relationship the writer obviously had with God that came through the main character. This alone has challenged me to deepen my own relationship with God. Secondly, the depth of understanding Biblical truth and the ability to communicate those truths in simple terms, even as those issues often deal with difficult questions that often are raised by seeking people, comes through. Pastors have a big responsibility to communicate Biblical truth that especially relates to the character of a compassionate, loving God. Any pastor could benefit just from learning ways to do that more effectively from this book. Unfortunately, multitudes of people have left the church in the past decade, most of them young people. After reading this first volume I would encourage those who have become disillusioned with the church as a result, often disillusioned with God, to give these books a read. You will find an accurate description of Biblical truths, especially your understanding of God will be illuminated in a picture too often missing in the modern-day church. My final observation regards dealing with grief. Again, the author displays an incredible understanding of grief as she recognizes that nobody handles grief the same and the journey of grief has no even pathway and no ending in this life, although, God is the "God of all comfort" who primarily uses other people to accomplish that. Anyone who has experienced the loss of a loved one would find comfort and encouragement here. One word to sum up, AWESOME!" -Don Allison, Pastor of 50 Years

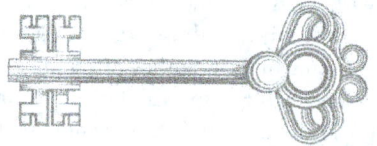

Chapter 1

Rachel tried hard to remain calm when she sensed Richard's initial shock from her asking the question out loud: "Is someone there?" It was clear he desperately wanted to reply but that he did not yet dare speak. *Perhaps he does not remember how?*

Trembling, she was too afraid to move or even blink as her wide eyes welled with fright. Although he remained just to her right side, she continued to pretend she could not see him, hear him, or feel his pain. Fully aware there was nothing she could do but await his response, she kept her gaze fixed straight ahead down the hallway and wondered what he might do.

Unable to answer her, Richard showed his frustrations as he grabbed a small table nearby. With a roar, he threw it up against the wall and stormed away, making her jump. Once he'd disappeared into a side door, she exhaled, alarmed by his instantaneous rage. Horrified by his outburst, she placed her hand on her chest, rising and falling like waves in a stormy sea.

Being around those who struggled with mood disorders was hard for Rachel due to her empathetic nature, but she found it exceedingly difficult pertaining to Richard. Worse than before, his strong emotions burned within her.

She closed her eyes tight and questioned her motives for pushing him so fast. *What was I thinking, trying to speak to him this soon? Praying aloud and reading the Bible to him is one thing, but this?* With a gulp, she swallowed back the fear that formed in her throat. *The severity of his illness must be much worse than I thought.*

Now, more discouraged than ever, weak, and nauseous, she clutched at her heart to hold back a flood of tears. When she was finally able to move, Rachel rushed down the hall and into the library to gather herself before meeting Richard's father, Master Nathan, for dinner.

Gripping the back of a chair, she cried, "Dear God, forgive me, but why won't You just heal him? After blaming himself for his family's death, being brainwashed as a child into believing he was a ghost by that horrible doctor, and wandering about this house all alone for ten years, has Richard not suffered enough? Lord, have mercy. I beg of You to do something."

She knew she'd better forget about rushing off to eat and took the time to calm herself. Following a bit of an internal struggle, with as much strength as she could find within herself despite getting so emotional, she dried her tears and headed down the stairs. Rachel knew how badly she needed food. More importantly, she had to admit, at this point, that she needed to be patient with Richard and with God.

"Oh, my! You look glorious, my dear," Master Nathan said, gasping as she entered the room. "I told you that I would beat you to dinner," he bragged, "but wow! I must say, seeing you in that dress was, ahh... Well, it was worth the wait." He looked up and to the side, wondering if his words even made any sense, and chuckled, not caring if they did or not. He then bowed as he reached out his hand, which she was happy to take. Rachel smiled politely as she curtsied.

"Are you quite well?" he asked, tilting his head, looking at her more carefully.

Worsening anxiety grew within her about sharing all that had unfolded with Richard since her arrival at Locke Mansion, having no idea how Master Nathan would react. The thought of upsetting him frightened her. *Will he be angry with me? Will he yell at me the way he did his servants? Or worse, will he fire me?*

Concerned about the outcome of any one of those possibilities, she chose to keep the news about his son to herself, for now, answering, "Yes, Nathan. I am well. Yet, I do believe I am famished."

Pleased she used his name, he kindly glanced her way before escorting her to a seat next to his at the head of the table, and said,

"I'm glad to hear that. Austin had the kitchen staff prepare a grand feast for us this evening. He told me that he wanted to treat us, knowing how hard we worked today cleaning out my family's rooms to donate their belongings to charity."

Rachel figured Austin must have been much relieved that Master Nathan was finally able to let go of his wife and daughters' things after a decade of watching his master grieve. She hoped, since Master Nathan had agreed to open up and air out their rooms, that area of the mansion would feel more like a home now than a museum.

"How delightful," Rachel whispered, attempting to keep her composure. The scent of delectable foods filled the air as several carts were wheeled in. Now parked right next to her, she could see they carried an attractive display of food on plates of silver fit for a king. Turkey, chicken, and beef, each covered in a different sauce, with several sides of vegetables, a variety of bread loaves, and more, made her mouth water.

Witnessing her excitement, Master Nathan looked pleased. Trying a bit of everything, they ate for over an hour while talking enthusiastically about their day. This time, he could not help but comment on her ability to eat more than any girl he had ever met. She shrugged, unbothered by his comment, and simply continued eating until she felt stuffed.

They laughed at one another's jokes and again enjoyed getting to know each other better. Once dinner was over, he stood and asked for her to join him in the parlor. "I would like to play something for you, my dear, if you would like."

"That would be splendid, Nathan. Thank you," she said, standing to walk with him. However, Austin stopped them unexpectedly as they began to make their way across the dining room. To her surprise, Austin took his master aside and whispered something in his ear. She stood at a distance and noticed Master Nathan pursed his lips, looking puzzled as Austin bowed and walked away.

Despite whatever news Austin had just shared, Master Nathan flashed a big smile in Rachel's direction, which made her wonder if he did so to hide something from her. Pretending everything was okay, he took her hand and slowly led her down the hallway.

3

"Is everything all right?" Rachel asked since he still looked somewhat baffled.

"What? Oh. Yes. I am sure there is nothing to worry about."

"What is it?" she inquired again, having a strong sense that something was amiss.

"I am sure it will be okay, but Austin has noticed that Richard stopped taking his medications."

"Oh? For how long now?"

He hesitated for a moment before answering, "Surely, it is just a coincidence, but it seems he stopped the day after you arrived."

"Truly?" she said, putting her hand on her belly as it sloshed unpleasantly with nerves.

"Yes. But I am sure it is nothing. And you must not worry. It is only medicine that helps him sleep during the day instead of in the night."

Rachel gripped her fingers together and asked, "How long has he been taking it?"

"To be perfectly honest with you, the doctor who convinced him he was a ghost prescribed it to him. We have had other doctors provide more of it for him each month for years now."

"What? That horrible doctor who muddled his thinking so terribly? I am sorry, but I do not understand. Has Richard ever gone without it before?" Rachel asked, greatly concerned for his well-being.

Placing one finger on his chin, deep in thought, Master Nathan answered, "You have a point. I wonder if I should just let him go without it for a while to see how he does...."

"Well, if he refuses to take it, it looks like we have no other choice." Rachel paused but then stated with determination, "I will pray that he will do better without it."

Upon entering the parlor, they sat down on the sofa, and Master Nathan surprised Rachel when he asked, "Would you be so kind as to pray right now? I fear I still do not even know what to say, and this seems too pressing to wait."

"Of course," she said kindly, glad he had asked. Taking his hand, she got down on her knees, closed her eyes, and bowed her head.

"Thank you," he whispered.

Already focused, Rachel prayed with boldness, "Heavenly Father, You know the situation we are facing and have heard Nathan's cries for his son. I know You want Richard to be well, for You are a charitable God. If this medicine has hampered his healing or has been making him worse, please make that clear. I ask that, as this medicine leaves his body, he will start to feel better, not worse, and perhaps even attempt to communicate with us again. I pray that he will someday, somehow find joy and, most importantly, that he will find a new desire to live—truly live, not just amongst the shadows of this house but also *with us*."

When Master Nathan squirmed in his seat, Rachel knew full well he doubted Richard would ever be able to live normally or even speak again, but his reaction did not stop her. "I ask that You free him from the bondage of oppression and condemnation. You are the great physician and have given Your followers the authority to bind and loose. So, in Jesus' name, I bind the spirits of confusion and frustration and claim victory over Richard's body, mind, and soul. If he needs new medicine, Godly counseling, or perhaps a different doctor, so be it. In the meantime, according to Matthew 18:18, I loose blessings upon him."

Raising her voice, she said, "I declare and decree on his behalf peace, restoration, a sound mind, happiness, and love. I claim Your protection over him and praise You in advance for shining Your light into Richard's heart. And Lord, above all things, You desire for us to live in surrender, trusting in You. So, I ask that You help us trust You in this situation, abandoned to Your will without fear. In Jesus' mighty name, amen."

"Amen," Master Nathan said. He shook his head and gave her a look of approval.

Unclear about his expression, she questioned him, "Yes?"

"Oh. It's nothing."

"No. What is it?"

He continued to smile and shrugged his shoulders. "I just love that you pray with such intensity and optimism. That is all."

"Well, you are supposed to pray with faith, remember, silly? In fact, God does not like for us to doubt Him. He forgives us when we do, but it still displeases Him."

"Displeases Him? How so?"

"Remember I mentioned in the chapel how one of my favorite stories my father used to read to me from the gospels talks about that? I can quote it word for word."

Master Nathan nodded and replied, "By all means. Be my guest."

Rachel grinned. "Matthew 8:23-27: 'Now when He [Jesus] got into a boat, His disciples followed Him. And suddenly a great tempest arose on the sea, so that the boat was covered with the waves. But He was asleep. Then His disciples came to Him and awoke Him, saying, "Lord, save us! We are perishing!" But He said to them, "Why are you fearful, O you of little faith?" Then He arose and rebuked the winds and the sea, and there was a great calm. So the men marveled, saying, "Who can this be, that even the winds and the sea obey Him?"'"

She paused. "Therefore," she said boldly, and began to pray once again with even more passion, "God, we can see from this verse that You do not like us to doubt your abilities, and You want us to have faith. So, I ask that You forgive our fear and doubt and that You calm the storm within us, within this house, all around us, and within Richard. In Jesus' mighty name, amen."

"Wow," Master Nathan said softly.

"What?"

"Nothing. It is just that if I were God, I would do whatever you said because I'd be too afraid of you not to!"

Her demeanor lightened. "Oh, stop," she said as she slapped his arm and got up to sit beside him. "There you go again, making jokes during a weighty moment."

"You are right. I am sorry. I will try to be more serious from now on," he commented, raising his eyebrows comically as he said the word "serious" before he stood. He then stepped back to look at her lovingly once again. "Mmm, mmm, mmm! You truly are a vision, Rachel."

She blushed and reminded him, "You were going to play something for me?"

Snapping out of it, he chuckled. "Oh! Oh, yes. Your beauty made me completely forget what I was doing. Do pardon me," he said with a wink as he picked up his violin to tune it.

"I wrote this song for Gloria to play for her when she was sick. I was hoping it would help her heal. It obviously did not work. I have not played it since, but I think it is quite pleasant and hope you like it. If not, just tell me, and I shall never play it again."

"I am sure I will love it. Please." Rachel kindly gestured for him to begin, thankful he felt safe enough with her to share a song that meant so much.

He stood by the crackling fire, closed his eyes, and waited a moment. Once he began, she was mesmerized from the very first note. She sat with her hands folded in her lap, staring at him wide-eyed, listening intently. The song was beautiful and alluring to her soul, like nothing she had ever heard. As a tear rolled down his cheek, her heart sank. She assumed he must have been remembering the last time he'd played the song for his wife while she was fighting the illness that ultimately took her life.

Rachel pondered what it must have been like for him to play his violin at his dying wife's bedside with hopes she would recover. She shut her eyes, unable to imagine how difficult it must feel to lose the love of your life.

A tear then ran down her own cheek as she allowed herself to feel his pain. She realized she had never loved a song more. Holding back her emotions over Richard and their unique situation, she did her best to listen to the music instead of her heart's cry. She could not believe how skillfully Master Nathan could play his instrument, especially with a song he had not performed in so long. She shivered when she felt the glory of God fill the room and was once again astonished by it.

The violin was one of her favorite instruments, and she had never witnessed anyone more accomplished. After a long while, he ended on a rich and smooth note. Lowering his violin and bow, he opened his eyes and looked up to see Rachel's reaction.

Noticing her tears, he quickly placed his violin down and fell to his knees beside her. "Oh, Rachel, how I hate to see you cry. I am so sorry. Did you not like it? Tell me," he said, looking at her intently. "I have never seen so many thoughts behind a pair of eyes."

Once she'd gathered herself enough to speak, she rambled on with a passionate response, wiping at her tears, "Did I not like it? Why, no. I absolutely loved it. I am only crying because of how beautiful it was. And because, well, because of how wonderful I think you are. While listening, I could picture you playing beside your wife as she lay sick in her bed, and it was so touching. I sensed that you were such a good husband to her, and to be honest with you, I was concerned that playing it must have brought back painful memories of her death. I simply do not want to see you sad anymore. That is all. Other than that, it was the most beautiful song I have ever heard. Truly, Nathan, I shall never forget it."

He chuckled at her long-winded response, relieved to hear she liked it so much. Overwhelmed by her kind words, he laid his forehead down on her knees to reflect and to recover from the intensity in the room, the emotions thicker than he would have liked.

Rachel kissed the back of his head and slowly laid her cheek against the spot she had just kissed. They sat perfectly still in reflection, absorbing the room's silence, letting it fill their minds with lingering notes of songs played and sung by loved ones past. Each precious note seemed to represent memories they both held so dear.

After a while, Master Nathan lifted his head and asked, "Will you play something for me now? And sing, please? By all means, you must sing."

She agreed with a smile, knowing the power music held to promote healing. She rose and fixed her dress as she sat at the piano bench. Before playing, she asked the Lord which song she should share and instantly thought of the perfect one.

"These lyrics were written by a man named Horatio Spafford, who also went through tremendous loss about fifteen years ago. He was a wealthy lawyer who had bought property in America, in the city of Chicago. Unfortunately, he lost everything in the Great Chicago Fire. Prior to the fire, he'd lost his only son to pneumonia at the tender age of four. Then, not long after, his wife and four daughters were in a shipwreck. You see, he had business to attend to and had sent them ahead on a voyage without him. His wife survived and sent him a telegram that simply said, 'Saved. Alone. What should I do?' Sadly, all his daughters drowned."

'Oh, how dreadful," Master Nathan said with a horrified expression.

"Agreed. And to say he was devastated would be an understatement. Days later, while journeying on a vessel to meet his grieving wife, he penned this song as he sailed over the exact location where his daughters' ship had gone down. This hymn, composed by Philip Bliss, has spread throughout many churches over the last few years. I hope it helps you to see that, in your grief, dear Nathan, you are not alone."

Rachel began to play and sing as skillfully as before. She took her time connecting to the piano keys with a soft touch, sounding as lovely as ever.

Pondering the words to the song, "It Is Well with My Soul," Master Nathan began to shake, as she finished. Appearing overwhelmed, he sat staring straight ahead with large, glassy eyes. He took a deep breath and blew it out slowly. "Oh, that was simply brilliant. Thank you," he told her quietly, looking at nothing at all, appearing lost, wounded, and exhausted.

"Nathan?" Rachel whispered, now at his side.

As if in a fog, he replied in a monotone voice, "Yes?"

"You look so tired. Shall we retire for the evening?"

"Oh, nonsense." He blinked a few times rapidly and jumped up. "Absolutely not! I wish very much to once again dance with you in that dress of yours, my dear. Now, come," he said, holding out his arm to escort her.

Although quite tired herself, Rachel did not want to disappoint him, so with a slight grin she rose to accompany him to the ballroom and said, "Perhaps just one dance."

"The night is still young, the storm has passed, and the moon is full. Tonight, I want you to see the ballroom without the lights. By the light of the moon, it is truly glorious."

She was pleased to see all traces of his sadness had vanished, and that he genuinely seemed excited once again.

"Come, my darling."

When Rachel realized he had not yet called her "my darling" and that he was acting unusually serious, she responded, "It would be my honor."

Chapter 2

Entering the ballroom, Rachel stopped in her tracks, awestruck by the moonlight flooding the room.

Master Nathan lit only one candle by the entrance and held her arm gently to guide her down the stairs. After starting the phonograph, he blew it out, took Rachel's hand, and politely led her to the ballroom's center. Just as before, he bowed low, stood tall, and raised her hand into waltz position, placing her other on his shoulder. Holding her firmly, he smiled down at her and listened to the music's timing.

While nervously waiting for him to lead, the moon, shining through the tall windows, struck the chandeliers' crystals, flashing thousands of miniature lights around the dance floor and across his face. Like live, excited blue fireflies, these tiny reflections began fluttering about the entire ballroom in a circle, accentuating several of the massive, arched glass windows and doors. Reaching the thirty-foot-high ceiling and its life-like paintings, each framed with gold trim that resembled vines and leaves, these lights seemed to be enticing her.

Rachel looked far up overhead and let out an astonished laugh, which pleased Master Nathan immensely. Never having been one to believe in magic, she knew that if anything could ever be magical, this room, in this light, indeed was. Still staring at her surroundings, she found it difficult to accept that this was her life now. She could not help but admire Master Nathan, looking handsome, fulfilled, and carefree, yet the instant the melody started, her mind floated elsewhere.

As they began covering the entire moonlit room, although she was thrilled to be dancing in such a gorgeous place, for some reason, she caught herself thinking of Richard. Trying to hide her thoughts, which Master Nathan always seemed to be able to read, she was glad the ballroom lights were off, and darkness hid her sentiment.

After a delightful spin on the floor with Master Nathan, Austin appeared on the balcony unexpectedly and held up a candle to get his master's attention, quickly making his way down the steps. Bowing, he spoke with hesitation. "Excuse me. I beg your pardon, master, but there is a rider at the door who says he has an urgent message for you. I am afraid, sir, that he has news from town. Something about one of your factories, I believe. Shall I tell him to wait, or would you like to see him now?"

"I will be right there," Master Nathan replied as he sighed in frustration before letting Rachel go. "I shall return promptly," he said, then bowed and winked at her. However, she noticed a flash of worry cross his face when he turned away. Then, he paused and turned back to take another look at her as if the sight of her brought him tremendous peace.

She stepped toward him and asked, "Shall I come with you?"

"No, no. There is no need. I am sure it is nothing for you to worry about, my dear. You wait here. I'll be back in a moment."

He walked briskly to restart the music, "You are not to go anywhere. I want one more dance with you, young lady. You can practice all by yourself while I am gone if you would like, but I will be right back." Dashing up the staircase, he disappeared through the double doors.

She smirked and shook her head as she watched him leave, and thought to herself, *That is not a bad idea. Perhaps I should practice.*

Near the center of the room, where it was rather dark, Rachel stood tall and held up her arms, imagining Master Nathan within them. Just like he had shown her, she listened to the music's beat and closed her eyes. When she opened them, she gasped and froze. Richard had appeared out of nowhere and was now standing directly in front of her.

Not knowing what to do, she swallowed back the scream building in her throat. Her breathing became heavy as her heart rate accelerated, yet she remained still. Even though he had frightened her terribly, she knew full well not to look at him and dared not move. Making every attempt to act as though she had not noticed him, Rachel began to tremble, uncertain of his intentions.

Thankfully, before she knew it, Richard stepped into a waltz position, bringing his chest almost up against hers. A shiver ran through her body when he took one of her hands and lifted it very carefully as if he did not want to frighten her further. He then gently placed his other arm around her, his hand resting on the middle of her back, and pulled her close.

Feeling the warmth of his touch, she blinked once slowly, enjoying his nearness. While still pretending to be alone, she did not move and allowed him to do precisely as he wished.

Rachel kept her gaze locked straight ahead, as though in a trance. Due to Richard's height, she found herself staring directly at his strong neck and jaw muscles, which she adored. Although her nerves were unsettled and she grew faint, his embrace calmed her, and she began to relax.

Afraid to enrage him as she had done earlier, she gathered the courage to place her hand on his shoulder and pretended he was an imaginary partner, hoping that was what he wanted. Inhaling deeply to steady her breathing, she noticed that now, instead of smelling like Christmas, his scent was clean and fresh.

She took a moment to study his appearance. There he stood in the most sophisticated suit she had ever seen, looking like a prince, just as he did in her dreams of him. Yet this time, he had his hair tied back out of his face. She wondered if he had gotten all dressed up specifically for her and blushed, flattered by the possibility.

The timing of the music was perfect, and Richard began to lead her, just like his father had only moments before. Rachel could tell right away that he was an excellent and commanding dancer as he moved in a precise rhythm. She wondered if he had spent time practicing by himself in this very room all these years, waiting *for her.*

Amazed by what was happening, she tried hard not to glance his way. But before she could stop herself, Rachel looked up, and for the first time, they made direct eye contact. She found herself staring into his spirited eyes, filled with more passion than she had ever witnessed in any man. She attempted to look away but could not. His glance pierced right inside of her, making her heart pound out of control.

Unsure of how she had not frightened him, she figured the lack of light in the room was responsible for him not turning away when their eyes met. She was glad that, instead, he appeared to quite enjoy it. As they went in and out of the moon's light, he studied her face. His gaze, filled with fierce desire, made Rachel grow dizzy with emotion, causing her lungs to swell and shrink rapidly to the beat of the music.

Knowing that it had been over ten years since Richard experienced the privilege of looking another human being directly in the eye, she was honored that out of all the people in his world, he had chosen to see her. Really see her.

Together, they danced with ease, like a match made in Heaven, as they moved gracefully about the floor. Again, she attempted to avert her gaze; however, she could not help but nervously smile up at him. Thankful to see that he seemed to enjoy her smile as well, Rachel exhaled, relieved.

She was surprised that, as they danced, he seemed perfectly normal to her in every way. He twirled her around the dance floor, appearing confident. For Rachel, that would have been enough, but then, to her delight, he flashed her a soft smile. She could not believe it, Richard was smiling! He looked like a royal prince who was no longer sad nor angry; instead, he seemed almost joyful. And not only that, what shocked her the most was that he appeared deeply in love *with her.*

Unable to help herself, she imagined what it would be like to marry him. She wanted him, body, heart, and soul, as he held her in his arms and led her across the room. His handsome face, romantic eyes, smooth skin, and strong stature were one thing, but his full lips seemed to be taunting her. She knew better than to ever attempt to kiss him, but she closed her eyes and imagined it, wanting more.

How can someone I'm holding so closely be so far out of reach? Father, I am aware that the only thing I can do is trust You and surrender to You fully concerning Richard. I know You want Your children to enjoy the journey with You, not just the outcome. But I want more than anything to talk openly with Richard, so I will wait patiently until that day. In the meantime, I will count my blessings and dance on with thanksgiving in my heart, knowing it is a miracle to be dancing with him at all. I ask that You give me the wisdom to proceed in silence and the strength to endure as we draw closer to one another while still worlds apart. In Jesus' name.

Surrendering to his touch, Rachel let go of her fears and let him take her to that place where nothing else mattered while they floated along. In an instant, as she let her imagination run wild, she pictured Richard and her dancing together in a room full of wedding guests and a full orchestra playing music loudly. For the full duration of the song, her heart ached for what she knew only dreams were made of. *Yet still.*

Wishing they could stay in this moment forever, sadly, her thoughts were interrupted. With a sudden thud that gave her a jolt, both doors swung open at the top of the stairway. Master Nathan had returned. Rachel let go of Richard and attempted to turn and face his father, the action, throwing her off-balance, made her spin. When Master Nathan began to run down the stairs, Richard vanished as quickly as he appeared.

Still whirling, she gasped and stopped without falling as the bottom of her dress continued to wrap around her ankles for a moment before settling back into place.

"Be careful there, my dear!" Master Nathan called to her when he approached the phonograph to start it over again from the beginning.

Glad that he had not seen Richard, Rachel was out of breath and did not know what to say to explain herself.

"Are you all right, darling?" he asked, laughing at her panting sounds. "You were practicing extra hard, I see."

Through her labored breathing, she replied, "Oh. Oh, yes," trying to regain her composure. She contemplated telling Master Nathan about Richard but was afraid he might still be in the room. Instead, she changed the subject. "What did the messenger have to say?"

Not wanting to answer, Master Nathan ignored her question and resumed dancing with her like he had never left.

Rachel was happy to join him, trying to keep his focus off the room. She then noticed an outline of Richard's tall frame in the darkest corner of the ballroom as the blue firefly-like moonbeams exposed him. He stood in the distance, watching them closely from the shadows like a phantom. She said nothing and made sure only to peek in his direction over Master Nathan's shoulder whenever possible, glad he seemed entirely focused on her and that he did not even notice his son standing there.

Finally, Master Nathan responded to her question, sounding almost amazed by the news he had to share, "Well, it is extraordinary, really. Do you remember how you were telling me tonight about that man who lost everything in a fire?"

"Yes. Why?" Rachel asked as they continued to dance.

"Well, apparently, today, there was a fire at one of my factories," he stated casually.

"What?" Rachel stopped moving immediately. "That's terrible! How bad was it?" she inquired, sounding panicked.

He ignored her response and pulled her close to start dancing again. It appeared he had no intention of stopping *to talk*, so she went along with it. "I do not know, really," he continued. "They sent a messenger straight away, apparently, as soon as the fire started. He informed me that they are doing everything they can and are sending another messenger in the morning with more details. It is unclear what time he will arrive, but I should find out more tomorrow. I am sure there is nothing to worry about. Besides, we have insurance for those sorts of things now. So, stop worrying about my boring factory, and let's enjoy our dance."

With a smile, he led her around the room once more.

Although it was evident to Rachel that he was still stressed, she figured he very much needed to enjoy this moment with her in order to hide his concerns. So, she held her tongue and stepped up her dancing, knowing Richard was still watching.

"There you go! That is splendid, my dear," Master Nathan exclaimed as she focused on dancing her absolute best. Then, out of the corner of her eye, she noticed Richard turn away and abruptly leave. She thought he appeared rather upset, almost as though he was hoping for another turn with her, and she felt terrible about disappointing him, yet smiled to cover her remorse. Because his father had returned, she knew it was no longer possible for them to dance and sensed Richard's frustrations floating around the room like palpable waves.

Once he'd left the room, again she thought about everything that happened between her and Richard thus far and wanted to tell Master Nathan, but again, she hesitated. Since he had just gotten such bad news about one of his factories, she decided she had better wait until later, not wanting to alarm him.

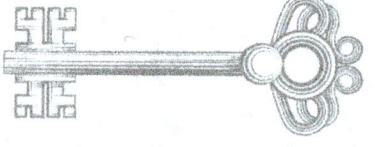

Chapter 3

Hearing the music stop, they bowed politely toward one another. Master Nathan happily led Rachel by the hand outside onto the terrace to gaze up at the moon. Standing with their shoulders merely inches apart, she grew more worried about what might happen if she remained silent and did not tell him every detail about Richard. She opened her mouth and started to confess all, but he spoke first.

"Rachel, I have a question for you. Do you promise to be honest with me?" Master Nathan asked, looking quite frazzled.

"Of course. What is it?"

He fidgeted slightly, acting nervous. "If I need to go up north tomorrow, I would like for you to come with me. Sadly, I worry about Richard. Since he just started to come into your room and listen to you read, I am afraid of what he might do if both of us were to leave right now. Disrupting him never goes well. Would you mind staying here without me, even if it is for several weeks? Be honest. Would you feel safe here alone while I am away?"

Picking up on the fear in his voice, she wanted to calm him but was hesitant.

Since she did not reply right away, he spoke louder and faster as he continued, sounding even more distressed, "The last thing I want to do is to leave you, especially if you will be afraid. I understand you hardly know anyone here, and Richard is so unpredictable." He paused a moment, then gently put both hands on her shoulders, looked into her eyes, and asked, "Rachel, will you be afraid of Richard?"

Wanting to give him some reassurance, Rachel said the first thing that popped into her head, "Of course not. I will be fine."

"'Fine?' There is that word again. Are you trying to be vague on purpose, or are you certain you will be alright?" He took a step back and began to rub the back of his neck with one hand, his other on his hip, making him look overly concerned.

"I promise. I am not afraid. And besides, Austin will be here to watch over me, right?"

"Yes. That is true," Master Nathan said, pacing a bit in frustration. "If only Richard hadn't stopped taking his medication. Why now, of all times, would he do that? We have no way of knowing how it will affect him, and to be perfectly honest, it troubles me a great deal." He sighed and stood still to look up at the moon as if to ask God what He thought.

"Nathan, we must have faith in this situation. I have been praying for Richard and have been seeking the Lord's peace for all of us. And, whether you believe he can get well or not, maybe there is a reason the Lord moved him to stop taking this specific medicine. Perhaps because it was doing him more harm than good? Or perhaps he needs something new or different: herbs, teas, oils, fresh air, or sunlight? Maybe he simply needs change, love, human touch, Godly council, or all those things combined. Maybe none of them. We cannot know for sure. All we know is, God knows, and we must ask for His wisdom concerning Richard. He will help us."

"You think so?" Master Nathan asked, turning to face her.

"Yes. I do. And we must remember that God is so much bigger than our problems. He can help us to discover what is best. We are just called to pray, listen, obey as best we can, and trust Him to work all things out in His way and in His timing, not our own. For His ways are not our ways. So, I will even trust Him with this fire at your factory."

"I wish I had your confidence. I am trying to remember what you said about God not being the one who causes tragedy in our lives as I ponder it all."

"I am sure God did not cause the fire, but He can turn this situation around and use any tragedy in time for our good. Possibly, if you travel to town to be a light and an exceptional leader to the community or to your employees, things might improve somehow? My father always said that good and decent people make good employers. So, who knows? Perhaps there is something that needs to change there—or here, for that matter—while you are away." Rachel paused then nervously mentioned, "As a matter of fact, I would like your permission to make some changes here when you are gone."

Squinting, he asked, "By 'changes,' what do you mean exactly?"

Rachel answered with animated movements, "Well, for one, I would like to open every curtain in the entire mansion to let in more light, if possible. Then, each day, when the weather is just right, I would like to open all the windows to allow fresh air in. I want to get rid of every speck of dust, organize each room, and bring in fresh flowers from the gardens."

He laughed at her excitement and pleasantly surprised her with his reply, "Well, actually, that sounds splendid. We used to do that very thing each spring, but because I've not allowed the servants to be seen since my family's death, I suppose it has been rather hard for them to do such a big task with me around. To tell you the truth, I have more than likely made it quite impossible for them to do their jobs at all."

"You think?" she said jokingly. "Which brings me to the other things I would like to do—with your permission, of course."

With raised eyebrows, he lowered his chin to look up at her. "You know, for a missionary girl, you are quite high maintenance and hard to please." He smirked, content with his remark.

She smiled. "I'm serious."

"Okay. What is it?" Master Nathan asked in a deep tone, making an exaggerated, serious face.

Rachel ignored his playful attitude and answered, "Well, I would like your permission to meet with each of your house servants."

"I beg your pardon. Whatever for?" Master Nathan pretended not to know the answer.

She knew he was aware of her quest and answered him anyway. "It is time to bring some joy back into this house, and we are going to need a great deal of help to get it back into tiptop shape. Once you return, I want you to try to get to know your staff as well. They are people too, you know, who deserve to be seen and heard just as we do. Do you not agree? And you cannot be such a snob all your life nor carry on isolating yourself. Besides, I think it would be just plain fun."

"Okay. Okay," he agreed, rolling his eyes at her.

She grinned, delighted. "You mean I have your permission?"

"Yes. Fine."

"Fine? 'There is that word again.' I want to have your permission for all of it. Do I?"

Due to her persistence, he chuckled. "All right. Yes. Yes, you do. You have my permission for all of it."

Elated, Rachel forgot her manners once again and threw her arms around his neck.

"Well, if I had known you would get *that* excited about it, I would have already suggested it by now," he joked.

"Oh, Nathan, thank you! It will make such a difference," Rachel said. "I promise you will not regret it."

Master Nathan did not reply as they held one another for a minute, until he slowly moved her away from himself to get a good look at her and asked, "Shall we have one last dance before we retire, my dear?"

She giggled nervously at his request. "But there is no music."

"Yes, there is! Listen, and you can hear the beat," he winked, "of my heart." He raised an eyebrow at her, daring her to comment. "Ready?" Then he waited for a second as if listening for his heartbeat. "Yes. There it is." Smiling, he instantly began twirling Rachel around on the terrace, humming loudly as they danced.

Laughing and having the time of her life, again, Rachel could not believe she was getting paid to live here in this magnificent place with such tremendous people.

"Nathan?"

He continued to hum a particularly upbeat tune as he danced with her. "Hum, mmm, mmm… Yes?"

"Are you real?" she asked.

"Hum, mmm, mmm... Yes." He continued to hum and dance, almost ignoring her at the same time.

"Is this spectacular terrace, this bright moon, your glorious gardens, and us dancing here together now... Is this all real, or am I dreaming?"

"Hum, mmm, mmm... It's real," he stated casually, resuming his humming.

Beaming with adoration for him, Rachel could not help but grin as they danced by the moonlight. Real fireflies flashed their lights randomly around them, and life enveloped the night sky. Crickets chimed in as if they, too, wanted to join in the fun.

After they enjoyed another romantic dance, Master Nathan bowed. "Thank you, my dear, for the pleasure of your company. It has been a most glorious evening," he said, kissing her hand with a satisfied grin.

"You are most welcome, Nathan." Rachel curtsied.

An expression of pure gratitude flashed across his face, and without warning, just as he had done outside the chapel, he picked her up by her waist, held her over his head, and swung her around in circles. Letting her down very slowly, he reached for her hands and kissed them both, one at a time. "Rachel, I have decided on something of vital importance."

"You have?"

"I have decided if I must leave," he paused, "to wait to tell you what it is until I return. And I promise to return as soon as I can, bringing with me a special gift for you. But it is a surprise," he stated, looking rather serious.

"Oh, how delightful. I'm learning to *love* your surprises."

As they walked back toward the house, Master Nathan swung her hand back and forth playfully and asked, "Did you notice anything different about me this evening?"

She looked at him confidently and said, "Yes, actually, I did."

"What?" he said with a squint.

"I noticed that you did not have any alcohol to drink, and to be honest, I am very proud of you for it."

"Why, thank you, my dear."

Unclear how to act, Rachel nodded. "No. *Thank you*. I appreciate it a great deal. I just didn't know if I should say anything or not."

"Well, I am glad you appreciate it, and you are welcome. However, not to be rude, I did not do it for you. I am aware that I have been drinking excessively for far too long. Clearly, drinking so much all these years has not helped me in the ways I thought it would, so I want to try to go without it. I need to do this for myself, but since it will not be easy, I would appreciate you keeping me in your prayers."

"I am thankful that you realize for yourself the importance of drinking less. So, of course, yes. I will pray for you. And I will ask God to answer your prayers as well."

"He did," Master Nathan said with a grin. "He answered my prayers when he sent me you, remember?"

Acting embarrassed, Rachel flashed a shy smile and looked down.

"What? You have nothing to say, Miss Talkative?"

She shook her head. "No. I-I just did not know if you had finished, and I did not want to interrupt you."

"It is okay for you to interrupt me… as long as you are agreeing with me, that is," he said with his usual wit.

They walked in silence as they entered the house, admiring one another before saying goodnight at the bottom of the grand staircase. After she gently kissed him on the cheek, Master Nathan firmly kissed her forehead and took her hand again, not wanting her to leave his side.

Feeling his strong desire, Rachel slowly backed up a few steps, holding onto the railing to keep herself steady before letting him go. She turned to retire to her room, so deep in thought that she did not even notice him watching her walk to the top of the stairs in her stunning dress, his eyes filled with love.

Whereas Austin, waiting to greet her at the top of the steps with a candle, quickly noticed Master Nathan's expression.

Since Rachel was oblivious, she thanked Austin, took the candle, and walked toward her room in a daze. She wondered how she would manage at Locke Mansion without Master Nathan if he were to leave and pondered what Richard might do if left alone with her.

Rachel was so distracted she did not even turn around to wave goodnight. In her mind, she was already walking toward an uncertain night with Richard. With her heart once again torn in two, a wave of regret washed over her. Not telling Master Nathan about her feelings for his son or the events that had taken place with him thus far went against everything she stood for. Honesty, transparency, and openness in a relationship meant everything to her. *Perhaps I will tell Nathan everything first thing in the morning?* she said to herself, grasping for a hint of peace yet finding none. *I know he is falling in love with me, and I, with him, but not in the way he wants. What am I to do now?*

Austin's thick eyebrows narrowed, but he said nothing and met his master at the bottom of the stairs. Master Nathan hugged him tightly, patting him firmly on the back. Then, shocking his faithful servant further, Master Nathan grabbed his shoulders with a firm grip. He put his smiling face right in Austin's, and exclaimed, "Well, my good man, I'm in love!"

"I hadn't noticed, sir," Austin said sarcastically.

Master Nathan made a funny face, wondering what Austin meant.

"Would you care for a drink this evening, sir?" Austin asked, ignoring his master's confession of love for Rachel.

"Yes, please... I will have some tea. Herbal tea of some sort, please. Thank you," he stated boldly.

Austin appeared dumbfounded that his master was not asking for something stronger like he did each night. *What? No brandy?* Although confused, he seemed relieved to hear Master Nathan's unusual request. He had wished for years that his master would cut back on his alcohol consumption and wondered if Rachel had something to do with his sudden change in character and spirit.

"Austin, I feel inspired to play my violin for a bit. So you can bring my tea up to the library in about thirty minutes. Thank you," Master Nathan announced before turning toward the music room.

"Yes, sir," Austin replied, wide-eyed, leaving to fetch his master's tea.

"And Austin," he said, turning back to address his faithful servant one more time, "just so you are aware, there will be a great many changes taking place in this house over the next few weeks. The staff, including yourself, are to do absolutely everything Miss Rachel says. Is that clear?" He smirked and cocked his head sideways to wait for Austin's reply, wondering if his sanity was about to be questioned again.

Confused, Austin blinked a few times, bowed, and said, "Of course, sir."

Master Nathan was glad to see him at least comply with his request. Since Austin did not congratulate him after he confessed he'd fallen in love with Rachel, he hoped that Austin might at least like her somewhat.

It had been another long day, but Rachel was pleased it had been so productive. Tired, she tip-toed to her room, wondering if Richard would even come to her this evening. Thinking back, she was amazed that he danced with her. She wondered what it meant and what he might be feeling.

Unsure if she should look him in the eyes again after their magical moment on the dance floor, she wondered if it would be almost impossible not to. But after carefully considering it, to be on the safe side, she decided to try to act as though their dance had never taken place. Even though she knew that looking deeply into his eyes had altered her soul for life, she was afraid that doing anything but reading to him would be too much too soon.

Entering her room, she locked the door behind herself, not wanting to worry, but she could not help it, especially if Master Nathan had to go away. Rachel wanted to make things better instead of worse for these two darling men she adored but felt inadequate. She recalled her mother asking her, "If God only gave us tasks that were easily completed, what would we need Him for?"

Thankful that the servants had built a roaring fire and turned down the bed for her, she placed her forehead up against the door to consider her predicament. She inhaled and let out a quiet sigh. Unable to come up with any answers, she turned to get ready for bed. Slipping behind the room divider to change, she heard a noise outside of her door and saw Richard's shadow moving underneath.

Again, Rachel took her time changing into an elegant new nightgown and robe. Gently placing the cross necklace beside her bed on the nightstand, she considered what to do with it. She told Master Nathan she would never take it off but was afraid Richard might get upset if he saw her wearing his mother's necklace. He was so temperamental, and she knew she had better be extra careful, but felt it would be okay to leave it out.

She placed several blankets and pillows perfectly in front of the fire and moved her mirror just to the right angle. Wanting to see Richard's reflection easily if he were to sit next to her again on her bed after she read, she lined it up perfectly.

Grabbing her Bible, she quickly unlocked her door before seating herself on the blankets and opening it to the gospel of Mark. When she started reading, she could hear Master Nathan playing another song on his instrument in the distance. As the notes that seemed to be crying out to her, snuck up the steps and into her ears, they settled in her heart. It almost made her cry to think of him all alone, playing without her. She placed her hand on her chest, thinking of him, lonely, serenading no one.

Suddenly, the door creaked open as Richard entered. Rachel did all she could to ignore him, but it was not easy. Out of the corner of her eye, she noticed that he was carrying a few things in his arms, and she was curious as to what they were. Thankfully, he walked right past her, allowing her to steal a quick peek. *Oh my*, she thought to herself as she returned her gaze to her Bible and continued to read.

Richard brought her a few very special gifts. He had selected a few items from the hall that he wanted to keep, yet instead of holding onto them for himself, he was giving them to her. Carefully, he placed the three teddy bears that resembled his family from Sophie's room, upon her bed. He sat them in front of the fancy pillows she never used on the empty side of her bed and took extra care to place the "boy" bear closest to the side on which she slept. Then, he slowly lowered himself onto his hands and knees and placed a small booklet next to her, which she assumed must have been a book from his childhood.

Her heart sank deeper as she wondered what all of this might say about his mental state. She did not know if he was regressing or making progress. Having never been trained in mood disorders or how to deal with this sort of thing. She thought to herself, *At least he did not get angry and throw his sisters' things around the hallway like he did with the small table.*

Rachel hoped this meant he might be getting somewhat better and thought that him letting some of their things go was a good sign. Wanting to trust that all the new things he had been doing recently—like dancing with her, giving her gifts, and keeping calmer around her—were, indeed, progress, she gained a spark of hope, making her grin.

She noticed that Richard spotted the cross necklace sitting on her nightstand and began to get concerned about how he might react. Picking it up and examining it, he held it against his chest with his eyes closed tightly, showing tender sorrow.

Perhaps he is remembering his beloved mother? Trying not to be frightened about what he might do if he got upset with her for having jewelry that belonged to Gloria, her nerves jumped. She suddenly wished she had kept the necklace hidden, but it was too late. Rachel continued to read, knowing there was nothing else she could do. She could feel him looking at her intently and began to tremble. It was a bit frightening when he looked at the necklace and then back at her several times.

Not clear if he was angry or not, she struggled to remain calm but became even more afraid as he approached her, holding the necklace in his hands. She thought of bolting for the door but was much too scared to move. Her mind raced with fearful thoughts, and she cringed. *What is he going to do? Choke me with it?* She prayed silently for protection so as not to mess up the words she was reading aloud. With zero inkling of what his next move might be, she braced herself and was ready for anything. But then he stopped.

To Rachel's surprise, Richard knelt close beside her and kissed the cross. Just as she was about to get up and run, he carefully placed the necklace around her neck. Her heart was racing and breaking at the same time. She could sense the gentle, sweet, and giving demeanor in Richard that Master Nathan described to her. Desperately wanting to stop reading, embrace him, and thank him for his kindness, her eyes welled. She was so ashamed of how foolish her thoughts and fears had been, once again, over nothing.

Seeming quite content now, watching her read with his mother's necklace on, Richard crawled, inch by inch, into position and lay down close to listen to her soothing voice. Reading in the middle of Mark, she hoped to share as many stories of Jesus' boldness and healing as possible. Her confidence grew, and a tremendous peace washed over her once they both settled. Relieved by his kind-hearted behavior, she assumed it was okay to read with a new intensity.

Rachel wanted him to know that there was no situation too difficult for Jesus and how compassionate He was to those in need, so she read Mark 1:29-34. She could feel Richard's child-like excitement as he stared at her, eyes wide with curiosity as to what Jesus would do next.

"'Now as soon as they had come out of the synagogue, they entered the house of Simon and Andrew, with James and John. But Simon's wife's mother lay sick with a fever, and they told Him about her at once. So He came and took her by the hand and lifted her up, and immediately the fever left her. And she served them. At evening, when the sun had set, they brought to Him all who were sick and demon-possessed. And the whole city was gathered together at the door. Then He healed many who were sick with various diseases, and cast out many demons; and He did not allow the demons speak, because they knew Him.'"

Rachel never got tired of reading about Jesus' power to deliver and heal those who were oppressed. It brought much hope to her heart, which she so desperately needed after suffering great trials herself. These stories had increased her faith through her most challenging times, even in situations that seemed hopeless. Therefore, she aimed to help Richard not only hear every word but grasp them.

He moved in closer, and she tried not to let her thoughts wander. But for whatever reason, though, the horrible events that had taken place when she was young suddenly flashed across her mind. She shivered upon recalling the wayward preacher's son who touched her inappropriately when they were on a mission trip together. *Oh, how he had hurt me so and wounded my soul.*

Chapter 4

Simultaneously pondering her past as she continued reading, regret wedged its way back into Rachel's heart. She wished she had told her parents about her abuse much sooner, having kept that painful event a secret for far too long due to unnecessary guilt and shame. Many years later, it was still hard not to get angry with herself for having believed the lie from the enemy that she would never be free from the painful memories. But she was thankful that she knew better now and wished she could share the lessons she had learned about freedom with Richard.

She remembered studying 2 Corinthians 10:5 about casting down strongholds, imaginations, and every high thing that is exalted against the knowledge of God. When she had first been taught about taking all thoughts captive, she knew her "negative thoughts" were not her own. Despite how difficult it was, that was the day she finally decided she'd had enough of the torment in her mind and mustered up the courage to tell her parents the truth.

Even though she did not want to attract attention to herself, Rachel knew that telling her parents and shining a light into the darkness could make all the difference. She had hoped that when she finally talked openly about her abuser, the evil chains binding her would break off for good. Thinking back, she was thankful that, when they'd prayed about it as a family, things quickly changed for the better.

Her ability to share her true feelings and ultimately forgive that young man, greatly helped her release any lingering anger, fear, shame, and resentment she'd held. It was like a weight had been lifted off her, and she wished to help Richard do the same.

Recalling how loving and supportive her father was during that time, she frowned, sad that Richard had no one to support him after suffering tremendous abuse. Rachel hoped his relationship with his father might one day be restored, so he could have a small taste of what she once cherished with hers.

After her father shed many tears about her abuse, his words of wisdom had such a lasting effect on her, and she never forgot them. That very day, he taught her that the young man who violated her had no right to harm his little girl and that it was of vital importance for her to know, beyond anything else, that it was not her fault. He wanted her to know that she was still pure, blameless, and deeply loved by God, and she always would be.

Her father explained, the only way to forgive the young man's vile behavior was to know that he did not know who *he was* when he hurt her. Her father also made sure she understood that what happened to her, although it had been very real and horrific, was in her past and that her past did not determine who she was. He had been adamant that her past did not define her and that, in Christ, she was and always would be a victor, not a victim.

His words about her being not only a spotless, beloved child of God but a priceless warrior princess, brought her tremendous peace when she needed it most. She recalled him saying, "Because you are a mighty warrior for Christ, you hold the power to forgive and forget. God has given you the strength to move on and let go of the past, like He does with each of us. Our past can make us better or bitter, but we must choose between the two. Just be mindful that, in your choosing, being bitter never helps anyone."

At first, she had been upset by her father's tough love, but after giving it much thought, Rachel realized he was right. Once she'd willingly chosen to forgive the most horrendous evil she had ever known, the power within her grew beyond measure. When she'd lain her anger toward that young man at the feet of Jesus and blamed the Devil instead, she was free. Knowing that her life radically changed after that decision, she was deeply grateful for her parents' support and wisdom.

Glad Jesus had miraculously healed her of her most painful memories, with a grateful heart, she shifted her mind back to Richard. Although she was reading in the New Testament, she remembered a scripture from the Old Testament that had gotten her through those dark times when she'd felt so alone: Isaiah 41:13, "'For I, the Lord your God, will hold of your right hand, Saying to you, "Fear not, I will help you."'"

While reading, she began praying for Richard. In her busy mind, she acknowledged that if she could be set free from torment, he could be too. To encourage him, she then proceeded in Mark 1:35-42 to convey how Jesus helped others overcome their trials, "'Now in the morning, having risen a long while before daylight, He went out and departed to a solitary place; and there He prayed. And Simon and those who were with Him searched for Him. When they found Him, they said to Him, "Everyone is looking for You!" But He said to them, "Let us go into the next towns, that I may preach there also, because for this purpose I have come forth." And He was preaching in their synagogues throughout all Galilee, and casting out demons. Now a leper came to Him, imploring Him, kneeling down to Him and saying, "If You are willing, You can make me clean." Then Jesus, moved with compassion, stretched out His hand and touched him, and said to him, "I am willing; be cleansed." As soon as He had spoken, immediately the leprosy left him, and he was cleansed.'"

Feeling groggy, Rachel took a few deep breaths to energize herself. She loved reading to Richard and did not want to stop, especially when he seemed to be enjoying himself so much. But to save time and to show Richard that Jesus did not care what other people thought of Him, she skipped forward to the story where the religious leaders of the day did not like Jesus healing a paralyzed man on the Sabbath. She hoped Richard would see that Jesus always did the right and loving thing, no matter what anybody said or thought about Him and read Mark 2:1-12.

"'And again He entered Capernaum after some days, and it was heard that He was in the house. Immediately many gathered together, so that there was no longer room to receive them, not even near the door. And He preached the word to them. Then they came to Him, bringing a paralytic who was carried by four men. And when they could not come near Him because of the crowd, they uncovered the roof where He was. So when they had broken through, they let down the bed on which the paralytic was lying. When Jesus saw their faith, He said to the paralytic, "Son, your sins are forgiven you." And some of the scribes were sitting there and reasoning in their hearts, "Why does this man speak blasphemies like this? Who can forgive sins but God alone?" But immediately, when Jesus perceived in His spirit that they reasoned thus within themselves, He said to them, "Why do you reason about these things in your hearts? Which is easier, to say to this paralytic, 'Your sins are forgiven you,' or to say, 'Arise, take your bed and walk'? But that you may know that the Son of Man has power on earth to forgive sins." –He said to the paralytic, "I say to you, arise, take up your bed, and go to your house." Immediately he arose, took up the bed, and went out in the presence of them all, so that all were amazed and glorified God, saying, "We never saw anything like this!"'"

Noticing that Richard was hanging on her every word, Rachel quickly flipped the pages to one of her favorite scriptures, Mark 2:17, "'When Jesus heard it, He said to them, "Those who are well have no need of a physician, but those who are sick. I did not come to call the righteous, but sinners, to repentance."'"

Since both she and Richard seemed to be getting sleepy, she decided to proceed only a bit further in Mark 3:1-5, "'And He entered the synagogue again, and a man was there who had a withered hand. So they watched Him closely, whether He would heal him on the Sabbath, so that they might accuse Him. And He said to the man who had the withered hand, "Step forward." Then He said to them, "Is it lawful on the Sabbath to do good or to do evil, to save life or to kill?" But they kept silent. And when He had looked around at them in anger, being grieved by the hardness of their hearts, He said to the man, "Stretch out your hand." And he stretched it out, and his hand was restored as whole as the other.'"

She paused right there so Richard could hear how Jesus restored a man entirely. Wanting him to have hope for himself, she finished with the stories in Mark 5:21-36, that showed God's limitless power, making a way where there was no way.

"'Now when Jesus had crossed over again by boat to the other side, a great multitude gathered to Him; and He was by the sea. And behold, one of the rulers of the synagogue came, Jairus by name. And when he saw Him, he fell at His feet and begged Him earnestly, saying, "My little daughter lies at the point of death. Come and lay your hands on her, that she may be healed, and she will live." So Jesus went with him, and a great multitude followed Him and thronged (pressed around) Him. Now a certain woman had a flow of blood for twelve years, and had suffered many things from many physicians. She had spent all that she had and was no better, but rather grew worse. When she heard about Jesus, she came behind Him in the crowd and touched His garment. For she said, "If only I may touch His clothes, I shall be made well." Immediately the fountain of her blood was dried up, and she felt in her body that she was healed of the affliction. And Jesus, immediately knowing in Himself that power had gone out of Him, turned around in the crowd and said, "Who touched My clothes?" But His disciples said to Him, "You see the multitude thronging (crowding against) You, and You say, 'Who touched Me?'" And He looked around to see her who had done this thing. But the woman, fearing and trembling, knowing what had happened to her, came and fell down before Him and told Him the whole truth. And He said to her, "Daughter, your faith has made you well. Go in peace, and be healed of your affliction." While He was still speaking, some came from the ruler of the synagogue's house who said, "Your daughter is dead. Why trouble the Teacher any further?" As soon as Jesus heard the word was spoken, He said to the ruler of the synagogue, "Do not be afraid; only believe."'"

Before Rachel continued, she hoped to get a feel for how Richard was responding. Luckily, he was not looking, and she was able to sneak a peek in his direction. The smile on his face made it clear he was enjoying the stories she was sharing, so she finished, "'And He permitted no one to follow Him except for Peter, James, and John the brother of James. Then He came to the house of the ruler of the synagogue, and saw a tumult (commotion) and those who wept and wailed loudly. When He came in, He said to them, "Why make this commotion and weep? The child is not dead, but sleeping." And they ridiculed Him. But when He had put them all outside, He took the father and the mother of the child, and those who were with Him, and entered where the child was lying. Then He took the child by the hand, and said to her, "Talitha, cumi!" which is translated, "Little girl, I say to you, arise!" Immediately the girl arose and walked, for she was twelve years of age. And they were overcome with great amazement. But He commanded them strictly that no one should know it, and said that something should be given her to eat.'"

Richard seemed thrilled to hear such powerful and hopeful stories, but Rachel could not stay awake a moment longer. She closed her Bible but then the booklet that he had brought to her caught her attention. Wanting to say thank you to him somehow, she set down her Bible and picked up the book. Seeing that it was the Lord's Prayer, she hugged it to herself and was happy to read it aloud, "'Our Father in heaven, hallowed be Your name. Your kingdom come, Your will be done, on Earth as it is in Heaven. Give us this day our daily bread. And forgive us our debts, as we forgive our debtors. And do not lead us into temptation, but deliver us from the evil one. For Yours is the kingdom and the power and the glory forever. Amen.'"

When Richard sighed, she wondered if, perhaps, he might have recalled his mother reading those very same words to him. She picked up on the spirit of serenity as it flowed throughout the room and smiled to herself.

Overtired, Rachel yawned, and even though she did not want her time with Richard to end, she knew she needed sleep. Daringly, instead of getting into bed, she moved her body lower on the blanket, closed the book, and slowly laid down, placing the back of her head on the pillow right next to Richard.

With her heart racing, curious about how he might respond, she stared straight up at the ceiling, waiting to see what he might do. To her surprise, he propped himself up onto his elbow to get a better view of her. He took a long time and studied every detail about her, combing her body with his eyes. She knew her mother would never approve, yet she was glad Richard seemed to be enjoying the view.

He reached up and carefully touched her face. She tried to ignore it, but upon feeling his touch, she inhaled and closed her eyes, giving in to the intensity of her emotions. Although Rachel attempted to remain calm, her mind began to race once again. *Why did I lay down next to him?* she asked herself. *What was I thinking?* Then, surrendering to his touch, she held perfectly still, except for her chest rising and falling. For some strange reason, she felt she could trust him.

Ever so slowly, he used only one finger to stroke her hair, the outside edge of her shoulder, and down her arm. He traced the curves of her face—eyebrows, cheekbones, chin, and finally, her lips. Seeming to relax, even more, he outlined her features several times.

The moment he moved his fingers down the middle of her neck, Rachel tilted back her head, knowing he was about to touch her chest. She grew faint over the unfamiliar, burning desire raging within her and clenched her teeth. But out of respect for her, Richard stopped himself from touching her breast and instead pulled back his hand and placed it over hers, which was resting on her stomach. He then laid back down and further inched his way next to her, getting his body much closer to hers than before.

She could tell he was still mesmerized by everything about her. Despite desperately wanting to roll over onto her side and talk to him face-to-face, she kept her gaze straight upward, letting him enjoy this much-needed human interaction. Thankfully, he behaved like a true gentleman. And although they had spent little time together, her emotions grew stronger for him with each passing minute. More than ever, she wanted to reach him, really reach him. After a long silence, she knew the only way to communicate with him now would be to pray. So, she chose her words carefully, closed her eyes, and whispered a prayer into the night.

"Dear Lord, I come before You, seeking Your face tonight. You know how I long to trust You. I know that You are faithful and that I have never walked alone. Every step of my life, You have been with me. I want to breathe in Your grace and walk in Your love for others, just as You do for me. You are my joy and my Salvation. You are the Healer, the Life, the air that I breathe, and I want to bring You praise all my days. I would lay down my life just to be by Your side. Lover of my soul, help me to be pleasing in Your sight. Fill me with Your supernatural love and strength. Use me to be a vessel of honor to bring healing, restoration, and joy to this house."

Richard gently stroked her hand with his thumb as she continued to pray.

"I surrender my all to You, Lord, for You deserve nothing less. I humble myself before You and ask that where the Devil brings sorrow, sickness, death, and confusion, You will use Your mighty power to remove all traces of his dirty work. Remove the ashes and replace them with Your indescribable beauty. Shine Your light upon this house through me, Your Word, the power of prayer, Your beauty that surrounds us, and Your unchanging love. I thank You that 'neither death, nor life, nor angels, nor powers, nor past, nor present, nor future can separate us' from Your strong love. You say to those who are weary to come to You. You say to come to Jesus, the Living Water, all who are thirsty. To the hungry, You say, 'come to the table to taste and see that The Lord is good,' and You, indeed, are. I will forever adore You, my God, and my King."

She paused and then continued with a prayer that was more focused on helping Richard grasp the concept of life beyond the mansion's walls. "Lord, my soul longs for You and You alone, but I also want to find my true love and future husband. I long to have children someday, to travel, to help others, and to live a life pleasing to You. I have faith that You will take care of me personally because Your mercies are new every morning."

Hearing Richard sniffle and clear his throat, she was glad to see that he had closed his eyes. He was now praying right along with her, and she grinned. "I know that we are Your beloved, precious in Your sight, and the heavens move at the sound of Your voice. My God, Your presence alone is enough, but I ask for swift, sweet, and wonderful changes to come to this home through Your tangible presence. Help us feel glory as we walk in the gardens, for we know that You created each flower, plant, color, and blade of grass just for our pleasure. I know that each ray of light and drop of rain speaks of Your undying love toward us. Let us be mindful of our surroundings and feel You beside us as we dance in Your moonlight under the magnificence of the many stars You placed perfectly in the night sky, just for us."

More than a few times, Richard fidgeted, but she did not let that stop her.

"Each day, as we feel the warmth of Your sun upon our faces, as our ears take in the delight of birds' chirping, the roar of the thunderclap, or the wind's song, let us be reminded of Your power. You are the Creator of Heaven and Earth, and we give thanks for all that nature provides. It is Your special gift to remind us of Your beauty and kindness."

Noticing Richard wipe a tear away from his eye as she continued, Rachel held back tears of her own. "Let us see Your majesty in everything around us. Not just in the flowers but in each petal. Not just in the trees but the details in the unique textures of the bark and the colors of each leaf. Not just in the sunshine but in every ray that shimmers before us. Not just in your book, The Bible, but as we read it, let it speak directly to our hearts."

Because Richard was still listening intently, Rachel finished with more personal prayers. "Father, I love You with everything that is within me. There is no love like Yours. Forever, You are my Abba Father and Lord of my life. You will reign in my heart always. In Jesus' name, amen."

Surprisingly, Richard moved even closer, lightly squeezed her hand and whispered, "Amen."

Smiling, she was thrilled and dared to lightly squeeze his hand back in response while quietly praising God for what seemed like a miracle. The fact that Richard had spoken *at all* was astounding. With only one spoken word, she fell in love with the sound of his voice, and it gave her tremendous hope.

Except for the crackling of the fire, all was silent. Rachel closed her eyes once more and did not even get up to blow out her candle. She was so comfortable with Richard now. She could hardly believe it and did not want him to leave. They held hands, lying next to each other by the fire until they both fell fast asleep.

After what must have been several hours, she felt his strong arms lifting her off the floor. Rachel pretended to sleep as he laid her in her bed and placed a soft kiss on her cheek. She could feel him covering her with blankets and tucking her in, just like her mother and father used to. Then he took the "boy" teddy bear that resembled him as a child and carefully tucked it underneath her arm to give her something to hold onto as she slept. As he sat next to her, watching her, she wondered if he would kiss her.

To Rachel's delight, instead of kissing her, he brushed a few stray curls off her face and acted like a proud father tucking his child into bed with her favorite toy. Her heart fluttered at his thoughtfulness. She could hear him blow out what remained of her candle before he tiptoed away. Sneaking a peek in his direction as he made his way out of her room, Rachel hugged her bear tight. And just like that, Richard quietly vanished once again. She pulled her blanket up under her chin, confident that she would rest safe and secure for the remainder of the night.

Nodding in and out of sleep, Rachel began dreaming of Richard lifting her out of bed. Unable to stir herself awake and sure she was only dreaming, she let herself relax into his arms as he carried her out of her room, across the hall, and down an unfamiliar set of steps to a back door that led directly outside and into the garden mist.

Confused, she blinked slowly, trying to wake her eyes. The few silver dots in the sky above, peeking through the clouds and thick fog, made her head fuzzy. Suddenly, a cool breeze blew several locks of hair across her face, tickling her nose. Wiping the hair out of her eyes, she stirred from her slumber to see that Richard was indeed carrying her past the ponds and far from the house. She panicked, and her muscles stiffened. *What is happening? Where is he taking me?* She wanted to leap from his arms and run back to her room, but she buried her face deep in his neck, trying to hide her fears. Yet it was of no use, and goosebumps raced across her skin.

The vibrating sound of crickets, peepers, and bullfrogs singing rhythmically in the night, which would normally soothe Rachel's nerves, only made things worse. Her brain, working overtime to organize their song and make sense of his sudden urge to drag her out of bed in her nightgown, made her imagination spin like a tornado. *Master Nathan never warned me about Richard doing something like this!*

While forcing herself to slow her breaths to keep from screaming, she decided it would be wise to pretend to sleep. Richard took brisk steps and showed no signs of stopping. His pace, this late in the night, to her, felt more like a death march in her panicked state. She wished he would change course and put her back in bed, yet he acted so determined, almost angry.

The mansion, far away in the distance now, called to her, but there was no escape. Sneaking another peek, she noticed a massive tree sprawling out in all directions ahead of them. Misshapen and showing no signs of life, its jagged branches reached out to grab her like bony fingers, making her withdraw inward toward Richard's embrace. It appeared to have been dead for many years and looked almost petrified, as she was.

"Hoot." Hearing an owl, Rachel looked to see it sitting high in the tree's clutches. She shivered as it made itself known with another loud "hoot" before leaving the scene with a great swoosh of its wings.

Worse yet, she could make out her fate directly underneath this monstrous timber. Three crosses, neglected and moss-covered, now lay in Richard's path. Instead of the inner peace the cross would normally bring her, the worst possible scenario crossed her mind, and she froze. *What is he planning to do with me?*

After he stopped, she wondered what was next. *Why has he taken me to a graveyard?* She squeezed her eyes tight and prayed for protection but questioned God in her predicament. Yet, when she was close to breaking down into tears, Richard planted a soft kiss upon her forehead once again, just as he had done prior to tucking her into bed.

Pretending to awaken slowly, she sighed, inhaled, and squirmed until he gently placed her bare feet upon the soft moss below. Feeling faint, she attempted to steady herself against Richard's strong frame.

Finally, after appearing steady on her own, he let her go, stepped forward, fell to his knees in front of the crosses and let tears spill out of his eyes like heavy rain from a black cloud. He held nothing back as sobs he had choked back for years broke free.

Terrified, Rachel focused on Richard and stumbled her way closer to him. To her surprise, he then reached out for her hand, grasping for support himself. Instinctively, filled with pity, she took it.

With great care, he gently pulled her down to kneel beside him, bowed his head low, and clasped his hands together, making a gesture as if he wanted her to pray. It was then that Rachel realized the three crosses directly in front of her were placed over his mother's and little sisters' remains, and she exhaled with a quiver in her voice. *He must want me to pray for them all,* she guessed, putting her hands together. *Oh my!* She pondered for a moment, now fully awake, shocked by where she was and what was happening, and thought, *what do I say?*

Bowing her head beside Richard, she put herself in his shoes as a spirit of compassion washed over her. "D-dear Lord," she stuttered, "I-I bow before you now in this most solemn and sacred place. Missing our loved ones while we are still here on Earth can feel unbearable. Our stomachs ache. Our minds race. Our hearts no longer beat in rhythm as they should. Everything feels out of place, and everything within us hurts when we remember them. But You, Lord, You already know those truths, and You care so deeply. Your compassion for those dealing with grief is more than I could ever hope to comprehend, and so I call on You now for help in our most desperate hour."

Because Richard was weeping, it broke Rachel's heart as she spoke, but she trusted her prayers would help him. "Regardless of being able to rest assured that those who have gone on before us are being cared for in Heaven and are perfectly fine, we, Lord, are not fine without them. We long for days gone by and, oftentimes, cannot see our way ahead. There are empty spaces in our present—and sometimes our future—that should be filled with their love and laughter, and the thought of going on without them can feel utterly impossible."

When Rachel noticed Richard swallow hard, she hoped he was okay, "Throughout this most difficult time, I ask for renewed strength from You that is supernatural. At times, when we think of what will never be, even breathing hurts. Help us to take the next needed breath of air. Help us put one foot in front of the other, for we are weak and cannot do it alone. Give us a clear vision and help us to press on, even when we feel like giving up. But mostly, help us to want to live. Truly live."

Those words seemingly affected Richard more than she would have liked. He let out a forceful breath and grabbed at his chest, pulling at his shirt as though his heart hurt, but she did not stop. "Help us to live our lives to the fullest to honor those we lost, with the understanding that if they could tell us anything, I believe they would tell us that they love us still and that they want us to not just survive but thrive. And even though it is impossible to let them live through our experiences, our laughter, and day-to-day comings and goings, in a way, they do because they have, even in death, shaped us into who we are."

As Richard sniffled and wiped at his tears, she finished, "If we had never met them, our lives would have turned out so differently. So, help us to live with a heart of gratitude as each moment passes, thankful for the time we spent with them on this side of Heaven. While this painful time ticks on until we see them again, I have no doubt that You will take amazing care of them for us. In the meantime, if possible, Lord, please do us a favor, and tell them that we will be okay as we walk side by side with You. Make sure they know that we will never stop loving them because love is eternal. In Jesus' name, amen."

After she'd ended her prayer, Richard laid facedown across their graves and continued to cry. This time, Rachel felt his expression of sorrow was healthy and perhaps long overdue. So she said nothing but stood and waited gracefully by his side, her hair and nightgown blowing in the wind.

Letting her eyes wander about, she could make out old bouquets of flowers, long since dried, scattered about the ground. Each one had been carefully tied with ribbon, now faded, and worn thin. She assumed they were from Master Nathan and figured that Richard had, more than likely, not visited their graveside since he was a child.

Wishing she could lie down, Rachel yawned loudly and instantly regretted it. Richard noticed and sat up straight, wiping his tears in haste. Despite the fact they could not speak, he reacted as though he wanted to be incredibly attentive to her needs. Without hesitating, he carefully scooped her up like she was as light as a flower and began making his way back to the mansion. Holding her snuggly to protect her, he seemed to want to make sure she was comfortable and warm.

This time, as he carried her through the dark of night, he took his time, and the walk in the gardens felt romantic and serene. No longer afraid he meant her any harm, Rachel rested her head against his strong chest as a grin crept across her face. The music of the night creatures' singing, mixed with the pounding of his heartbeat, finally comforted her. She realized how much he must respect and trust her to bring her to his family's graveside to pray for them with such urgency and hoped he was beginning to understand the power of prayer at any time, in any circumstance.

He slowed his steps, acting like he did not want the night to end as he continued to hold her. She, too, could have stayed in his arms forever. Rachel was surprised when he was strong enough to squat low and pick a tulip with one hand as he held her in his other arm. He carefully placed the flower in her hand before sitting on a bench below an enormous willow tree near the pond. With her tucked safely in his embrace, he began rocking her gently back and forth, like a sweet father trying to rock his child back to sleep.

His scent aroused her as she nuzzled into his neck, melting into his touch like a snowflake on a warm mitten. Then, to her delight, Richard began humming a sweet hymn that her father used to sing, called "Amazing Grace," and she was surprised he knew it at all. His deep tone, precisely on key and powerful, vibrated within her, and she sighed. *Oh, Lord, please make this man well so I can hear his voice loud and clear someday*, she prayed. He had the voice of an angel, and it soothed her to the core.

With her head getting heavier by the minute as sleep fought to take over her, Rachel rested, fully trusting him to put her back into bed when he was ready. In the meantime, she chose to simply enjoy their adventure and the warmth of his skin next to hers and drifted back to sleep.

Once back in her room, Richard placed the tulip on her night-stand, kissed her forehead, and slipped out the door. Rachel was exhausted, yet restless. She stared up at the ceiling as the shadows of the leaves from the tall trees outside her window made their way to and fro in waves across the angels and clouds over her bed.

Aware she had never felt like this about anyone, she mulled the sound of Richard's voice over and over in her head as she felt an ache for him growing within her. Forcing herself to steady her breaths, she wondered what the Lord was doing. *Is there any hope for him? And if so, when? I recognize I am not really his teacher, but I know better than to get involved with a student to such a degree, especially one who struggles as he does. It is not right*, she told herself, trying to rest, but sleep eluded her for hours as she thought about Richard, unaware of what the future and even the next day might hold.

Drifting off, she suddenly sat straight up in bed, as flashes of her outing with Richard raced through her head. She reached for the tulip, but it was not there. Frantically searching for it on the floor around her nightstand and even amongst her pillows, she grew frustrated and questioned if her evening with Richard was even real. *Was I only dreaming? Could my imagination have possibly run away with me so wildly?* Blinking rapidly, she thought, *How could something that seemed so real have been just a figment of my imagination?* She laid back down and prayed, trying to make sense of it all, but to no avail.

It was not long before she fell back asleep while thoughts of Richard and everything that she had experienced that day troubled her. Yet, after hours of uninterrupted sleep, instead of dreaming of Richard, she battled a horrific nightmare. In her dreams, something terrible happened between herself and Master Nathan. He was furious with her, had grown violent, and was yelling at her with tear-filled eyes. Her dream was so upsetting that Rachel began crying in her sleep and was only awoken by a loud knock at her door. Still half asleep, with tears in her eyes, she jumped up and opened the door without thinking or even asking who it was.

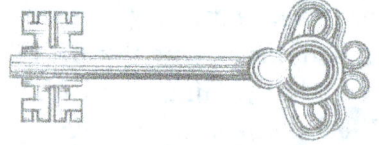

Chapter 5

Relieved to see that it was Master Nathan standing in the hall, overcome with emotion, she flung her arms around him, crying, "Oh, my! Thank goodness you are here!"

"Well, good morning. If I had known this is how you would greet me, I would wake you up early every morning," he teased, hugging her back. Quickly sensing something was wrong, he asked, "Rachel, what is it? Are you quite well?"

As she became fully awake, her eyes opened wide. Realizing she was still in her nightgown and that her chest was inappropriately pressed up against him, she suddenly felt very exposed. The satin material of her nightgown was relatively thin compared to her dresses, and she knew that if he let her go in this daylight, he would see her, *fully* see her. She also knew that if she kept holding him, he would be able to feel her body, and that would not be good either. Panicking, she stepped back.

"Oh, Master Nathan, I am so sorry. Please forgive my rudeness. I was in the middle of a bad dream when you knocked on my door. It was about you, and it was horrible," she said as she turned away from him and grabbed her robe off the foot of her bed to cover herself.

"You were dreaming about me? No need to apologize. I am flattered," Master Nathan chuckled. "What was your dream about?"

"Oh, it was awful. You were in a rage, crying, yelling, and so angry with me, but I do not even know what it was about. All I know is I was so upset that you were angry with me. I think I was actually sobbing in my sleep and begging for your forgiveness, but you would not listen to me."

Quickly taking hold of her hand, Master Nathan pulled her to himself and hugged her once again to comfort her. "Oh, Rachel, come here. It is okay. It was just a dream, my dear." He rocked her a little and said, "There, there. I am not angry with you, silly. In fact, I feel quite the opposite. I came to your room this morning to ask if you would have breakfast with me. I may need to leave to go up north this morning after all, and to tell you the truth, I want to spend as much time with you as possible before I go."

"That sounds splendid," she said with a sigh.

He took hold of her shoulders. "Can you get ready soon? I am afraid our time this morning will simply vanish. Although I do not wish to leave you at all, I fear I must. But it is a lovely morning, and I want to show you something before I go."

Thankful her dream was not real, Rachel was glad Master Nathan was easily able to calm her fears. She smirked at how dramatic she had been. "Yes. Yes, of course. I will get dressed right away."

"Do you need any help with that?" he said with a comical expression.

Rachel gasped and looked directly at him, wide-eyed, pretending to be shocked by his comment, despite knowing full well he was only making it in jest.

"I'm kidding! I'm kidding! I am leaving. Goodbye!" he said, hurrying out the door.

Shaking her head, she replied before closing the door, "I will be down shortly."

Turning to find the right dress for the day, she heard him raise his voice in the hallway.

"And Rachel," he shouted, "dress comfortably today. Well, never mind. Just wear whatever you want."

"Go away," she yelled to him with a laugh.

He chuckled. "Okay. Okay. I will meet you in the library. Take your time. But hurry!"

Smiling, Rachel rolled her eyes over his comments and did not bother to reply. Instead, she went through her remaining dress choices and picked out a gorgeous, light green cotton dress covered in tiny pink, pale blue, white, and yellow flowers, remembering that green was Master Nathan's favorite color.

After cleaning herself, she put her hair up into a quick bun, slipped into her dress, and started to head out the door. She took another quick peek in the mirror, but upon looking at her reflection, she could not help but remember Richard.

Still in awe over the fact she first met him in a dream, she wondered what God had in store for their relationship. Unsure what was going on with Richard's mental state, Rachel again wrestled with telling Master Nathan everything before he left and pondered the possible outcome if she did not. She decided to inform him of the details immediately and headed for the library in haste, wanting his opinion on the events that had taken place with his son thus far. In truth, she hoped for some advice to follow while he was gone.

Unfortunately, as she entered the library, what looked like a new messenger boy was just leaving. She noticed Master Nathan sitting down on the sofa with a look of complete shock. Wondering what had happened and about the news that he might have just received, she stood in silence before approaching him with great care. He sat staring straight ahead and appeared horrified as he crumpled a written note and threw it into the smoldering fireplace.

"Nathan, dear, is everything all right?"

The moment he saw Rachel, he sat up tall and forced a grin, one that she could see straight through.

Ignoring her question, he commented, "Oh, my. You look quite glamorous, my dear. And in a green dress even. Good choice."

She sat next to him after she curtsied and asked, "What has happened? Tell me."

He turned to her with heavy eyes, "I have just received word from the city."

"What is it?"

"Well, I have just been informed that the factory of mine which caught fire yesterday has burned to the ground." He sighed.

Rachel gasped, "Oh, no! How dreadful!"

He leaned back in his seat. "It was not my largest factory, but it was not my smallest either. I must go up north straight away. I will more than likely need to purchase another building along with new equipment. Or I will need to move things around in one of my larger factories to get production up and running again as quickly as possible. Yet, that is not what bothers me the most."

"What's wrong?" Rachel asked, leaning towards him.

"I am concerned about my workers. They rely on their jobs to feed their families and pay for their homes. I am worried about getting them back to work as fast as I can to keep them earning money. But there's more." He paused.

"Oh?"

With sorrow in his tone, he said, "Last night, the fire took the life of one of my workers. His name was Eric. He was about Richard's age. His father worked for my father, and his grandfather worked for my grandfather. I have not seen him since he got married last year." He shook his head, "Rachel, he has a new baby daughter, and well, I just feel terrible. I wonder what I should do for his widow and child."

Rachel felt his pain and put her hands over his. "First, let me just say that I am deeply sorry for your loss. And about Eric, I am so proud of you for not being worried about the financial side of this great tragedy as much as you are about your employees. That is very admirable of you."

He offered a weak grin. "Thank you."

"Second, I do not want you to leave me for a moment, but I feel you need to address the situation and figure out how to get everyone back to work as quickly as you can. More importantly, I think you should help this widow and her baby girl financially somehow. Perhaps you could tell her in person how sorry you are for her loss and even bring her a gift?"

As his eyes widened with new hope, Master Nathan sat straight up. "What a splendid idea! Quick, come with me. I just had an epiphany!"

Focused on his new task, he took her by the hand and pulled at her as she ran behind him. Leading her directly to the other wing of the house, with his daughters' toys and clothes still sitting in the hall, he pointed to the pile. "Rachel, will you help me pick out some things to take with me as gifts? I think it might mean a lot to Eric's wife to know that these special things belonged to my children. Would you agree?"

"Yes, Nathan. That's a lovely idea."

Enthusiastically, he started grabbing toys, little dresses, and other things to bring up north. "I am going to save most of my wife's jewelry for Richard, but I feel that I should bring up some of Gloria's dresses, too. What do you think?"

"Brilliant," Rachel said, proud of his willingness to donate some of the very expensive clothes that his wife had once worn. The dresses were a tad out of fashion, but she figured that since they were so expensive, Eric's wife would not mind.

"I could not be prouder of you than I am right now," Rachel told him.

"Oh, stop! Now, do not just stand there. Make yourself useful," he said, picking on her.

They gathered armfuls of items, making several trips back and forth as they fumbled their way down the steps to plop it all by the front door.

"Austin!" Master Nathan yelled loudly.

"Yes, sir?" Austin said as he entered the room.

Now thoroughly excited about his trip, Master Nathan asked, "Austin, are my carriage and luggage ready?"

"Not quite, sir."

"I am bringing these items along with me as well." He reached for Rachel's hand once again to lead her out the back doorway and raised his voice to finish his instructions, "I will be back and ready to go momentarily. Please prepare brunch for me to eat on the way instead of breakfast. And be sure my carriage is loaded with as many of these gifts as it can carry. Understood?"

"Yes, sir!" Austin responded as he bowed in the direction of Rachel and Master Nathan, who were now quickly heading out back and into the gardens.

The warm rays of the sun shone brightly across the landscape. The blue sky adorned with glowing, white, fluffy clouds, and a slight breeze cooled down the air.

"Come!" Master Nathan declared.

Again, he rushed Rachel through a part of the garden that she had not yet seen.

"Now, cover your eyes and promise only to look down at your feet. Take care not to trip, but do not look up until I say. Do not peek. You promise?"

"I promise," she said with a chuckle.

As he helped her walk, all she could see was the ground beneath her feet. Noticing that the white path had turned into a crooked path of slate stepping stones, she wanted to look up. In between each stone grew bright green and golden moss with tiny, low-growing flowers of white. It looked inviting but was hard to walk on due to its uneven nature. Since it was difficult to see anything, Rachel wondered just what Master Nathan was up to. She had never met anyone so excited about surprising people, but she adored him for it.

Finally, he whispered, "Okay. You can look up now."

Opening her eyes, she was flabbergasted. "Why, Nathan! Oh, my. This is the biggest tree I have ever seen. It's-it is unbelievable." She looked up high and turned around in a circle with her arms open wide, in awe at the size of the glorious tree canopy spreading out over her.

Thrilled that she liked it, he exclaimed, "And look, my favorite part: it has a swing!"

"Oh, what fun," Rachel stated enthusiastically. She enjoyed swinging as a young girl. Sadly, the split-leaf maple tree that she grew up playing on next to her house had been destroyed in a storm a few months after her father's death. It had since been removed except for the enormous trunk that still stuck up about two feet from the ground, reminding her of her childhood.

"Have a seat, my dear," he said with a wink. Holding the ropes, he let her know that he wished to push from behind.

Rachel sat down on the seat, grabbing the ropes tightly. "All right."

"Do not be afraid, but I am going to push you extraordinarily high," he teased, really planning to be ever so gentle with her.

"Me? Afraid? Of course not. I enjoy heights!" she proclaimed, flashing back to how daring she was as a little girl.

Surprised by her enthusiasm, he said with a chuckle, "Okay. Well, here goes. I am going to run right underneath you."

"Go ahead," Rachel said fearlessly.

"Hold on!" Master Nathan exclaimed as he took several steps backward, holding onto the ropes just above her seat. He backed up just enough to run full speed ahead and go directly beneath her. Grunting as he gave her an extra push over his head, he jumped off the ground to get her as high as he could. Rachel let out a loud squeal of excitement as she reached the peak and whizzed backward away from him.

She recalled how much she'd loved it when her brother, David, used to do the very same thing on their old swing back home. Swinging like a child, so undignified in front of Master Nathan, she was thankful she did not feel embarrassed. Instead, she felt alive and free, elated to be so high.

After a great deal of fun, he slowed her down and pushed her gently to enjoy pleasant conversation and the natural beauty around them. Talking about nothing in particular, they listened to the songbirds together when Rachel asked, "Did you know that the birds begin their song exactly an hour prior to the rising of the sun? My father said he'd observed the leaves on the trees opening the instant they would start singing. He believed it was so they would be prepared to receive the sun in advance. Isn't that astounding?"

"It is," Master Nathan replied, sounding distracted.

Rachel then remembered she still had not told Master Nathan anything about Richard, and her heart grew weary. Although it was the perfect time to tell him, she worried that the fire at his factory must be weighing heavily on his mind, so she kept the news to herself once more and continued to talk with him about the wonders of nature instead.

When it came time for him to go, she remained seated while he slowed the swing and stopped her. Coming around to the other side of the swing, he knelt on one knee directly in front of her. A severe demeanor came over him as he nervously cleared his throat to speak. "Rachel, I…" He hesitated. "I want to apologize for being such an emotional mess since your arrival. I am ashamed of the anger I displayed in front of my employees years ago. But now, now I am ashamed of letting you see me get so upset. Can you forgive me?"

Rachel's eyes softened. "My dear Nathan, there is no need for apologies. Emotions are what they are, but the thing we must remember is that they are windows to the truth of what we value. If you get angry or frustrated when you want to talk to Richard but cannot, it shows that you want to have a relationship with him and that you cherish connectivity. Clearly, that is honorable. When you feel sad, lonely, or depressed over the loss of your girls, it shows that you valued your role as their father and the ability to nurture them and watch them grow. Their early death took that from you, and you have every right to be sad. When you feel lonely and sullen when missing your wife, it shows you cared about her deeply as a wife and that you miss the love you shared with her. In that, there is no shame."

He lowered his head as though she was once more, tugging on exactly the right heart strings he had kept covered for so long. Swallowing hard, he thanked her, "My sweet Rachel, I am afraid I must be leaving now. Austin will prepare brunch for you in the solarium if you wish. I will need to eat on the way, as I have a long journey ahead. But before I go, I want you to know something." He paused and took a deep breath.

"Yes?"

"You, my dear, in this short amount of time, have come to mean a great deal to me. You have helped me in more ways than you will ever know, and I will forever be grateful. Honestly, I do not know how I could ever be content in this house again without you here. Be careful. Be safe. And tell Austin if there is anything you need, anything at all. Be sure to inform him straight away if anything frightens you. Clearly, you can tell that Richard means the world to me, but I know how angry he can get at times. I am just not sure where he gets it from," he said with a humorous look.

Rachel giggled, knowing Richard's temper was just like his father's. "I will."

"My dear," he paused again, "if you are afraid to stay here by yourself, I would completely understand if you wanted to go home for two or three weeks while I am away. Of course, I would pay you just the same. I promise I would not be upset nor think any less of you if you left. Sadly, you know I worry about Richard as well. And as I said yesterday, I am afraid of how he might react if we both were to leave."

"Nathan, no. I am not leaving. I will be fine." Hearing the concern in his voice, she was glad she'd decided to wait until his return to share any news of his son's behavior as of late, not wanting to worry him further.

"'Fine.' Are you truly going to use that word again? I want you to tell me honestly: are you quite certain you will be okay?"

Trying to reassure him, Rachel smiled and spoke with a laugh, making light of the situation, "So far, Richard has been a perfect gentleman, and I am not afraid of him in the least. Trust me. Everything will be better than fine. In fact, I am confident that all will go swimmingly. Nathan, you must not concern yourself with me right now. Do as you must, take care of your business and your workers, and return to me as soon as you are able. Fear not, I will be all right, except for missing you."

He sighed loudly, thankful for her words of confidence. Looking down at the ground, he tried not to get emotional but told her, "I will miss you, too, Rachel."

She touched his hand to comfort him. "Do you want me to come to the house and see you off? I will be happy to come up and wave goodbye."

"No, please. Saying goodbye has become exceedingly difficult for me, as that was how I last saw Sophie. She was standing outside the front door, waving her goodbyes as I left for town the day she died. I am sorry, but I truly cannot handle that right now. Why don't you stay here and enjoy the swing all to yourself? Even though it will not be much fun without me here to push you," he said with a wink.

It was clear that he wanted to stay, but Rachel knew he had a long journey ahead of him. So, she stood and hugged him without saying a word. He held her softly, squeezed his eyes shut, and whispered, "My wife and I never said goodbye without saying, 'I love you,' as our last words, just in case we never saw each other again. Would you mind?" Master Nathan asked, anticipating her reply.

"No. Not at all," she answered.

He hugged her tighter and said, "I love you, Rachel."

She swallowed, breathed in deep, and whispered back, "I love you, too, Nathan."

With a mixture of emotions, before letting him go, she gripped him tighter and prayed just loud enough that he could hear, "Dear Lord, please protect Nathan in his travels. Help his trip be peaceful, productive, and pass quickly so that he can return to us soon. We will all miss him so. In Jesus' name, amen."

"Amen," he said. He kissed her cheek softly, and slowly backed away, still clinging to her hand. Reluctantly, he peeled himself from her fingertips, and she could see that he did not want to let go of her. His eyes held a melancholy look, and his eyebrows knitted together.

As Rachel stood in silence, watching him walk away, she put her hand on her stomach. She was pleased to see that, when he was halfway down the path, he turned and looked at her one last time. Putting up his hand to wave, he gave a feeble grin. She returned an exaggerated smile and waved goodbye, trying to make him feel better, but she, too, felt despondent and covered her mouth before giving one last wave.

When he'd disappeared from sight, she felt ill, as though she were missing him already, but more so because she had told him nothing about Richard. Unsure about what the weeks ahead without Master Nathan might bring, she decided she was much too sad to eat and sat back down on the swing.

Feeling led to pray, she focused on listening to the songbirds and used her feet to swing herself lightly. Rachel grew weary at the thought of Locke Mansion without Master Nathan's smiles and silly jokes. She would miss him, but she hoped to surprise him with significant progress pertaining to Richard upon his return. Aware of how much he loved and worried about his son, she found herself once again trying to shift her thoughts away from Master Nathan and began praying for Richard, *Lord, as I sit under this majestic tree, I am reminded not only of Your beauty but of Your strength and how You shelter me all the days of my life. I pray that You will watch over me here and work a miracle in Richard these next few weeks. I ask for a radical breakthrough within him. Help me to reach him. Holy Spirit, please give him a passion for life again. Show him Your glory, love, beauty, and light. Mostly, show him his own beauty and his immense value and worth to You. Let him see how much he moves Your heart and how much he means to You. In Jesus' mighty name, amen.*

Unexpectedly, she felt a gentle push of the swing from behind. *Nathan has returned for one last goodbye hug,* she thought. Jumping up, she quickly turned around to dive into his arms and hug him tightly. But once she embraced him, she suddenly realized that it was not Master Nathan at all. It was Richard!

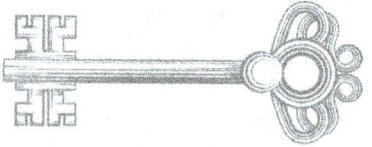

Chapter 6

Panic rushed through her veins. Rachel almost fainted, and her face turned white. Confused, she held on tightly with her cheek pressed firmly up against Richard's chest, afraid to move. At first, he didn't even hug her back, and she felt every muscle in his body stiffen instantaneously. Squeezing her eyes shut, she feared that she must have shocked him and waited for a violent outburst.

But after a few moments passed, little by little, she could feel his muscles loosening. Because he had not been hugged in so many years, it made her wonder if he even knew what to do. She then felt him ever so slowly place his arms around her. To her delight, he gently hugged her back and began breathing deeply. She thought she might have even heard him sniffle.

Unsure of how to handle the predicament, she hugged him back tighter still. He slowly increased his grip on her as well. Rachel felt relieved for an instant; however, once she could tell he was crying, she swallowed back sorrow. Not only had Richard lacked human touch (except for hers the past two nights), he'd not been held in ten lonely years. It didn't take long before his muscles softened into her embrace.

Feeling his pain as though it were her own, she continued holding him as her heart raced. Before she knew it, she felt him kiss the top of her head and squeeze her just a bit more, as though he could see how much she cared.

Once she realized that he was relishing her touch, she pondered all the changes Richard had made since her arrival, and her confidence in his progress grew. Rachel's eyes shone with excitement at the possibility of his recovery. Yet, she knew it would be wise to remain calm and hold still. She remembered asking God for a breakthrough for him only moments before and was genuinely thankful that Richard was outside and interacting with her.

Uncertain about what she should do, she held him firmly while he cried. To her, this was one of the most beautiful moments of her life.

Without looking up, Rachel loosened her grip, turned to face the other direction, and let him hold her from behind. At that precise moment, the sunshine greeted her from between the leaves above.

Richard watched as she lifted her chin to let the sunlight warm her rosy cheeks, admiring her beauty until the sun hit his own face. He inhaled, visibly astonished by it. Closing his eyes, he emulated her and leaned his head back. His skin had seen little direct sunlight in years, but he appeared to love the feeling as it washed over him.

To see this precious moment taking place, Rachel couldn't help but look up, deeply moved by Richard's beauty as he interacted with the blessing of light. He looked like he was healing right before her eyes as his face relaxed. Grinning, she waited for a long while before stepping away from him to sit back down on the swing.

Acting very gentlemanly, he stepped into position behind the swing and began to push her, but he did so with an extra gentle hand. Not a word was spoken between them, but there was no need.

When the sun was high overhead, Rachel stopped the swing with her feet, stood tall, and took three steps forward. She then stopped and stretched her hand back toward Richard to beckon him without looking in his direction. After a moment, she felt him place his hand into hers, which pleased her immensely. They began walking hand-in-hand on the pathway through the flowers, leading them further from the house and closer to one another than she'd ever thought possible.

Smiling, Rachel got the impression Richard was during their silent stroll while taking in the sounds and sights of nature. The apple blossoms yielded their sweet aroma and appeared to uplift him as he inhaled deeply. Eager to get closer to the babbling stream and brightly colored tulip gardens that ran alongside their paths, he took the lead and began directing her instead. She happily followed as the birds serenaded them from all directions.

After climbing several steps that led past many other plants, flowers, and unique trees, the winds picked up, as did Richard's excitement. Exploring together, he seemed to rediscover the beauty of God's creation he'd once known, making their little outing feel like a page out of a romantic fairy tale.

Circling the pond with the swans floating by and willow trees swaying gently in the breeze, they could hear several crickets growing louder as they approached. Rachel lightly chuckled when Richard appeared almost entertained when they passed by a cricket, and it grew completely silent to hide. He grinned while he turned his head and listened carefully to hear when it would resume its unique sound, after it felt safe. *He must know the feeling.*

To Rachel, crickets reminded her that, even when God is silent, He never leaves us alone. She was thrilled that Richard was awake to share the day with her and questioned, *I wonder if that was why he stopped taking his medicine?* She assumed he wanted to spend time with her during the day instead of just at night when she would need sleep. Unsure, she was thankful for his presence regardless and thought, *How handsome he looks with the breeze blowing wisps of his hair away from his face.*

When they approached an area with huge boulders scattered throughout, Rachel assumed that Master Nathan must have had the rocks brought in from far away and had them placed just so, making her think of him. She could not wait to tell him that Richard had gone outside on his own and hoped he would be cheerful, hearing that magnificent news.

Another hour slipped by, and while looking around, Rachel realized she had no idea where she was and once again felt lost. Knowing she needed food and water soon; unease rose within her. Leaving Richard's side was not an option, for fear she would quickly lose her way. In truth, Rachel did not want to leave Richard at all but felt lightheaded and wished it was possible to just talk to him. Still too afraid of how he might react, she realized something needed to come about, and fast. So, she attempted to communicate her needs to him through prayer.

Holding his hand, she began praying aloud while he listened intently, "Dear Lord, thank You so much for this day and for these glorious gardens." She paused as a wave of unsteadiness hit her. "And right now, thank You for helping me find my way back to the solarium so I can get some food and water, as I am feeling quite weak. In Jesus' name, amen."

Before she knew what was happening, Richard swept her up into his arms and was carrying her quickly back toward the house. Overwhelmed and dizzy, she hugged him tightly, feeling loved and protected. Closing her eyes, Rachel assumed that, since he had spent years looking out the windows that overlooked the gardens, he knew exactly where he was going.

The winds blew briskly upon them as they moved along in haste due to his long strides. Thankful for the birds that were sweetly singing, she remained in perfect peace. During this precious moment in Richard's loving arms, walking through the gardens, Rachel felt like she was in Heaven on Earth.

Once he arrived at the terrace stairs leading to the solarium, he set her feet down gently on the third step from the bottom so that, when she stood, they were almost face to face. She still didn't dare to look into his eyes in broad daylight, so she closed hers and took him by the hand. Holding her breath while at the same time feeling extra daring, she squeezed his hand tightly before turning away to head indoors.

Her heart was heavy, leaving Richard's side, but she was encouraged by his progress. Looking back toward him one last time, he had already disappeared. Upon entering the solarium heightened emotions overtook her at the thought of their encounter and she collapsed.

Falling to her knees just inside the door, Rachel wept tears of joy while praising God for answering her prayers, "Oh, Lord, Your sweet Holy Spirit is so evident in Richard. He not only takes after Master Nathan but after You, too. Truly, I can see Your compassion and desire to help others is reflected in Richard's outstanding character. Thank You, Father, for the changes he has made and for the favor You have so lovingly bestowed upon me. I praise You for bringing me here to this place to serve Your beautiful Richard. I pray that I will be a source of peace for him as I strive to help him draw him closer to You. This is like a dream come true. Still, I promise to pursue You, the Dream Giver, not just the dream itself, as You are the One I adore. In Jesus' precious name, amen."

Hearing a familiar voice, she stirred.

"Good Heavens! Miss Rachel, are you quite well?" Austin asked, sounding worried when he entered the solarium and saw her crying in a heap on the floor.

Smiling up at him as he knelt beside her, she reassured him, "Yes. I-I guess I just need some food and water."

"Forgive me, Miss, but you are much too thin to skip breakfast. Here. Sit," Austin said, boldly helping her to the table. He then raced to get her food and drink he'd prepared for her hours ago. Returning promptly, he said, "Here you go, Miss. Please eat. You have not had any breakfast, and it is well past lunch."

"Thank you, Austin. I was in the gardens and must have lost track of time."

Uncovering the food, he asked, "Would you like me to...." He was going to offer to warm it up, but Rachel was already eating fast. She grabbed a bite of this and a bite of that and then downed some water, spilling a little as she drank in haste. "Are you all right, miss?" he asked again.

She wiped her chin and ate a bit more before coming up for air. "Austin, I must tell you, something wonderful has happened."

He looked puzzled and raised his caterpillar-like eyebrows.

But when she had inhaled a few more bites, she told him everything. "Austin, it's Richard! He has been amazing. He even came outside today," she said, blurting out the details of the changes in Richard thus far.

Austin gasped, "What?"

Rachel chuckled, "Isn't that wonderful?"

"I don't understand. He has not gone outside for so many years. Why would he venture out now?" Austin inquired, and then his face changed as it dawned on him. "It's you, Miss Rachel. He must fancy you a great deal. That would explain everything. Now I see why he stopped taking his medicine, why he has been so calm and dressed up each night, and why he cleaned his room."

"He cleaned his room?" she asked quickly as she continued eating.

"Why, yes. It has been a disaster for many years, but soon after you arrived, it was organized and spotless. I was so perplexed by this, but this all makes perfect sense now," he said, looking stunned.

"Well, don't look so shocked, Austin. Are you surprised he would fancy me? Am I that bad?" Rachel said jokingly.

He sighed. "Of course not, miss, but..."

"But what?"

"No. It's wonderful and quite extraordinary, really, that he has progressed so much since your arrival, but..."

"But what?" she asked again, genuinely wanting to know his opinion.

"Miss Rachel, pardon my boldness, but Master Nathan, well, surely you must see that he fancies you, too. And..."

She squinted and questioned, "And...?"

"What will happen to Richard if you love Master Nathan? And if you love Richard, I am just wondering how Master Nathan will react to that news? Miss Rachel, Master Nathan loves you. I am certain of it," Austin told her gently.

"I love him, too," she said as casually as she would announce her love for a brother or a father. "I mean, of course, I love him. He's positively darling," Rachel stated, but she knew what he was getting at.

Austin picked his chin up and raised a brow to let her know she wasn't fooling anyone.

"Okay, Austin. You are right, of course, and I know what you are implying. But you must trust me; my love for them is genuine, and I have the purest of intentions. I promise to do everything I can to bring joy, peace, and unity to them both, instead of division and sorrow. In fact, I have been praying for it. They are both wonderful and special, and I would never want to hurt either one of them. I hope you believe me," she sighed.

"I do, indeed, Miss Rachel. Yet, I'm just warning you to..."

"Yes, Austin? I honestly believe love will prevail in all of this and that my prayers will be answered."

"Just be careful, Miss."

"Be careful?" she asked.

"To protect their hearts, Miss Rachel. They mean the world to me and are both so fragile."

Although distraught by Austin's warning, she was happy to have someone to discuss it with. "Oh, Austin, I agree. And thank you for sharing your heart with me. I will be careful. I promise."

He finished, "And if I were you, I would be cautious to protect your own heart as well." Since he still wore a face of concern, Rachel lightly touched his hand to comfort him. He grinned in reply, so she changed the subject.

"Austin, can you help me with something?"

"You mean besides picking you up off the floor?" he inquired sarcastically, reminding her of Master Nathan.

She chuckled. "Yes, besides that. Thank you."

"Of course. What is it, Miss?"

"I would very much like to meet the staff today. Master Nathan let me know that since the accident they have been instructed to hide while still doing their tasks. We discussed this, and he agreed, now is a good time to change things back to the way they used to be. Thankfully, he's asked me to address this directly, for I am deeply concerned over how difficult it must be for them to do their jobs under these conditions. I want to reassure them they no longer need to remain in hiding and thank them for their years of hard work. Also, I know fresh air and sunlight is vital to maintain proper health. So, for Richard's sake, I hope to speak to the staff about cleaning and airing out the house while Master Nathan is away. Could you possibly arrange that?"

"Well, yes, actually. If you follow me to the kitchen, most of them are there at this very moment. Would you like to meet them now?"

"Oh, that would be perfect!" She stood quickly to hurry to the kitchen but was still a bit dizzy. She sat back down instantly to keep from falling.

"Why don't you finish your meal first and let me go and gather them to prepare for your introduction? I will come right back to get you. Will that be all right, Miss?"

Rachel nodded politely. "Yes. That will be just splendid. Thank you."

Austin promised Master Nathan he would take excellent care of Rachel while he was away, and her dizzy spell made him quite worried. Wanting her to finish her food, he turned to leave the room.

She took a deep breath and ate until she was content. Using her time alone to think of what scriptures to read to Richard that evening, she decided on several. While reminiscing about her walk with him, she stood and looked out the windows. Her longing eyes roamed over the gardens, hoping to catch another glimpse of him.

Although he eluded her, he stood hidden amongst the trees, watching her from a distance, hoping she was all right.

When Austin returned, he asked, "Are you ready, Miss?"

No longer feeling weak or lightheaded, Rachel replied, "Yes. Thank you." She took care to rise much slower this time. Relieved that the room was no longer spinning, she curtsied to show her gratitude before accompanying him to meet the staff. She didn't know whether she had cause to be nervous and grasped at her skirt.

Chapter 7

When Austin and Rachel entered the kitchen, about thirty staff jumped to attention. She quickly noticed they almost looked frightened. Seeing them react that way made her extra glad she had come.

Austin addressed them formally, "Good afternoon, everyone. This is Miss Rachel. Please give her your full attention. Master Nathan has left her in complete charge of the estate in his absence. Thank you." He bowed toward Rachel and stepped aside, leaving the floor all to her.

She curtsied and spoke sweetly yet with boldness to make herself clear, "Good day. I have come here to meet each one of you in person to say thank you. You have done a marvelous job caring for this house, Master Nathan, and Richard, who have grown to mean a great deal to me in a short amount of time. While he is away, Master Nathan has allowed me to make some changes around here. We shall see how well Richard tolerates these changes, and we will do our absolute best to keep him as calm as possible. Understood?"

There was a long silence as concern filled the room. Finally, her young, smitten, stableboy friend spoke up. "Pardon me, Miss, but what sort of changes?" he asked, wringing his hat in his hands nervously.

"Good changes, I assure you," she said, leaning forward and smiling his way. "My goal is to remove the spirit of fear and sadness from this house and to bring new life, light, laughter, and joy to all who live here." She stood tall, and her voice grew louder. "First, I want every window opened wide to let in as much fresh air and sunlight as we can. Weather permitting, of course."

Feeling the energy in the room shift, she continued, "I would like for us to clean and unclutter every room and place bouquets of fresh flowers in those Master Nathan uses most often, including Richard's room. The fresh flowers displayed in the foyer should be exceptionally colorful and grandiose." The staff began to glance around at each other excitedly.

"We shall start with the first floor, then work our way up toward Richard's area." She paused. "He has made tremendous progress this week, and he even went outside today."

Rachel could hear many of them gasp in disbelief upon hearing the news of Richard venturing outdoors, and some began to murmur, but that did not stop her. "For the time being, I recommend you continue to ignore him, for he is still unwell, but I believe there is great hope. Those of you who believe in prayer, I implore you to do so on his behalf. I trust God can work a miracle of restoration in his life, yet I will take any suggestions you may have."

Since no one commented, she looked around the room and asked, "Where are our cooks?"

"Here." Two women and two men raised their hands.

"Congratulations to you. You do such a wonderful job; the food since my arrival has been outstanding. Truly brilliant. But I request, from now on, you take care each day to give Richard whatever foods grown from the gardens you can, when they become available. Please be sure to include fresh meats, fish, and herbs, along with vegetables from every color of the rainbow for lunch and dinner. And if you could give him an array of fruits for breakfast, even if they have been canned, as well as fresh eggs each morning, that would be ideal. This way, we can provide him with a variety of foods to help him heal. But I ask that you give him very little in the way of sweet treats. Is everyone in agreement?"

"Yes, Miss," they replied.

After that, a staff member spoke up, "Is it okay to remove Gloria and the children's things from the hallway today?"

"Indeed, it is. As a matter of fact, I ask that each item be donated to the church in town, so they can in turn donate things as they see fit to the poor, per Master Nathan's request. And please, be sure to take great care as you transport everything to town. Any more questions?"

"What about Richard? Won't he be upset if we remove their things?" someone asked from the back, sounding deeply concerned.

"That is a good question, but I truly believe has already picked out what he wants to keep and that he will be all right."

"How can you be so sure?" someone next to her asked.

Rachel smiled, satisfied to hear the staff cared so much about Richard's well-being and answered, "Last night, Richard gave me some of their things as a gift. It was quite extraordinary. So, I am sure he has already gone through everything."

In awe, the staff whispered amongst themselves over how surprising Rachel's news was, but their expressions suggested most felt at ease.

"Do we need to continue to hide?" someone else asked.

"No. No, you most certainly do not. It is high time this home felt normal and friendly again. We must always show love and respect and give space to those we serve, but you must never be afraid here again. Is that clear?"

Nodding their heads with big smiles, they agreed, and a few even appeared to have tears in their eyes.

All were happy to oblige when Rachel delegated many jobs to rearrange and freshen up the house. "Now, before we get busy with our new tasks, I would very much like to learn your names. I want us to feel like a family here from now on." Since only Austin had ever asked their names before, they acted surprised to see she was genuinely interested in them. "Will you help me learn your names?"

The room filled with glee as, one by one, they each began giving their names and positions. Many thanked her for her kindness and told her they were thrilled by the changes she wanted to make. Others volunteered to take care of the new tasks Rachel had invoked right away and rushed off to get to work. Austin, too, looked satisfied. Rachel was having so much fun, but she knew she had better find Richard quickly before the commotion started.

"Excellent speech, Miss." Austin bowed toward her as she shamelessly grabbed another piece of food off her tray before it was taken away to be cleaned.

"Thank you, Austin," she responded proudly and lifted her chin to show fulfillment in a task well done. Dusting her hand off with two claps to remove a few crumbs, she gave Austin one last curtsy, left the kitchen, hurried down the hall, and headed up the stairs, seeking Richard.

In the middle of the lower staircase, Rachel paused for a moment to pray, knowing that, so far, she had only been to the second floor, never the third, where she assumed Richard's room was. She felt uneasy about finding him and was even more uncertain of what to do if she did not. Hoping to assess the area in which he lived, she wanted to open a few curtains to let in the light and perhaps even some windows for fresh air.

As Rachel headed up the grand staircase, she turned and looked back toward the stairs that she figured must lead to Richard's room. Her nerves twitched as she wondered if she would be welcome. This area of the house was his domain, after all, and she had not officially been invited.

A bit out of breath, she arrived at the top of the second floor of the grand staircase and to the base of the third-floor steps. Something caught her eye, and she put her hand up to her mouth in surprise. Much to her relief, Rachel knew she was not only going to be welcomed but that Richard was expecting her. On the bottom step leading up to the third level, there lay the single tulip from her visit to the gravesite with him. It had wilted, but still, it beckoned her. A look of satisfaction made its way across her face, knowing that her trip with him in the night was real.

A few stairs up, there was another newly cut tulip, and then another, and another. She picked them up one by one, forming a multi-colored bouquet as they led her up the staircase, down the hall, and then directly to what Rachel assumed was Richard's bedroom. She wondered if his room was almost directly over hers, but she was more intrigued by the music she could hear coming from inside.

Before stepping into his doorway, she blinked slowly, feeling the significance of what lay ahead. She asked God for guidance, again wondering if she should look at Richard or not. Though she desperately wanted to explain to him about the changes that were about to occur within the walls of Locke Mansion for his benefit, she knew in her heart it was not yet possible. Besides, even if she could explain, she had no idea how he would respond.

Standing outside in the hall, she peeked through the cracked-open door and noticed how dark his room was. Concerned about what his reaction might be, she knew it would be better to take her time. She was determined to bring some light into his bleak and lonely world but had learned to be extra careful, fearing she would bear the consequences otherwise.

Cautiously opening his door, Rachel held her breath. When she entered his room, she was pleasantly surprised by how neat and clean it was, just as Austin described. She was also astonished by its size. She thought that her room was huge, but Richard's appeared to be at least four times the size of hers. It was almost like a second ballroom. Although it was hard to see, she could tell that it was spectacular and wished it wasn't so gloomy so she could see better.

Even though it was daytime and there was plenty of light outside, the room had over thirty massive, thick, dark red, tightly closed, velvet curtains that refused to let any of the light into the room. The few lit candles sporadically spread about the room illuminated little. She narrowed her eyes to look around, taking it all in, and then she saw him, reminding her of the first time she'd ever seen Master Nathan. He had his back to her, staring out the one window where the curtain was pulled back about seven inches. His hands, clasped behind his back, made him appear deep in thought until he noticed her presence and slowly turned around.

Entering the room quietly, Rachel made sure not to look in his direction and pretended to talk to herself as she looked around. "Oh! This room is spectacular."

His room—filled with exquisite furniture, shelves with an extensive collection of books, a large grandfather clock, a few chairs, and a fireplace—was beyond glorious. Near the fireplace was a massive bed that looked inviting and lush, with a large canopy overhead. A few feet past his bed, the second phonograph in the house, created by Thomas Edison, captured her attention. It was playing the music she heard from down the hall, tempting her to dance.

While looking the other way, Rachel set down the armful of flowers she had collected on a nearby table. Her gaze elsewhere, she did not even notice that a few fell to the floor. Turning from side to side, she put her arms up and began to sway to the music to let him know she very much wished to dance with him.

Aroused by her presence, he did not hesitate. But first, he picked up the flowers she dropped and carefully placed them on top of the pile, stepped directly in front of her and lifted his arms into position. She shivered as his hands touched her skin, and before she knew it, they were once again whirling together as one.

Sensing that he was staring down at her intently, her heart began to race. She felt as though she would burst if she could not talk to him somehow, someday, and soon. After swallowing back her frustrations and taking in a few breaths, she allowed herself to relax and enjoy the dance. When she did, she felt a tremendous joy come over them both. Her emotions stirred so strongly that she almost laughed out loud, but instead, she remained silent and let him sweep her mind away so she could forget the rest of the world.

Richard was kind and gentle and such a strong dancer. Much like his father, he led her with each step as though on a cloud. Rachel could not believe how incredible she felt around him and held back a giggle, hoping he felt the same way.

By candlelight, dancing together step by step without missing a beat, they spun gracefully together as time stood still. Not yet daring to meet his gaze, she let her eyes wander about the room. When she did, a vision flashed across her mind just like it had before in the ballroom. She could envision a live orchestra making melodies with perfection. A room full of guests dressed in their best with her family and friends dancing about flashed across her mind. It was a festive occasion like none other, but when the music stopped, silence filled the room and her vision vanished as fast as it had appeared.

Letting go of Richard, she danced across the room by herself without any music at all, feeling light and free. After a while, she remembered why she had come up to his room in the first place and began gently touching each curtain as she danced past. Not daring to open any quite yet, she began humming to herself as she explored the outer edges of his bedroom.

Then, in an instant, the most enchanting sound she had ever witnessed slid into her ears. Stopping dead in her tracks, she listened intently to the exhilarating tune surrounding her.

Wanting to communicate with her but not knowing how else to do so, Richard had sat down to play his cello for her.

Moved by the passion he displayed throughout his body while he played, Rachel could not help but smile. His head bobbed to and fro in time to the music while his hands flowed smoothly, manipulating the bow and strings. His hair, wildly covering parts of his eyes, reminded her of her first dreams of him. Standing motionless, in shock over his skill level, she covered her mouth with one hand, watching him in awe. He looked so charming, and his music simply took her breath away.

A rush of confidence hit her. She resumed dancing alone again but this time to his music, wearing an enthralled grin as she allowed herself to fall deeper in love with this man of many talents. In no time, it became clear that song was his way of openly communicating his desires for her.

Dancing past the curtains, Rachel reached out and touched them one by one, letting in one sliver of light at a time. Then, believing so strongly that Richard needed sunlight, fresh air, and a connection to nature, she knew what she had to do next. Wanting him to get well, her burning desire to help him grew with the intensity of the music. She could not hold back the urge any longer. Ever so slowly, she pulled back just one curtain, revealing the bright sunlight, to see if Richard would do anything out of the ordinary. Since he continued playing, her eyes lit up.

The light was too bright for him at first, but his eyes soon adjusted, and he fixed his gaze directly on her. He watched her every hand and foot placement while she twirled in graceful circles before pulling back another curtain. As the music rose to its crescendo, she ripped open another curtain and then another and another without holding back.

Enthusiastically, she opened each curtain while Richard played, as though they had choreographed the entire display until the whole room was filled with radiant sunlight. Rachel was astounded, and her gaze widened. The light, beaming through thirty, twenty-feet-tall windows, as well as a few that were stained-glass and colorful, revealed the true immensity of his room.

His song began slowing, with quieter, more solemn tones that soothed Rachel while she opened a window to let in some fresh air. A sudden breeze rushed in and hit Richard directly, blowing his hair away from his face. He inhaled and finished with a few beautiful, lingering low notes and closed his eyes. Dropping his hands to his sides, he lifted his chin to enjoy the wind and sunshine upon his skin as he had in the garden. He carefully set his instrument down and, after taking a few deep breaths, began to rush in her direction, looking determined.

Quite nervous about what he might do, Rachel held still. Worried he was upset with her for opening his curtains and window, she wondered, *Will he close them?* Instead, he went directly to another window. Grabbing it firmly, he flung it open wide and stuck his head out to take in the delicious spring scent. He shut his eyes and inhaled so deeply that, to her, it looked as though the breeze was healing his soul. In haste, he made his way directly to another window and opened that as well, and the next, and the next. Exhilarated, he let out a chuckle as a big gust of wind blew all the candles in the room out simultaneously with a *whoosh*.

When the last window was opened, she joined him. Standing beside him, she, too, closed her eyes, taking in the warm rays and the sweet aroma of spring.

He turned to watch her and smiled. Reaching up with trembling hands, Richard gently stroked the wisps of tight curls that glowed in the sunlight as they fell around her face.

Keeping her eyes shut, Rachel remained motionless for a long while, not wanting to ruin a single ounce of his joy. But after opening her eyes, she stepped backward and continued to look out at the landscape as Richard circled her to inspect her like he had done the first night they'd met. It was as though he wanted to examine her again in the brightness of daylight, unable to get enough of her. Breathing heavily with her heart pounding hard against her chest, she silently hoped to impress him.

Standing behind her, he became very daring, pulled her hair to one side, and softly kissed her exposed neck. Surprised, she quickly stepped forward to stand in the window, but that did not stop him. He stepped up behind her, brushed her hair to the other side, and kissed her neck with firmer pressure.

Rachel's passion for him rose to new heights as she tilted her head and exposed more of her neck for him to kiss. His soft lips on her skin made her feel weak. Gripping the windowsill tightly, she almost collapsed. The powerful emotions rising inside of her from all that was happening caught her off guard. She thought he might get angry with her for opening his room to the elements, but this... this was unexpected.

He kissed her neck again and again, sensing she was falling more in love with him and his touch. Knowing she was allowing things to progress much too fast, she inhaled deeply and put her hand on her heart. Unaware of her thoughts, he kissed her again. This time, she felt a strong urge to turn and kiss him back directly on his lips but realized that she had better step away instead. Slowly and gracefully, not wanting to hurt his feelings, she positioned herself on his left side.

Spotting a shiny object from across the room, she briskly walked toward it. Rachel gasped upon noticing many unique machines of various shapes and sizes along his room's entire inner wall. She wondered if these creations were things he had designed. They appeared to be set up on display and were quite impressive. Seeing what looked like his desk or workstation covered in perfectly arranged tools of every sort, she was amazed.

Without speaking a word, Richard came up behind her and demonstrated precisely how one of his inventions worked. Ignoring him as best she could, she watched the workings of his device intently and dared to speak out loud, "Oh, my goodness. That is outstanding!"

Going down the row, he demonstrated one product after the next, and she was glad to see that he seemed extremely proud of his craftsmanship. She thought to herself, *I wonder if anyone has ever complimented him on his work before?* Then speaking out once more, she said, "I have never seen anything so incredible in my life. Look at the details!"

Feeling his enthusiasm building while he revealed many of his projects to her, he seemed almost giddy as she admired them. "This craftsmanship is like nothing I have ever seen. Each so unique and useful." Clearly, Richard was a genius, but more importantly, she could tell that he desperately wanted to speak with her about his work. She sighed and thought to herself, *Oh, how I wish he would.*

She took a long time to inspect everything he had created, but not wanting to wear out her welcome, Rachel knew that she should leave soon. After he'd finished, she walked back to her flowers and gathered them into her arms. Not wanting to leave him without coming up with a plan to see him again, she hesitated and thought about what to do. While keeping her eyes down, as though talking to her bouquet, she shared her plans aloud. "After I help the staff clean and air out the house, or perhaps following dinner tonight, I shall play the piano in the parlor and practice dancing again in the ballroom a bit more," she said with a soft grin before walking toward the door, hoping he would take the hint that she wanted him to meet her in the parlor later on.

Although Richard remained silent, she could feel his eagerness to spend more time with her. So, she slowly turned and left him standing alone in his room to walk down the hall, deeply satisfied as the sun coming from his room lit her way.

Stepping out of his doorway into the hall, he watched the sway of her hips from behind. When she was close to the staircase, she heard a noise that sounded familiar, as though Richard opened yet another curtain at the other end of the hall. She turned to check, and, seeing her assumption was correct, her smile became even more prominent. Knowing that the last thing a person needs is darkness and solitude when fighting sorrow, she was hopeful he understood the vital importance of what she was trying to do.

In high spirits, Rachel listened to him open all the hall curtains and glanced back before heading down the staircase. A sense of victory came over her spirit, and she grinned. With a single nod, she acknowledged that, again, God had intervened, and she could not have been more thankful.

Approaching the bottom of the grand staircase, she felt a buzz in the air and could smell the scent of spring flowing all around her. Workers were busy cleaning, opening windows, organizing rooms, and bringing flowers in from the gardens and greenhouse. The mansion felt more vibrant and alive than she anticipated. Praising God, she whispered, "Thank you."

"Miss Rachel is it okay if we rearrange furniture, too?" a member of the staff named Dean asked her.

"Yes. That is a great idea. Just be sure to be careful with Master Nathan's papers and be careful with the musical instruments, will you?"

"Of course, Miss," he stated as he bowed and then returned to work.

Excited for Master Nathan to see the changes in the house and share the news of Richard embarking on his journey outside, her feelings were again mixed about his return. She grasped her hands together, genuinely concerned about how he would react to Richard falling for her. She told herself, *I had better figure something out, and fast! But what?*

Rachel was torn, having no idea what to do. She remembered the strong desire for Richard she felt in her dreams, even before meeting him. Still, in the first few days at Locke Mansion, she had unintentionally fallen for Master Nathan as well, assuming that Richard was only a figment of her imagination. She had no idea that he was real. But now, loving them both for different reasons, the last thing she wanted to do was to hurt either of them. Rachel knew Austin was right: she needed to be careful with both of their hearts as well as her own, and she sighed.

Praying about her predicament while working hard, she reminded herself to slow down since she had not felt particularly well that morning. Aware that worrying never helped in any situation, she decided to pace herself. Thankfully, Austin found her and brought her some refreshments so she could keep busy.

"Oh, Austin, you are so thoughtful."

He explained with a lift of his brow, "As I told you before, Master Nathan made it very clear that I am to take excellent care of you while he is away. I fear I am not doing my job."

Rachel responded hastily, "Don't be silly. Of course, you are. Why would you say such a thing?"

"Well, this morning, you almost fainted due to having breakfast much too late, and now it's well past time to eat again, and here you are, working. Won't you come to sit in the dining room to eat, please?"

To appease him, she agreed. "All right. Since you asked so nicely, I will."

They walked together to the dining room, and she openly shared with him a little about her time spent with Richard. "Austin, it is so exciting. Richard just let me into his room, and he allowed me to open all of his curtains and windows."

Austin froze. "I beg your pardon, Miss Rachel, but what did you just say?"

"I know! It's like a miracle, isn't it?" she said with childlike animation.

He stuttered, "I-I don't know what to say, Miss. In ten years, Richard has not allowed anyone to open his room or let in the fresh air. To keep the air from stagnating, I had to sneak in on occasion to air things out when he was not around. Miss Rachel, this truly is hard to believe," he stated, still shocked, but resumed walking.

She then exclaimed, "Austin, I honestly believe in the power of prayer. You see, Richard not only let me open his room, but he helped me. And he seemed gleeful while doing it. Let me just tell you, it was so thrilling. More importantly, as I left him to come back downstairs, he continued to open the rest of the upstairs rooms and hallway windows himself."

"What?" Austin asked, dumbfounded.

"I know!" Rachel said with a chuckle.

"You are right, Miss Rachel. It is a miracle, indeed," he stated.

She sat down to eat, but this time, one servant after the next brought her food. They were so kind; she could tell they were delighted to no longer remain in hiding.

She addressed the staff in between bites and reiterated the importance of ignoring Richard until she let them know otherwise. She explained that they might be seeing more of him during the day but made it clear again, they were not to pay any attention to him just yet. They bowed and promised to pass that news on to the others before they left her alone so she could finish her meal.

Hoping it would attract Richard to spend more time with her, Rachel went to the parlor to play the piano. She believed the more time he spent with people, the more progress he would make. Sitting down, she began to play softly. In no time, she could sense Richard standing behind her. Thankful he had come, she simply continued to stroke the keys, pretending she did not notice his arrival.

Within herself, she could feel his emotions building as he slowly walked about the room, watching her. When he cautiously sat next to her on the piano bench, just like he loved to do with his mother, Rachel swallowed back her tears, overwhelmed with compassion. She knew how long it had been since he had sat next to Gloria on this very bench, and her eyes welled up just thinking about it.

She played and sang to the best of her ability but kept it soft and sweet, concerned about how he would respond to any level of intensity. After a while, he laid his head upon her shoulder, acting just as Master Nathan had described. She was thankful to be a part of helping Richard heal, but she wished she could simply hold him in her embrace.

The more Rachel thought about everything he had lost, she had to stop herself from crying since Richard sounded like he might be weeping. She lowered her chin and played on, glad he seemed to enjoy her voice as a look of contentment came across his face.

Never had she felt so moved by the Holy Spirit. She realized her fingers and voice sounded anointed. Ending her song with a lightest tap of the keys, she laid her hands in her lap. Then, as if to thank her, Richard reached over and placed his hand over hers, touching her heart immensely, making her inhale slowly to keep from shaking. She thought to herself, *growing up alone in this big house, he must miss his mother terribly.*

After moments of peaceful silence, he stood but did not let go of her. As they walked together holding hands, Rachel could not help but wear a shy smile. She wondered just what he had in store for her next and where he was taking her.

Chapter 8

Walking by Richard's side through the mansion, Rachel was heartsick as she pictured him roaming the halls of his house alone all these years. She guessed that he was leading her to the ballroom and grinned as she anticipated spending her evening dancing with him.

When she and Richard arrived, Rachel noticed that someone had already turned on the ballroom's many lights, and she thought, *I wonder if Richard turned them on? Perhaps he was hoping to see me better while we dance this time?*

He led her down the staircase, similar to the way his father had, and started the music, but the song was different this time. It was lovely, yet more passionate.

Pleased to think that they were going to be able to dance together again, she covered her mouth with one hand. Being with him in this magnificent place made her feel as though she was living in a dream world. It was like the Heavenly home she had always imagined. Keeping her eyes down she placed her hands over her heart while she waited for him, *I hope he can tell I love every minute of our time together.*

Whirling around the room, Rachel felt his eyes admiring her face, and she could no longer stand it. She wanted more than anything to look into his eyes, and without thinking, she tried to make eye contact with him like she had the first time they'd danced together by the light of the moon.

The instant she lifted her gaze, their eyes locked. But to her dismay, Richard stopped dancing and his entire body froze. He abruptly turned away from her, as if he couldn't stand being seen. It had been years since he'd felt as though anyone had the ability to truly *see* him, and he acted unsure of how to handle the attention. For a moment, he started to walk toward the terrace in anger but stopped himself. A few steps away, he stood motionless, staring out the window, gasping for air, panicking.

Rachel visualized the turmoil seething within him. To her, he looked torn between clinging to his past—continuing to believe he was a ghost—and what he desired for his future: her. He wanted her. She was sad that he appeared to be shaking, disoriented, horribly frustrated, and unable to move, paralyzed by his fears.

Not wanting to hurt him further, Rachel considered rushing off to her room, but she hated leaving him alone. She quickly prayed for guidance and was reminded of how God relentlessly pursues those whom He loves with the utmost gentleness. So, trying to be Christlike, she made a choice and swallowed back her concerns. Ever so slowly, she walked up behind Richard and put her hand on his shoulder.

Drawing her lips inward to hold her tongue, it was clear he was crying, which broke her heart. When he turned his body away from the window and stood still, Rachel drew closer to his side. She traced the edges of his shoulder and ran her fingers down his arm, then waited for a moment. Growing rather daring, she took his hand into hers, and stepped directly in front of him. His eyes remained focused on the floor, yet she moved his hand onto her waist. Knowing it was risky, she took her other hand and lifted his chin, trying to look into his eyes once more as if to tell him that everything was going to be all right.

She kissed his other hand firmly and lifted it into position as she glanced his way. It had been so long since anyone had looked upon him with such love, his eyebrows narrowed in confusion.

But thankfully, despite his bewilderment, instead of leaving in a rage, Richard chose something different. Vastly different. He chose to look deep into her eyes without fear, and right then and there, he chose to dance.

Taking Rachel's breath away, he moved about the room with more passion than before as they twirled again as one. But this time, they did not take their eyes off each other, and she could tell that he loved it as a smile grew more pronounced upon his face. And with each move he made, as she admired him, she noticed that he looked more stable than ever.

Their hearts beat perfectly in sync, interlacing into each other's world as the music moved them along in a dream-like state. She grinned, proud of his progress, but she still felt it best to take things slow, and so she remained quiet.

Covering every square inch of the ballroom for the entirety of the song, *I could dance with Richard like this forever,* Rachel thought to herself. When the music stopped, they strolled outside onto the terrace holding hands just as she and Master Nathan had done. This made Rachel wonder if Richard had been watching them the entire time and if he was trying to imitate his father.

She still did not dare to speak to him directly, but without saying a word, Richard's eyes suddenly lit up. He seemed to want to explore as he led her down the terrace stairs in haste, so she followed close and continued to hold his hand, excited about where he might lead her.

Once they made it to the rose garden, he slowed his pace and circled the fountain before investigating the archways with her. They proceeded to enjoy a quiet stroll in the gardens, and once again, he appeared amused while listening to the crickets' song. Meandering through the mansion's beautiful grounds for over an hour, they exchanged glances of admiration. Rachel, smiling at him, almost blurted out what she was thinking, *I cannot believe this! I am so grateful.*

When he grabbed a lantern sitting on a nearby bench seat and motioned for her to follow him further away from the house, Richard surprised her again. The lantern's light led them closer to the trees, yet Rachel let him lead, trusting him. She looked pleased once she realized they had made their way back to the swing.

Acting like he wanted to push her like before, he set the lantern down and stood holding the ropes, as though he was waiting for her to take a seat.

Happy to indulge him, grasping each rope one at a time, she sat gracefully. Rachel closed her eyes and enjoyed the softness of the tepid breeze against her face as she swung forward. His touch on her back made her grin. Not a word was spoken, but peace flowed between them, and the back-and-forth motion of the swing seemed to connect them somehow.

Finally, still holding hands, they walked back to the terrace; occasionally looking at one another and grinning wide. Now standing side by side, Richard looked up at the house and took in its splendor. With its windows lit up from the inside, Locke Mansion looked picturesque, but as Rachel witnessed Richard admiring his home, she could not take her eyes off him. She adored watching him experience things anew and exhaled, wearing a satisfied expression.

When they re-entered the ballroom, they climbed the staircase and walked down the many hallways leading back to her room. Rachel was so glad Richard was no longer alone and squeezed his hand before letting it go. Upon entering her bedroom, she noticed that the windows and curtains had been opened by the staff as instructed. The evening breeze felt refreshing and invigorated her. Unfortunately, not knowing how to proceed, no moment had ever felt more awkward between them. She knew it was time to change and get ready for bed, but she did not want to do so with him in the room. Thinking quickly, she prayed aloud, "Thank you, Lord, for this glorious day. As I change into my nightclothes, please help me to think pure thoughts. In Jesus name. Amen."

At that point, thankfully, Richard stepped back, smiled and bent forward at the waist, bowing low toward her as if she were a member of the royal family. Rachel held her breath, watching him. He then gracefully backed out of her room and closed the door to leave her alone to change. *What a gentleman he is turning out to be.* Not wanting to waste a single moment, she got ready for bed as quickly as possible while he waited for her in the hall.

Putting on a few dabs of vanilla-scented perfume and her best nightgown and robe, she took down her hair and let it flow since Richard seemed to like her curls so much. She laid several blankets and pillows down in front of the fireplace but further back from the hearth, so they would not get overheated. Although it was getting a bit too warm outside for a fire, Rachel had instructed the staff to continue to make one in her room in the evenings for Richard's sake. She was glad they had, because sitting by the fire with the gentle breeze blowing into the room, made her room feel gloriously connected to nature.

Determined to not ruin their progress, while she continued to ready herself, she silently took a moment to ask God for guidance on how to handle the rest of the night with Richard. *Dear Lord, I know that You did not put stories in Your Word of others achieving breakthroughs, having divine encounters, receiving promises, blessings, and healings to simply tease the rest of us. Nor did You mean to cause our hearts to grow weary due to hope deferred when our expectations are unmet. I'm confident You shared those stories so that we can recall Your goodness, mercy, and authority over loneliness, illness, and darkness. Your ability and desire to heal, show how You long to shower Your love on those in need so that our faith can grow to believe in our own breakthrough. I ask that You help me not only to consider the stories of You healing others throughout history but that You show me Your desire for Richard's healing as well. I trust in Your ability to restore his mind and transform his life. I refuse to believe that he cannot recover. I thank You that each time I read Your Word to Richard, You increase his faith as well as mine. Guide me by Your gentle hand and lead us beside still waters this night. In Jesus' name, amen.*

Taking in a deep breath, with a soft smile, Rachel opened the door to let Richard back in. Eager to share the Word and pray with him again, she led him until they were facing each other. Hand-in-hand, while gazing into one another's eyes, they knelt together ever so slowly. After making themselves comfortable upon the blankets and pillows beside the crackling fire, they inched closer to each other than they had the night before. She sat up to read, but Richard laid down next to her and looked up at her expectantly.

Before Rachel grabbed her Bible, she chose to pray out loud in front of him first. Longing to teach him many things about God, she prayed, "Dear Lord, as I look into Your eyes of mercy, Your eyes of love, I remember that Your heart is for me, not against me. I am holding on to Your divine love, and I am never letting go. When I am weak, You are strong; when I let go, I fall into Your arms. You are so wise, generous, and kind. I thank You for the beauty of today. I praise You for shining Your light and love upon this house and ask for true meaning and joy to fill the hearts of all who live here. Thank You for the splendor of Your gardens, the gift of dance, inspired inventions, human connection, and Your perfect peace, which comes from Heaven above. I steady my hope on the unmoving, solid ground of Your goodness. When I feel heavy with sorrow, I will lay it down at Your feet. Through trials, I will lift up my eyes to the hills from where my help comes."

Richard squirmed a bit, but she proceeded, "I will listen intently to hear that majestic sound of Your voice that speaks to me in the silence. And when the storms rage all around me, I will praise You, my God. Your rod and Your staff, they comfort me. You make a table before me in the presence of my enemies. You will never leave me or forsake me. And I thank You, my King, for the love You so freely give, so we can share it with others, for that is where we find our true selves and the purest form of joy."

Wanting to share more about Jesus, Rachel hoped that Richard was listening carefully. "Father, I praise You for Your Son and His willingness to leave His riches in glory to come and save us from our sins. Thank You that He came and humbled Himself by giving up His throne. His choice to be born as a baby in a manger and walk this Earth as a child and man of sorrows, caring for the sick and healing all who had diseases, forever changed history. The way He stood up to injustice and defeated the enemy on our behalf is astonishing. He did not have to come and live as a man nor die upon the cross for our sins, but He chose to so that He could redeem us. Because of His love, You can now forgive us and have fellowship with us for all eternity. And we, too, can forgive others and ourselves, setting us free from suffering. I know the Devil wants us to live in the past and wallow in sorrow and self-pity, yet Jesus died so we can have peace and a new life, a life that we can live, as Your Word says, more abundantly."

It was clear that she now had Richard's full attention and finished, "Thank You that Jesus went to the grave for us so we would never have to suffer that same fate. I am in awe that after His death and burial, He rose again on the third day to visit His people on Earth, proving the truth of His resurrection power to overcome even death. I cling to the eternal truth that—in Jesus' life, death, burial, and resurrection—the enemy, who roams around like a roaring lion seeking whom he may devour, was defeated forever. I praise You, Father, knowing that Jesus is once again seated at Your right hand where He will rule and reign as our High Priest. I have confidence that He is standing up for us daily as our faithful Brother until His triumphant return. In the meantime, help me to walk out my life as a living sacrifice, serving others so Your joy may be complete in me. Help me now to read Your Word with focus so I can hear what You have to teach me this night. I love You deeply with all that I am. In Jesus' name, amen."

Richard wiped a tear away before he whispered, "Amen." He then laid his head down on her lap to fully enjoy her reading, with a meek expression.

Delighted to hear him say, "Amen," Rachel grinned. Hearing him at all amazed her. Thinking of how significant it was that he had spoken (a small miracle of its own), she yearned for the possibility that he might one day believe in his full recovery.

She opened her Bible to the gospels that showed more healings, hoping it would strengthen Richard's faith. Having learned her Bible so well, she was able to quickly find each one. "John 4:46-54: 'So Jesus came again to Cana of Galilee where He had made the water wine. And there was a certain nobleman whose son was sick at Capernaum. When he heard that Jesus had come out of Judea into Galilee, he went to Him and implored Him to come down and heal his son, for he was at the point of death. Then Jesus said to him, "Unless you people see signs and wonders, you will by no means believe." The nobleman said to Him, "Sir, come down before my child dies!" Jesus said to him, "Go your way; your son lives." So the man believed the word that Jesus spoke to him, and he went his way. And as he was now going down, his servants met him and told him, saying, "Your son lives!" Then he inquired of them the hour when he got better. And they said to him, "Yesterday at the seventh hour the fever left him." So the father knew that it was at the same hour in which Jesus said to him, "Your son lives." And he himself believed, and his whole household.'"

She continued reading since Richard leaned in and acted intrigued by the words she spoke. "Mark 1:21-28 and Luke 4:33-37: 'Then they went into Capernaum, and immediately on the Sabbath He entered the synagogue and taught. And they were astonished at His teaching, for He taught them as one having authority, and not as the scribes. Now there was a man in their synagogue with an unclean spirit. And he cried out, saying, "Let *us* alone! What have we to do with you, Jesus of Nazareth? Did You come to destroy us? I know who You are - the Holy One of God!" But Jesus rebuked him, saying, "Be quiet, and come out of him!" And when the unclean spirit had convulsed him and cried out with a loud voice, he came out of him. Then they were all amazed, so that they questioned among themselves, saying, "What is this? What new doctrine is this? For with authority He commands even the unclean spirits, and they obey Him." And immediately His fame spread throughout all the region around Galilee.'"

Although Richard looked perplexed, she continued but wondered if he might be fighting some sort of demon of his own. She hoped that one day soon, she would be able to discuss it with him and pray over him with boldness. Despite her concerns, Rachel still claimed victory in her heart for God to unlock his mind, trusting that he would be completely set free in due time.

Because Richard, having reacted so strongly with each verse, appeared to want more stories of Jesus healing people, Rachel skipped ahead. "'When the sun was setting, all those who had any that were sick with various diseases brought them to Him; and He laid His hands on every one of them and healed them. And demons also came out of many, crying out and saying, "You are the Christ, the Son of God!" And He, rebuking them, did not allow them to speak, for they knew that He was the Christ.' Luke 4:40-41."

Feeling Richard's excitement grow, she shared, Matthew 8:5-10, and then went on to read verse 13, "'Now when Jesus had entered Capernaum, a centurion came to Him, pleading with Him, saying, "Lord, my servant lying at home paralyzed, dreadfully tormented." And Jesus said to him, "I will come and heal him." The centurion answered and said, "Lord, I am not worthy that You should come under my roof. But only speak a word, and my servant will be healed. For I also am a man under authority, having soldiers under me. And I say to this one, 'Go,' and he goes; and to another, 'Come,' and he comes; and to my servant, 'Do this,' and he does it." When Jesus heard *it*, He marveled, and said to those who followed, "Assuredly, I say to you, I have not found such great faith, not even in Israel!" Then Jesus said to the Centurion; "Go, your way; and as you have believed, so let it be done for you." And his servant was healed that same hour.'"

She then read about a young man that Jesus raised from the dead in Luke 7:11-15. Unsure how Richard would respond, she read it slowly, so he would see that nothing is impossible for Jesus. "'Now it happened, the day after, that He went into a city called Nain; and many of His disciples went with Him, and a large crowd. And when He came near the gate of the city, behold, a dead man was being carried out, the only son of his mother; and she was a widow. And a large crowd from the city was with her. When the Lord saw her, He had compassion on her and said to her, 'Do not weep.' Then He came and touched the open coffin, and those who carried *him* stood still. And He said, 'Young man, I say to you, arise.' So he who was dead sat up and began to speak. And He presented him to his mother.'"

Skipping through the New Testament, Rachel shared scriptures about freedom, desperate to bring Richard some peace. She read Colossians 1:21-22: "'Once you were alienated from God and were enemies in your minds because of your evil behavior. But now He has reconciled you by Christ's physical body through death to present you holy in His sight, without blemish and free from accusation.'"

Showing signs of distress, Richard sat up. It was unclear what he might be thinking, so she read Ephesians 3:12, attempting to comfort him. "'In Him and through faith in Him we may approach God with freedom and confidence.'"

Rachel finished, closed her Bible, sat it down, and prayed aloud, "Lord, help us to witness Your power to heal and change lives. Thank You that You long to set us free, as Your created beings, so we can choose our own destiny. Help us to live out our lives, pleasing in Your sight."

Having hoped her prayers and Bible reading would calm Richard, she noticed that, instead, his face was red, and his fists clenched. It seemed to her that he had many questions, making him more desperate than ever to speak with her, but he did not know how.

Afraid to say another word, she covered her mouth. With each passing moment, she grew more nervous as he fidgeted but remained quiet to give him time to process. But to her surprise, Richard jumped up and ran out of the room in a rage with what almost sounded like a growl. Rachel scrambled to her feet, tripping on the hem of her nightgown, and rushed to follow him. Unfortunately, he ran down the hall and up the stairs so quickly, she could not catch him. Once she had decided to let him be, she lowered her head.

Frustrated and panting heavily, she looked at the floor and questioned what she had done wrong. She rubbed her hands together for warmth and went back into her room to ask God to envelop Richard and herself with peace. "I need to be more careful," she muttered under her breath as she paced back and forth, "Father, forgive me."

Getting a sense that Richard was torn between continuing to believe the horrific lie he had lived with for so long and accepting a potential new reality, she feared she may have introduced those scriptures too quickly. Because he'd been convinced for so many years that he was a ghost and could not speak to anyone, she knew that it would be difficult for him to admit the truth. Rachel understood that accepting change was always hard, even when it was the right thing to do.

She realized that at this point in his life, altering his normal activities might be nearly impossible for him. Yet, she had to trust that the Lord would give him supernatural strength to embrace his desires for a bright future, strength beyond the powers which controlled his dark existence.

Rachel recalled Master Nathan telling her that Richard once had a dream of living life like a normal man, yet sadly, it was a dream he had left behind long ago. Despite that, she hoped he could see the unlimited power of God to alter a soul's cry. Filled with remorse, she grabbed at her stomach, knowing that when he learned about God's forgiveness, he would have to decide between staying the same or line up with the truth of what she was reading to him.

Thinking back as she re-entered her room, she questioned herself again. *Hearing that he is a man, has been given freedom, and that he has the power to choose his own destiny must have hit him like a slap in the face. But once he can grasp these possibilities, will he continue to live a lie—alone and afraid, filled with guilt and shame—or will he choose to live... perhaps even live a life with me?*

She sat by the fire again and asked aloud, "God, of course, You love people right where they are, but out of pure love, You also gave Your Word to help us grow. And although it is nearly impossible for some people to receive love, I ask that You help Richard *feel* Your love for Him throughout the scriptures. And help him *want* to understand Your love more. He needs You so."

Long ago, Rachel had learned the hard way, change was never easy, but that it was vital when one wanted to thrive, not merely survive, so she sighed. *If Richard could only see that he is alive, and not a ghost but a beloved child of God, then he might have a chance.* She pleaded with God, "In order for him to be able to speak to me directly, he will need to confront his fears head-on, let go of the past, and forgive himself. So, I beg of You to help him do just that."

She listened carefully and figured; *I must have pushed him too far too fast.* She rubbed her arms as goosebumps raised high on her skin. Clearly, he was distraught. Even though he refrained from throwing things around his room this time, there was no mistaking the sound of him overhead clawing at the floor, crying out loud to God.

Hearing Richard's cries in the night echoing throughout the halls of Locke Mansion, her heart ached for him. Kneeling, Rachel clasped her fingers together tight. She interceded for him once more in front of the dwindling fire, with the fire in her soul burning hotter than ever.

"Please, God, heal Richard. Heal his wounded soul from the grief and the loss he has endured. By now, he must realize that he not only lost his family but years of his life. Father, You are the One who parted the Red Sea when all looked hopeless. I beg of You to heal his mind from all confusion and painful memories. Help him to forgive himself for the accident and the grief it has brought into this home and to his father. Help him to see that it was not his fault and that the burden he carries over the loss of their lives is not his to bear. Please, hear his cries. In Jesus' mighty name, amen."

Wiping her eyes, she laid back down on the floor and buried her face deep into his pillow and wept while listening to his sobs. Interceding for what seemed like hours into the night until slipping into dreamland, she slept with tears still wet on her cheeks.

The next morning, oddly, Rachel found herself curled up in her bed. Disoriented, she remembered falling asleep amongst the pillows by the fire. *I wonder if Richard snuck back into my room and put me into bed?* Unable to remember climbing into bed on her own, she pondered the possibility. *He is obviously strong enough.* She was relieved to think that, after he prayed, he must have calmed down enough to return to check in on her. Once she realized that he had taken such care to move her without waking her, she looked astonished, with raised eyebrows.

She wanted to trust that Richard's prayers for himself would make a big difference, but again, she was unsure of his progress. Recalling how he sounded in the night as he pounded his fists against the floor directly above her, sobbing, she scratched her head. *It might be his way of begging God for healing; perhaps he finally longs to be free? Or perhaps he begged God to help him because he longs to be with me?*

Glad the night was over, Rachel looked up at her window and saw it was again raining and stormy outside. Choosing not to get up just yet, she lay still, drifting in and out of slumber, tired and weary. Then, unexpectedly, a vision came to her. She was sure it was from the Lord, but it startled her.

Chapter 9

Clear as could be, in her vision, Rachel saw herself approaching God as her beloved Father. Yet she was tall and strong, like a giant, and instead of Richard carrying her, *she* was carrying him. The thing that shocked her was when she looked down, she could see Richard at every age. From even before infancy, to when he was a baby, to a small child, to his teen years, to now. As she held him tightly in her arms at his current age, the Lord told her, in a clear and loud voice, that it was safe to let him go. She saw herself laying Richard at the feet of her Lord, showing God that she trusted Him to take care of the one for whom her heart ached. Her Heavenly Father then spoke to her in a gentle whisper, "Fear not, my child."

Pleased by God's comforting words, she closed her eyes and promptly fell back asleep.

Hours later, she heard a light knock at her door. "Yes? Who is it?" she asked in a groggy voice, half awake.

She heard a soft-spoken, unfamiliar voice coming from the hallway. "Miss Rachel? May I come in?"

"Yes, you may enter," she replied, sitting up with a yawn.

When a young girl opened her door, Rachel recalled she was one of the girls who attended to her on her first morning at Locke Mansion, *the one who smiled.* She had accompanied Miss Sarah that day and seemed kind. Entering cautiously, the timid girl set down a tray covered in a display of delicious breakfast treats for Rachel before she turned and hurried off toward the door.

"Wait! What is your name?" Rachel asked. The girl stopped in her tracks and seemed nervous, wide-eyed as she turned back toward Rachel.

Shyly, the girl asked, "My... my name, Miss?"

"Yes. Come here. Please, sit. Tell me your name." Rachel sweetly motioned for the girl to sit beside her at the foot of her bed, wondering why they had not met during their staff meeting the day prior.

The girl acted timid, but she obeyed and sat with caution.

"My name is Jeanne," she mumbled.

"Well, Jeanne, I am Rachel. It's nice to meet you, officially," Rachel spoke out with cheer, hoping to pull Jeanne out of her shell. "That is a unique name. What does it mean?"

"It is French. It means, 'God is gracious,'" Jeanne replied quietly.

"Oh, that is interesting. Was your father French?"

"No, my father was Irish, and my mother was French."

Rachel turned her head, and gave her a sweet look of approval, "Why are you so quiet, my dear? You do not have to be afraid of me, Jeanne. I am a servant in this house just like you," Rachel said, trying to reassure her.

Jeanne, acting surprised, inquired, "You are, Miss?"

"Yes. I am. I beg your pardon, but may I ask how old you are?"

Jeanne replied, "I'm eighteen, Miss Rachel."

"Me, too! Tell me, how long have you worked here at Locke Mansion?"

"Just a year."

"What is it that you do here?"

"Well, before, I did whatever Miss Sarah told me. But now that she is gone, I'm just helping Austin. This morning, he told me to bring you food."

Rachel chuckled. "I see. And are you happy here, Jeanne?"

"Well." She paused, contemplating how best to answer. "Miss Sarah used to be..." she hesitated again.

Reaching out and touching Jeanne's hand for a moment, Rachel reassured her, "It's okay. You can tell me."

Jeanne sighed, "Miss Sarah was angry and mean to me a lot, but Austin is much nicer."

"That's good that Austin is nice. I like him, too."

"Will that be all, Miss Rachel?" Jeanne asked, gave a shy grin, and stood to leave.

"Yes. But Jeanne, if you please, from now on, just call me Rachel. You do not have to call me 'Miss' Rachel. Thank you for bringing me this wonderful food. I really appreciate it," Rachel told Jeanne, knowing she probably had never been adequately thanked before.

A big smile came across her face, proving Rachel's assumption was correct. "You're welcome, Miss—I mean Rachel." Jeanne curtsied, "Will that be all?"

"Yes, Jeanne. Thank you."

Jeanne turned to leave, yet she stopped before closing the door, "Rachel?"

Lifting her chin, Rachel asked, "Yes?"

"Thank you for saying 'thank you.' That means a lot. And well, I am glad you are here. This house was pretty scary and sad until you came along, but it is getting much better now."

"That is good news," Rachel nodded, "and you are most welcome."

Jeanne curtsied one last time before she exited and shut the door.

Practically inhaling her breakfast, Rachel then cleaned herself up and got ready for the day. She unwrapped another new dress in a large box and pulled it out to find that it was extra full from the waist down. Its soft, cotton, cream-colored cloth and lace—adorned with raised silk embroidery and flowers—and a velvet sash, made Rachel love it. Although it was not quite as fancy as the one she had worn the day before, she figured that might be for the best, having no idea what the day might bring.

Fixing her hair with several thin braids, she put them up into a loose bun and admired herself in the mirror once again before heading off to see what was going on downstairs. Hopeful that the staff was making significant progress on cleaning and organizing, she wondered why it was so quiet.

Unexpectedly, just outside her room, on her way down the hall toward the library, she spotted Richard up ahead. Seeing her, he hurriedly crossed the hallway, slipping into a doorway to the left.

Surprised she had not yet noticed the door existed, as though it were some sort of secret door, it piqued her curiosity. He seemed to be acting *extra* mysterious, which she thought was strange, and squinted, trying to figure it out. She stopped walking and began to fidget with her fingers. Waiting anxiously, Rachel told herself that most of her fears, thus far, had been unmerited.

Richard then stepped out again, crossed the hall and vanished into another hidden door, but on the hall's right side this time. Staying put, she prayed that God would help her to overcome her fears, stand her ground, and wait to see if he would show himself again.

She was glad that he did indeed appear once more, but when he went from one side of the hall to the other, still acting cryptic, she was tempted to return to her room. Yet, as he re-entered the concealed door on the left again, he kept it cracked open and motioned for her to follow. Hesitant and a bit frightened by his odd behavior, she wished that he would just talk to her. It was difficult to remain silent, so she asked God for patience and reminded herself that love is patient.

Even though her heart was in her throat, she remembered how sweet Richard had acted just the day before and chose to believe that it was perfectly safe to follow him, *even through a wall.*

However, she was surprised to discover this hidden door led to an enclosed area shrouded in darkness. Light from the hallway exposed the top of a massive spiral staircase. She leaned over the railing and shuddered. It descended ominously into an abyss. Peering with keen eyes, she noticed, at about the halfway point, a light from a candle was moving downward. When she caught a hint of Richard's face illuminated by the glow, she made the decision to chase after him. Afraid he might slip out of sight once he reached the bottom, she lifted her skirt with her right hand and began her pursuit. Her left hand sliding over the railing, she made sure she could grab it easily if she tripped before she quickened her pace.

Upon feeling that the staircase plunged much further into the depths than she would like, she clenched her jaw. It even seemed to go below the first floor of the house. *Is this a dungeon?* Rachel asked herself, following him, step by step, down into the gloom, *What am I doing?*

Reluctantly dipping her toe onto the black, moist ground, she peeled her fingers from the railing and steadied herself before moving with caution to get nearer to Richard. The air was damp and grew colder with each stride. Rachel shivered and paused; her breathing heavy. Musty smells bit at her nose as though she was inhaling dirt. She figured that she was now in the basement of the mansion and wrapped her arms about herself to massage away the cold.

Rachel never liked basements and wanted to get out of there as soon as possible. Yet, when she was about to turn and flee back up the stairs, curiosity got the better of her. Inspecting her surroundings, she pressed on slowly. Ducking her head, she was reminded of a frightful basement from her childhood with similar low ceilings. It had many spider webs and large spiders crawling about, which she detested in every way, and she began to panic just thinking about it.

Her fear over those tiny eight-legged creatures often enraged her. Questioning herself, she thought, *It's absurd. How am I supposed to fight demons, when even tiny bugs bother me?*

Her anger then switched toward Richard for leading her to a place she had quickly decided she did not like. *Where is he leading me?* Her body began to tremble, and she wondered if she was the one dealing with mental illness, instead of Richard, simply for following him. *Or perhaps I am just foolish.*

The floor's moisture made it clear that she was now far underneath the mansion. Inhaling deep, rapid breaths, she felt like she was suffocating and stopped once again. Up ahead, the glow of Richard's candle was getting dimmer as the distance grew between them and Rachel knew she had better catch up with him and quick! She was most uncomfortable, disoriented, and chilled to the core, but she wanted to trust him.

Finally, Richard stopped and waited for her since it was now pitch black. It seemed to her that he did not want her to run into anything or get hurt, which soothed her fears but only marginally. Once she was directly behind him, she grinned, thankful to be near him again.

Extremely glad for the light, up ahead, the darkness loomed. She swallowed back her fright, feeling that, without the candles' light, the thickness of the pitch-black surroundings would swallow her whole. She bent forward and tightly clutched the sides of her dress near the hem, lifting the skirt high to keep it dry. Barely able to make out shapes of cobblestone halls and rooms branching off the path on both sides, she drew even closer to Richard.

Feeling the humidity hit her skin as she passed one of the most dismal, cave-like rooms, she trembled wildly, *Are we in a root cellar?* But when Richard held the candle up, she caught a glimpse of what appeared to be a massive canning room. There were shelves upon shelves from floor to ceiling filled with glass jars. Some were empty, but most appeared to be full of vegetables or fruits. In the middle of the room, long tables holding empty jars and lids of every size, stood as straight as possible, given the condition of the stone floor.

Although afraid and unsteady in her steps, Rachel pressed on. At the end of the path, they entered an enormous room held up by large stone pillars. Her eyebrows narrowed when she noticed Richard placing the candle down on the floor in the very center of the room. *What is he doing?*

This room was different from any other as its ceilings were high. The exterior walls were covered with thousands of wine bottles in neatly stacked rows. She was surprised at how pretty they looked, sparkling by the candles' dancing light.

Once she figured out that Richard had led her deep into the wine cellar, for whatever reason, he vanished. She turned from right to left, hoping to see him, but he had disappeared. She inhaled deeply, her heart racing now, and she wrung her hands together as her eyes darted about the room, searching for him.

Alone and abandoned, she stood grinding her teeth in the middle of the room and waited near the candle. Listening carefully for him and hearing nothing, she wanted to yell for help. But before she had the chance, she noticed Richard was returning to her side, and she exhaled.

When he reappeared, he was carrying a small wine glass, a bottle of wine, and a tiny wooden object crafted from sticks. She watched as he carefully placed the wine glass next to the candle on the floor, filled it to the brim with wine, and then carefully leaned what seemed like a tiny little ladder up against it. He stood slowly, stepped back, and then gently took hold of Rachel's hand to pull her back, away from the wine glass and ladder, off to the side of the room.

They were now about ten steps from the glass and the candle, and Richard stood, staring at it with eyes wide. A long time passed, and nothing happened. Gravely concerned, Rachel scanned the scene, stared up at him and then back at the glass and candle. Wondering what on Earth he was doing, she began to get upset and drew in her lips to keep from crying. *I must have imagined every single ounce of his progress. Oh, dear. Is he much more troubled than I want to believe?* With a frown, she waited quietly beside him, afraid to flinch.

More time passed slowly by, and yet there was nothing. In the distance, the unmistakable sound of a clock ate at her patience, one tick at a time. Its repetitive rhythm caused her to become more perplexed by what was, or was not, happening, tempting her to simply let go of his hand and run away. But Richard remained still, staring in silence at the glass as if expecting something to happen to it.

Growing sadder by the second about his mental state, Rachel went to move a bit, but Richard squeezed her hand harder, not allowing her to leave. Due to his unwillingness to let her so much as shift her weight, she contemplated what other options she might have and gulped back her fears.

With her heart pounding hard, it sank deeper, and she glanced over at him once more, this time with great pity. But then, a smile came across his face, which, to her, was so strange, considering he was seemingly staring at nothing but a wine glass. Instantly, his eyes widened, and he pointed toward the glass. In a flash, a fat little mouse, cute in every way, scurried across the floor. It ran up the ladder and, much to Rachel's amusement, began to drink the wine with zeal.

Richard chuckled at the sight, but Rachel could not believe her eyes. *How adorable!* What was even more precious was how Richard seemed to enjoy this display and the plump little mouse so much. It took a moment for her to get over her initial shock, but then she, too, chuckled softly.

After the mouse had his fill, he ran down the ladder and weaved back and forth across the floor and disappeared under a shelf.

Laughing out loud at his little friend, Richard let go of Rachel, picked up the glass and ladder, set it down on a nearby shelf and reached back for her hand. Thankfully, he smiled in her direction before slowly showing her around the rest of the wine cellar by candlelight in silence.

No longer in fear, Rachel managed to now see that the cellar was quite pleasing in its own way. There were a few exquisite pieces of artwork displayed on the walls. As she leaned forward for a better look, Richard took note of her curiosity about the paintings and grinned.

She observed several empty vases sitting on round tables with chairs that had been placed just so for a person to enjoy an occasional wine tasting. With row upon row of wine bottles and a large slate blackboard hanging nearby to keep track of every bottle, she figured that the entire cellar must have cost Master Nathan an absolute fortune.

Richard appeared to enjoy leading Rachel down more hallways filled with wine bottles and then up a different set of stairs altogether. She was glad this set of stairs was not in a spiral but was next to the outside wall leading straight up two levels. He then snuck her past the kitchen, down the main hallway, and into a room a few doors down. To her astonishment, it opened to an enormous art gallery.

The walls in the room were extra high, like that in the ballroom. There were no exterior windows or doors leading to the outside, yet it had many more paintings than any other room in the entire house.

She loved that the ceiling was designed with only glass held together by thin brass frames, so the sky above was clearly visible and was surprised by how much light it let in since it was beginning to rain again.

One by one, Richard led her to his favorite paintings, which quickly became hers. There were many paintings of the mansion, the gardens, children, older men and women, other families, several mothers with their children, and some of Jesus with His disciples. There were paintings of people enjoying picnics and a few of the chapel where Master Nathan and Gloria were wed. She stood, shaking her head in disbelief at the painting of the chapel's magnificence before its roof had been almost fully destroyed.

Looking around the room, Rachel then realized that most of the paintings must have been of Richard's family. She guessed that some were of his grandparents and great-grandparents, as well as other people she did not know.

She loved one that she assumed was of Gloria with her babies. But her favorite was clearly one of Richard as an infant in his mother's arms, with Gloria lovingly gazing into his eyes and kissing his tiny hand.

With Rachel by his side, he stared at it for a long time as tears began to form. She moved in closer and laid her head on his upper arm and admired his mother's immense beauty. Rachel imagined how lonely he must have been all these years without his family. To have been by himself long enough to make friends with a mouse and teach it how to climb up a ladder and drink wine, she felt sorry for him, and exhaled.

Yearning to speak with him, she placed her hand upon her heart, wishing she could soothe the ache he displayed. Aware of how much he must have loved and missed his sisters, she found herself hoping to be able to comfort him somehow and that he would soon realize he was no longer alone.

Pacing themselves and strolling about the room, before long, they were staring at a life-sized painting of Master Nathan, making Rachel miss him terribly. *I wonder how he is doing on his trip.*

While staring at his father's portrait, she observed that Richard's demeanor turned to one of exceptional sadness. He reached out and placed his hand over the top of his father's, which fit over Master Nathan's perfectly. Rachel's grimacing face showed she thought, *They look identical.* Seeing him hold it there, as if trying to touch his father somehow, more than anything, she wanted to be able to help restore what was left of their family. She knew how much they missed each other, but sadly, there was no way for them to communicate or spend time together anymore. Richard had not even come to listen to his father read in months, which was why Master Nathan hired Rachel in the first place. Although she was grateful for the position, she longed for things to be different between them.

She wondered if Richard was aware of just how wonderful his father was. She doubted he understood the blessing of having a father who loved him, was still alive and abiding under the same roof. Knowing how desperately Master Nathan longed for a relationship with his son, it was hard for her to remain silent.

Richard stepped back from the painting, took Rachel's hand, lifted it to his lips and kissed it gently, squeezing his eyes shut. She felt as though he was saying thank you, which was very moving, but she wished he would just tell her outright. She sighed, feeling as if she was dying inside a little more every moment they went without words.

After spending a great deal of time admiring the artwork together, it started to rain harder as they walked hand-in-hand to back to the solarium. Once inside, they both raised their eyes skyward and were amazed. The rain poured down like buckets of water overhead on the glass roof held together by brass that had greened, like that of the art room. It towered two stories above them and was a glorious sight.

The rain was almost deafening and a bit unnerving, yet exciting. Hearing the thunder roar in the distance, Rachel knew that the solarium, with its high glass ceiling and glass walls, was probably not the safest room in the house to be in during a storm but was unafraid. She thought of how much fear she'd felt in the cellar and was displeased with herself. Determined never to be in fear of Richard again, no matter what he did, she stood tall.

Leisurely walking along the solarium, they admired the different plants together while listening to the songbirds that had somehow ended up inside. Next to the manmade waterfall near the back of the solarium, Rachel recognized many of the tallest plants were from the tropics. Her father had been on a six-month trip to the islands of Hawaii two years before his death and had brought his family back many detailed drawings. She recognized Royal Palms, her favorite Coco Palms, and the Silver Fan Palm. Underneath, she noticed the orange Angel's Trumpet flowers as well as a yellow and red Bird of Paradise. She loved the huge leaves of the Elephant's Ear and Monstera, yet the orchids of various colors caught her eye. Those were her father's favorite.

Acting as though he liked them, too, Richard inspected them closely, turning his head to one side and then the other. Seeing his interest, Rachel questioned if it had been a while since he had entered the solarium, for he seemed to enjoy it immensely.

When the storm subsided, and the rain stopped, the sun emerged from the dark clouds, gleaming brightly through the roof. Its glorious rays shone directly upon them, and again, Richard turned his face upward to let the sun warm his cheeks. He looked so handsome and at peace as a smile crept across his face.

It was beginning to hurt Rachel that she was still unable to reach out and hug him, and she lowered her gaze to the floor. Taking in a deep breath, she let it out, sounding frustrated, which caught his attention. She thought, *I wonder if he knows how badly I wish to communicate with him.*

Appearing remorseful over his inability to speak, he let go of her hand, turned away, and walked deeper into the solarium to surround himself with the tallest and widest plants.

Is he trying to hide away from the world and maybe even me? Rachel sensed he wanted to be alone, so she, too, walked away, respecting his needs. Sitting down at the small round table to give Richard some space, she was glad to see Austin enter the room.

"Ah, there you are, Miss Rachel," he said. Out of the corner of his eye, he spotted Richard in the distance. Ignoring him, he asked, "Would you like to have your lunch here today, Miss?"

She put up her fingers to show Austin to bring enough food for two. "Yes, please. That would be lovely," she answered with a wink. "And Austin?"

"Yes, Miss?"

"Can you bring me a Bible, please?"

"Of course, Miss."

"Thank you, Austin."

He refrained from showing any excitement, bowed, and then left the room to fetch her a Bible and enough food for both her and her quiet companion. Even though she was unsure if her attempt to encourage Richard to eat with her might anger him, she wanted to try it anyway.

Chapter 10

Quietly, Rachel sat and listened to the cries in her heart for Richard growing louder by the minute. *Dear Heavenly Father, what is going to help Richard pull out of this? How can I share Your love—and now my love—for him if we cannot even communicate? You will need to speak to his heart for me and set him free from his confusion. I cannot do this alone. Please help him want to be free, not for his father nor me, but for himself. Help him to see Your beauty, Your grace that abounds, and Your mercy. Give him the desire to come to know You through the reading of Your Word and my prayers; I implore you.*

Peeking around some branches, Richard appeared to be checking up on her. It was as though he was making sure she was all right, which only made her pray harder. *Father, I know love is patient, so I ask that You help me be patient with Richard, myself, and, more importantly, with You. For if I say that I love You but get impatient with You for not fixing things as quickly as I would like, I am not loving You well. Thank You for being protective over me like a big brother and singing over me, my good father. Give me childlike faith and increase my confidence for Richard's recovery by filling me with Your perfect love that casts out all fear. I pray You unlock a new life for him by clearing the cobwebs in his mind as he learns he is Your favored one.*

Rachel's stomach hurt for Richard's wellbeing, and she prayed like a starving child, begging for scraps of food from the banquet table. *Lord, I am willing to fight for him, so lead me onward into battle over his soul. With You by my side, there is hope, for love always hopes for the best. You, the steady hand that guides me, placed the stars in the sky and set the universe into motion. All I have to do is stand strong as You hold me in the palm of Your hand.*

Watching Richard in the distance as she continued to pray silently, she wished he would join her. *You hold us together, even when we feel like we are falling apart. I humbly ask that You help me be the bridge that connects him to the truth of who he really is and who he is meant to be. Your love for him, as Solomon writes, is as strong as death; jealousy fierce as the grave. You adored him even before he was formed in his mother's womb. Waters cannot quench the thirst of Your everlasting love for Your children, for we are the desire of Your heart.*

When Richard looked out from the leaves, she grabbed at her cross necklace. *Set a seal upon his heart and awaken love. Let him feel Your tangible presence as never before, and help him understand that anytime he needs, You will firmly hold his hand as his mother and father once did.*

Looking up to see if Richard had moved closer or further away, Rachel sighed. Sadly, he had retreated deeper into the solarium. *Richard has floated around this house by himself, feeling lost and alone for far too long. I plead with You to set his feet on the solid ground of Your sacred love. Help him to walk on his own but not alone, so he can stand firm against the enemy. I know the battle over him was won on the cross; therefore, I am confident that the Devil no longer has claim over him and praise You for that truth. Cast out all fear within him so he can finally be set free from the bondage of his past, for there is no bondage so heavy and no chain so thick that Your selfless love cannot break. In Jesus' mighty name, amen.*

Inspired, once again, to never give up on Richard, Rachel finished and stood. She was determined to love him with a relentless, undying, and Godly love. Leaving the table to look for him, she found him deeper inside the solarium. He was still surrounding himself with sunlight and plants that were unique and beautiful, much like he was to her.

Now beside him, she took his hand and made the bold decision to speak out loud about what she thought of him. "These plants are unique and beautiful, just like someone I am getting to know."

She waited for his reaction and was happy to see that Richard blushed and looked down, playing shy. Thankfully, he showed no sign of getting upset and actually seemed to enjoy the compliment.

Nodding toward Austin, she wanted to let him know everything would be all right as he delivered the tray of food and set the table for them. After Austin left the room, she turned toward the table and gently pulled at Richard's hand to come and sit with her. He hesitated but only for a moment.

Since Richard, for years, only had food brought to his room, he appeared apprehensive and unsure how to act, so he moved with caution. At first, his eyes were downcast, but soon, he followed Rachel's every move, trying to remember his table manners.

The moment she placed her napkin across her lap, he did the same. When she picked up the correct fork to eat her salad, Richard copied her. She took a small bite, and so did he. Looking at him while chewing her food, Rachel smiled, and to her astonishment, he returned it. Yet, his smile was much more than a polite gesture; he honestly looked the happiest she had seen him. It was clear that he'd missed dining with someone and was thrilled to be eating with her.

Bite by bite, Richard mimicked her, almost like a young boy learning a new skill, and she could tell he was trying to impress her. Once they had eaten everything on the tray, she decided to speak as if to no one. Wiping her mouth with her napkin, she set it on the table and said quietly, "Delicious."

He again copied her, wiped his mouth, and stated faintly, "Delicious."

Ecstatic to hear his voice again, she did her best to stay calm as she reached for the Bible. Richard remained seated and listened to her peacefully—at first.

Feeling led to read more stories about Jesus being gentle and loving to sinners—such as Mary Magdalene, a prostitute, and Matthew, a tax collector—Rachel began. She wanted Richard to grasp that, although the religious leaders had hated Jesus for being kind to sinners, He was consistently compassionate toward everyone, no matter who they were or what they had done in their past. She read how darling Jesus was to the little children, how He healed many who had given up hope, how He helped the needy, and that He was not judgmental or critical.

The more she shared, Richard seemed to fall more in love with Jesus. She wondered if he could now see more clearly how caring and wonderful her Savior was.

Rachel chose to read only the lighthearted stories about Jesus for almost an hour, yet she felt led to finish with the most intense Bible story of all. Wringing her hands in her lap, she read to him about Jesus' death, burial, and resurrection.

While she read, Richard could no longer sit still. Restless, he stood and closely listened, pacing back and forth within earshot. She could tell the pain Jesus endured disturbed and shocked him immensely. Concerned about how he might react, she admitted to herself that she had to trust God to work in Richard's heart before daring to say more. Yet, when she read about the torture that Jesus endured, Richard seemed irate.

Trying not to worry, she paused until he calmed back down before resuming. "Mark 15. 'Immediately, in the morning, the chief priests held a consultation with the elders and scribes and the whole council; and they bound Jesus, led Him away, and delivered Him to Pilate. Then Pilate asked Him, "Are you the King of the Jews?" He answered and said to him, "It is as You say." And the chief priests accused Him of many things, but He answered nothing. Then Pilate asked Him again, saying, "Do You answer nothing? See how many things they testify against You!" But Jesus still answered nothing, so that Pilate marveled.'"

Richard huffed while Rachel continued reading difficult scriptures about the day Jesus was to be killed. "'Now at the feast he was accustomed to releasing one prisoner to them, whomever they requested. And there was one named Barabbas, who was chained with his fellow rebels; they had committed murder in the rebellion. Then the multitude, crying aloud, began to ask him to do just as he had always done for them. But Pilate answered them, saying, "Do you want me to release to you the King of the Jews?" For he knew that the chief priests had handed Him over because of envy. But the chief priests stirred up the crowd, so that he should rather release Barabbas to them. Pilate answered and said to them again, "What then do you want me to do with Him whom you call the

King of the Jews?" So they cried out again, "Crucify Him!" Then Pilate said to them, "Why? What evil has He done?" But they cried out all the more, "Crucify Him!" So Pilate, wanting to gratify the crowd, released Barabbas to them; and he delivered Jesus, after he had scourged Him, to be crucified."'

It was hard for Rachel to watch as Richard paced more quickly with firmer steps, but she was determined to finish. "'Then the soldiers led Him away into the hall called Praetorium (that is, the governor's headquarters), and they called together the whole garrison. And they clothed Him with purple; and they twisted a crown of thorns, put it on His head, and began to salute Him, "Hail, King of the Jews!" Then they struck him on the head with a reed and spat on Him; and bowing the knee, they worshiped Him. And when they had mocked Him, they took the purple off Him, put His own clothes on Him, and led Him out to crucify Him."'

Knowing how important it was for Richard to learn the truth of how Jesus died to make the lowly wretch His treasure, Rachel pressed on, even though he groaned like he could feel Jesus' pain. "'And when they crucified Him, they divided His garments, casting lots for them to determine what every man should take. Now it was the third hour, and they crucified Him. And the inscription of His accusation against Him was written above: THE KING OF THE JEWS. With Him they also crucified two robbers, one on His right and the other on His left. So the scripture was fulfilled which says, "And He was numbered with the transgressors." And those who passed by blasphemed Him, wagging their heads and saying, "Aha! You who destroy the temple and build it in three days, save Yourself, and come down from the cross!" Likewise the chief priests also, mocking among themselves with the scribes, said, "He saved others; Himself He cannot save. Let the Christ, the King of Israel, descend now from the cross, that we may see and believe." Even those who were crucified with Him reviled Him. Now when the sixth hour had come, there was darkness over the whole land until the ninth hour. And at the ninth hour Jesus cried with a loud voice, saying, "Eloi, Eloi, lama sabachthani?" which is translated, "My God, My God, why have You forsaken Me?" Some of those who stood by, when they heard that, said, "Look, He is calling for Elijah!" Then someone ran and filled a sponge full of sour wine, put it on a reed, and offered it to Him to drink, saying, "Let Him alone; let us see if Elijah will come to take Him down." And Jesus cried out with a loud voice, and breathed His last. Then the veil of the temple was torn in two from top to bottom. So when the centurion, who stood opposite Him, saw that He cried out like this and breathed His last, he said, "Truly this Man was the Son of God!""""

Rachel was heartsick when Richard dropped to his knees onto the floor beside her. He was panting strenuously now, as if striving for air that was too thick to breathe in. She could tell he was terribly upset to learn what happened to Jesus but did not want to end the story there, so she continued. "'Now when evening had come, because it was the Preparation Day, that is, the day before the Sabbath, Joseph of Arimathea, a prominent council member, who was himself waiting for the Kingdom of God, coming and taking courage, went in to Pilate and asked for the body of Jesus. Pilate marveled that He was already dead; and summoning the centurion, he asked him if He had been dead for some time. So when he found out from the centurion, he granted the body to Joseph. Then he (Joseph) bought fine linen, took Him down, and wrapped Him in the linen. And he laid Him in a tomb which had been hewn (cut) out of the rock, and rolled a stone against the door of the tomb.'"

To Rachel's dismay, Richard appeared to be weeping now, so she read faster, trying to get to the good news. "'And Mary Magdalene and Mary the *mother of* Joses saw where He was laid. Now when the Sabbath was past, Mary Magdalene, Mary the *mother of* James, and Salome bought spices, that they might come and anoint Him. Very early in the morning, on the first *day* of the week, they came to the tomb when the sun had risen. And they said among themselves, "Who will roll away the stone from the door of the tomb for us?" But when they looked up, they saw that the stone had been rolled away—it was very large. And entering the tomb, they saw a young man clothed in a long white robe sitting on the right side; and they were alarmed. But he said to them, "Do not be alarmed. You seek Jesus of Nazareth, who was crucified. He has risen! He is not here.""""

Appearing excited, Richard gasped as she read the story of the resurrection.

""'See the place where they laid Him. But go, tell His disciples—and Peter—that He is going before you into Galilee; there you will see Him, as He said to you." So they went out quickly and fled from the tomb, for they trembled and were amazed, and they said nothing to anyone, for they were afraid. Now when He rose early on the first *day* of the week, He appeared first to Mary Magdalene, out of whom He cast seven demons. She went and told those who had been with Him, as they mourned and wept."'"

Richard shifted from his knees to sitting on the floor. Wiping his eyes, he listened with a keen ear. Concerned for his wellbeing, Rachel finished in haste. "'And when they heard that He was alive and had been seen by her, they did not believe. After that, He appeared in another form to two of them as they walked and went into the country. And they went and told *it* to the rest, *but* they did not believe them either. Later He appeared to the eleven as they sat and ate at the table; and He rebuked their unbelief and hardness of heart, because they did not believe those who had seen Him after He had risen. And He said to them, "Go into all the world and preach the gospel to every creature. He who believes and is baptized will be saved; but He who does not believe will be condemned."'"

She could sense Richard looking up at her, with a face full of concern about his own salvation, so she ended the reading, "'And these signs will follow those who believe; in my name, they will cast out demons; they will speak with new tongues; they will take up serpents; and if they drink anything deadly, it will by no means hurt them; they will lay hands on the sick, and they will recover." So, then the Lord Jesus, after He had spoken to them, was taken up into Heaven and sat down at the right hand of God. And they went out and preached everywhere, while the Lord worked with them and confirmed the message by accompanying signs.'"

Thankfully, Richard appeared relieved once he heard the good news of Jesus rising from the dead, but he looked deep in thought.

Knowing what she had just read was difficult to hear, and since she still could not talk to him, there was nothing else to do but pray.

"Dear Lord, words cannot express how thankful I am for the immensity of Your love for me."

Richard noticed Rachel praying, so he remained on his knees, scooted closer toward her, and placed his hand in hers. He then bowed his head and laid his forehead on her knees.

"Thank You so much for sending Your one and only Son, Jesus, to die for me. I know I do not deserve it, but I receive it. It is a gift like no other. Because of Jesus, I am set free and can talk to You openly. I can have a fellowship with You that is live, tangible, and continuous. Through Your Word, Your Spirit, and prayer, I can get to know You, which is the thing in the world I cherish most. I do not understand everything You do, nor Your timing, yet I do not doubt the vastness of Your adoration for me. Because You sent Your Son in my place to die such a horrible death on a cross like a common thief, although He was pure, spotless, blameless, and without sin, I will never again doubt Your love for me. For it is written, 'There is no greater love than he who lays down his life for his friends.' So, I know that I am Jesus' friend, which warms my soul."

Since Richard was growing fidgety, Rachel wondered what he was thinking. It was almost as though he wanted to pray as well, so she continued, hoping that he might. "Thank You so much, Father. I know that if You had not chosen to give up Your Son and if Your Son had not chosen to lay down His life, there would have been no hope for me. I would have been lost with all humanity in a downward spiral of eternal separation from You, which would cause me to suffer beyond belief. So, Lord, I promise to no longer allow the Devil to try to make me feel guilty, ashamed, sorrowful, or sinful. Instead, I will cling to the story of the old, rugged cross, which shows I am worth everything to You."

Rachel snuck another peek and was delighted to see that Richard was squeezing his eyes tight as if he was praying right along with her. "Oh, Father, Your thoughtfulness and mercy overwhelm me. Your grace is more than I can even comprehend, but I gladly receive it. I welcome You into my heart and life from this moment on because Your Word teaches that when I surrender to You, all things will be made new, and I will be set free from the bondage of sin. Lord, Your desire for me is nothing less than a fulfilled life. Even though You do not promise our lives will be easy, You wish me to prosper and be in good health as Your royal daughter, the apple of Your eye. Help me to hear Your Holy Spirit's gentle whisper more clearly instead of the enemy's constant lies, whose goal is my destruction."

Pausing, she pondered what to say before she finished since Richard still seemed so engaged. She then asked God, "Help me overcome the things of this world as I give my life, time, focus, heart, and energy to serve You by serving others. Nothing on Earth brings greater joy than loving You and others through You. Everything else is like chasing after the wind and will never satisfy my soul. May I receive Your comforting presence as we walk and talk in union. May I live out my days with soundness of mind, a clear conscience, and heartfelt thanksgiving. Knowing that I have been redeemed for all eternity by the blood of the Lamb, I accept Your precious gift of salvation and will praise You forevermore. In Jesus' sweet name, I pray, amen."

Taking in a deep breath, Rachel exhaled, and sat quietly for a bit to observe Richard. When she rose to stand, he removed his hands from hers to dry a tear rolling down his cheek. She hoped he would follow her, yet he remained on the floor, staring wide-eyed at the ground, reminding her of Master Nathan. Hoping he surrendered his heart to God during that prayer, she waited for him.

Seeming disheartened, Richard struggled to rise and dropped back down onto his knees. Witnessing this, Rachel was hit with so many different emotions she placed her hand on her forehead, not knowing what to do. She then remembered how much it helped Master Nathan when she'd left him alone to pray in the chapel and decided to sneak away and leave Richard alone with God.

Since the rain had stopped, she grabbed a pair of gardening shears from the table by the door and slipped outside alone into the gardens. Even though everything was soaking wet, the bright sun warmed her shoulders. Rachel loved how the moisture on the flowers reflected the light. She noticed how the bright droplets on their petals sparkled like jewels from Heaven and wiped one with her fingertip. Cutting a pink flower, she smelled it, enjoying its aroma.

Making her way further into the garden, she cut a few more flowers, hoping to fill a vase, but then changed her mind. She thought it best to stay on the terrace so Richard could easily find her, climbed back up the steps, wiped a seat dry for herself with the hem of her skirt, and sat in the sun, waiting. Inspecting the few flowers she'd cut, she admired the handiwork of her heavenly Father.

A sense of peace enveloped her as a butterfly circled her three times and landed on the top of the chair beside her. Again, remembering her mother's lessons on butterflies being one way the Lord tells us we are right where He wants us to be, she watched while her new friend slowly opened and closed his brightly colored wings as if waving to her. When he flew away to kiss the various flowers in the gardens, she had a feeling that her mother was right.

Time passed, and Rachel hoped the storm in Richard's heart would pass as well. She knew he would need counseling, time, love and understanding. Still, she had hope for him. Wishing he would soon join her, she exhaled and looked up toward the solarium door, expecting him at any moment.

Chapter 11

A fter having waited for Richard almost an hour, Rachel was relieved to see that when he stepped outside to accompany her, he acted almost cheerful. But before he reached her, she stood and walked down the terrace steps to stroll along the paths surrounded by yellow daffodils and tulips of every color.

Without speaking a word, she selected and cut random flora here and there, taking care to shake off the remaining water on each one. Wanting to make an impressive arrangement for the round table in the foyer, she did not rush herself.

Richard followed closely behind in silence, so she waited for the perfect timing. When he happened to be standing directly beside her, she immediately made her move and handed him all the flowers she had cut without even asking for his help. He looked a bit surprised with wide eyes, but he took them regardless. Cutting one stem after the next, Rachel made it a point to smile and look in his direction as she handed them to him. Their connection deepened as their eyes met, one smile and one flower at a time.

When Austin and Jeanne entered the solarium to clean off the table, they quickly noticed the beauty of what was taking place outside. Jeanne inhaled deeply and covered her mouth to hide her shock. Witnessing Richard helping Rachel in the garden during daylight hours was a miraculous sight.

As they watched in amazement, he seemed to blossom right before their eyes. Austin knew full well the significance of what was happening and that the best thing for someone in Richard's sorrowful condition was to get outdoors, serve, and be with others. It appeared that Rachel, the scriptures, prayer, the beauty of nature, and God Himself were radically changing him from the inside out. Astonished, Austin thought about how brilliant Rachel was and how much she had helped Richard, given how few encounters she'd had with him.

"Isn't it wonderful?" Jeanne said, half laughing and half crying tears of joy while wiping her cheeks with her sleeve.

"Indeed. It is," Austin replied, happy for Richard. Yet, in the back of his mind, he was still wondering what might happen when Master Nathan arrived home. Uncertain, he shook his head. "Come along," he said, wanting to give Rachel and Richard some privacy. Moved by this heart-warming display, Jeanne had difficulty turning away but reluctantly obeyed.

Richard's arms were overflowing with so many flowers; Rachel looked at him and chuckled. "Come on," she said, speaking directly to him for the first time. "Let's go put these in a vase."

At first, he stood motionless. But as she walked further and further away from him toward the solarium, he quickly followed to catch up. She did not look back but grinned.

Rachel opened the door to let them in and regarded how careful he was being to not hurt any of the blossoms. She led him to the big arrangement table at the back of the room so he could lay the flowers down and begin organizing them.

Watching how gentle he was, as if the flowers were precious children, she was again surprised by his sweet spirit. She placed her hand on his shoulder but remained quiet, hopeful that he would not become angry at her touch. Keeping the tone of her voice extra soft, she said, "Thank you," as she reached to the back of the table to pick out the perfect vase from the variety of choices lined up in a row.

Glad he did not get upset with her for saying 'thank you,' Rachel was much relieved to see that he actually lifted his chest, like he enjoyed the praise.

Anticipating his help, she moved extra slow, carefully selecting and placing the blossoms she had chosen into the tall vase. Richard watched her for a few moments, but then, much to her delight, he joined her, picked up a flower and placed it into the vase. Although she was giddy, she said nothing and simply continued working on the arrangement, pretending that their working together was nothing out of the ordinary.

Before she knew what was happening, Richard stepped over to stand close behind her, just like he had done in her dreams. His boldness astounded her. It almost felt like he was hugging her as she worked. Rachel quickly lost her train of thought as his body pressed up against hers. His strong arms reaching around her ever so slowly made her shiver as he helped her finish what was now "their arrangement."

Feeling love and desire for him growing stronger within her as she listened to his deep breaths, her pulse accelerated. She was keenly aware that the beauty before her was no longer just in their floral arrangement. It was now also flowing out of Richard and his eagerness to try new things. Despite the appearance that he was eagerly trying to make a fresh start for himself, she planned to take things one step at a time so as not to harm him. But something had shifted greatly, and she welcomed it.

With each flower they set into place together, Rachel prayed that the broken pieces of Richard's heart would be replaced with hope. Little by little, as he began to surrender to the truth that he was real, forgiven, capable of being helpful, and deserving of love, he was indeed changing.

Upon noticing new signs of internal peace, she wanted to believe that he was, perhaps, beginning to want to live again. Not only was Richard coming out of his shell, but he also showed signs of understanding God's gifts and blessings of creation. *Lord, I thank You that Richard's new awareness will lead him towards complete healing and transformation.*

As the arrangement neared completion, she let him put the finishing touches on it. Getting lost in his embrace, she inhaled deeply to admire his scent. She laid her head back upon his chest, closed her eyes to feel his beating heart, and said to herself, *He smells so amazing.*

Rachel never knew how quickly she could fall in love with someone, and it almost upset her. Random thoughts of the possibility of them being together once he fully recovered flashed across her mind. She knew she was willing to wait for him to get well, no matter how long it might take, and refused to care what anyone would say. She loved him enough to wait forever if need be.

When Richard noticed that she had forgotten all about the vase and was only interested in him, he stopped working. Sensing her desire, he gently pulled her hair to the side and began to softly kiss her neck just as before. A shiver ran down her spine, but she smiled, her nerves pulsing with the sensation that she was both dying and coming to life at the same time. Her breathing grew heavy, as did his.

She swallowed hard, knowing it would be best for him to stop, but she did not want him to. After convincing herself that there would be no harm in allowing him to continue, she surrendered entirely to his touch. And just like that, Rachel knew she could no longer stand to be without him. Wanting him in every way possible, without thinking, she quickly turned around and kissed him fervently on his lips.

Richard responded by kissing her back with every ounce of his heart's cry. His pent-up loneliness and desire to be loved flowed from his lips directly onto hers. He held the back of her head with both hands to press her sweet mouth against his.

Overwhelmed by unfamiliar physical senses spreading across her body, Rachel knew that there was no turning back now. *Is this really happening?* She drank in his passion as though she had been lost in a dry and weary land for far too long, and he was the much-needed cup of cold water she was longing for. He felt so good and tasted delicious. To her, amongst the tropical plants, being with Richard felt like paradise, but it did not take long before the intensity of his kiss was more than she could bear. Worried about how moving too fast might affect him, she forced herself to break their kiss and turn away.

Dizzying thoughts began to swarm around inside her head like a disturbed bees' nest. *Oh, no… What am I doing? What was I thinking? What will Nathan say?* Stumbling backward, she bumped up against the table, feeling lightheaded and more confused than ever. Not knowing what to do next, she was tempted to jump directly back into his arms, but seeing the hurt look on his face, overcome with conflicting emotions, she darted away.

Poor Richard, perplexed by her fluctuating behavior, was not about to let her go. So without delay, he chased after her, following closely behind. The panicked look on his face made it clear that Richard was now worried about Rachel.

For whatever reason, Rachel thought of one place to go and hurried up to the tower. Running as quickly as possible, she wrestled hard with her thoughts, wanting to clear her head.

Richard could have easily caught her, but he respectfully let her get a good lead. Without letting her out of his sight, he stayed on her trail up one flight of stairs after the next. She knew he was directly behind her at every turn but was unsure of what else to do since she was unable to talk to him directly.

Finally reaching the top, she ran into the tower and stopped just shy of the wall of windows facing the west gardens. Out of breath and afraid, she knew there was no place left for her to go. Ashamed over how she'd given into her lustful desires, aware it might ruin every inch of his progress, she buried her face in her hands and began to weep.

Richard, being cautious because she was now in tears, gently placed his hand on her shoulder to comfort her.

At his touch, Rachel felt faint. Unable to stop herself, she spun around to face him and looked deep into his eyes. Kissing him once again, more passionately than before, she knew there was no denying it: despite everything, she had fallen for him. Parts of her innermost being regretted the decision to kiss him at all, and she questioned, *Why am I suddenly feeling so weak?* Another part of her just didn't care anymore and wanted to trust that Richard could get better with God's help. She convinced herself they would be able to make things work and that she would rather die trying than live without him.

They shared a powerful yearning for one another physically, but before things got out of control, she stopped him once again and stepped back. Richard looked at her with an intensity that seemed to connect with her innermost hidden parts. He had a way of staring right through her, and she loved it and hated it simultaneously.

Knowing how much he wanted her made it almost impossible for her to contain her true feelings or resist him. She watched his chest rising and falling fast as he panted for air after their kiss, and his jaw muscles flexed, showing he could no longer wait to have her. There was no doubt he wanted her, but more importantly, she truly believed that he loved her.

Unable to look at his enticing face any longer for fear she might give in, Rachel closed her eyes and turned away again. She knew that having sexual relations before marriage was a sin, and she wondered if they might ever be together that way at all. *How can I marry someone with so many issues?*

Crying again, she grew even more upset with herself, aware that her unstable emotions were not healthy for Richard to witness. *If there is any hope for us to ever have a relationship, I must at least try to speak to him.* Taking the risk of a lifetime, she outright disobeyed every instruction Master Nathan had given her pertaining to his son.

Her back was turned to him, still, Rachel spoke with a love that burned hot on her tongue. Her words were like wild animals that had been caged for far too long and just had to be released, but she began as clearly as possible through her sobs. "Richard?"

His eyes grew wide, but he said nothing. No one had called him by his name in years. He froze, shocked, unable to process his name being said aloud. Having no idea how to react, he grabbed at his chest, twisting his shirt in his fist.

"Richard, I know you can hear me; you can see me. And I know you can feel me."

She waited. Yet, he said nothing. Because she continued to face the windows and couldn't see his reaction, she was unaware of the look of pain that fell across his face. She had no idea that he was turning away from her, shrinking to his knees like a melting snowman in the most unbearable summer sun. Unable to handle being spoken to so directly, her every word tormented him to the core.

Still, oblivious, Rachel carried on, hoping for a miracle. "Richard, I can see you, hear you, and I can feel you too. You must realize by now that you are not a ghost but that you are, indeed, a man; a man who is very much alive. Not only are you alive, but you are amazing.

You-you are magnificent. To me, you are an incredible man who is extraordinary in every way, flaws, and all. You are more caring and compassionate than any man I have ever met. And you, more than anyone I know, deserve to live your life to the fullest *now* while you are still alive."

Overcome, Richard covered his ears and crouched down onto the floor. After all these years, he was still unable to cope with being spoken to so directly. He moaned loudly like a man being tortured.

Alarmed to hear his moan, Rachel quickly spun around to witness his severe reaction. She gasped when she saw Richard cowering with his ears fully covered by his hands. He looked as though her words were deafening, with his eyes shut tight like he was in tremendous pain. Her heart shattered, but she continued, determined not to give up. This time, she stripped herself of all pride and pleaded with him, laying her soul bare.

"Richard, please listen to me," she begged. "I'm sorry about what happened in your past and that it hurt you. I am sorry that the doctor you saw as a child harmed you and lied to you the way he did. That horrible man had no right to even touch you. Richard, I know your life took a wrong turn, but none of it was your fault. That is all behind you now. It was long ago, and I beg of you to forgive yourself and not let the past cause you anguish any longer. You were just a boy when the accident happened, and of course, you are not to blame. You are not at fault whatsoever. You have tortured yourself long enough and deserve to be free. Please, Richard. Talk to me! Come back to me. Come back to your father. The pain of your silent loneliness is so loud, and we can no longer bear to see you hurting. You are so special, incredibly important, and precious to us. Do you understand?"

Because Rachel strongly believed in her convictions and wanted desperately to help him, she continued pouring her heart out, "Richard, you must listen to me. The key to unlocking your mind, to finding freedom and joy in this life, no matter what happens to us, is trusting in Jesus." She paused. "But you cannot trust whom you do not know." She waited again before finishing with a whisper, "I want to help you get to know Him. I want to help you see His beauty because when I look at you, I see nothing but His beauty *in* you. You, Richard, are the darling of my heart. More than anything, I want you to be happy again."

She began sobbing when he did not reply. Unable to look at him in his wounded state any longer, she turned back to face the west windows again in utter despair. Unsure of what to do, she did not want to finish her failing speech, knowing she was getting nowhere fast. Her heart pounded rapidly with dread, just thinking about the possibility that, instead of helping, what she was saying might have made Richard worse—much worse! *How could I be so foolish? Why can't I just keep my big mouth shut? God, forgive me! Please help me! Help Richard!*

Suddenly led by the Holy Spirit, Rachel prayed in her heavenly language as tears streamed down her face like a flood. Then she whispered, "Oh, Lord, I'm deeply sorry for once again trying to fix someone. I know it is Your job, not mine. I surrender Richard to You once again. Please help me to trust You more, to fear not, and to believe in You. Please, increase my faith. I love Richard, and I pray for his mind and his life. Just like in the vision you gave me, I lay him at Your feet. Your will be done. I pray in the name of Jesus."

Bowing her head low, she wept in full surrender and prayed, *Why did I allow my impatience to ruin our day and possibly our future? Why would I speak to Richard directly before he was ready? Oh, Lord, what have I done?*

Shame instantly tried to bind her as anxiety stepped in, but she refused to allow it to control her. Despite knowing she had made a terrible mistake, she did well to not to let her negative thoughts take over and forced herself to stop crying. She used her pain to pray with zeal, knowing that fervent prayer moved the heart of God more than anything. Feeling a release, she finished what she wanted to say, in love. Even if it meant it might be months before she could speak to Richard again, she knew she had to keep trying.

Sadly, Richard remained on the floor with his hands covering his ears and his eyes tightly closed, rocking back and forth like an injured child. She decided to keep her back turned and speak to him as softly and gently as possible, especially after making such a mess of things.

Gripping her hands together over her heart, she felt the Lord nudging her to continue, and—similar to her interview with Master Nathan—she held nothing back. "Richard, I love you. I am certain of it. I love you with all my heart and everything that I am. I want to be with you forever. I know it's sudden, but in this short time I have spent with you, you have become a part of me. I can no longer imagine my life without you. Forgive me for being impatient and speaking with you directly before you were ready. The Word teaches that love is patient. I promise, from now on, to be patient with you. I will wait for you for as long as it takes. And I will believe in God for your complete healing, in *His* timing, not mine. God has given me visions of you well, carefree, and confident, so I trust He will guide us through this. Richard, I-I want to marry you. I want to be your wife and be with you forever. I promise to stand by you through whatever this life may bring if you will let me. If that is not possible or is not what you want, I promise, no matter what you decide, with my every breath, I will love and support you always."

She buried her face in her hands, and her shoulders shook as her sobbing resumed. Yet, she was no longer crying out of fear but out of submission to God, just as her mother had done when her brother died in her arms. Rachel pictured letting Richard go and giving him over to a loving, trustworthy heavenly Father. It was excruciating, but she knew it had to be done.

Regardless of how she felt, Rachel forced herself to surrender Richard's mental health and life entirely over to the Lord, aware that she needed to trust God completely. All she could do was continue to intercede for him. She proclaimed her authority and rebuked the enemy for all he had stolen from this man she adored—demanding reimbursement—and as she did, several tormenting spirits left Richard all at once. And, in their letting go, Jesus gave back in return.

In no way did Richard understand it, but he knew something extraordinary was happening. The tension between how good his usual comfort zone felt versus the innate calling of his God-given potential tugged at his soul. Suddenly, a spark within him was lit by love, and because of it, deep down, he refused to remain comfortable with being alone any longer.

Due to her immense sorrow and since she still had her back to him, Rachel did not notice that as she spoke about loving him and wanting to marry him, Richard's eyes shot open. And when she rebuked the evil that attacked him for so long, they opened even wider.

Rachel was unable to see that, directly behind her, a miracle was taking place. She had no idea that Richard lowered his hands from his ears and looked astonished as if he was hearing a heavenly choir singing over him joyfully due to his return. His eyes had become clear like a sliver of unfamiliar light had revealed the truth to him. As the colors in the room from the setting sun became more vivid than before, the dark cloud he had been living under suddenly vanished.

Inch by inch, Richard slowly began to stand, repeatedly hit with inexplicable yet positive emotions, one after the next. He corrected his posture, looking more like royalty, redeemed, and refreshed than ever, as new strength, clarity, and boldness overtook him. It was as if, all these years, his frame—which had felt empty and weak—began to fill with renewed vitality. The usual look of pain on his face vanished, while every drop of shame, timidness, and doubt within him disappeared, and courage and hope took their place. Although in shock, he began to smile.

As each second passed, the heaviness seemed to lift. For the first time, Richard was choosing to open the door to his future. He was choosing to fight for it, knowing that Rachel was correct. Right then and there, he decided to forgive himself and let go of his past once and for all. He was choosing life, so he could be with his father, with others, with God, and he was choosing to be *with her*. I am free! Thank You, God! I am finally free!

Unaware of Richard's emotions and afraid to look his way, Rachel cried on, not knowing that, at that instant, God was answering hers, the households, and Master Nathan's prayers for Richard. She had no idea that God had unlocked his mind and was releasing his soul from the Devil's grip.

Then without making a sound, Richard stood taller than he ever had, astonished by what he was about to do. For the first time in ten long years, he was confident and determined enough to talk to someone outright, but not just anyone.

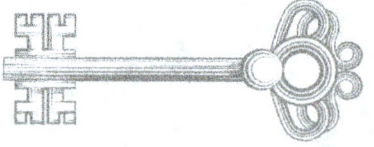

Chapter 12

Utterly fascinated, Richard inspected his hands from front to back, like they had materialized out of thin air. He put them on his chest to feel it rise and fall while air filled his lungs. He touched his face, grabbed his arms, and looked down at his feet as if he were seeing his own body for the first time. His breathing grew deep as he finally realized that he genuinely was not a ghost but, indeed, a man—*alive*, just like Rachel said.

Thrilled, he started to laugh a little, but at the same time, overcome, his body began to shake as he spoke softly. "Rachel," he said, trying to get her attention. But since she still stood with her back to him, crying so hard, she could not hear his voice. Lifting his chin high, he placed his hands by his sides and said, in a much louder tone, with boldness, "Rachel!"

She raised her head instantly, stopped crying, opened her eyes wide, and her ears perked up. Taking in a deep breath, she held still, unsure if Richard truly said something or if she had let her imagination run away with her once again.

Raising his jawline, he then declared in a deep voice, "Rachel, my lady."

In shock, Rachel spun around and gasped. She looked into his eyes, and instantly could tell he appeared different. She had no doubt that Richard *was back* and in his right mind.

"Richard!" Rachel sobbed as she yelled his name and leaped forward into his arms, kissing him with a desire that only true lovers know. He kissed her back with intensity, thoroughly enjoying the blessings of being a man; a man in love. After hugging her tight,

Richard picked her up and swung her around over his head as they each laughed, praising God.

"Oh, Richard! It's a miracle!" Rachel exclaimed, amazed by God's gift of answered prayers.

He slowly let her down and held her in his embrace.

Squeezing Richard and nuzzling her cheek into his chest, she whispered, "Oh, Thank you, God, You are so good to me!"

After much celebration, a severe look fell back across Richard's face, and he said quietly, "Rachel?"

"Yes, my darling?" she asked, partially ignoring him, giving his cheeks quick, soft little kisses over and over before she stopped to listen.

He held her away from himself for a moment and whispered sweetly, "I want to be with you always, too."

Rachel covered her smile. She almost started crying again, but instead, wrapped her arms around his waist tighter, letting out a sigh of relief. Due to the depths of her love, she could no longer think straight, and now it was Rachel's turn to be speechless. Yet, after a long while they collected themselves and sat down close to one another, talking excitedly.

"I have so many questions and so much to tell you. But first, I must ask, what made you come back? What I mean is, why did you decide to speak to me today after all this time?"

He grabbed her hands and held them to his heart as she blinked several times and contemplated his answer. "I don't know. It was several things, really. It was you—reading to me, teaching me how much God adores His people, how much He loves me, and how He longs to forgive even the worst of sinners when they come into repentance. You made me want to learn everything about Him. I wanted so much to talk to you about it, and when I could not ask you questions, well, I thought I would burst. Then, something you said today… It felt like the winds switched direction within the darkest and most stormy places of my soul."

"What part? What did I say that affected you so?"

"You said that the key to unlocking my mind—to gaining freedom and joy—is trusting in Jesus, but that I could not trust whom I

128

do not know. When you said that, I knew I simply could no longer go on the same way that I have been. I knew that if we were able to talk directly and perhaps read His Word and pray together, that would be the best possible way to get to know Him. So I, of course, *had* to speak to you."

"I see," she said with a slight smile.

He continued shyly, "There is something else."

"Yes?" Rachel asked, dying to know.

"When you told me that you loved me, I found it nearly impossible to stay silent a moment longer. I absolutely had to tell you how much I loved you too. Rachel, you have given me back my will to live. I never thought I could feel so genuinely happy as I did the instant you confessed that. But when you said you wanted to be my wife, the negative thoughts in my mind that had been swirling out of control since the accident suddenly stopped. Right then, everything became clear. It was like my entire world shook in sudden violence—as though an earthquake hit, and everything shifted—but in the most positive way. At that moment, I knew, all that I cherished remained; however, the bad had vanished." He leaned in closer and lowered his head. "Rachel, I had given up on ever feeling loved by anyone a long time ago. But by being with you, forgiving myself, and finding out that God actually loves me just as I am, I feel as though I have finally been liberated."

Her smile grew as he continued, "Also, to be upfront with you, I have had a feeling for a while now that I was not a ghost. And since I have never actually seen one in my entire life, I began to question if ghosts were even real. Sadly, I did not know how to approach the situation because everyone acted so terrified of me. But then, you came along, and you were different. You were not scared of me. You have shown me nothing but love, kindness, and compassion since you arrived, but..." He paused and sighed loudly, acting incredibly nervous. "Even so, I am afraid to tell you something that I have been longing to share with you since the first moment I saw you. But Rachel, I am so worried you will not believe me."

Tilting her head to the side, Rachel asked, "What? What do you want to tell me?" Noticing that he genuinely seemed concerned, she attempted to reassure him, "Richard, darling, I love you, no matter what. You can tell me anything. I promise."

Still acting nervous, he fidgeted with his fingers, wringing them together. He stood and began to pace back and forth on what little floor space the tower had to accommodate his long strides. "All right. I'll tell you, but to be honest, I am fully aware of how mad this sounds."

"Go on. It's okay," she urged.

"Well, you may not believe this, but days before you came to this house, I saw you in my sleep." He stopped and looked right at her, judging her reaction to his bold declaration. "Rachel, it sounds impossible, I know, but I dreamt of you three nights in a row."

Rachel put one hand over her mouth, and although she gasped, she said nothing.

"In a small room, I watched you for a moment by the light of the fire as you stood looking into a mirror. You were stunning, in a white dress, with your beautiful hair flowing down that revealed your curls. You wore a crown of flowers on your head, made of white roses, tiny, violet flowers, and blue thistles, with hints of green cedar. I remember every detail it like it was yesterday. I had been hiding in the darkest corner of your room, concealed by a black, hooded cape, because I feared showing my face. Drawn to you, I could not help myself and came up behind you as though I were floating. But as I got closer to you, my confidence grew. I then dared to remove the cape that seemed to be covering my very existence. After it fell to the floor, it vanished in the mist around my feet. Underneath my cape, I wore clothes fit for a prince, and suddenly, my fear turned into a feeling of royalty. Instantly, I dared to reach out and touch you."

Almost interrupting him, she stopped herself, covering her mouth with both hands now. "I…"

He resumed, "As I touched your hair and then your cheek, my heartbeat raced as it never had before, like it would thump right out of my chest. And Rachel, the moment I touched you in my dreams, I fell madly in love with you. When I awoke the next day, although I had not prayed in years, I found myself praying that you were real. Each time I envisioned you, I fell in love with you deeper still. As strange as it sounds, I felt like the Lord told me He was sending you here to help change my life. I swore I heard Him say I would soon be cherished more than any man could ever desire and that I was to marry you. It felt as if God Himself, told me that you would adore me as He does, with an undying, relentless love. But I... I did not believe Him."

Almost fainting from the intensity of his words—words that she had felt and even spoken herself—Rachel placed her hands on her chest and exhaled sharply, amazed by the resemblance to her own dreams of him.

Richard could tell right away that she was shocked and grew worried that she might think that he truly wasn't in his right mind because of what he'd just shared. He quickly knelt in front of her to further explain and get a feel for her thoughts. "Rachel? I am not making this up. You do believe me, don't you?" he asked anxiously.

She started weeping but then, oddly, began laughing. "Richard, I do believe you. I do. The Lord, He-He gave me dreams about you as well!"

"Wait. What? He did?" Richard sputtered. Staring wide-eyed, he slowly sat close on the bench beside her. "Tell me. Tell me about your dream, please," he said as his heart pounded wildly.

In awe of God's hand in their relationship, Rachel could barely speak. "Yes, Richard. I, too, experienced that exact scene three nights in a row, including the night before I came here."

Rachel described her own dreams, accentuating how every detail mimicked his, and told him, "When you softly touched my cheek in my dream, my heart melted. You were more handsome than I ever thought a man could be, and I knew that you were gentle and kind. I instantly fell head over heels in love with you. Yet, when I awoke, I forced myself to dismiss my strong feelings for you, telling myself it was just my imagination. I tried so hard to forget about you and did my best to block out my emotions until I saw you with my own eyes here at Locke Mansion the first night you came into my room."

Now dumbfounded, he began trembling. His dazed eyes started to well up again, and his jaw dropped in disbelief.

"Oh, Richard! Because my dreams were so real, I knew God had a plan for me, but I did not know if *you* were real. I had no idea who you were. I am ashamed to say that my faith was weak, and after spending a few days in this house, I stopped believing in the possibility of your existence. I then did what I could to forget everything and focus on helping your father. Even though I felt led to come to this house, I only came for employment. And when I heard the details of your story, I still did not know who you were. I just knew that I really wanted to help you and decided that no matter how difficult your situation might be, I wanted to be the hands and feet of the Lord to bring healing into your life. God gave me a heart of compassion for you. But now that I have gotten to know you, my feelings for you have grown into so much more."

"This-This is incredible," Richard muttered.

Inhaling deeply, she explained further, "When I saw you for the first time—for real—in the mirror in my bedroom, I almost fainted. Truly! I knew that you were the man of my dreams, but since I was given specific instructions by your father to never speak to you, I had no way of telling you how I felt. So, Richard, I, too, loved you even before I met you. Since then, I have been dying to talk to you, hold you, and tell you how much I adore you. Yet, because of your situation, I knew I needed to wait, so instead of talking to you directly, I prayed for you. I prayed daily for patience and the right time to speak to you. But today, Richard, after we kissed, I just couldn't wait any longer. It felt as though I was being tormented. I simply had to share my affections for you and tell you that I desperately wanted to be with you. I think you are one of the most remarkable, Christlike men I have ever met, and well, I'm sorry. I just couldn't keep my feelings bundled up inside of me any longer. Forgive me."

Now smiling, laughing, and wiping tears away, Richard, much relieved to hear that she believed the truth about his dreams, kissed her once again and hugged her tightly. "Oh, my lady, do not be sorry. I am so glad you dared to tell me how you felt today. Clearly, the timing could not have been better. It's just that I-I never knew God worked through dreams like this," he said, wholly astounded just thinking about all that God had done to bring them together.

"I know! It is hard to believe. I have heard He does, at times, but I do not doubt that it is rare and special. He has blessed us beyond what we ever imagined for ourselves, and I am so grateful."

Rachel and Richard, overcome with thanksgiving, knew that their story would be a testimony of God's passion and love for them both for eternity.

"We really should pray and thank Him. Don't you agree?" Rachel asked.

"Actually, yes. I would like to try. May I?"

"Of course. Please!" Rachel replied, ecstatic.

Together, they got down on their knees as Richard questioned, "Rachel, I'm a little nervous. I am afraid I won't know what to say. Can you give me some advice first?"

She said softly, "Just say whatever is on your mind. Ignore me, focus on Him, and talk to Him, knowing how much He loves you. Pray with thanksgiving as though you have already received whatever you are asking for in faith. Do not be afraid because you never have to be in fear around Him. Remember that He reached down to us through His Son, so we would not have to try to attain anything or work to gain a relationship with Him. That is the one difference between Christianity and all other religions of the world. God reached down to man instead of man reaching up to God. His love for you is perfect, as 1 John 4:18 says, 'perfect love casts out fear'. So, speak to Him truthfully from your heart."

He exhaled, acting nervous. "Is there anything else?"

"If I may, I suggest you invite Him into your heart, mind, and life. If you feel you need forgiveness for anything, simply ask for it, and that's all you must do to receive. And when you finish, you might want to end your prayers by saying, 'in Jesus' name.' Because Jesus taught in the gospel of John 14:13, 'And whatever you ask in my name, that I will do, that the Father may be glorified in the Son.' But truly, just be yourself." Rachel kissed his hand. Beaming with joy, she admired him for his willingness to pray in front of her.

Before he began, she took the time to explain the importance of salvation, forgiveness, God's mercy, and how to obtain eternal life. Encouraging him to not be so hard on himself, she said, "I'm going to be quiet now," knowing it was time for Richard to make up his own mind about what to pray.

"Okay. I shall try," Richard said as he squeezed Rachel's hand, bowed his head, and closed his eyes. "Dear Heavenly Father..." He paused, getting emotional. Then, he surprised her, stopped himself from crying, and prayed with a firm tone, "Thank You for sending Your Son to die for me. I am so sorry for being angry with You all this time. Please forgive me. I know You delight in me despite my rage, but I still want to say that I am sorry. Rachel has taught me that nothing compares to Your strong love. So, with a thankful heart, I receive Your forgiveness. Come into my heart. I invite You. I invite You into my life and my mind so that I, too, can walk in the newness of life. Thank You that You love me so much that, when You look at me, You see me as Your perfect son, for I know I do not deserve it, but I believe it. Help me to serve You all the days of my life. I surrender to You, Lord, with no turning back. In Jesus' name, amen."

Rachel put her hand gently underneath his chin and lifted it to kiss his forehead. "I am so proud of you, Richard." Laying her head upon his chest, she noticed fan-like rays of the setting sun reaching up from behind the clouds as they rose high into the sky. She smiled as their vibrant colors filled the tower.

After a long talk, while they rested in one another's arms, Rachel pondered their day and could not help but be grateful. She whispered softly, "2 Corinthians 5:17: 'Therefore, if anyone *is* in Christ, he is a new creation; old things have passed away; behold, all things have become new.'" As much as she cherished that verse, for some reason, it reminded her of Master Nathan. She knew she better start praying for everything to work out with Richard's father when he returned home. Despite the fact that she was confident he would be thrilled over his son's return, Rachel worried that he would be deeply hurt over losing her. And the last thing she ever wanted was to break his heart. Just thinking of it pained her, so she hugged Richard tightly to appear calm and allowed herself to get lost in his embrace.

Keeping her thoughts to herself, fear sought to grip her throat. She kept her head cushioned against Richard's chest, finding solace, and hoped everything would be okay. But she did not want to lie to herself. *Oh, God, You know my heart. I give You all the glory for today, but please tell me what to do now. I long to bring both Richard and Master Nathan joy, but I need Your wisdom now more than ever.*

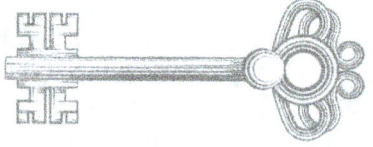

Chapter 13

Their joy was unmistakable as she and Richard spent the rest of the evening in the tower, wrapped in one another's arms, talking. Rachel never felt so comfortable or relaxed with another human being in her life. Yet, even though Richard's progress was extraordinary, she knew that he would still need lots of prayer and time in the Word. Sitting there beside her sweet Richard, she could not help but wonder if he might also need some Godly counsel or rehabilitation to recover from his years of trauma.

Sensing God leading her to stand and pray over him, she asked his permission. "Richard, I feel like the good Lord wants me to pray *over* you right now, not just with you. Would that be all right?"

"Of course, yes. Thank you," he replied as he sat up straighter to pay close attention to her words. He had grown to respect Rachel's relationship with God significantly and was trying to learn from her.

She looked pleased over his willingness, bowed her head, closed her eyes, and began to pray over him confidently, "Dear Lord, our Healer, we lean not on our own understanding and know it is vital to trust You. We give our hearts to You and call on You. When I envision the cross where You were bound on our behalf, I see Your precious gift of freedom. You have brought us from death to life, so we will sing Your praises as our souls receive Your grace. Through Your scars and Your resurrection, we are victorious. Jesus, there has never been a man that is more alive than You. Our risen Savior, we surrender all to You. Because of You, our chains are gone, our debt is paid, and the enemy can burden us with his lies no more. We will forever be grateful to see the truth of Your love and hear from Heaven."

Richard sat up straighter and opened his hands as though receiving a gift.

"I ask that You remove the spirit of fear and crippling inner critique Richard listens to. Let him know each day how incredibly rare he is and how loved. Help him to know not just who he is but *whose* he is. He is Yours. I specifically ask that You tear down all strongholds in his mind, strengthen him, and give him power to overcome the enemy from this day forth. Align His thoughts with Your thoughts and strengthen his heart. Help him to let his mind dwell on things that are pure, noble, good, and lovely, so he can more easily see Your beauty. Help him to see Your glory on this Earth, which You have so lovingly created for our enjoyment."

As Richard fidgeted in his seat, she paused but then went on, "Thank you for allowing Richard to see Your beauty that surrounds him as well as the acts of courage displayed in others. Help him feel the majesty of Your presence. Let him get to know Your precious Son, the King of kings, as his Brother, so that he never again forgets that he truly is royalty—which is likely the reason why he was wearing royal clothing in our dreams. I ask that when he looks at himself in the mirror from now on, he will know that he is a beautiful reflection of You, created in Your image. Thank You for strengthening him so he can hold his head high, knowing he is forgiven, accepted, and more than enough. In Jesus' mighty name, amen."

Feeling the intensity in the room as she prayed, Richard swallowed the lump in his throat. He sensed that Rachel's prayers would affect him for the rest of his days, so he waited for her to go on.

Reaching into her dress pocket, she pulled out a tiny bottle filled with Frankincense oil to use on Richard as in Isaiah 61:1-4. She wanted to anoint him with a spirit of gladness instead of mourning. From a young age, Rachel learned to always keep a bottle with her to use on herself, like in Leviticus 8:30 in case she needed to use it during her prayers for protection. She anointed her forehead and prayed, "Lord, render me holy unto Yourself. Forgive my sins and seal and protect me with the precious blood of Jesus."

She instructed Richard to kneel before her as she anointed his forehead with oil, saying, "Lord, render Richard holy unto Yourself.

I thank You for forgiving him by your divine mercy and seal and protect him with the precious blood of Jesus. Thank you for replacing the spirit of mourning that has been upon him with a spirit of gladness. In Jesus name." She put the oil back into her pocket and again began to pray out loud for Richard with one hand on his shoulder, the other lifted high toward the sky. "Lord, I pray over Richard's past, present, and future." Her thoughts then changed course slightly, and she altered her prayers accordingly to speak change into his life. "I ask that You, God, completely and permanently rebuke and remove the spirits of fear, doubt, guilt, shame, and condemnation from Richard. By the power of Your Holy Spirit, I break the curses that may have been put on him through that man who claimed to be a doctor years ago. I break off any curses that may have come upon him from any members of his family in any generation, all the way back to Adam and Eve. I break off all demonic strongholds and spirits that may have blocked him from hearing and seeing the truth about You and his identity in Christ these many years."

Rachel's prayer encouraged him so much he began to shake. Feeling the influence from the Holy Spirit, he lifted his chin to listen to her prayers more carefully.

"Lord, I am fully aware that our words have a tremendous impact on us, even though I do not fully understand it. So, I ask that, from this moment on, You help Richard to think uplifting thoughts and speak words of life over himself. I pray that the enemy will no longer have influence over him. For I know that the Devil has power but no authority except what we give him, whether intentional or not. As a believer and Your daughter, I have more power and authority than the Devil. I am not interested in glorifying Satan in any way by dwelling on him, yet I am fully aware that I am a soldier for Christ. And when any soldier is fighting a battle, they need to know their enemy in order to defeat them. And if I aim well, by focusing on him long enough to shoot my arrow exactly where it will do the most damage, I trust You will bring me victory through Your guidance. By following the Holy Spirit and seeking His wisdom, walking in love, living in the light holy devoted to You, taming my tongue, speaking life, quoting scripture, rebuking the devil's attacks and pleading the blood of Jesus over difficult situations, You will help me to defeat the darkness."

Shifting from praying to God, to rebuking the enemy, Rachel opened her eyes and declared boldly, "Right now, through the power of the Holy Spirit, I render all assignments against Richard null and void. I also render any assignments the evil one and any of his kind has against Richard's father null and void. I break off all curses that may have been put on Locke Mansion residents—past, present, or future. With Christ's authority and by the power of God within me, I am officially condemning all demons influencing people in this house to receive their full punishment for failing in their assignments to cause further harm. Go! I command, in the name of Jesus, that all spirits intending Richard, me, my family, our loved ones or anyone else in this home, pain, confusion, or loss in any degree, depart this instant. You must leave us alone, never to return, in Jesus' name!"

Once she'd finished her prayer, Richard told her that he felt as if years of burdensome weights had finally been lifted off his shoulders. He shared with her that he could see the cobwebs of his mind being swept away. Rachel thought he was adorable when he asked her to pray a little more, and she smiled.

"I thank You, God, that Richard's mind is now free to worship the One found worthy, the Lion of the tribe of Judah, the root of David. Jesus, You became a man. You took on flesh for us. There is only One—the Lamb who was slain for the sins of mankind. We will worship You all the days of our lives. Jesus, You are the key to unlocking our potential. You are the key to our peace and joy as we get to know You more. Let us encounter You as we set our faces to seek You through the wisdom and revelation of the Holy Spirit. We love You and claim victory over our lives through You. For when You said, 'It is finished!' that is precisely what You meant. Chains were broken on the cross the instant You gave up Your life, and we give You all the glory with heartfelt thanksgiving for the gift of freedom Your sacrifice provides. Help us to fall more in love with You daily, for we know that there is nothing else that satisfies. I praise You for setting Richard free this day and for dispatching your angels to protect him now, and forevermore, in Jesus' mighty name, amen."

Richard's eyes flowed with priceless tears of joy as he climbed up from his knees to sit beside Rachel. They sat without saying a word for a while, gently embracing one another. Then, placing his forehead softly upon hers, he let out a sigh of relief, as did she.

"I cannot explain it, but I have not felt this light since I was a small child," he said, closing his eyes to enjoy the moment while the birds sang sweetly around the tower windowsills.

Beyond thankful for Richard's breakthrough, Rachel was annoyed that she felt conflicted. As much as she wanted to enjoy this moment, her mind swirled with thoughts of Master Nathan. *How am I supposed to break the news to him about my love for his son?* Again, afraid of how he might respond, she exhaled. *I am such a hypocrite.*

Rachel understood, when she could not see her way ahead, that was when she needed to trust the Father the most, but she feared how Master Nathan might react. Despite being aware she needed to tell him the truth as soon as possible, she did not want to ruin their relationship. She loved him dearly, but it would never be the kind of love he needed.

Of course, Master Nathan loved Richard more than anything, but she still wondered if he would be heartbroken over having to let her go, even to his own son. Not wanting to flatter herself, she held Richard tighter at the thought of how difficult the conversation with Master Nathan might be when he returned and prayed quietly in her head, *Lord, I cannot do this on my own. I need You to work all of this out. Please. I beg of You.*

Completely unaware of her dilemma, Richard hugged her back.

Realizing there was no possible way she could even explain her predicament to Richard, again, she kept it to herself. When contemplating what to do, she remembered her father telling her, *"There are bad things, good things, and better things. When you must make an important decision in life, choose the better thing."* Yet, still unsure of the best way to handle the situation, she continued to ask God for wisdom, hoping for some revelation.

While they stood to watch the remaining sunset, Richard put his arm around Rachel in awe of everything he saw and felt. "Rachel, I really think I can see colors more clearly now. Perhaps I can even see colors that I could not before. I can't be sure, but this sunset, with its orange and red sky, and purple and pink clouds, is by far the most magnificent one I have ever seen."

In agreement, she said, "Actually, I have heard of many people who had a similar experience after the Devil was forced to flee from them. God longs for His children to see the splendor of His creation as it was designed to be seen. I am so glad you can see better now, Richard. That is such a gift, and I cannot think of anyone who deserves it more."

She fully enjoyed his embrace once more and nuzzled closer to Richard as the sun lowered itself over the purple hills on the horizon. With her desire for him so strong, she decided to speak with him about the importance of being careful not to sin. She explained that she would greatly appreciate it if they could wait until marriage to kiss one another again. Knowing full well the intensity of their passion, she shared her concern that they might be tempted to come together in inappropriate ways too soon. And although he was hesitant, they talked openly and agreed to study the Bible verses that discussed the importance of remaining pure for the one they loved. However, resolving they would commit to solely enjoy holding hands and hugging until their wedding day, she acknowledged how trying that would be.

Leaving the tower, while walking to her room, she wondered if Richard felt disappointed with their decision for physical boundaries but did not ask. She changed her clothes as he patiently waited outside her room. After letting him back in, they spent a few hours talking next to the fireplace. He shared how he'd survived the past ten years and what it had been like to spend each day and night alone amongst the shadows. He told her how difficult it was to have no one to talk to and how much he'd wanted to reach out and hug his father daily.

Her heart ached as he described how disconnected he'd felt from his father, the world around him, and his own soul. She tried to understand what he meant when he said that there always seemed to be something blocking him from ever allowing him to do or say the things he wanted. But she had never experienced anything like that, so while he poured out his painful memories, she listened intently. Her attention made his heart glad. Her curiosity showed how much she cared for him and about his struggles.

Afterward, they agreed to end each night still reading the Bible, but now Richard would read to Rachel. He started reading and she sat watching him, grinning and twining her curls around her fingers, a twinkle in her eye. She loved listening to his voice and felt she was witnessing another miracle with each word that flowed from his lips.

Richard read long into the night until Rachel fell asleep with her head on his lap. As he sat by the firelight, stroking her hair and admiring her face, she lay peacefully in his care. Getting tired himself, he cradled her head, lifted her into his arms to place her in the bed, and tucked her in as gently as possible to avoid waking her. *Thank you, God, for sending Rachel to me. Thank you so much.*

Dreading leaving her side, Richard curled up beside her bed on the floor and rested his head on his arm to admire her until he closed his eyes and slipped off to dreamland. However, this time, for the first time in years, his dreams were sweet and filled with thoughts of love.

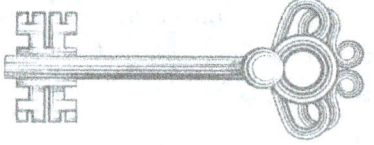

Chapter 14

Getting to know one another better, for the next several days, Rachel and Richard were inseparable. Touring more of the mansion, the rose gardens, and the maze, they revisited the rhododendrons and azaleas that were practically in full bloom. Both were in awe over the striking variety of colors and plants as they talked about their pasts, their families, and hopes for a bright future.

Like he used to with his sisters, they even played hide-and-seek and tag. On occasion, he would carry her around on piggyback, or in his arms just for fun, through the winding paths. Listening with delight to the songbirds and flowing fountains, they walked to the garden's edge.

Upon entering a nearby forest, Rachel found it fascinating. Although Richard had not been in the woods for years, he enjoyed following her into the expansive tree line and exploring the wood-lands surrounding the Locke property. The trees were some of the most magnificent she had ever seen; some seemed over seven feet wide at the base. Everything was exceptionally green now, and life was teeming all around them.

Before long, their path was blocked by a wide stream. They sat down next to it on one of the many large rocks and enjoyed holding hands, talking, and skipping whatever small, flat stones they could find.

The sparkling waters babbled in the crisp air of the day, forcing them to raise their voices. White water bounced off the rocks as the rapids poured throughout the stream, and a few boulders that were worn smooth caught Richard's eye. He stood and decided to jump from rock to rock, just inches from a good soaking, as he climbed about in his fancy clothes. Rachel stayed put but enjoyed watching him have a good time. He appeared fearless, pleasing her immensely and making her laugh.

Once he'd had his fun, they found another large, flat rock, further upstream where it was quieter. This large boulder, now eroded smooth, seemed like God had carved a seat for them. It sat perfectly placed on the stream's edge about a foot above the waterline. They took off their shoes and socks to dangle their feet in the cool waters. Sunlight danced off the ripples they made together, as they splashed and kicked like a couple of children.

Richard asked her some questions about her prayer life and how she had learned so much about God's Word. She answered each question with humility and love.

Then his eyes narrowed. "Rachel, do you remember your prayer over me in the tower?"

"Yes."

"Well, you prayed that the Lord would tear down strongholds. Can you tell me what that means?"

She looked happy to explain. "'Strongholds' are incorrect thinking patterns that greatly affect our lives if they are not corrected."

"Thinking patterns?"

"Yes. Thinking patterns. When it comes to finding joy, it is of the utmost importance to control your thoughts. And when it comes to your thoughts, you must remember this teaching above all else." She paused and thought through how to make her answer crystal clear. "We cannot afford to have any thoughts about ourselves that God does not have about us. Any thoughts contrary to His are lies and must be dealt with swiftly for us to overcome strongholds." To reflect on her wording, she stopped, thought, but then decided she was pleased with it.

"I am still unclear exactly why wrong thoughts are called 'strongholds.'"

Rachel replied, "All right, picture this: say you are at war with a terrible enemy's army, and you and your men have set up camp in a certain location you feel is safe."

Richard nodded. "Yes. Okay."

"Then, let's say that your enemy and his military come along. Without opposition, you let them build a large fortress right next to your camp. From this fortress, your enemy can constantly attack you with fiery darts and cannons from over his tall walls. And in his fort, he will be protected from your counterattacks. Are you with me so far?"

"I am," Richard answered, "but that doesn't sound wise. Why would I let him do that? I mean, why would you allow your enemy to build, right next to your camp, a fortress from which he can easily attack you? I apologize, but that just does not seem smart."

Proud of his insight, Rachel said, "You are correct. That would not be wise because now he would have a powerful fort, like a stronghold—where he could protect himself and his army—from which he could easily destroy you in the meantime. It would put him into a position where he could cause you great harm, but people do this exact thing in the spirit world with their thoughts all the time."

Richard squinted, "How so?"

"Well, when we continue to have the wrong kind of thought patterns against the truth of God's Word and against ourselves, the Devil uses those thoughts. Picture him using our negative thoughts much like bricks. When we believe his lies and allow these negative thoughts to remain in our heads, we give him brick after brick to build a stronghold or fortress for himself."

"Okay," he replied hesitantly, still trying to figure it all out.

"Richard, darling, it may seem harsh to bring up your past so soon, but in order to help you understand and overcome any strongholds, let's look back at your life and dispel the lies directly. Shall we?" Rachel waited to make sure he was okay with such an up-front discussion about himself.

Inhaling deeply, he let out his breath and said, "All right. By all means."

Rachel said kindly, "Stop me if this is too much for you, okay?"

"I will."

She spoke softly, taking her time, "For years, you presumed that the accident was your fault when, in fact, the Bible is clear that the Devil is the one who kills, destroys, and steals our loved ones. Now,

I do feel that sometimes people go on to be with the Lord before it's their time, but the lie about you being responsible for their untimely death was a huge brick with which he could start building a fortress for himself next to your camp. After persuading you of that first lie— or *brick,* so to speak—he could lead you to accept the lies that your father was angry with you, that he blamed you for their deaths, and that you were better off dead. Those were like three more massive bricks to build his fort with."

Richard sighed.

"He then confused you until you accepted the lie that you were a ghost. That was another gigantic brick. Then you were convinced that, since you were a ghost, you could never again interact with another human being. That was another brick, along with several other lies, which completed the foundation of his fortress. Are you with me so far?"

"Yes. Go on," Richard said, sounding profoundly interested.

"So, since you could never interact with another human being, you started to agree with the lie that you would forever be alone, which was another massive brick. The Devil told you lie after lie after lie. He used each one like bricks stacked on top of one another until he had you believing so many lies that, eventually, he had a huge fortress from which he could attack you."

Though silent, Richard clenched his fists. *How could I have let this go on for so long?*

Noticing his frustrations, Rachel finished, "Once these lies were established in your mind, his strongholds were complete, and then from there, he continually threw fiery darts at you, like fear, loneliness, guilt, shame, condemnation, thoughts of suicide, anger, and more. Richard, you were young and vulnerable, especially after the accident. But I can promise you that none of what the Devil said about you is true. Absolutely nothing."

Richard, upset and confused, asked, "What kind of person would attack a child this way? It's unthinkable!"

Rachel said in agreement, "Indeed. Not only is it unthinkable, but it is inhuman. You see, the Devil is not human. He is pure evil and does not care whom he attacks. He hates every single human being on the face of the planet. He attacks innocent people from all walks of life. It does not matter your age, religion, race, gender, economic status, or what you believe, even if you worship him. He hates all and will utterly destroy anyone he can."

"This is infuriating. I'm not sure if it's wrong to hate him, but I do."

"That is understandable, but he doesn't deserve your hatred towards him to take up any of your energy. He's just not worth it. The good news is that through Jesus' death on the cross, we now have authority over him and his minions: the demons who do his bidding. We simply must know this fact and claim our rights as sons and daughters of the Most-High God. Only then can we walk in victory over our thoughts, our lives, the Devil's deception, and even death. You see, Jesus paid for it all. And when the Bible says all, it means all."

Since Richard looked like he felt all right, Rachel continued, "The truth is this: it was the Devil who destroyed your family. You were just a sweet, innocent child who simply wanted to play the trumpet. It was not your fault the horses got spooked. And, of course, the lie that you would be better off dead was a horrible thing to instill into a young boy by the Devil who spoke evil to you through that doctor. Yet, as I said, he does not care about you or anyone for that matter. He is the picture of selfishness, and Jesus is the shining example of the exact opposite. Jesus is and always was selfless, even to the point of death. And that is one reason I love you the way I do. I see Christ's light in you. You remind me of Him."

He absorbed the compliment with a shy grin as she went on, "It will take time for you to learn about the kindness of God. The good news is that it will be an honor to teach you if you like, and I'm not going anywhere. You now have your whole life ahead of you. These past ten years are just that: the past. You now know that you are loved no matter what. You are a child of the King, free and forgiven. Although I cannot promise that things will be easy, I can promise that your life will never be the same again. And Richard, just so you know, you are not the only one who struggles with needing to tear down strongholds. It happens to all of us. The Devil is called 'the father of lies' because he deceives each of us without letting up until we learn to defend ourselves. He lies to everyone. No one is immune to his attacks. Now that you are aware of it, you can recognize it and defend your mind with the truth of God's Word. Does that make sense?"

"It does. In fact, it makes perfect sense. You are saying that the Devil used my own thoughts against me to keep me in bondage all these years?"

"Yes. That is exactly what I am saying."

Richard looked down and exhaled heavily. "I've wasted years of my life, haven't I?"

"Well, you could think of it that way, but that would be another lie. When someone learns from their experiences, then it is never a waste. Even though you have endured a great deal of pain and trial, the fact remains that you did, indeed, endure. It's astounding. The Bible says that, for all eternity, we will be known by the word of our testimony. Just think of the testimony you will have to share for all eternity. The victory of God in your story will forever be amazing because you went through tremendous trauma, loss, and heartbreak, but you survived. Richard, although you may not see it this way, you are an overcomer."

Hearing her encouraging words, his countenance changed, and the sparkle returned to his eyes.

"I am so proud of you. All will be well. You will see," she said, kissing his cheek.

He inhaled sharply and grinned as she taught him teachings she learned from other Bible verses she'd studied. Scriptures about hope when all seemed lost, and about the power of renewing the mind. Lessons she claimed saved her life.

"In fact, allow me to elaborate. Hopefully you can clearly see the power of the mind and our belief system and how it can be used against us to cause us great harm. The opposite is true when we focus on God and His Word. He is the one who has given us the power of our mind, and our words, to shift our circumstances for the better. It can help us tremendously.

Now, if you will indulge me, I want to encourage you to try to use your imagination for good. Close your eyes and picture yourself, brick by brick, dismantling all the strongholds we discussed. After you have dealt with those, envision yourself forgiven, close to God, deeply loved by Him, stronger, wiser, completely healthy, constantly smiling, and living without fear. Think of the dreams you walked away from long ago and then vow to bring them up into your remembrance every single day. Speak out loud to God in prayer for them, fully believing that you will receive them. Picture yourself, happy, at peace, dancing, meeting new people, and building new relationships.

Allow yourself to enjoy visions of your new life, from the grandest scale, down to the smallest detail. See yourself able to stand tall with confidence in front of a large crowd, having the courage to speak boldly in front of them. Your voice is strong, commanding, and revealing your heart causes you to be excited, instead of nervous.

Imagine riding horseback with your father again, or me for that matter, and having tremendous fun doing it. Imagine how that would make you feel mentally, emotionally and physically. Let yourself experience those wonderful feelings over and over."

Looking astonished by what Rachel was sharing, Richard said nothing.

"Some people say you should ignore your feelings, but my father taught me, the feelings I felt were the *felt sensations* from my own thoughts. Sometimes they helped me, sometimes they hurt me. In other words, the thoughts I allowed myself to think greatly affected my feelings, my body, my heart, and my soul. Yet, no matter what my day was like, he encouraged me to go to bed and recount my day with gratitude, even for the difficult lessons I'd learned. He said to pray for guidance as I went to sleep, reflecting on the quality of my thoughts. This way I could more easily discern if they were positive or negative, serving me, or harming me; whether they were ideas that helped me to trust in the Lord or not.

Wanting me to wake up each morning with mindfulness, he requested that I try to think healthy thoughts and ask good questions. Questions like: I'm curious as to what God will surprise me with this day? I wonder what insightful lessons He might teach me. I am curious if God will bring someone new into my life today or not? Someone, like Jesus? I wonder, what is one small change I can make today to improve things for myself or others?

He said it was wise to ask simple things like, I'm curious as to what my life would look like if made sure to wake up with the sun each day or how I might feel if I went for a daily walk, or if I slept better or ate well? I'm curious how sharp my mind would be if I memorized more verses or read my Bible more? I wonder how doing those things would strengthen my faith and my relationship to God? I wonder, if I stopped complaining, what He will bless me with next?"

She snickered, "My mother always says, 'Allowing yourself to complain is like drinking poison, and the sooner you stop, the better,' but she is a saint, not like me," she said bobbing her head to one side. "I tried to do that, especially after my father passed away, but it was not easy. She also made me say kind things to myself in the looking glass and praise God for how, and who, He made me. Although it was a struggle, I made myself, knowing it was best for me. So, not always, but most days, this leads my mind towards seeing the good. That way, I can better communicate with myself or with God about what I am thankful for. You see, communication is an art. How we communicate our thoughts with ourselves, the enemy, with our Savior, or with others, can greatly alter our day.

You can't change everything at once, but one thing you can change is what you say to yourself inside your own head. Therefore, if the Devil speaks lies to you again, and he will, just rebuke his deception and cling to the truth of God's Word. We can't control everything around us, but we can control what we think, feel, choose to believe, and what comes out of our own mouths. I am not great at it, but one thing I try to do is never complain. So, if you ever hear any complaints come out of my mouth, big or small, promise me you will stop me. Sometimes, I too, need help renewing my mind."

Placing her hand on her chest, she said, "It doesn't matter how I feel. When my heart is not right, I need to shut my mouth. This stops the momentum of a complaining attitude and negative thoughts, which then generates just enough strength to move me to ask better questions and shift my mindset."

Smiling at the thought of it all, Richard promised to try to renew his mind each time he entertained a negative thought or a lie from the enemy. He closed his eyes and sighed, letting his imagination run free. Longing for change, he sighed. Finally reaching for renewed hope, wanting to trust in God, He began to see each detail of his future differently.

Over the next few days, Richard asked Rachel many questions about the news of the world, her life, her family, and the Lord. He wanted to know everything. She shared openly with him her thoughts on the church, love, relationships, politics, her travels, and her favorite verses from the Bible. He seemed to be maturing in the Lord at an unheard-of rate, and she was thankful for it.

Several glorious days passed, and one afternoon as they sat by the pond on the park bench to read to one another, the swans floated nearby with their new babies. Richard thought for a bit and named them out loud, "Here, Jack, Lori, Jo, Linda, and Hayley. Come here."

Rachel chuckled at his creativity and how he reminded her of Master Nathan. As they observed the swans gracefully swimming about, Rachel did not tell him his father already named them and had even picked similar names.

Then Richard jumped and sat up straight as though he were listening to something in the distance. He seemed focused on a bird that was repeatedly singing the same two notes.

"Do you hear that bird?" he asked excitedly.

"Yes," she replied, giving him a perplexed look.

He shifted in his seat from excitement as he explained that those notes reminded him of his mother. "Rachel, this may sound silly, but I vividly recall my mother telling me when I was little that I was an exceptional child. As we listened to a particular bird singing, I remember it was unique. She was so sweet and shared with me that God had the birds sing specially, just for me. She said it was calling my name, 'Rich—ard,' as it sang its two notes, one high and one low. Can you hear that?"

"I can. How darling." Rachel put her hand on her heart. "I can just imagine you as a boy with your mother while she told you about your very own special songbird. I sure wish I could have met Gloria at least once before she passed. She sounds incredibly dear."

For over an hour, Richard shared about his mother and sisters. Rachel knew it was healing for him to express his love for them and how deeply he missed them. He explained the games they used to play and what books they loved most. He remembered how he enjoyed sitting next to his mother in church and recalled looking up at her to admire her beauty and grace as she snuck him small candies to keep him quiet.

Rachel loved witnessing him pour out his feelings about his life and his past before the accident. Just listening to him speak at all brought her joy, knowing what a radical transformation was taking place within him. Since he held nothing back, she had a twinkle in her eye.

He then asked about her family. She explained her mother's current state, but not wanting to worry him, Rachel made sure he understood that she had high hopes for her mother's full recovery. She opened up about several of her favorite memories, but she shared them carefully, not wanting to provoke him to jealousy over how close her family still was. And when he asked how she survived after her father's death, she paused and replied sweetly, "Not by my own strength."

Looking at her with compassion, like her answer softened his heart even further, he hugged her close.

His questions then shifted back to Jesus and the Bible. She was glad to expound on verses such as John 5:24, where Jesus said, "'Most assuredly, I say to you, he who hears My word and believes in Him who sent Me has everlasting life, and shall not come into judgment, but has passed from death into life.'"

She would ask Richard to read specific passages that she believed would help him the most as well. One such scripture was Psalm 34:17-18. He sounded noble as he read aloud, and she inhaled, proud of him. "'The righteous cry out, and the Lord hears, And delivers them out of all their troubles. The Lord *is* near to those who have a broken heart, And saves those who have a contrite spirit.'"

Rachel read a passage from Philippians 4:4-9 that she'd shared with Master Nathan, knowing how vital it was to live by. "'Rejoice in the Lord always. Again I will say, rejoice! Let your gentleness be known to all men. The Lord *is* at hand. Be anxious for nothing, but in everything by prayer and supplication, with thanksgiving, let your requests be made known to God; and the peace of God, which surpasses all understanding, will guard your hearts and minds in Christ Jesus. Finally, brethren, whatever things are true, whatever things are noble, whatever things are just, whatever things are pure, whatever things are lovely, whatever things are of good report, if there is any virtue and if there is anything praiseworthy— meditate (let your mind dwell on) on these things. The things which you learned and received and heard and saw in me, these do, and the God of peace will be with you.'"

They talked extensively about the importance of listening to the truth in God's love letter to His people, the Bible. Rachel admitted she enjoyed reading other books, too, but explained that the Word of God was the only thing they were to live by and cling to, especially in times of need.

He agreed, and then he grew quiet for a bit. Speaking slowly, he admitted that he used to hear voices in his head that were incredibly destructive. He let her know that they often told him to harm himself and that he was better off dead. He shared that these voices had him believing no one loved, cared for, or even missed him.

Once again, Rachel's heart broke for him, but she did not interrupt.

Richard explained that since the day in the tower when he'd prayed and surrendered his life to God, everything had been different. He let her know, the second she prayed over him and anointed him with oil, all the horrific voices in his head seemed to have been silenced at once. And for that, he was exceedingly grateful. He was ecstatic that he could now genuinely hear the Word of God without mental blockage or confusion.

"Before that day, organizing or controlling my thoughts was next to impossible. I even found it difficult to take in the sounds of nature let alone God's voice."

Rachel was dumbfounded as he continued to describe how he could only see darkness and said that perceiving God's beauty within nature or himself had merely been a distant memory since the accident. Yet he clarified, that now, everything seemed to be shifting and felt vastly different.

They strolled hand-in-hand amongst the roses, taking the time to smell them. While watching Richard react like an excited boy, marveling at each rose's unique scent, Rachel chuckled to herself. He shared how he enjoyed comparing the different varieties growing near one another.

While trying to pick Richard a rose, Rachel cut herself on a thorn, and he jumped to her aid. Kissing her wound, he looked into her eyes, desperately wanting to kiss her, but resisted and shifted his focus to the rose. Inhaling deeply, he greatly exaggerated the effects of its scent. Taking in another big whiff, he pretended to pass out from the enticing fragrance. Rachel played along and pretended to catch him, making him laugh.

Knowing there was no way she could hold him up, she shouted, "Richard!"

He jokingly fell past her and lay on the grass, then reached up for her hand and pulled her down next to him. Now face to face, the urge to passionately embrace one another and give into their desires was overwhelming, but they resisted. Lying next to each other in the sun for a long while, they looked up at the blue sky filled with puffy white clouds, resting while they enjoyed the soft, warm grass.

"Rachel?"

"Yes?" she answered, propping herself up on her elbow to look at him directly.

"Do you think my mother and sisters are happy in Heaven? Because I have often wondered if Heaven is real."

Again, he reminded her of Master Nathan, who had asked the very same question about Heaven during their picnic, and she smiled. "Some people do not believe in Heaven, which is their choice, but I do. And to answer your question, yes. I am sure they are with Jesus, among others who love Him up in Heaven. I am confident they know no other feeling but eternal bliss."

"Do you think they know how much father and I miss them?"

"I'm not sure. Perhaps. But one thing I do know is they are not sad. What kind of God would allow people to feel loss or sadness in Heaven? I think that if they know you are sad, well, that would not be very 'Heavenly' now, would it? Life on this Earth is so short compared to eternity, and I'm sure they know that you will all be together soon. They are probably doing amazingly well and looking forward to spending eternity with you, too. In fact, I am sure they are rejoicing that you have finally surrendered your life to the Lord, just as all of Heaven rejoices when someone lost comes to Jesus. Because now, they know, without a doubt, that when you die, you will forever join them."

"That will be incredible," he said, looking at peace as he turned and faced her. "Rachel?"

"Yes?"

"Are you sure I can't kiss you until our wedding day?" he teased.

"I'm sure," she responded with an embarrassed giggle.

"What if I catch you?" he said as he raised his eyebrows up and down.

"Oh, no!" Rachel fake cried as she scrambled to her feet.

Acting wild, resembling his father, Richard ran after her like a madman, letting her stay just out of reach until they got to the swing, where they spent the rest of the afternoon. Yet today, she pushed him. She was delighted to witness him enjoying something he loved from his childhood.

On occasion, just to have fun seeing her blush, he would beg for a kiss as he got near her on the swing. Each time she would refuse him with a shy smile. She knew that Richard would patiently wait until their wedding day. But because she wanted to kiss him too, she was grateful he respected her wishes.

Rachel could feel the beauty and presence of the Lord surrounding them as they grew closer to God and one another. With each passing day and as they read together each evening, she had the plea-sure of witnessing her beloved heal more and more. His newfound joy and their developing love were undeniable, and she praised God for it.

Sadly, still torn about how to handle Master Nathan's return, she tried to lay her concerns at the feet of Jesus and not fret, but her attempts were futile. For some reason, the worst-case scenario continued to rummage through her head. Although spending time with Richard was lovely in every way, everything at Locke Mansion reminded her of Master Nathan, who was due to return any day now, and she shivered, knowing she had yet to come up with a plan.

Chapter 15

Weeks passed since Richard's *awakening* from being lost in the darkness within his mind, and he had learned a great deal. He now acted, looked, and talked like a completely new person. His transformation was truly remarkable, and everyone was in awe of this new young man who had blossomed right before their eyes practically overnight.

One evening, Rachel and Richard were sitting in the tower, hoping to watch the sunset together, when, out of nowhere, Rachel thought about Master Nathan once again. Panic hit her like an unwelcome wave from the cold sea, splashing water upon her peace. She was instantly reminded of what she soon must face and did not understand why she felt afraid.

After preaching strongly against fear and tearing down strongholds, she tried to deflect it. But her heart ached at the thought of disappointing Master Nathan. She wished that she had at least written him a letter while he was away so that the news of Richard would not be such a shock when he returned. *I am such a fool. Why did I not heed Austin's warning?*

Then, at that moment, she saw it! Master Nathan's carriage was approaching from around the tall hedge and coming up the carriage-way rapidly. "Nathan!" Rachel cried out as she jumped to run and meet him, partly out of excitement to see him again and tell him the good news about Richard, but mostly because she knew she needed to tell him the truth as soon as possible.

Richard stood perfectly still, his eyes wide and filled with fear as he stared out the window, watching Master Nathan's carriage approach the house. Rachel noticed that he looked anxious and was trembling. She took his hand, kissed it firmly and then held it up to her cheek as if to hug it, hoping to calm him.

Putting her hand under his chin to turn his face, she looked directly into his eyes and said, "I have an idea: why don't you wait here and let me go and tell your father the wonderful news of your... well... of your return? The last thing we want to do is startle him, and I have no doubt that, even though he will be thrilled, he might go into shock when he sees you. So, give me some time to tell him, and then, when you come down the stairs, he will be so happy to see you. He should be able to handle the news much better that way. Does that sound all right with you, my love?" Rachel asked, hoping he would agree.

"I..." He paused. "I don't know why, but I am a nervous wreck. So, that will be the best way to handle this, I suppose."

Because he was breathing heavily and sweat beads were forming on his forehead, Rachel laid her head on his chest and felt his heart racing. So was hers. Wearing a fabricated grin, she held him close and gave him a warm embrace. After kissing his hand one last time, she ran down the stairs as quickly as she could without falling.

Calling back to Richard, she yelled, "Do not worry, my love. It will be all right. You'll see!"

She tried not to fret and to trust God to work everything out, but she was struggling to breathe. Once she approached the bottom of the grand staircase, Master Nathan swung the front door open wide. By the look on his face, Rachel could tell that he was downright excited to see her too. She ran down and jumped into his arms.

As he swung her overhead in a circle, she proclaimed, "You're back!"

He set her feet down quickly and grabbed her by the hand. "Yes, I am! And I have much to tell you!" he exclaimed, pulling her into the parlor.

Almost shouting, Rachel replied, "I have a lot to tell you, too! So much has happened since you left; you will not even believe it."

Once she was seated on the sofa in front of the fireplace, he blurted out, "Me first!" acting giddy with beaming eyes. Rachel had never seen him behave like this. He let go of her hand and began to pace back and forth, not knowing where to begin. But then, to her surprise, he stopped and got down on his knees directly in front of her, talking rapidly, unable to contain himself.

"Rachel, I prayed the whole way, and my trip was truly incredible. First, I purchased an empty building down the street from our old factory that ended up fitting our needs precisely. I was then able to organize each of my factories quickly. I got manufacturing back on track, encouraged my employees and staff, and more importantly, gave them all big raises. The most fun part was I brought several gifts, love, and hope to the families that needed it most, and it felt so good. It really did!"

"Oh! That is such good news, Nathan."

"Rachel, you were right. You were right about everything. God worked out my entire trip just perfectly. And I was even able to find time to get you that gift I promised you."

"You were? Oh, what fun! What is it?" she asked, excitedly moving closer to him on the sofa's edge.

"As I said, I prayed all the way home. And well, there's a great deal more I need to tell you." He grew serious. "Rachel, I..." He paused for a moment and then rose and paced a bit longer before he once again knelt in front of her. "I never expected this, but Rachel, I-I love you."

"I love you, too," she replied casually, still excited.

"No. No. You do not understand. I really love you."

She replied once again, "I love you, too, Nathan." Only, this time, she looked bewildered.

Master Nathan leaned closer to her to repeat himself with a look of desperation, and this time, his tone was deep, and his words slow. "No, Rachel. You do not understand. I love you. I really love you. And I-I want to marry you."

Rachel gasped as he pulled a large engagement ring covered in diamonds from his pocket and took her hand to place it on her finger. She did not want to hurt his feelings, but she was stunned.

Nowhere in her mind did she ever imagine him asking for her hand in marriage. Especially so soon.

The instant she saw the ring, although it was stunning, she thought of Richard. Rachel knew right away that she could not allow Master Nathan to place it upon her finger, not even for one split second. Her heart skipped a beat. Not knowing what to do, and without hesitation, she pulled her hand away and placed it over her mouth as she began to shake.

Seeming quite distraught by her reaction, he squinted. "Now, I know this is sudden. But I promise to do whatever it takes to make you happy. You do believe me, don't you?"

Utterly dumbfounded, she said nothing, and in an instant, her wide eyes began to well with tears.

Noticing that she did not look happy, he became confused, and his eyebrows scrunched together. He'd thought she would say "Yes!" right away and stammered, "Rachel, I…."

Rachel stopped him and quickly attempted to explain herself, "Nathan, please. There is so much to tell. Please, I must speak with you."

Master Nathan looked upset as he slowly realized that she was not going to happily accept his ring or his marriage proposal as he had anticipated. He held onto the ring and, with a look of sorrow in his eyes that broke her heart, sighed, lowered his chin, and crawled up next to her to sit on the sofa. "Okay. I'm listening."

She chose her words very carefully. "Nathan, I, I am honored by your proposal, but I must speak with you first."

Letting out another loud sigh, he said, "Well then, go on. Speak. What is it?"

After Rachel inhaled and exhaled slowly, she began, sensing he was quite offended now, but she tried to explain, "When I first came here to Locke Mansion, I did not know what to expect. I was unsure, and—well, as you know—I was a bit afraid of you. But then, I met you and I could not believe how wonderful you were. And to be honest, I fell in love with your charm, your wit, your brilliant sense of humor, and, well, just everything about you."

With renewed excitement, he turned toward her and asked, "Then you do love me?"

"Yes. Of course, I do. Very much, but please, I have more to say. I beg of you to let me finish."

"My apologies. Do go on," he said with a perplexed look.

"You are wonderful to me in every way. I am flattered by your proposal of marriage. And I am fully aware that, for a poor missionary girl like me to get a proposal of marriage from a man like you is unheard of." She sighed once again. "I think the world of you. Truly, I do. I know that I do not even deserve your friendship, and I am so thankful for it. But..."

He was starting to get frustrated as Rachel went on, and his excited look slowly turned into a glare. It was becoming clear to him that her words did not appear to be getting to any sort of point that might lead to their wedding someday. In fact, her speech sounded a lot like there might not even be a possibility of their being together at all. He looked down at the floor and loudly exhaled before he once again rose to stand.

Leaning forward toward him as he walked across the room with a blank stare, Rachel fumbled over her words, "Please understand. So much has happened since you-you left."

He tried to remain polite. "I am listening. But you said that already. Go on. What has happened?" he asked abruptly as he stood motionless, now staring straight ahead at the liquor cabinet.

She breathed in deeply, worried about how he might take the news of her wanting to be with Richard instead of him and tried to keep her speech as positive as possible. "I have something extraordinary to tell you, but I am worried that you may not believe me."

He did not reply but focused on the liquor in the cabinet in front of him as if it were tempting the deepest parts of his wounded soul, claiming it would soothe him.

Rachel, sounding rather desperate now, jumbled her words together, "Before I came here, before I met you, three nights in a row, I had the same dream." She paused. "I dreamt about a young man looking at me and my reflection in a mirror. I did not know who he was, but I knew that he was in love with me. And I…" She paused again.

"Yes?" he said rather lethargically as he slowly opened the door to the liquor cabinet, only half listening now.

"I was in love with him, too," she said quietly. "At the time, it was only a dream and therefore I dismissed it. Then I came here, I met you, and you excited my heart like no man ever had before."

The bottle that was more than half full of whiskey was now directly in front of him. It beckoned him. He grabbed a glass and placed both the glass and the bottle on the shelf in front of himself. Staring at it, he said, "But?"

"But then something happened after you went away."

Torn about what to do next, he poured a glass for himself and just stood there looking at it. Now curious about her news, he wondered how she had met another man while he was away, but he did not say a word.

"It's… It's Richard."

A look of confusion and pain crossed his face. "What about Richard?" he asked with a snarl before he picked up the glass and began to drink it.

Rachel tried to finish quickly so he would stop drinking, but she was too late. "It's a miracle, really. He has been amazing. He has been going outside, spending time with me daily, and is even praying now. He is better. He is talking now! Nathan, Richard truly is back! And…"

Clearly, Master Nathan did not believe what she was saying. His face turned red, and his eyes glazed over. He refused to acknowledge her efforts and simply got more glasses out of the cabinet and lined them up beside each other. He poured for himself more drinks than any man would ever need and began drinking them quickly, as his anger grew.

Not knowing what else to do, she spoke faster. The more she tried to convince him about Richard's return, the angrier he became. Despite that fact, she attempted to conclude her failing speech. "And he-he loves me, and he wants to marry me. And-and, Nathan, I want to…" She sighed, knowing just how unstable she must sound. At this point, she realized Master Nathan obviously did not believe a word she was saying. Regardless, just to get the torment of the conversation over with, she blurted out, "And I want to marry him, too." Rachel put her hands on her chest as tears began flowing freely down her cheeks.

She went on and on, explaining all that had taken place since his departure, but he did not respond and simply continued drinking. "Nathan, are you even listening to me?"

He finished tipping back each glass, and then consumed what was left of the bottle practically in a single gulp. Looking bitterly at it, he realized he'd given into temptation and had just drunk it all down by himself. And he blamed her. He blamed her for his fury and slipping backward into drinking so quickly after he vowed to himself never to drink again. Suddenly, he turned toward Rachel with a look of resentment as his chest lifted high and then fell. He spoke in a low growl with dark, piercing eyes as his infamous temper began to emerge. "Rachel, what have you done?"

Sadly, she was crying so loudly now, she did not hear him through her sobs, and did not reply.

His eyes narrowed as his agitation flared even more, waiting for her response. Still, she said nothing, and he was unable to hold his tantrum back any longer. He yelled with a loud voice, repeating himself, "Rachel, what have you done?" And then, with all his might, he shouted, "Ahhhhhhhh!" violently throwing the empty bottle right over her head, breaking it into a hundred pieces on the wall behind her.

Rachel jumped and began shaking like a leaf in the wind, but she resumed her pleading, "Nathan, it's true! Why won't you believe me? Richard is back. He-he is in his right mind, and he no longer thinks he is a ghost."

Master Nathan bellowed even louder this time, "Rachel, stop! This is madness! You know that is impossible. How dare you disobey everything I told you? I explicitly instructed you to never speak to him directly. How could you?"

Trembling, she covered her mouth with both hands but was too scared to reply.

He looked and sounded furious and broken at the same time. It was plain to see that he genuinely did not believe that Richard would ever be healed. Once again, to release his pain, he yelled at the top of his lungs, and his rage echoed throughout the lower levels of the house. "Auuuuustiiiiinnnnn!"

Out of desperation, she pleaded with him to believe her, still sobbing uncontrollably. But he refused to listen to another word from her quivering lips. Turning his back to her, he tuned her out entirely while rummaging for a new bottle of whiskey. Finding none, he looked at the engagement ring he had just bought her and stood there, staring at it as his eyes welled. He had such innocent intentions and high hopes that were now crushed. Adrenalin rushed through his veins and he threw the glass forcefully straight down onto the floor, shattering it, just in time for Austin to witness his master outlandish display.

Frightened by the scene, Austin stiffened, but he attempted to remain professional and calm to defuse the tension. "Yes, sir?"

Master Nathan took one last look at the ring and gripped it tightly before he threw it, too, against the wall over Rachel's head. It hit the wall behind her and bounced off, landing on the floor on the other side of the room. Looking defeated, he placed both hands on the liquor cabinet in front of him to steady himself and slumped forward, leaning over it, his breathing still labored. He then spoke with a harshness that she had not yet heard pass through his lips. It sounded as though it came from deep within him, and it frightened her.

"Austin, we no longer require Miss Rachel's services. Call back my carriage to bring her home at once!" Then his voice changed to utter sadness after a loud exhale. "We can send her belongings to her later. Just get her out of my sight." It sounded as though he was crying now as well, but since he refused to look in her direction, it was unclear.

Austin snapped his fingers, summoning a nearby servant to fetch the carriage. He did not want to leave Rachel alone with Master Nathan in such an enraged state. After he relayed the message to the stable boy, who had just entered the foyer, he quickly returned.

Austin wished to be of service but knew his master all too well. Everyone was fully aware that when his mind was made up, there was no changing it.

Rachel tried once more to reason with Nathan, but she was shaking so severely now that she could only muster up a whisper through her tears. "You-you don't understand. Richard is well. We walked in the garden in the sunshine. He showed me his inventions. He showed me the wine cellar, and-and we even danced."

Unfortunately, the news of her dancing with someone else did not help whatsoever. In fact, now that the alcohol had hit his system, hearing that she danced with Richard seemed to anger Master Nathan further as he snarled under his breath.

"Nathan, please! Please listen to me!" Rachel begged.

Austin, knowing how unruly his master could get when he'd had too much to drink, began to help her up in haste, doing his best to rush her out the door for her own safety. But since Master Nathan had already tuned her out, she directed her pleas toward Austin instead.

"Please! Austin, tell him. Tell him that it is all true. Tell him about Richard," she cried.

"Now is not the time, Miss," he told her as he pulled her toward the front door.

"Nathan, please!" she pleaded one last time.

He turned and looked at her with mad, wounded eyes. "Miss Rachel, from now on, you will address me as 'sir,'" he said with a hateful tone.

The instant he stated so boldly that he no longer wanted her to call him by his first name, she almost fainted. Rachel felt the implications of calling him "sir" once again instead of Nathan stabbing right through her heart, and she crossed both hands over her chest.

In an attempt to steady herself, she took in a big breath. Her exhale, now filled with sobs, echoed off the foyer walls as she began to cry even harder. It was now clear that trying to reason with Master Nathan any longer was of no use. She started to bolt for the front door, her spirit in tatters. Turning back with a longing glance up the staircase behind her, she hoped for one last glimpse of Richard, yet he was nowhere in sight.

Covering her mouth with the back of her hand to keep from turning back to yell at Master Nathan in her sorrow, she wished she could turn and run up to the tower to notify Richard of what had taken place. She wanted him to prove to his father that she was telling the truth. Unable to do so, she ran out the door.

Climbing into the carriage took every ounce of strength she had left. The footman closed the door behind her as she turned and attempted to push it back open, desperate to run back into the house to find Richard and make things right. But all she could do was fall to her knees on the floor of the carriage, her hands grasping the edge of the open window, panting for air. The stress of it all was making normal breathing difficult, and Rachel felt herself go limp. She gave up and simply let her tears wash down her cheeks.

Austin, deeply concerned for her wellbeing, approached the carriage. He reached up for her hand with a look of disappointment over all that had just transpired. Clinging to the outside of her window, he placed his other hand over hers as the carriage began to pull away. He did not want her to leave either, knowing that she never meant to hurt Master Nathan and was, indeed, telling the truth. He felt partly responsible, wishing he had been more straightforward with her about the dangers of upsetting his master. He, of all people, knew how stubborn Master Nathan could be, especially when he was drunk.

Rachel stuck her head out the window and begged him for the last time, "Austin, please! Please tell him the truth. I do not want Richard to encounter him like this. Promise me that you will try."

"I will, Miss. Keep praying and have faith, child. It will all work out in the end. You'll see." Although he did his best to comfort her as the carriage accelerated, he could not keep up with the horses' pace and let her go. He answered her with a shout and a final wave of goodbye. "Stay strong, my dear."

It was clear Austin was upset too, so she tried to flash a smile to make him feel better. But she noticed the look of horror in his eyes as the carriage took off and the distance between them grew.

The horses began picking up speed. Rachel turned her gaze upward to the north-facing windows of the tower where Richard last stood. Her energy was completely drained, but she climbed onto the rear seat and pressed her hand against the back window to wave goodbye to her beloved. She was hoping he would be able to see that she was all right but was being forced to leave quickly against her will and without saying goodbye. Sadly, there was no sign of him.

Trying not to let fear grip her as the carriage turned the corner and Locke mansion moved out of sight, she attempted to catch her breath. Disappointed with how poorly she handled the entire affair, she wondered how the reunion with Master Nathan and Richard would go now after the mess she had just left behind. She feared they would be extremely agitated, for different reasons, before they even met and that it might not go well once they saw each other.

Rachel blamed herself. She had made so many mistakes since arriving at Locke Mansion. She squeezed her eyes shut, faced forward, and grabbed her head with her hands. Dropping it low, she tried to stop the negative thoughts from racing through her mind. *What was I thinking? Why was I so selfish? So foolish?* She wondered how she would survive living without them and wished she could start her entire day or her entire month over again.

If only I had been honest with Master Nathan from the very beginning about Richard's progress before leaving for his trip. Why did I keep everything to myself? If only I had been honest with Richard and told him the truth, too. We should have both run down to welcome his father together, and I would probably still be there with them now. I am such a hypocrite. Dear God, help me. Please. I beg of You.

Her crying resumed, but she began to pray with more determination than ever for reconciliation between the two men she dearly loved. She knew that giving these two precious men back to God was all she could do. *Pray and trust. Pray and trust.* She told herself before crying aloud, "Please, God, forgive me for allowing my pride to get in the way, thinking that I would be able to fix this relationship between them simply by loving them so strongly. I should have known better. Forgive me for not telling them the truth sooner and for not trusting You more. Obviously, I was living in fear of how Richard would react to his father falling in love with me instead of walking in faith that You would help him process the truth well. Oh! What a mess I have made of something so important. Please, God. Help their reunion to go well. In the name of Jesus, I pray."

After giving it some time, Austin ventured back into the house to try to talk some sense into Master Nathan, but when he saw the painful look on his master's face, he dared say only one word: "Sir?"

Master Nathan spoke sternly, in a raised voice with a slight slur due to his drunken state, "That will be all, Austin."

He tried again. "But sir?"

Master Nathan bellowed, "That will be all, Austin!"

Austin bowed low and then stood slowly. Discouraged, he reluctantly turned away, leaving his dear master alone, and quietly went back outside just in time to see the dust from Rachel's carriage settle to the ground. He stood firm as he watched all traces of her vanish around the corner from where she first arrived. As he thought about his first meeting with her, it seemed like ages ago. Closing the front doors before shaking his head in disgust, he wished Master Nathan would listen to reason, but he knew better. He only hoped Richard would have the courage to face his father and set the record straight.

While the carriage bumped along, Rachel could no longer sit up straight, and her shoulders slumped. She lay back on the seat, feeling lifeless and crushed. But then, in an instant, she felt the Lord say that He had already forgiven her for everything. Discerning that He was asking her to surrender and trust in Him again without reservation, she thought hard about what to pray for until it came to her. Leaning forward, she fell to her knees and knelt on the carriage floor, placing her elbows on the seat across from her.

She bowed her head and closed her tear-filled eyes while clasping her hands together to cry out to God in her most desperate hour.

"Forgive me for not trusting You, Lord. Help me to see, beyond my limited vision, what You can do in this unusual situation. You are almighty, and nothing is beyond Your abilities. I pray that You will intervene and give Master Nathan and Richard more blessings than I could ask or imagine. You know I have made so many terrible mistakes since I arrived at Locke Mansion, but even so, I beg of You to do what You do best and make a way where there is no way. I lay this entire situation at Your feet. I know You are listening, hear my cries, and that You will rend the heavens and come down. I know You will not relent until You have it all, so I give You my all in all. I promise to do my utmost to let Master Nathan and Richard go. I surrender them both to You now, knowing You love them more than I ever could."

Looking up, Rachel noticed they were passing by the site of the accident, and her heart sank, remembering all the loss these two, beloved men had endured. Realizing that they were now going to have to cope with the pain of losing her, too, she felt nauseated and put the back of her hand over her mouth to keep her food from coming up.

Despite getting tossed about, she continued to ride in the carriage on her knees. In talking with God, Rachel hoped peace could be found in the chaos. To make herself feel better, she attempted to sing a worship song that her mother had taught her, but it didn't help. Her broken voice cracked with sorrow as though she was choking on the notes.

She knew that being unable to make amends with Master Nathan would be unbearable, but she feared that her heart would break in two without Richard. Her song turned into sobs as she pleaded with God. Now painfully aware that her relationship with Master Nathan and Richard was no longer in her control, she acknowledged that clearly, it never was.

As Rachel recalled her dreams about Richard, confused, she still felt strongly that God had ordained their meeting and their love. Believing this truth made it extra hard to admit that she had ruined everything with her poor decision-making. Now, it was time to obey, wait, and trust God to work things out. This meant that she had to have faith and stop worrying altogether, and she knew it. "Fretting is not faith," her mother would always say. Yet, no matter how hard she tried to take courage, she was unsure if it was possible to get over having to leave Locke Mansion and the men she loved.

She permitted herself to be sad about her circumstances, knowing that her days would be bitter without her sweet Richard after having tasted such goodness. The thought of not being able to hold him in her arms again made her queasy. Grabbing her stomach and turning to climb up and sit on the seat behind her, she leaned her head back to rest, but trembling overtook her. She exhaled and tried to come to terms with the fact that her trip was coming to an end and that this would be her last few moments in one of Master Nathan's plush carriages—her last connection with Locke Mansion.

Rachel turned her puffy red eyes to the streets to look for solace outside the carriage walls. She could not help but notice the grim-looking grey sidewalks and a pile of horse manure caught her eye. Wondering if the rest of the world might look ugly to her from this day forward, compared to the beauty of Locke Mansion, her attitude worsened.

Shaking her head, trying to rid it of all unhealthy thoughts as though they were unwelcome guests, Rachel rebuked them aloud, one by one. She knew better than to allow herself to entertain such *doom and gloom* and closed her eyes tightly, trying to renew her mind. Fighting back the spirit of depression, she attempted to obey scripture, to focus on what was good, noble, pure, and lovely, just like she had advised Richard only days before.

Desperately wanting to remember God and His goodness instead of her circumstances, she realized she needed to practice what she preached about tearing down strongholds. The rest of the trip, trying to be selfless, she found that praying for someone other than herself helped tremendously, and she prayed for everyone at Locke Mansion.

Climbing out of the carriage was one of the hardest things she had ever done, and she stumbled before she reached her door. Steadying herself, she gripped the door handle as her tears resumed. After the coachmen and footman said their goodbyes, she covered her mouth with both hands and watched the carriage and her dreams disappear into the distance. And with it, what little strength she had left, vanished too.

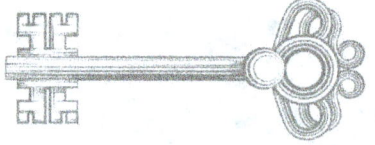

Chapter 16

Still horribly drunk back at the mansion, Master Nathan grumbled to himself under his breath. Stumbling around the room with tear-filled eyes, he somehow managed to notice a table adorned with a large vase of flowers on it, then another, and yet another. When it dawned on him that Rachel had likely arranged them to welcome him home, he placed his hands on his chest and winced at the pain of losing her. Just thinking about it, his nostrils flared as despair overtook him once again. In a blind rage, he grabbed the nearest vase and hurled it across the room, smashing it against the wall, spilling its water and flowers all over the floor.

The thought of not being with her and living all alone again was more than he could bear. He stumbled over to where the vase had landed and practically fell as he turned and pressed his back against the wall with a thud. Sliding down onto the floor, he sat listlessly. When he found himself beside the remains of Rachel's floral bouquet, he scowled. His legs and feet were so widespread in front of him that he figured he must look like a stuffed toy clown on a child's shelf—*That, or simply a fool.*

He reached over and attempted to pick up one of the blue flowers, remembering that he and Rachel had discussed them. Clawing at the floor he inched his fingers toward it until he was able to grab it. Squeezing it tight, he looked down at the flower with an exaggerated frown and counted its petals. It reminded him of her striking blue eyes, which he had grown to adore. His heart ached so deeply for her that as he held the flower close, and grabbed at his chest once more, he scratched at it with his fingernails as if he were in deep pain. He was. His hopes of joy, love, and marrying her had been destroyed, and he could not help but envision growing old and frail, spending the rest of his days alone.

How will I ever live in this house again without her? His mind began to whirl out of control, but then it shifted back to Richard. *And what if... what if Rachel was telling the truth? What will become of Richard? What if he genuinely does love her? How will* he *live here without her now? How will she survive this?*

The whiskey and his negative thoughts seemed to bump into one another at the front of his head, making him dizzy. He dropped the flower and picked up what was left of the broken vase. The top half was completely missing, and the exposed edges of the bottom portion were jagged. He looked at it with longing, and his speech slurred as he began a conversation with it, sounding rather comical. "You know what? We-we are so similar, you and I. Broken. And... and empty. What do you think I should do now anyway?" He asked his question to the vase directly, talking to it as if he had lost his mind, his head spinning like a top.

It was a good thing he was holding the remnant of the vase in his hands because, without warning, he could not help but vomit straight into it as his body tried to clear itself of the toxic poisons he had ingested. Making horrible noises that echoed out from the vase, he retched over it until his stomach was empty.

Once he finished heaving, without thinking, he looked inside and made a disgusted face at the sight. He then held it as far from his nose as he possibly could and apologized to it. "Ugh. I am so sorry," he said aloud before setting it down, being careful not to spill its contents.

Leaning his back against the wall, he slumped even lower, trying to clear his head. Thankfully, he avoided getting cut on the broken pieces of the vase that had shattered all around where he was seated, as he was unaware of the danger.

His fingers fumbled their way to his pocket, and he pulled out his handkerchief to dab at his face, but it, too, reminded him of Rachel. After wiping the residue from his lips, he was too intoxicated to notice the stench of vomit covering the fabric as he lovingly held it against his face to remember her. He frowned as an ominous feeling of sorrow hit him right in his gut, thinking back to the first time he shared his handkerchief with her. He was glad he'd had it handy when she first cried in front of him during her job interview upon hearing the stories about his life, the accident, and Richard.

Slurring his words toward the vase once again as though it was his only real friend left in the world, he spoke to it with regret, "You know, although she was a real…" he hiccupped. "…a real pain in the…" he paused, trying not to use profanity similar to when he was talking to God in the chapel. "…*behind*, she was a good listener, you know? A bit preachy at times, but still," he muttered with another hiccup and a wave of his hand to make his point.

He sat up and chuckled at the thought of her preaching to him, and a smile came across his face. It was quickly replaced by a wide-eyed stare of sadness, his upper body wavering back and forth as if blowing in an unseen wind. His eyes remained fixed straight ahead on the floor, watching nothing at all until he came to. He inhaled and exhaled an exaggerated breath.

His mind quickly jumped to their last conversation, and he contemplated how irrational he had been when she was simply trying to talk to him. He shook his head out of shame when he realized how he had cut her off and did not even let her explain herself. *How could I have just yelled at her and sent her home like that? I am such a madman.* The thought of it all sobered him up a bit. Wobbling excessively while fighting gravity, he climbed to his feet, picking up the ring along the way. And after gazing at it for a moment, he put it in his pocket and clumsily ran outside to chase after Rachel, bumping into the wall.

The residual alcohol in his system hit him so fast that, as soon as he'd flung the front door open and stepped out, he stumbled down the front steps sideways. He then staggered onto the carriageway before realizing that he was too late to catch her. Falling to his knees with a crash, he landed hard, practically on his face.

Slowly, he crawled back onto his knees and lifted his fists toward the heavens. With a loud cry, he yelled at God much like he had done after the accident, and roared loudly for all to hear, "Whyyyyyyyy?"

Falling forward in defeat, he then made every effort to crawl on his hands and knees down the carriageway as he sobbed, inching toward Rachel's house. Already missing her, he wanted her back with every ounce of his being. He felt horrible and wanted to apologize for his cruelty and for making her sad.

Disoriented, Master Nathan quickly abandoned his attempts at crawling and stayed for a long while on all fours, sobbing, feeling sorry for himself, defeated, and beaten. Once his mind shifted back to Richard, he grew deeply worried about his son all over again. *If he loves Rachel as much as I do, there is no way he could handle the pain of losing her. If I cannot bear losing her, Richard certainly would not be able to. Oh, no! What if he...*

Thoughts of Richard possibly trying to end his own life again after he found out that Rachel was gone hit Master Nathan like a sack of bricks to his gut. With a heave, he almost threw up a second time. He could not bear the thought of losing his son and knew that for Richard to even think of taking his own life... Well, it was simply not an option. He found himself praying for forgiveness and asking God to help them all. "Please, God!" he appealed toward the sky with a vulnerable tone.

He then felt the Lord speak to his spirit so clearly that his eyes grew large, and he froze, staring at the ground while trying to listen. He thought he heard the Lord tell him something that he did not want to hear. *"I won't relent until I have it all. Surrender your heart to Me. I have set you as a seal upon My heart, as a seal upon My arm with love that is as strong as death and jealousy as demanding as the grave, but you must let your family go. Let your son go, let your addictions go, let Rachel go, and trust in Me."*

Master Nathan squeezed his eyes shut and grabbed a handful of dirt. He threw it as hard as he could toward the sky while he growled, "Why? Why do You demand so much of me?"

The Lord repeated Himself, *"I won't relent until I have it all. Surrender your heart to Me. I have set you as a seal upon My heart, as a seal upon My arm with love that is as strong as death and jealousy as demanding as the grave, but you must let your family go. Let your son go, let your addictions go, let Rachel go, and trust in Me."*

Master Nathan continued weeping until he could not take it anymore. "Fine! You win, God! Finally, I surrender." Yet, he knew his bitter heart would never be accepted the way it was, and he began to cry even harder. Then, suddenly, he felt a shift just like he had in the chapel. He was humbled to the point that he knew surrendering to God's leadership and letting go of control in his life was his only option, and he broke down.

Still sobbing and slurring his speech, rocking back and forth, he did the best he could to repent. "Forgive me, God. You are right. I surrender fully. From now on, I let everyone and everything go. I know that everything belongs to You anyway. I will let go of Rachel. I will let go of Richard, and I will trust You to forever take care of the ones that I love, knowing that You cherish them more than I ever could. And I will stop questioning You. I will obey Your Word and rage against You no more. I promise that I will no longer drown my sorrows in liquor, and I will strive to trust You in all things. Forgive me, Father. I repent. I am sorry."

Unexpectedly, he felt someone run past him, almost hitting him as they hurried by, but Master Nathan was nearly too weak to look up. Tears that were now pouring out from his eyes and flowing down onto his cheeks blurred his vision.

To see who had run past him on the ground, knowing they were much too fast to be Austin, Master Nathan lifted his head. Then he heard the man shout in a loud voice, "Raaaaachelllll!

In his drunken state, Master Nathan narrowed his gaze and could barely make out a young man standing down the carriageway. Having no idea who it was, he shook his head as it whirled with confusion. He tried to wipe at his tears so he could see more clearly, but in the process, he wiped dirt all over his face and into his eyes, making his vision even worse. But after a few moments, he began to get some clarity and started to tremble uncontrollably. "Richard?" he asked, thinking his mind was playing tricks on him. "Rich—Richard?"

Then, he thought maybe he was actually seeing a ghost, or perhaps he just had far too much to drink. "Richard?" he said once again, trying hard to stand but to no avail.

Richard turned around to see his father drunk, unable to stand, dirty, and in tears. *Oh no, where is Rachel? What has father done?* he questioned, with anger consuming his mind. But then, he suddenly realized how broken Master Nathan looked and covered his mouth with one hand as his heart filled with great pity. He had been angry with his father for so long, he sighed, and his face looked as though he too was in agony. *It is time.* Stepping toward Master Nathan, Richard knew right then and there that he needed to forgive his father at once. He had to go to him, but more importantly, he had to *talk* to him.

Master Nathan still questioned if it was actually his son. In complete disbelief, he asked again, stammering, "Rich... Richard?"

Running toward his father, Richard fell to his knees on the ground directly in front of him. He could tell that Master Nathan was in shock and severely inebriated, so he grabbed him and helped him to his knees. He let the years of missing his dear father take over as he threw his arms around him and hugged him tightly.

Now tearing up, Richard leaned back and looked tenderly into his father's eyes. "Yes, Father. It is I, Richard, your son."

Shaken to his very core, Master Nathan looked as though his only son had just been raised from the dead. Astonished, he could hardly speak. "My... my son?" he muttered through his sobs, a tremble in his voice. For the first time in ten long years, he gave Richard a hug, albeit weak, due to the pure shock controlling his body. Trying to gather himself, he wobbled terribly.

With much effort, Richard helped Master Nathan to his feet and then hugged him once more as he spoke softly into his father's ear, "I am back, Father. I really am back."

Disoriented and crying hard, Master Nathan almost collapsed, but Richard held him up so that, instead, he was able to push his son back into full view. As he looked upon the face of his beloved child, it took some time for his vision to focus. After a while, Master Nathan's look of pain and confusion turned into extreme delight as he searched Richard's face. He continued to cry, but this time it was mixed with sobs of thanksgiving and bewildered laughter.

He then finally hugged his son tight, and every drop of sorrow he ever harbored fled him all at once. He could see that Richard was indeed real. He was back, and there was no doubt that he was in his right mind.

Master Nathan's demeanor shifted, and he began to cry out loud as he begged Richard to forgive him. "Richard! Oh, my son. My dear, sweet son. I am so, so sorry. Please forgive me. I was such a fool. I love you so much, my precious, beautiful son!" He hugged him tightly once again.

This time, Richard held Master Nathan away from himself to stare intently into his father's eyes. "No, Father. It is I who am sorry. For over three-thousand, eight-hundred, and seven days now, you have wanted a relationship with me. Yes, indeed. I know it sounds mad, but I have been counting. Because every single one of those days, I have longed to speak with you. Yet, out of my own unwillingness to forgive God, you, or myself for the accident, I refused to even try. I have been so blind, and I am so sorry. I love you, Father. Can you please forgive me?"

Broken, Master Nathan responded in humility as tears streamed down his face, "Son, there is nothing to forgive. I am to blame. In fact, I have something to tell you."

"Wait, Father. Here, sit." Richard helped his father sit on the step, since it was difficult for him to stand on his own, and then sat beside him so they could talk. "Thank you, son," Master Nathan said as he reached up and squeezed Richard's entire face with one hand to admire him. Although he made Richard's lips and cheeks look like a fish, Master Nathan sat grinning, thinking of how handsome his son was.

With his father still squishing his face, Richard tried to speak, but it was too muffled to understand.

"What? Oh," Master Nathan said, letting go of Richard's cheeks. "Tell me son. Tell me everything! How is it that you came back to me today. I need to know every detail."

After a long talk about Richard's return, how he had survived all these many years alone, and about Rachel, Richard reminded him, "Father, what were you trying to say?"

"Was I saying something?" Master Nathan asked again, confused. "I don't want to speak anymore. I just want to hear you talk. Hearing how deep your voice is now, it has changed completely. It's astounding."

"Yes, but you said you had something to tell me, remember?" Richard said, laughing at his father's forgetfulness.

"Oh. Yes." Master Nathan said. Then he instantly made a face of absolute regret. "Son, I do have something I need to tell you, but you are not going to like it."

Since his father resumed shaking terribly, Richard, worried for him, asked in a compassionate tone, "What is on your mind?"

As though mortified by what he was about to share, Master Nathan closed his eyes and shook his head. He looked up, "Son, I cannot even tell you how much it has bothered me all these years that you have blamed yourself for the accident. None of it was your fault. It was all mine. But I fear it may be too soon to tell you why I say that. I am not sure if you can handle the truth or not."

"Father, I am not a child anymore. And I'm not the same man I was when you left. You do not need to be afraid for me. I am not going to slip back to the way I was. Tell me, father. What is it that troubles you so?"

Taking his time, Master Nathan sighed and then began, his speech sounding hurried as tears streamed down his face, "Yes. I can see that you are a grown man now, so I will do my best to be honest with you."

Richard put his hand on his father's shoulder. "Go on."

Lowering his head, Master Nathan sputtered, "The day of the accident, your mother told me she did not have a good feeling about going to town. She told me the Lord warned her not to leave the house. She begged for me to listen, but before I left for the city, I dismissed her. I told her she was being paranoid, and I insisted she take you and your sisters shopping despite her pleas."

"But father, why? Why did you insist she go to town if she told you she had been warned against it?" Deep concern could be heard in Richard's tone.

Unable to look at his son any longer, Master Nathan turned away, swallowed back his pride, and admitted, "This will be hard for you to hear, but I must tell you the truth. I cannot allow you to believe the accident was your fault any longer. This is something I have never told anyone, and it has been eating me alive. I do not expect you to understand this, but..." he paused and covered his face with one hand, ashamed beyond consolation.

"Yes, father?"

Finally turning around to look back at his son, he removed his hand from his face and placed it on his hurting stomach. He exhaled loudly as though trying to muster up the courage to tell his son about the worst mistake of his life. "Richard. When you were young, it was quite customary for men my age to have several mistresses. But I never did. I swear to you. Not even once. However, on the day of the accident, I made a grave mistake. I did not go through with it, but due to a persistent urging from a friend in London, I was tempted..." He hesitated and resumed with a sorrowful tone, "I am so sorry, and I regret having to admit it, but that day I planned to meet another woman for lunch. I figured your mother would not suspect if she were busy entertaining you children."

"Father, no!" Richard shook his head, greatly disturbed.

"I know how this sounds, but I must finish. I can no longer bear to think of the guilt you carry because of me," Master Nathan pleaded with his son to not interrupt.

Richard closed his eyes as though the words he was hearing hurt. He cocked his head to the side while Master Nathan went on.

"So, to cover my discretions, I made her spend the day with you and your sisters in town, regardless of her concerns. Once I arrived in London, I knew I could not go through with meeting this other woman. As the snow began to fall around me, I was reminded of how much I loved your mother, since she adored snow. I then refused to meet with my friend's acquaintance. Although he called me a coward, I was relieved that I did the right thing and remained faithful to your mother. After I vowed never to attempt such a foolish thing again, I spent the day working at the factory instead. Sadly, when I was on my way home, I felt quite proud of myself. But just when I was getting cocky, I saw the carriage in the river and instantly feared the damage I had caused just by lying to your mother."

Richard sat in silence, now staring at the ground, his jaw muscles flexed tight in frustration.

Unaware of his son's reaction, Master Nathan continued, "So, if anyone is at fault here, it is me. Because of my lust, my selfishness, and my foolishness, I lost my entire family that day. It was all my doing, son, not yours. I beg of you to no longer blame yourself for any of this. Not even for one moment."

Still dumbfounded, Richard sat motionless as his father buried his face in his hands and cried.

After weeping bitterly, Master Nathan said, "Oh, Richard. It breaks my heart every day to think of how I ruined your life. I know that I do not deserve for you to return to me as a son. Nor do I deserve Rachel. I deserve nothing. But I am begging for your forgiveness. I am so, so sorry. And if you could ever possibly find it in your heart to forgive me, I would never need anything else in my life."

Grinding his teeth and turning away to think as his father sobbed, Richard could not believe what he was hearing. He knew the pain lies could cause, but he never imagined the truth could be so excruciating as well.

He recalled how, when Rachel prayed over him in the tower, it was like a heavy weight had been lifted from his shoulders. Somehow, with this news it felt like a new one had taken its place. Embarrassed for his father, Richard sat for a while with no response. Yet, after some time passed, in his mind, he sighed and acknowledged the fact that his father had never been disloyal to his mother.

Allowing himself to experience the pain his father must have endured all this time, he closed his eyes and felt the sorrow in his father's confession. He thought of how the past ten years would weigh so heavily on anyone's soul and how unbearable that must have been. Pondering it all, instead of rage, he thought of Luke 7:47 and how much God had forgiven him. Instantly, his heart filled with mercy instead of anger.

With his gaze turned upward toward the Heavens, he prayed, stood, pulled Master Nathan to his feet, and hugged him close. "I forgive you, Father. I do. The burden of the past and your sin are no longer yours to carry. It, too, was nailed to the cross."

They embraced tighter and patted one another firmly on the back, both in tears. "You sound just like Rachel," Master Nathan stated, then, in unison, their cries turned into laughter—deep laughter from their bellies. Master Nathan felt his strength return to his muscles as he praised God for the return of his son and for the forgiveness of the cross.

After giving his father some time to sober up a bit, Richard took hold of his shoulders and, with a serious expression. said, "Father?"

"Yes, my son?" Master Nathan asked, sounding as though he would give Richard the entire world right then if he would only ask for it.

"Father, speaking of Rachel, where is she?"

Master Nathan jumped to attention, and his eyes widened. "Oh! Oh, no! I-I did not believe her when she told me about you getting better. I became so angry with her that I-I sent her home!" he said, covering his stomach with one hand and putting the other on his forehead once he fully realized the gravity of what he had done.

Then, as if to wake him, Richard shook him slightly. "Father, we have to get her back!"

"Yes. Yes, of course. Let's go. Let's go get her," Master Nathan said, looking flustered.

Right on cue, Austin, who had seen what was happening, came out of the stable with two horses saddled up and ready to ride. Master Nathan looked at Richard, Richard looked back at Master Nathan, and at the same time, they both asked each other, "Are you sure you can ride?" Laughing out loud at one another's question, they appeared thankful to see they still thought alike.

Richard boldly declared, "Of course, I can ride. Let's go!" And he hurried off toward the horses with a final hard pat on his father's back. Unaware of his own strength, he was oblivious to the fact he made Master Nathan stumble and fall forward, right down onto his knees again.

While watching proudly as his son rushed to the horses to jump fearlessly onto one of them, much faster than he had as a young boy,

Master Nathan chuckled. He could only kneel on the ground and thank God for what he saw. Ecstatic, rising to his feet with some effort, he realized that seeing Richard outside at all was a miracle. But witnessing his son sitting on a horse's back caused him to beam with pride.

"Father, come on!" Richard reached out his hand to motion for him to hurry while laughing at the sight of his father just standing there.

"Oh, right," Master Nathan said, shaking his head and snapping out of his dazed stare. He instantly transformed back into his silly self and stumbled once more. But before he climbed onto his horse, he thanked and hugged Austin profusely.

Although Austin had to help him up because he was still a little drunk, it did not matter to him, for he was delighted that his master and Richard had reunited and were rushing to find Rachel.

Master Nathan was thrilled to be riding horseback with his son like they used to. "I would not miss this for the world."

"Are you ready?" Richard asked.

"Are *you* ready?" Master Nathan replied with sarcasm and a quick raise of his brow, challenging his son.

Richard appeared almost giddy as he challenged, "Race you?"

"Race?" Master Nathan questioned, looking astounded.

Without fear, Richard shouted, "Hyah!" and kicked his horse so it would take off at a gallop.

Master Nathan did not budge while he sat proudly watching his son with his eyes glazed over. When he finally realized that Richard had left him in the dust, he yelled, "Oh. Oh! Hyah!" Spurring his horse in an attempt to catch up to Richard, he had not felt so alive in years and sprang into action.

At the start of his ride, while remembering that racing on horseback was his son's favorite thing when he was young, Master Nathan could not help but wonder if he was dreaming. He also knew he loved Rachel, but if he had to lose her to another man, Master Nathan was glad it would be to his beloved Richard.

Racing away from the mansion, they made their way down the long, winding road through the woods that led to the river. Master

Nathan was behind Richard the whole way, only a few horse lengths back, until they reached the area where the accident had taken place.

Richard abruptly stopped, yet his horse did not seem to want to wait as it pranced around, showing its impatience. As it fought him and started running again, Richard was hesitant and pulled back on the reins hard to force his horse to stay put, causing it to rear on its hind legs. Thankfully, he managed to stay in his saddle when the horse landed back on all fours.

Once Master Nathan arrived, he stopped beside Richard, concerned about his son having flashbacks of the worst day of his life. "Son? Are you quite well?" he asked.

"I… I just… I realized that I don't know where I am going," Richard declared, not really answering his father's question.

"It's all right. Follow me," Master Nathan replied, wanting to give Richard time to process, yet he also felt that it would be better if they just kept going. Wanting to see his son press on toward the goal ahead instead of dwelling on the past, he was unsure if Richard was capable of facing his fears. "Hyah!" Master Nathan yelled, once again kicking his horse so it would run, leaving his son to decide for himself how to proceed.

Thinking back to that horrid day, Richard hesitated, but only for a moment. Then he prayed for the strength to face his most traumatic memories. Trusting that the demons that had kept him in bondage were finally defeated, he chose to move along, more determined than ever.

"HYAH!" Richard shouted, showing gumption, spurring his horse on to resume a full run across the part of the road closest to the river's edge. Racing across the spot where he played his trumpet all those years ago, he felt confident. He reminded himself that the accident was not his fault. In short order, he caught up with his father.

Proud of Richard for facing his fears head-on, Master Nathan grinned as they raced side by side. But to be safe and not hurt anyone, they slowed down and rode more carefully through town, bringing their horses to a trot. Seeing Rachel's cottage in the distance, they dismounted and walked their horses quietly the rest of the way.

Now outside her house, they tied the horses to a post near a water bucket. As they reached Rachel's front door, Master Nathan stopped Richard and asked, "Son, if you do not mind, I would like to speak to Rachel first, please. I was so cruel to her today, and there is much I need to say. I simply must apologize to her before I burst. If I may?" He looked down at the ground, then up at his son with pleading eyes.

Master Nathan's look of regret made Richard feel sorry for his father all over again. "Of course, Father. I will wait for you out here," he replied with a gentle smile showing his respect. "Besides, I am quite nervous and unsure of what to say to her. So, in a way, I am glad to have a moment alone to think."

While heading over to knock on the door, Master Nathan smiled at his son's nervous tension. But first, looking deep in thought, he turned and walked back to Richard, pulling something out of his pocket. "Son, in case you decide you need this, I want you to have it," he declared as he handed him the engagement ring he had bought for Rachel.

Confused but thrilled at the same time, Richard looked up at his father.

"Don't ask," Master Nathan requested with a laugh shaking his head as he strongly patted his son on the shoulders. "Just don't ask."

Dumbfounded, Richard stood staring at the ring, but complied with his father's request and did not ask.

Amused at his son's reaction, Master Nathan appeared pleased before turning away to knock on the door. Even though it was inappropriate, he entered the house without waiting for a reply. Thankfully, Rachel's mother and brother were out for an evening stroll. But then, as he stepped into Rachel's house without an invitation, he sighed loudly, saddened by what he encountered just inside.

Chapter 17

Earlier, when Rachel made it home, she arrived right as her mother and brother had decided to take a walk. Wanting to be alone, Rachel politely requested some time to herself, but accepted some much-needed comfort before they left. She was thrilled that her mother had beaten her illness and felt well enough to go outside, but she was still devastated by how poorly Master Nathan's return had gone.

After seeing her family out, Rachel collapsed, falling to her knees. She curled up on the floor and cried to the Lord, asking Him for mercy. Trembling, she wondered if she would see Locke Mansion, her sweet Richard, or Master Nathan ever again.

Desperately wanting to trust that God would intervene, she fought off negative thoughts that were once again trying to invade the wounded spaces of her mind. Rachel knew better than to entertain any dialogue with the Devil. So, although it was not easy, she made a conscious decision to rebuke all the lies the Devil had been whispering to her since she left the mansion.

The fiery darts of shame, guilt, and condemnation over how poorly she handled the whole affair pierced her heart. It was as though the Devil, like an evil blacksmith poking at her repeatedly with his red-hot rod, would not let up. Knowing these jabs were too hot to push away herself, she sobbed as they burned intensely within her, forcing her to surrender to God once again.

Praying for peace, she suddenly remembered her father's famous teaching on the subject. He often taught that peace was not a state of mind nor a process but a person. "In the world," she recalled him saying, "peace comes with the absence of things: things like fear, financial troubles, confusion, shame, hunger, lack, war, and so on. But in the Kingdom of God, peace can come regardless of our struggles when we are thankful and hold fast to one person. The only thing that can bring peace when all seems lost is our relationship with Jesus and the abiding presence of the Holy Spirit. When the world around us feels like it is crumbling, if we express gratitude, acknowledging His beauty and undying love for us, leading to our trust in Him, everything becomes clear. Even Jesus, on the night He was betrayed, knowing He was about to be tortured and killed, gave thanks."

Although her struggle was real, wanting to find peace in her pain, Rachel admitted to herself that her father was right. In her mind, organizing a long list of things to be grateful for, she especially appreciated meeting the Lockes and the time she had spent at their home. *I will never forget it.*

Despite feeling weak, Rachel forced herself to sit up and proclaim aloud what the Word of God declared about her instead of listening to any more of the enemy's lies, just as she had instructed Richard. "I am a child of the most-high God, and He loves me with a furious love. I am called, chosen, redeemed, and a daughter of the King of kings. I can do all things through Christ who strengthens me. I was created in His image. Yes, I have made many grave mistakes, but I have been set free by the blood of the Lamb and am forgiven. My mistakes do not define me, for His Word says there is no condemnation for those who are in Christ Jesus. And for that, I give thanks."

Although breathing heavily due to the intensity of her proclamation, Rachel focused on all the good things her Heavenly Father had done for her these past few weeks instead of panicking. She tried to be brave, but the thought of losing Richard overwhelmed her, so she whispered Romans 8:28, "'And we know that all things work together for good to those who love God, to those who are the called according to *His* purpose.'"

Wondering what she was going to do without Richard and feeling nauseous, she grabbed at her stomach. She felt almost like she did after her father's death. Rachel remembered the day after his funeral and how she asked her mother questions like, "What are we going to do without Father? How can we go on? How will we survive this?"

Her fretful breathing slowed as she envisioned her mother answering her questions with a firm resolve that could only come from above. "Rachel, dear, I do not know what we are going to do," her mother had told her, "but remember, it is okay not to know. If I've learned one thing from spending all these years with your father, it's that life is a fascinating mystery. If we knew everything in advance, or if everything in life was certain, we wouldn't need faith. Faith functions best when you do not know. It compels you to rely on God to supply all your needs, especially in times of great trials. So, although we are hurting immensely, and this season may not be easy, I trust that God has the ability and the will to do amazing things out of love for us. Fear not, my child. We will obey His Word, which is His will, and we shall pray with thanksgiving for His abounding goodness toward us."

Rachel lifted her chin as she recalled the strength her mother displayed through difficulty, hoping to be just like her one day. She quoted one final scripture, Lamentations 3:22-23, to comfort herself, "'The steadfast love of the Lord never ceases; His mercies never come to an end; they are new every morning; great is Your faithfulness.'"

Quoting that verse encouraged her, but still crying, she asked God, "Lord, I know You love me. But please, I need reassurance that You are going to be with Richard and Master Nathan to work all things out for their good. Your will be done. And if it is Your will that I see my beloved, and perhaps Master Nathan again someday, I will forever be thankful. I am trying to have faith, but I ask that You increase my faith once again. Regardless of what You choose to do with this mess I've made, I give You all the praise. In Jesus' name..."

Instead of holding in her sorrow, she lay back down on the floor and continued crying to let out her pain, hoping God would show her the mercy she was begging for. After asking Him to deepen her faith, she began singing worship through her pain, knowing that was one of her strongest weapons against the enemy.

Right then, Master Nathan knocked and then opened the door with caution. Upon entering, he found her in a heap on the floor in front of a cold, dark fireplace, crying and singing. The guilt he felt all over again for causing her needless pain made his heart race.

She glanced up with a runny nose and red puffy eyes to see who had stepped into her house as Master Nathan fell to his knees before her. "Rachel, I..."

Still in a daze, Rachel realized that she must have been a mess and quickly wiped her face to appear more presentable.

Somewhat sobered, thanks to his encounter with the vase and the dash on his horse, he could see how hurt she seemed. Remorseful, he began pleading with her, "Oh, my dearest Rachel, I am so sorry. Please forgive me. I am a horrible person. And apparently, I am an atrocious drunk. I had no right to yell at you and treat you the way I did today." Shaking his head, he confessed, "I could not be more embarrassed."

Overjoyed to see him, Rachel hugged him around his neck and blurted out a longwinded reply. "Oh, Master Nathan, you are not a horrible person. I know it was not you who was yelling at me today. It was your pain. I am not embarrassed by you. And I beg you to never forget that I love you, whether you are drinking or sober. I do forgive you and promise that I will always love you, no matter what."

Squeezing his eyes shut, he hugged her back, relieved to hear her kindhearted words, but her sweet spirit made him feel even more guilty. His shame, due to getting drunk so quickly because of his disappointment over losing her, reddened his face. Once she let him go and looked up at him, her eyes, filled with compassion, made him realize she really meant what she said.

For a moment, Master Nathan felt as though he was staring directly into the eyes of his Savior, which startled him. He blinked a few times from confusion, humbled himself, and asked, "Rachel, you saw how angry I got today. Now you know why I have the reputation that I do. I am ashamed that I slipped right back into my old habits so fast and turned to drinking instead of God. I am sorry you had to witness that. What is wrong with me?" He hesitated. "I know I need help. But..." After a long pause, a miracle took place, and Master Nathan found the courage to directly ask for help for his excessive drinking. "Rachel, I-I know I need to stop drinking, but I fear I cannot do this on my own. It has been such a crutch for me for so long. Will… Will you help me?"

Knowing how vital it was for those battling addiction to ask for help out loud, Rachel politely responded, "We all struggle with something. You are no exception."

He looked at her with wary eyes as if he knew Rachel was being much too kind, and his voice trembled. "But I get so easily frustrated and angry and can't help but drink. And I know… I know that is bad."

She flashed him a loving glance. "Of course, I will help you, but when difficulties come, may I suggest you decide for yourself in advance where you are going to go for comfort? You see, instead of letting your frustrations lead you to drinking, each morning, you must decide that no matter what happens, you will turn to God instead."

"I know. You are right. When I got frustrated with you today, I lost all sense of reason. I let myself get angry, and then I immediately turned to my liquor cabinet for comfort instead of God. I do know better than that, but I cannot seem to stop. It is almost as though I am addicted to it, and it is so humiliating," Master Nathan confessed.

With pity, she said softly, "It's okay."

He paused, appearing downcast, as his eyes welled. "Rachel, there is… there is something else important I've not yet told you. During your interview, when I explained what happened to my family, there is something that I did not reveal to you."

Rachel looked at him with questioning eyes, "Oh?"

"In fact, I lied to you because I'd never wanted to tell anyone about this, ever," he went on, shaking his head in frustration.

"I see," she said. Curious now, she sat up straighter.

He let out a deep sigh, "I know you say the accident was the Devil's fault, but in truth, it was mine." After confessing his guilt to Rachel by telling her the same story he had disclosed to Richard about potentially meeting another woman the day of the accident, he broke down.

Instantly sickened by his confession of the truth, she swallowed back the first words that came to her mind and remained steadfast.

Showing extreme pity, she lifted his chin and said, "Sir, I cannot imagine how difficult it must have been for you to keep that truth to yourself all these years. What an enormous burden for you to bear."

Rubbing both his eyes with one hand as though they hurt, he told her, "To tell you the truth, it has been eating me alive. Sadly, I know I deserve all the pain it has brought me. So you see, the accident, my family's death, and Richard's struggle with mental illness is all my doing."

Rachel's face showed she felt all his pain at once, and in an attempt to comfort him, she said, "I am proud of you for telling me, but please, you still mustn't blame yourself for the accident. Yes, if you had made different choices, things might have turned out differently, but you must realize the Devil's hand in tempting you to lie to your wife. Thankfully, you did not go through with your plans. The way I see it, he is still the one to blame, and you simply must forgive yourself."

Astounded that she did not get upset with him for lying to her, and because she instead showed him her usual portion of grace, it brought him further to tears. Holding his hand, she reassured him repeatedly that he was not to blame.

He then admitted, "Rachel, you are so full of mercy. I cannot believe I had the nerve to yell at you today." He peered up at her. "After you left, I realized how much I must have hurt you with my violent outburst, and I ran outside after you. Sadly, in my drunken state, I fell flat on my face. Then, once I saw that I was too late to stop you, every ounce of guilt I thought I had left behind me in the chapel came flooding back."

Despite being worried he had fallen, she was delighted to hear he had run after her. Not wanting to pour salt on his wounds by telling him she agreed he had an issue with self-doubt, which often led to drinking, she reminded him how loved he was instead. "Master Nathan, you know the enemy likes to make you feel guilt-ridden, but you also know that guilt is not from God. Romans 5 says that our faith in Jesus transfers God's righteousness to us, and He now declares us flawless in His eyes." She paused. "So, my friend, what if... What if you saw yourself that way? As flawless?"

Unable to process what she meant, Master Nathan squinted. He had never heard that scripture before and could hardly believe that after showing his true colors—which were not at all pretty—she was trying to tell him that he was flawless.

Noticing how dumbfounded he seemed, Rachel repeated herself, "What if you could see yourself through the eyes of the Father? As flawless?"

Since he looked too shocked to answer, she went on, "We need to repent of our sins daily, but once we do, we are seen by God as spotless. In Romans 5:1, it says that we have been justified by faith, and so we have peace with God. Therefore, we must see ourselves through the eyes of the Father, not our own eyes or the eyes of the world."

He sighed and bowed his head. "I do try to see myself as forgiven and loved, but for some reason, when I fall short, I instantly feel horrible."

"I understand, and I hope you realize that most people struggle with that; therefore, you are normal." She smiled. "But to improve your life in any way, you first must *want* to improve it."

"Of course, I want to!" he said, rolling his eyes exasperatedly.

Rachel chuckled. "Well then, that's the perfect place to start, but it is crucial after you repent to make peace with yourself just as you are, imperfections and all. You see, God is glad when people are repentant, but He does not like His children wallowing in guilt. Remember, shame ruins relationships. All relationships. It puts a barrier between people, and God hates that. God longs to wipe away your feelings of condemnation because He longs to be close to you."

"Even after what I have done?" Master Nathan replied, absorbing her encouragement, but still sounded doubtful.

"My father always said that he had been justified by faith, just as if he'd never sinned. Clinging to that belief, he walked through life at peace with God, even though he made mistakes all the time. I, too, make mistakes daily. In fact, I have made a great deal of them since I met you, especially today. But the Bible is clear that we all fall short of the glory of God and give in to temptations at times. Today, we both made some big mistakes, but I know that not only is it satisfying to claim our forgiveness and walk in peace with God, but it is of vital importance."

"Vital Importance? Why?"

"It is imperative we remember we have been bought for a tremendous price and that God the Father is not only *able* to see us as flawless, but He also *chooses* to. In that peace, we have power over the enemy despite feeling like we are at war. We must see ourselves as God sees us: without spot or blemish. The Bible tells us that He wants us to confront and confess our sins, not dwell on them. That way, the enemy no longer has power over us."

"I do sometimes feel like I am fighting a war."

"Make no mistake, if you are at peace with God, you *are* at war with the enemy, but you can rest assured that the battle has already been won. However, you must remain kind to yourself in order to live in peace. Only after you repent, know that God has forgiven you, and have forgiven yourself, can you release your guilt. Afterward, you will be able to love others in return, and when you learn to love yourself, overcoming temptation is much easier the next time you are faced with it."

Looking defeated as he shared his struggles, Master Nathan acknowledged, "I have tried not to let my guilt consume me, but it has been nearly impossible."

Hoping to help, she explained, "The Devil knows that a guilty conscience causes disconnection from the Father. It is one of the most significant barriers to your relationship with God, others, and your sense of self-worth. Shame tries to steal your identity. This is the reason the Devil continually tempts people to sin. He wants you to feel remorseful and, therefore, unworthy. God, on the other hand, wants nothing more than to remain close to you and wipe the guilt and pain away."

Master Nathan huffed. "But doesn't He get angry with me? Aren't *you* angry with me?"

Rachel put her hand on his cheek to comfort him. "True, you drank too much today, yet you are repentant and remorseful; therefore, God is not angry with you. And no one likes to get yelled at, so I was hurt by you, but I am not upset with you. In fact, I am immensely proud of you."

"Proud of me? How on Earth could you be proud of me?" Master Nathan pushed his bottom lip up and angled his head to the side.

She answered softly, "In life, you cannot get where you need or want to be when you cannot face where you are. By humbling yourself and asking me for help today, well, that was your way of facing where you are right now. For that, yes, I am proud of you."

He remained quiet, listening intently as he pondered her explanation.

"As I said, we were created for connection, for it is in those connections we learn who we are. I also believe it is impossible to have connection without humility, which itself takes great courage. Today, when you arrived home, you opened up to me with complete vulnerability when you asked me to marry you. You shared your whole heart with me, and that was beautiful."

Master Nathan's eyebrows knitted together as he scowled. "Beautiful? I was rejected, remember? Then, because of it, I drank over half a bottle of whisky. I turned into a raging lunatic and kicked you out of my house. How is that beautiful?"

Placing her hand over his, she said sweetly, "After all the loss you have been through, today you were brave enough to ask me to be your wife without knowing the outcome. You had the strength to face possible rejection, and I am proud of you for that. In your vulnerability, you let me see you, really see you. You asked me to marry you with a wholehearted passion that is to be commended."

"But…" Master Nathan sighed, unsure of what to say.

Since he did not finish, Rachel continued, "It is in the living out of our lives with wholehearted passion that leads to fulfillment, even if things do not always turn out as we hoped or expected. Many people fall apart or get depressed when they have unmet expectations. And you did temporarily fall apart today, yes. Yet still, you got up the courage to be vulnerable again. You came here to my house just moments after I hurt you so deeply, asking for forgiveness with humility and sincerity. Because of that, I have even more respect and admiration for you than ever."

Mulling over the truth behind all she had said, he made light of the situation to cover his embarrassment. "You know what? I guess I *am* braver than I thought. Either that or I am a glutton for punishment."

Chapter 18

A smirk snuck across Rachel's face over his comment, and she replied kindly, "Good sir, you must believe me when I tell you, although I did not accept your marriage proposal, that does not mean I do not love you. It does not mean you are not worthy of my love. In fact, I love you more now than ever because of your willingness to trust me with your heart, and as I was trying to tell you at the house, I am deeply honored by your proposal. But when I declined you, it was apparent that you felt rejected. For that, I am sorry."

He took some time to respond but did not deny he was hurt, "Yes. I did feel the sting of rejection. And I will admit that I was not too fond of it. So, from there," he grimaced, "I allowed disappointment to harden my heart, which quickly turned into anger, which led me to drink too much. I know. I know."

Rachel asked gently, "The question is, have you ever thought about why? Why do you think you turn to alcohol when you are frustrated or in pain? Is it so that you can numb your feelings?"

Master Nathan thought for a moment before he shrugged his shoulders and said, "I suppose."

"Well, did it work?" Rachel inquired, trying not to sound judgmental.

Turning his chin down with his head to the side, his eyes showed his annoyance with himself, and he answered, "No. Clearly, not."

Rachel's voice softened further. "I love you enough to tell you, although I understand the desire to numb your pain, the truth is that no matter how much you drink, it will never work. The only thing I know that decreases the pain of loss, fear of rejection, or sorrow is facing things head-on, dealing with them individually, and then letting them go. Then, by the power of the Holy Spirit, you can turn your pain into power. And if someone in particular has hurt you, not just a situation, forgiving the person who hurt you is key."

"Of course, you would say that," he said with a chuckle, "knowing that, besides forgiving myself, you are the only one I have to forgive."

"Am I?" Rachel asked, digging deeper.

He cocked his head to the other side and squinted, "What do you mean?"

"Oh. You're not fooling anyone. I know you still harbor resentment toward your father. And you know that lingering unforgiveness toward people in your past can harm all current and future relationships. Therefore, I am concerned that if, in your heart, you do not forgive your earthly father and let go of your bitterness, it might even interfere with the relationship with your heavenly Father. Not only that, but some say unforgiveness can affect our health. So, would you consider working on that?"

Master Nathan agreed with her, sounding submissive, "As always, you are right. Yes. I will. I promise."

"I know you will. I trust you see the importance of forgiving him and letting go of any resentment you feel toward him. It may take a little time, but there is a reason the Bible says to not let the sun go down on your anger. Staying angry is the root of bitterness and being bitter is never healthy," she explained in a gentle tone.

"Well, that is true."

She sighed softly, "Now, as far as what happened today between us, what's done is done. Today was a big misunderstanding. We did not handle our discussion perfectly, and that is normal. You are not perfect, and neither am I. I am just as much at fault as you are. Misunderstandings with others are unavoidable, but we must be patient with one another, ourselves, and God. In times like this, we can only hope He is working all things out for our good, despite how messy things get."

"Messy. That is probably the ideal word to describe me." He made a comical face hoping to amuse her.

Rachel giggled. "Life is messy. But that is what keeps it interesting," she said with a grin and a quick raise of her brow, "especially life with you."

Master Nathan nodded and acted more at ease.

Making sure to end their conversation on a positive note, Rachel inquired, "Will you do me a favor?"

Looking at her suspiciously, his eyes merely slits, he said, "That depends. What?"

"Although we can encourage one another to become better versions of ourselves in time, I believe you are always deeply loved and accepted by God and that you are enough. Will you strive to recognize your imperfections, yet trust that you are enough? I will acknowledge my shortcomings, too, and we can choose to love each other unconditionally despite our flaws, no matter what. After that, we can help each other to grow. Deal?"

He flashed her a pleasant grin. "Deal."

She paused. "Remember when we talked about baptism?"

"Baptism?" Master Nathan asked with a scowl.

"Yes. We discussed how it can clean your conscience, but over the years, I have come to know many people who struggled with addictions, behaviors, and attitudes that they tried to change on their own and couldn't until they got baptized. Miraculously, I witnessed them totally set free once they were baptized by water. Now, I am sure it had nothing to do with the water itself. More than likely, it was the fact that they fully surrendered to the Lord in obedience. Then, after baptism, the power of the Holy Spirit became a part of their daily life, and that is where our strength comes from."

"Truly, you think it might help me stop drinking?"

"It might. After all, God Himself says, 'Not by my might, nor by my power, but by my Spirit.' So, being led by the Spirit becomes vital for overcoming our struggles. When the Devil tempts us in our weakness, the power of the Holy Spirit can lead us to do the right thing. Jesus commands water baptism. He was baptized Himself, and frankly, I have seen it help hundreds of people in radical ways."

Master Nathan's face lit up with a look of hope.

Rachel encouraged him, "I believe in you and have no doubt that you can overcome this and achieve any goal you set your mind to. And may I just say, once again, that I am so sorry to have hurt you today when I did not agree to your marriage proposal. Hurting you was the last thing I planned. Please forgive me."

He took her hand as she confessed, "You are so dear to me. Despite hoping to be a help to you, instead, it appears I ruined what should have been a memorable reunion between you and Richard. I should have written to you before you arrived home to tell you that he and I were communicating and developing a relationship, but I was afraid you wouldn't believe me." Rachel lowered her head. "Honestly, I know the news about Richard is hard to believe, especially without witnessing the changes he has made, with your own eyes."

Noticing how sorrowful she was, Master Nathan wondered how he'd let himself get angry with her. "You are right. I probably would not have believed you and gotten angry with you anyway. When will I learn to keep my temper under control? You have been so good to me." He put his hands on her shoulders to move her back and then lifted her chin to observe her closely once more. "Rachel, I am sorry I did not believe you about Richard. Thank you from the bottom of my heart. I do not know how you did it, but you did. After you left the house, Richard came downstairs. He *is* back. Richard truly is back! It is nothing short of a miracle."

Much relieved, she was glad to hear that Richard had come down from the tower and that they'd reunited. Letting out an exaggerated sigh, she proclaimed, "Oh! Praise God! I hoped that he would." Hugging Master Nathan again, they held each other tight, rejoicing over the miracle of his son's return.

"Rachel, I am astonished and will forever be in your debt. How can I repay you?"

They released one another, and still half crying, she looked up at him and chuckled, "Sir, have I taught you nothing? I did not do it, silly. *God* did. Richard's improvements are a miracle of God. Give Him all the glory, sir, not me."

Master Nathan flashed his brown, repentant eyes up at her before he asked, "Rachel, can you please stop calling me 'sir'?"

She nodded and gave him a soft grin, and answered, "Of course."

Pausing briefly, his mannerisms seemed to revert to his comical self so he could ask something weighing heavy on his mind. "Now, will you please try to forget my horrible behavior and come back to the house? Richard will never want to live in that house without you again. And well, as for me, never in my life have I had the pleasure of a best friend. No one has cared enough about me to be so *brutally honest* with me the way you have been since your arrival. The truth is, Rachel, that I need you. We all do. Locke Mansion will not be the same without you. So, there it is. You simply must return to us, no exceptions." He flaunted his charming grin, begging.

She whispered, "Perhaps." Rachel could not help but think about how much she wanted to return to the mansion to be with her beloved Richard, with Master Nathan, the gardens, and the staff, but she missed her family and felt torn. Deep down, she was unsure of how everything might work out with Master Nathan now if she and Richard were to wed someday.

"Please, Rachel. I implore you," he pleaded.

Despite his begging, she remained silent and pondered her and Richard's future; *I wonder if living at Locke Mansion would be suitable for him after everything he has been through there? He needs to be the one to decide where we are to live. But how could we leave Master Nathan all alone?*

Unable to hold still, dying to know just what she was thinking, he fidgeted and gulped down a sick feeling that quickly crawled into his throat from the pit of his stomach when she did not say "yes" right away. *If Rachel and Richard marry, will they leave me and the mansion for good?*

Negative, random thoughts of him dying at Locke Mansion—old, frail, and alone—flashed across his mind, which made him nauseous. He put his hand over his belly and thought, *how could I ever live without either one of them now?*

He stood and took hold of both of her hands to help her rise. Yet, when they were face to face, he did not let go of her but looked down at the floor, deep in thought, and then back up at her once again with imploring eyes.

"Yes, what is it?"

Since she had not answered him after he'd asked repeatedly, Master Nathan decided to try a different approach. He cleared his throat and attempted to reassure her—to ease her mind—that living under one roof with him would not be awkward. "Rachel, you know that I will always love you, but I vow never to interfere with you and Richard. That is if you decide you wish to be with him. I will give you both my most heartfelt blessing. But..." He paused as his nerves took over, making him fumble his words. "...only...only if you are sure that is what you want. Just promise me that you will not agree to marry Richard out of pity but only out of the purest love for him."

His intense look, with his head angled to the side, reminded her of Richard, and he seemed to be hurting all over again. Rachel could tell that the way he worded the question was his way of asking her one last time if, she was sure.

Even though his voice cracked, and he sounded heartbroken over losing her, he agreed to support her either way, whatever she decided. Right then and there, Rachel knew that he loved her with a godly love and that he wanted nothing more than for her and Richard to be happy. Her tears resumed at the thought of his sacrifice.

"Oh, my dear, sweet Master Nathan, I will always love you, too, but as a friend only. And yes, if he is able, I want to marry Richard, not out of pity but out of love. I genuinely do love him. And I can assure you that it is for all the right reasons. I give you my word." She bowed her head sweetly in an intentional gesture, almost as if she were saying goodbye to what might have been between them.

A single tear rolled down his cheek before he grinned, accepting her heart's desire and hugging her one last time. After a moment of silence, he then kissed her forehead. This time, his kiss seemed more like he was taking the role of a proud father, not just of Richard but of her, as her potential future father-in-law. "Well then, my dear Rachel, I shall proudly remain your truest friend. As a father, I pledge to love you and Richard to the best of my ability. That is, if you will let me."

She slowly nodded. "It will be an honor to remain your friend. And no matter what, please know that I will forever feel that you are wonderful beyond words."

"Beyond words? For you? Now, that *is* a miracle."

With a laugh, she slapped his arm for making fun of how talkative she was but said nothing, knowing he was right.

He chuckled, choking back mixed emotions. Although he was sad to be losing Rachel as a potential bride, he was pleased that he was gaining back his precious son and Rachel as a daughter all in one day. He put his hand gently upon her cheek to look at her lovingly, stood tall, and spoke kindly, "And it will be an honor to watch you and Richard join as one someday. I know the joy you will bring my son, and no one deserves it more than he."

"Thank you," she said softly.

Then, snapping to attention, Master Nathan practically yelled, "Richard!"

"What?" Rachel's eyes grew wide.

"Oh, my stars! I must still be drunk. Richard is outside!" he answered abruptly like he had just remembered.

"Excuse me? He's been outside this entire time?" Rachel asked, fumbling with her hair and dress, concerned about her appearance.

Right then, there was a gentle knock at the door. "That must be Richard now," Master Nathan stated in a panicked whisper.

With Master Nathan's help, Rachel fixed herself the best she could. Knowing they both were a mess, they quickly helped one another freshen up. He fixed her hair, wiped a few remaining tears off her face, and swatted at a spot of soot on her dress where she had been sitting on the floor. She fixed his tie and messy hair and wiped his dirty face.

Seemingly satisfied, they both laughed at the same time as they shouted, "Come in!" Rachel sprang to the couch and sat down, adjusting her dress, and patting it into place. Master Nathan rushed toward the fireplace and rested his elbow on the mantle. Leaning against it casually, he crossed one ankle over the other, acting as though nothing was amiss.

The door opened slowly, and it creaked as Richard entered Rachel's house, glancing at his father, hoping he might help him *read the room* before he came inside. "Pardon me. May I?" he asked nervously, wide-eyed and shaking.

His father gave him a nod to reassure him that all was well.

Richard carefully closed the door and turned to face Rachel. Showing grave concern for her well-being, he dashed to her side, trying to remain as dignified as possible. Kneeling before her, he kissed her hand and lifted his gaze to speak with her directly. "Rachel, are you all right, my dear?"

Overjoyed to see him, she answered, "Yes, I am fine. I am relieved to see you. I am sorry if I caused you and your father any distress today, my love."

He kissed her hand once more and said, "You have done nothing of the sort, my lady." Looking to his father for approval, he turned back to Rachel after getting a smile and a wink from him. "Rachel, if I may be so bold… I love you more than anything. I have decided that I never want to be without you. You have fought for me, prayed for me, and believed in me, and I will forever be grateful. As long as the Lord wills it, I want to spend the rest of my days discovering the undeniable gift of God that you are, as well as the beauty of God within you. Rachel," he paused and swallowed back his nerves, "will you do me the honor of marrying me?" Pulling the ring his father had just given him out of his pocket, his eyes excited her heart as they pleaded with her to forever be his.

Astounded as she marveled at the ring, Rachel turned to Master Nathan for clarity. She could see that he was smiling as a tear rolled down his face. He then gave her a single, firm nod with an emotional wink of confirmation.

Rachel quickly glanced back at Richard. Once the expression of shock wore off, it did not take long before her eyes twinkled as she stared back at him. Never had he looked more handsome nor appeared more alive. She giggled and covered her mouth to hide her exaggerated smile. Even though she wanted to blurt out, "Yes," she attempted to keep her composure, hoping to respond to his proposal in a distinguished way.

"Richard, I am honored by your proposal. I love you with all my heart and wish to marry you more than anything. But even though my father is no longer alive to ask his permission, I must honor him. I know he'd insist that you get David's permission first, and he would have advised that we seek marriage counseling before we wed. So, I beg your pardon, but would you kindly agree to meet with my brother, David, to seek his permission and Biblical counsel prior to our wedding? He is far wiser than any man I have ever known, and he'd be much obliged if you asked him."

"Of course, my lady. I shall ask him the moment I see him if you wish."

"In that case, if he agrees, then yes!" Rachel practically shouted.

Now glowing with a prideful grin, Richard placed the ring on her finger. Both laughing, they stood to embrace.

Keeping his distance, Master Nathan watched, but only for a moment before he decided he could not take it anymore. Jumping forward, he wrapped his arms around the two of them and squeezed them tightly as he pressed his smiling cheek firmly against Richard's arm.

Just then, the front door opened, and Rachel's brother and mother walked in. They were taken aback to see two strange men hugging Rachel so tightly in their home and simultaneously gasped.

Master Nathan quickly let go of Rachel and turned to show her family the courtesy of an introduction. He tried to bow, but when he saw Rachel's mother, instead, he almost fell over. His eyes grew wide, and he stumbled again, acting like a man in a comical play or vaudeville act. He caught himself, almost knocking over the end table. Once he stabilized the table and regained his balance, he quickly stood to face everyone, then suddenly froze stiff.

"Mother!" Rachel shouted as she turned to her, taking the focus off Master Nathan, and quickly hugging her. She turned to her brother. "Brother! I have the most wonderful news."

"Oh? What is it?" David asked, with peering eyes, baffled and having no idea what was going on.

"Mother, David, this is my employer, Master Nathan, and his son, Richard. Richard has just asked me to be his wife, and—with your permission, Brother—I've agreed to marry him. Isn't that wonderful?"

Although they were very confused by this sudden announcement, they politely smiled. It was clear that Rachel was eager to share her news with them, so they rejoiced with her to avoid hurting her feelings.

Sensing the sudden tension in the air, Rachel stated, "I know. I know. It is a long story, but you are just going to have to trust me. This is wonderful news. I have no doubt that God Himself has joined us together. We are deeply in love, and we are so excited to be married! So, David, Richard has something to ask you."

Richard stepped forward, cleared his throat, and asked, "David, it would be an honor, sir, if you would be so kind as to give us your blessing for our union. And if you are inclined to grant us this blessing, we humbly request your Godly counsel preliminary to our marriage. Rachel has informed me that your father would have insisted upon it, and we would like to honor him. That is, if you are willing, of course. As for the counseling, we would gladly pay you handsomely for it, should you require it."

Unsure, after a bit of questioning geared toward both Richard and Master Nathan, David courteously replied, "Indeed, you have my permission, and the honor will be all mine."

Taken aback, Rachel's mother covered her true feelings, turned to face Rachel, and said, "How extraordinary. We are delighted for you, my dear." At the same time, she glanced in Rachel's direction, asking her with just her eyes, *"What on Earth is going on?"*

Rachel gave her mother a funny look in return as if trying to tell her, *"Trust me."* They hugged once again so Rachel could whisper to her mother, "I'll fill you in later."

Flashing a quick smile Master Nathan's way, Rachel's mother curtsied. Then, turning to Richard, she reached out to shake his hand.

Richard, however, bowed before her and kissed her hand instead, treating her like royalty.

She blushed for a moment, but her flattered expression showed she was pleased. "Welcome to the family, Richard. I look forward to getting to know you. You may call me Lydia."

"Lydia!" Master Nathan stammered loudly as though he was in awe of both her and her name. Everyone turned their attention back toward him, looking puzzled. He tried desperately to rectify his uncouth behavior, yet he appeared unable to speak coherently or move a muscle. Like a mannequin, he stood, staring at Lydia with bulging eyes, making Rachel wonder if he might still be intoxicated.

After a moment of awkward silence, Master Nathan realized he must have appeared foolish by not introducing himself. He thought quickly of how to remedy the situation and turned into a perfect gentleman. Locking eyes with Lydia, he walked right up to her and bowed even lower than Richard had to kiss her hand before he stood. "Forgive me, please," he said with a dashing smile. "It has been an eventful day thus far, and I fear we are all a bit dazed. It is a pleasure to meet you, Lydia."

She curtsied in return yet held her tongue.

Mesmerized by Lydia's face, he somehow managed to shake David's hand without removing his gaze from the sparkle in her blue eyes. "David, it is a pleasure to meet you," he stated, giving him a rushed grin and sidewards peek before placing his focus back on Lydia.

Lydia started to speak, but Master Nathan continued blundering through his introduction. "Yes. Well, congratulations to all. Lydia, since our children are about to be married and we are going to be family, would you indulge me with a walk so we might have a chance to get to know one another a bit? That is, if you are feeling well enough," he asked rather boldly with another small bow in her direction, still holding her hand.

She was rather bold herself as she replied, "Actually, I am quite well. Thank you for asking; however, I have just come from a walk." Noticing the look of disappointment on his face, she continued, "But I'd join you for a ride on your horse."

Pleasantly surprised and smiling, Master Nathan perked up yet fumbled his reply, "Of-of course! Yes. Splendid. What a lovely idea."

Richard and Rachel could tell he was trying to hide his excitement and attempting to remain calm. Since he was failing at it miserably, they snickered.

"Rachel, you never told me that you were the spitting image of your mother," Master Nathan said as he turned his head in Rachel's direction and raised his eyebrows up and down quickly.

"You never asked," she said with a grin as Lydia and Master Nathan headed out the door together, arm in arm, gazes locked.

Chapter 19

Everyone said their goodbyes and followed Lydia and Master Nathan outside as they left the house. Watching Master Nathan attempting to help her mother onto Richard's horse, Rachel heard him ask her if she would require him to fetch a lady's saddle.

When Lydia answered, "There is no need for that," and climbed up herself, Rachel noticed a spark between them.

Chuckling under her breath and shaking her head, she thought, *I wonder just what God is up to now?*

Master Nathan gave Richard and Rachel a raise of his brow, eyes alight with excitement.

While heading back inside, David said, "Well, I guess I will go start dinner."

"No, no, no. Tonight is a celebration!" Master Nathan exclaimed.

"Tonight, we all will dine at my house. Lydia and I will ride up and send the carriage back for the rest of you. Be ready in an hour, all right?" Then, he directed his focus back to Lydia. "Does that sound pleasing to you, Mrs. Thompson?" he asked politely.

"That sounds..." She paused, noticing his engaging brown eyes were filled with adoration as they beamed up at her. Feeling a flutter in her heart she had not experienced in years, she simply said, "... wonderful."

He grinned wide at her choice of words and then began to mount the horse to sit behind her, assuming she could not ride by herself. Yet, before he climbed up, she asked, "Pardon me. Would you be so kind as to take the other horse instead? That way, we can race."

"Oh! Oh, my! Are you sure you are comfortable riding alone?" he asked, worried about her ability to handle Richard's horse.

"Yes, thank you kindly. I am sure," she replied with confidence as he stepped back.

"Yes, Ma'am."

Winking in Rachel's direction, Lydia shouted, "Hyah!" and galloped away with a commanding kick to the horse's side, leaving Master Nathan standing aghast.

"Wow," he whispered as he climbed onto his horse. Before he chased after her, he waved back to everyone and declared, "Love you! See you soon."

"Love you! Have fun!" Richard shouted back.

As they watched their parents race off toward the mansion, Rachel put her hands over her heart and leaned against Richard's shoulder. She was thrilled that Master Nathan seemed back to himself after the anger she had witnessed in him earlier.

Once they were out of sight, David firmly put his arm around Richard. "Well, Richard, tell me. Do you like fishing?" he asked as he led him back into the house.

"Actually, I do not really know. I have never been fishing before," he said with an expression of childlike wonder.

David inquired, "How about I teach you? Would you like that?"

"Indeed," Richard replied.

Rachel stood just inside the doorway and listened to the two of them talking as though they had been friends for years. Pondering the events of the day, she smiled and held up her hand to admire her ring, overjoyed to be engaged to Richard. Then, the ring's tremendous beauty made her realize something, and her heart skipped a beat.

Everything that day had happened so fast, her thoughts flashed to Master Nathan. Assuming he'd picked out the ring himself, just for her, she was floored by the incredible selflessness he displayed by simply giving it over to his son. His kindness as a father astounded her. She figured that he must have given the ring to Richard as soon as they arrived at her house so he could propose. Mindful that it was only moments after she had broken his heart, she sighed. Hoping that he was truly going to be okay, she hugged the ring against her chest with both hands.

That evening, Lydia and David were speechless as Master Nathan gave them a partial tour of his home. Never in their lives had they witnessed such a glorious place. Rachel giggled quietly, recalling her first visit to Locke Mansion. She fully understood why they were stunned as they beheld each area, eyes filled with astonishment.

After enjoying a most impressive dinner, music around the piano, and a spin on the dance floor in the ballroom, Master Nathan whispered back and forth with Richard for a moment before they addressed everyone. "We have an idea. Richard and I would like to be baptized tomorrow. What do you think?"

"What? That *is* a splendid idea!" Rachel proclaimed.

"We can even invite the staff!" Master Nathan declared proudly before turning to David. "David, would you do the honor of baptizing us both? Perhaps as early as tomorrow afternoon?"

David bowed with a contented smile and said, "Why, of course. I would be delighted." He had wanted to be a preacher for as long as he could remember, following in his father's footsteps, but had given up his dream when his father grew ill. Years ago, he'd been sent a proposal by a church in need of a pastor, but the location of the assigned parsonage was over one hundred miles away. He'd declined the offer, knowing he needed to be there for his family in case of his father's passing. And since his father's death, he refused to leave his mother and sister alone. So, the opportunity to baptize Master Nathan and Richard excited him tremendously.

Upon saying their goodbyes for the evening, it was evident both families hated to part ways.

Before David arrived the following day to share the importance of baptism with them, Rachel and Richard spent time visiting his family's gravesite. They cleaned the area and planted flowers around their crosses while Richard shared pleasant memories of time spent with them. Knowing it was healing for him to talk openly about his family, Rachel kept quiet, only asking questions that would encourage him to tell more fond stories about days gone by.

Afterward, they washed their hands in the stream and then enjoyed a romantic morning together on Richard's horse, exploring the grounds as he hugged her from behind. Riding in a direction Rachel had not yet explored, she was filled with a sense of reverence. As they passed expansive herb gardens and fields filled with other horses and barns that she knew nothing about, she wondered what other treasures Locke Mansion might hold. *I could ride with Richard like this forever*, she thought to herself.

At the crest of a hill, they stopped overlooking the most incredible vineyard Rachel had ever witnessed. She inhaled deeply. "Oh, Richard, it's glorious."

He nodded. "It is, indeed."

Once they toured the vineyards, they rested beside a vine that had recently been pruned. Rachel asked, "Richard, have you read about Jesus' teaching of the vine and the branches?"

"No. Will you teach it to me?"

"Of course." She quoted parts of Jesus' lesson with ease as they strolled along: "In John 15, verses one through five, Jesus said, 'I am the true vine, and my Father is the (gardener) vinedresser. Every branch in Me that does not bear fruit He takes away; and every *branch* that bears fruit He prunes, that it may bear more fruit. You are already clean because of the word which I have spoken to you. Abide (remain) in Me, and I in you. As the branch cannot bear fruit of itself, unless it abides in the vine, neither can you, unless you abide in me.' And in verses 9 through 12, He says, 'As the Father loved me, I also have loved you; abide in my love. If you keep my commandments, you will abide in my love, just as I have kept My Father's commandments and abide in His love. These things I have spoken to you, that My joy may remain in you, and that your joy may be full. This is My commandment, that you love one another as I have loved you.'"

Regardless of being impressed with her ability to quote scripture so easily, he joked, "Well, a commandment for us to love each other, that should be easy."

Rachel chuckled, "True, but did you catch its meaning besides that?"

"Of course. We must stay connected to Him and His Word in order to live fulfilled and productive lives that glorify Him," Richard stated casually.

Proud of his insight, she showered him with compliments as they made their way through the dense trees. They followed a meticulously landscaped woodland path leading down a curvy, steep hill until they reached the bottom of a deep valley. Richard dismounted and took the reins to help Rachel down.

Strolling hand-in-hand to the sound of the horse's footsteps, they walked under several enormous trees that were fully landscaped all around them. Several tall clumps of yellow grasses and flowering shrubs of dark and light pink stood next to a babbling brook. Up ahead, an opening with three large, arched bridges painted bright red, that connected a few smaller ponds, caught Rachel's attention. Before crossing the first one, they loosely tied their horse to the end of the bridge, allowing it to drink from the pond and enjoy the thick green grass growing near the bank.

Walking to the center of the middle bridge, they stopped to behold Richard's favorite garden and leaned over the railing. The winds picked up and he said, "Rachel, welcome to the Japanese Garden. I have not been here since I helped my father design and create it as a small child. I can still see the drawings in my mind so vividly. It is astounding how it has developed. It's just as we envisioned it."

Rachel could hardly believe it. "Oh, darling... Why, it is simply marvelous. The beauty of Locke Mansion never ceases to amaze me." She squeezed his hand as she looked about.

Japanese Maple trees of assorted shapes and sizes, arrayed in maroon or light-green leaves, greeted them at every turn. Evergreens, trimmed into rare forms filled the landscape, and were accented by flowers that flashed orange, red, purple, and yellow in the sunlight.

The fine grains of pure white sand raked to perfection, resembling ripples in water, formed around several large rocks of unique shapes. Each rock was placed precisely to look like islands standing tall amongst the ocean waves.

Different fences that matched various wooden structures one would find throughout the Orient were also painted red or stained dark brown. Having been erected to provide shade and comfort throughout the gardens, one interesting building was home to several bonsai trees that Richard explained were well over a hundred years old. They had been started by his great-grandmother and passed down over the years within the family. Since Rachel had made many attempts to grow bonsai trees of her own over the years and had failed miserably, she was greatly impressed.

This area of the gardens instantly became Rachel's favorite part of Locke Mansion too. "Oh, my. I don't think I have ever seen anything so lovely."

With a grin, he explained, "Historically, the Japanese have tried to emphasize the virtue of restraint in their gardens. They aimed to conceal beauty so that it might be discovered by the individual to provide pure enjoyment to the soul. Much like the joy that comes from doing a good deed in secret, Japanese gardens are designed to satisfy the cravings humans have for nature by offering a spiritual retreat, teaming with life."

Rachel stood, mesmerized by the reflections shimmering off the water, and pulled Richard to the other side of the bridge. The hills and valleys around the ponds each shared their own display of splendor. The steppingstones mixed with moss that covered the curved paths leading to and fro across the grass called to her.

Reaching one of the largest wooden buildings that seemed to hover directly over the water, Rachel squeezed her hands together and raised her shoulders excitedly when she noticed a table set for tea. The finest silver cups and tea pot rested casually on top of glistening silver tray. "What is this?"

"Ah. Good old Austin. We enjoyed a pleasant talk this morning. He suggested you and I share a spot of tea here and must have set this up, especially for us. Would you be so kind as to do me the honor?" Richard asked as he motioned with his hand for her to make her way to the extra-large white pillow on the floor.

Having sat with a little help from him, Rachel fixed her lavender dress skirt, removed her hat, and lifted her gaze. Admiring her fiancé, she took his hand and shared her heart, "Richard, I need to tell you something."

He gave her an attentive look, "Yes?"

"Never in my life did I think I would be so blessed. You. This place. And my life now. I don't deserve it. Regardless, I am overjoyed by all the Lord has provided me."

Smiling, Richard objected, "Of course, you deserve it. And yes, everything you have seen so far has been quite spectacular. I agree. But you wait until you see where I am taking you next."

"Oh?"

"I would like to surprise you," he said with a smile, "so don't ask."

After a suspicious look and a great deal of flirtatious banter, Rachel did her best to boost his confidence and show him the utmost respect with her every word. She knew that respecting him openly to edify him would be her most important role as his wife one day.

While waiting for Rachel to finish her tea, Richard looked at his reflection in the silver teacup, and smiled. Curious as to what he was thinking, Rachel asked, "What is it?" Pausing, he answered. "This week, David and I studied Malachi 3:3. It says, 'God will sit as a refiner and purifier of silver.' After our study, I traveled downtown to visit the silversmith to watch him work. I wanted to learn what this verse meant about the nature and character of God. As I watched him refine the silver, he held it in the hottest part of the fire, right in the middle, because he said that is how you burn away the impurities. I asked why he had to sit there the entire time during the process. He explained that it was of vital importance to keep his eye on it, holding it carefully in just the right place for the exact amount of time, because if the silver sits in the flames just a moment too long it will be damaged. So, as I pondered what he said, I realized that all these years, God was with me the entire time. Although he did not cause me hardship, in His goodness, I know he used it to refine me before setting me free. After that, I then asked the silversmith, how do you know when the silver is fully refined? He said, 'That's easy, when I can see my reflection in it.'"

Thinking back on everything her fiancé had been through, Rachel marveled at the meaning of what he'd just shared. She, too, could easily see the reflection of God in her beloved and reached for his hand, to show her gratitude.

As they continued to explore, Richard led Rachel to sit with him on a bench where the full view of the Oriental Garden was outstanding.

"Goodness gracious. You are right. This is spectacular," she commented.

"No, not this. Here. Take off your shoes."

"My shoes?"

"Yes. Take off your shoes and stockings."

Unsure, Rachel watched Richard remove his shoes and roll up his pant legs, revealing his strong leg muscles again. Aware of how inappropriately they were behaving by showing their legs to one another, like they did in the river, she chuckled. Yet following his lead, she removed her shoes and stockings that were hitched high up her leg under her dress. As he admired the view of her reaching high up beneath her skirt, she blushed and finished just in time for him to stand and take her hand.

"You know, I have a confession to make," he said.

"Yes?"

"Well, when you first came to Locke Mansion, I used to watch you change through the keyhole. I fell so in love with you in my dreams. I could not help myself. Will you please forgive me?"

Surprising herself, she stated boldly, "There is nothing to forgive."

"But I am so embarrassed. I was unsure how you would feel if you were to ever find out."

"Oh, silly, don't you know?" Rachel gave him a sly smile and pulled him down to her level by his tie to whisper in his ear, "I had a sneaking suspicion you were watching me."

Wide-eyed, Richard stood tall and replied, "Oh. I see." After a hearty laugh, he instructed her, "Now, close your eyes, my dear."

With a nod, showing complete trust, she obeyed. Keeping her eyes shut while Richard acted almost giddy, he led her across a large patch of the softest grass they had encountered thus far.

Rachel could feel the blades bending gently under her feet and grinned. Excited to think of how she wished to walk barefoot at Locke Mansion since she arrived, she was happy to be doing so with Richard. After taking several steps with him leading her, she asked, "Can I open my eyes now?"

"No. Not yet."

Hands clasped together, they enjoyed the feel of the grass and connection to the earth for a while. "Where are you taking me?" Rachel finally asked with a chuckle.

After a few more steps, Richard answered, "Okay. Now!"

Rachel's breath was stolen away. They had crossed the enormous lawn and rounded the bend to a new area of the gardens. Hidden by a large patch of trees, a massive, smooth, stone building with large arched windows covering the full length of its walls, now stood before her, resembling the mansion's ballroom. But it had a row of enormous pillars on all four sides, reminding her of the detailed drawings of several buildings her parents had sketched from their trip to Greece they had taken before she and David were born. They were quite impressive, leaving a significant imprint on her memory.

He hesitated, raise an eyebrow her way, then opened the doors, saying, "This, my sweet, is what I wanted to show you today."

Venturing inside, Rachel gasped and looked around in awe. The building was one big room that was over a hundred feet long and forty feet wide. The glass ceiling, similar to the one in the solarium, appeared to be forty feet high. There were no paintings or gold, just the grey cement pillars and the exterior walls of tall, arched windows with white grilles.

Just inside, another row of pillars around the outside edges of the structure's interior appeared to be holding up the building. They were at least three feet across each, reminding her of some of the extravagant cathedrals she had seen over the years. Yet, it was the floor that held her gaze. Nearly eight feet into the room on all sides, there was a single step leading into an enormous pool of water that took up most of the building's floor. Even though it was only four inches deep, it looked clean, fresh, and inviting.

Inside the pool, every seven feet or so, there were large cement pots with small trees that were perfectly round at the top. Around the base of each tree, tiny white and blue flowers, mixed with greenery of various lengths, hung low toward the pool.

Richard, stepping down into the water without reservation, turned to face Rachel. With one foot in the water and one on the step, he reached up for her hand and asked, "May I have this dance?"

Seeing his beautiful face looking in her direction with anticipation, she gave him a starry-eyed nod and placed her hand in his. Although there was no music, they hummed as they danced, splashed about, and strolled together in the water, falling more in love with each glance. Talking for over an hour until it was time for David to arrive, when they exited the building, Rachel commented, "What a glorious place this is."

Richard happily made Rachel blush as he bowed low and kissed her hand, "Indeed. Fit for royalty, like you, my lady."

While returning to the mansion on their horse, Rachel leaned her back against Richard's chest. Gazing up at the clouds as they rode, she questioned, "Richard, do you ever feel like this is a dream? Maybe it sounds silly, but sometimes, I feel the need to pinch myself to see if this is all real. If *you* are real."

With a grin and a quick pinch to the back of her hand, he said, "It's real."

"Ouch!" she exclaimed. After sitting up, she elbowed him and laughed, thankful to see his sense of humor emerging even more. "Goodness me, you are such a rascal. Must you always be so much like your father?"

He chuckled, quickly apologized, and kissed her hand where he pinched it. "I try my best," he joked. "But yes. I, too, oftentimes wonder if this is just my imagination." Kissing her hand again, he finished, "My dearest, forever I will praise God that you are indeed real and such a gift. I am so thankful."

"You had better be," she smirked, flirtatiously elbowing his side again.

He laughed over the fact he had irritated her, "Of course, I am."

Up ahead, Rachel noticed her mother standing amongst the roses. "Oh! Mother and David have arrived. He must be waiting for you in the solarium," she exclaimed before she slid out of the saddle and jumped down to spend some time in the rose garden with her mother.

"Good day," Richard said with a tip of his hat toward Lydia. He then winked at Rachel and rode off to the mansion to meet his father and David.

Noticing how Rachel watched Richard ride away with a dreamy stare, Lydia chuckled and took her hand gently. "Come, child. Let's pray about today's baptism. Your head is in the clouds anyway. So, let's lift it a little higher, shall we?"

David, Richard, and Master Nathan gathered at the small table in the solarium to study the importance of baptism. Richard was having the time of his life. He had grown to thoroughly enjoy reading the Gospels. More importantly, for the first time since he was ten, he felt the camaraderie of sitting around a table, talking with other men. "May I read first?" he asked David in a lighthearted tone.

"Of course. But might I first suggest we take turns reading each scripture I have listed here? Then we may address any remaining questions or concerns afterward," David said.

"That sounds splendid," Master Nathan replied.

"Agreed," Richard stated before he began. "Acts 22:16: 'And now why are you waiting? Arise and be baptized, and wash away your sins, calling on the name of the Lord.'"

Master Nathan sounded uncommonly serious as he read. "Mark 16:16: He who believes and is baptized will be saved, but he who does not believe will be condemned.'"

"1 Peter 3:21: 'And this water symbolizes baptism that now saves you also—not the removal of dirt from the body but the pledge of a clear conscience toward God. It saves you by the resurrection of Jesus Christ.'" David read.

"Acts 8:36-39: 'As they traveled along the road, they came to some water and the eunuch said, "Look, here is water. What can stand in the way of my being baptized?" And he gave orders to stop the chariot. Then both Philip and the eunuch went down into the water and Philip baptized him. When they came up out of the water, the Spirit of the Lord suddenly took Philip away, and the eunuch did not see him again, but went on his way rejoicing,'" Richard read loudly.

Studying these and several more verses related to baptism, great faith stirred within them. "Well, what are we waiting for?" Master Nathan practically yelled, jumping up from his chair.

"I love your excitement, but let's make sure Richard does not have any questions first." David turned to Richard. "Do you?" he asked with a laugh.

"Oh, right. Sorry, son. Do you?" Master Nathan said before he slowly sat back down with an embarrassed expression.

Richard thought for a moment. "Let me make sure I get this straight." He paused. "So, when we go under the water, our sins get washed away for good, no matter how big or small?"

David replied, "It's like we are being buried with Christ, dying to ourselves, and our sins are gone. We are then completely forgiven for all our past mistakes. But please understand, it isn't the water washing our sins away, per se. The act of getting baptized is a public display, showing to God, to those in attendance, and to the spirit realm, that we accept the gift of Jesus dying for us on the cross. However, it is the fact that He shed His blood for us that makes forgiveness possible. Does that make sense?"

Incredibly focused, Richard continued without answering David's question. "And then, when we come up from the water, it's like when Jesus rose from the dead three days after His crucifixion, and so it will be as though we, too, are being raised with Jesus to a new life. Right?"

"That is correct. It is His resurrection that makes a new life available to each of us," David said.

Smiling, with a look of peace, Richard finished, "And we will be made new?"

"Well, yes. That's about it. Since you were saved in the tower, and from this day forward, God, through His Holy Spirit, will transform you, moment by moment, from the inside out as you surrender to His Word. Because the Word of God is His will for us."

"Let's go, Father! What are we waiting for?" Richard exclaimed, standing quickly to his feet as his father had done.

Right then, Lydia and Rachel entered the solarium, and Master Nathan and Richard declared, "We are ready!"

Austin gathered the staff to join Rachel and her family to witness the baptism. Master Nathan, having much to say, hopped up onto the edge of the fountain to address them. "If I may? I would like to thank you all for coming today. But before we begin, I feel the need to apologize to each of you and beg your forgiveness," he said, clearing his throat. "I know that since the death of my family, I have been sullen, a bit of a brute, and extremely rude to many of you. For that, I am deeply sorry," he apologized, making a painful face toward Austin, who simply bowed, showing he had already forgiven him. Master Nathan flashed a grin toward his old friend and then turned his eyes toward Lydia to finish. "But I promise you, from now on, I am a changed man."

Smiles of gratitude were abundant, and many reassured him all was well, glad he was recovering from his trauma. Master Nathan then turned toward his son. "Richard, come up here!"

Richard was hesitant but climbed onto the fountain's edge beside his father regardless, while Rachel stood in awe beside Lydia and David. She knew how long the staff had been praying for this day and whispered that fact to her family so they would understand the importance of the moment. David grinned while Lydia covered her heart, thankful to be witnessing such a miracle.

At first, Richard, wringing his hands, seemed uneasy as he talked directly to the staff he had watched over in the night for so many years. Despite his shaking, he spoke boldly to show his gratitude. "I know that you are all fully aware of my story, and with my whole heart, I wish to thank each one of you. I know you have been patiently praying for me for a long time, and I will forever appreciate it."

To help stop his shaking, Rachel reached up and took his hand. His fear left him instantly, and his hand stilled. "I am getting better daily and looking forward to my new life. The Lord has freed me from my sins and unlocked my mind. I no longer believe in ghosts. And I am certain I am *not* one. Clearly, I never was since there is *no such thing*. In fact, I know that I am a very blessed *man* indeed. I am a man in love and want to live," he said. Turning to Rachel, he bent down to kiss her hand. "Not only that, but I am engaged to be married!" Although he was smiling as the crowd cheered, he jumped down and asked Rachel with a concerned tone, "Are you sure there is nothing else I need to do before I get baptized?"

She put her hand on his cheek trying to calm him. "No, sweetie. Just close your eyes and take a deep breath before David dips you back under the water."

With wide eyes, he nodded, deep in thought.

"You will be fine. Just focus your mind on your sins, your past, your guilt, your shame, and anything that bothers you about yourself. Picture God washing it away. He will remember your sins no more, and neither should you. Don't forget, baptism is a profession of your faith and like washing your conscience clean before your Creator. You are so loved by Him and by all of us. Truly, Richard, we could not be prouder of you."

Feeling the love from Rachel, her family, his father, and the servants, who seemed overjoyed to finally meet him face to face, he grinned wide.

Once Master Nathan got down to join them, he said, "Richard, I am so proud of you, too, and we are not even wet yet."

He turned to Rachel, tipped his chin down, and looked up at her with grateful eyes. "None of this would be happening if it were not for you. You know that, right?" She started to reply, but he interrupted her, "Ah, ah, ah! Rachel, I know you will say this is God's handiwork, not yours, but I am still going to thank you. You simply need to say, 'You are welcome.'"

She bowed and blushed. "You are welcome. It has been my pleasure." Then, she asked, "Master Nathan, did I ever tell you about the time my father shared with me he struggled with a very bad habit? An addiction of some sort that he could not shake?"

"Really? No. I always imagined him as a perfect saint."

"Oh. He was far from perfect. And there is no such thing as a 'perfect saint,' just forgiven sinners. But yes, it's true. He said it troubled him no matter how hard he tried to fight it until he committed his life to Jesus and was baptized. He said that, after his baptism, he never felt the pull of its temptation again. I want to let you know I have been praying for that exact thing for you. I am asking the Lord to help you never crave alcohol again after this day. I am trusting He will fill you so full of His Holy Spirit and joy that you never even need it." She turned her head to the side. "If I may, I would like to suggest, as you get baptized, that you pray a similar request for yourself. Who knows? Perhaps, as He washes the guilt and pain of your past away, He will answer us."

"Wouldn't that be a miracle?" Master Nathan said, half-joking, giving her a wink and stepping close to Lydia, who then smiled and curtsied to him. He took a moment to pause and inhaled as though seeing her face comforted him. But then he turned and focused on Richard, asking excitedly, "Son, let's say we wipe our slate clean. Shall we?"

After their baptisms, the celebration luncheon went on for hours so Richard and Master Nathan could get to know their staff better. Rachel, David, and Lydia introduced themselves to everyone as well. Since most of Master Nathan's employees were believers, it was like they had gained an instant family all in one day. Rachel never felt more at home, and smiled, *I wonder what God has in store for the household now.*

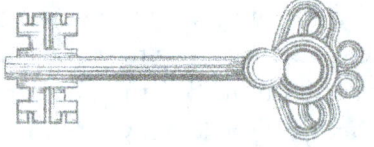

Chapter 20

Fondly thinking back to their baptisms that had taken place almost a year prior, Rachel practically floated about the garden. She was grateful to her brother for all the Godly counsel he'd given to both Richard and Master Nathan, as well as her and Richard regarding marriage. They were now closer than ever, and their past struggles seemed like a distant memory.

After months of preparation, the wedding day had finally arrived. The colorful fall leaves were at their peak. Red, amber, gold, and bright orange glowed brilliantly in the trees above and throughout the gardens. Those in the distant hills almost appeared to be ablaze in stark contrast to the hunter green grasses below. Each one seemed to be showing their excitement for the happy couple with their magnificent display as they fluttered in the wind.

Townspeople and visitors alike said they had never seen the foliage so vivid. Several mentioned it reminded them of their trips to New England in the Americas, making Rachel long to visit there one day. Her father spent years there before she was born, and she remembered how he described the autumn foliage in the state of Maine as though it was nothing short of divine.

Relieved there were only a few puffy white clouds in the royal blue skies above, she inhaled the fresh air that seemed extra clean and crisp. She sighed, thankful for the scents of fall that filled her lungs with each breath. What sparkling dew remained from the night before clung to everything exposed to the elements as the sun elbowed its way in for the morning. It was early; however, she was confident the day would be perfect for a three o'clock wedding.

A multitude of birds sang sweetly around her in unison as the full orchestra busily set up their instruments on one side of the terrace. But nearer to the fountain, a brand-new Steinway grand piano and a single chair for the cellist were placed directly on the lawn in the gardens to the fountain's left side for a surprise she'd planned.

Organizing the entire outdoor area meticulously, Rachel had the servants set up the white wooden chairs on the grass twenty feet from the terrace steps in seventy-five neatly laid out rows. Large stone containers overflowing with glorious fall, floral arrangements, stood every seven feet on either side of the white crushed-seashell path. These attractive pots were filled with different colored sun flowers of various sizes, purple cone flower, light blue and pink hydrangeas, orange roses, yellow and orange blanket flowers, hot pink dahlias, white daisies, golden straw flowers, pansies, and lavender-colored verbena. However, flowing down around every pot's edge, green sage mixed with succulent, honey scented, white alyssum, made the path extra inviting as it curved down toward the archway.

The day prior, the wedding party practiced walking through the ballroom's middle set of double doors, across the terrace, descending the grand steps to the path, through the central aisle of the chairs, and to the ceremony area in front of the fountain under the archway. This was the same fountain in which Master Nathan and Richard were baptized not so long ago and, therefore, it had become a special place to everyone.

Rachel strode down the aisle and around to the backside of the fountain and lifted her eyes to admire the grandeur of Locke Mansion. Sitting on the fountain's edge to take a break, she let her mind wander back to that glorious day. Oh, how she wished her father could have been there. *I'm glad that at least David was able to baptize them.* She smiled, recalling the three men she loved most in the world standing in the fountain together as a family.

Having attended hundreds of baptisms, Rachel thought she'd never felt the presence of the Lord so strongly as on that day. When Jeanne began singing an old Celtic hymn throughout David's preaching and the ceremony, one could sense the love flowing amongst everyone. Rachel remembered, it was like she could almost see Jesus in robes of white, walking amongst the cheering crowd to reassure her that nothing would ever go back to the way it was.

Since their baptisms, there were a great deal of changes Rachel never expected, yet she was thankful for them just the same. Knowing the Lord was showing her how everything in life that came her way didn't have to be exactly like she'd planned in order for it to be from Him, she thought, *That is true.*

Over the months, through their frequent visits, the kinship between their two families flourished. Richard and Master Nathan had rekindled the most loving father and son relationship Rachel ever witnessed. Seeing the two of them so close proved that God was always faithful to restore seven-fold what the Devil attempted to destroy.

As they visited their family's graves together weekly to adorn them with flowers after years of neglect, that area, too, was carefully restored. Even the old tree seemed to come to new life when they added a swing and its' leaves finally emerged. Near the tree, they installed a white bench seat that Master Nathan commissioned to look just like the one in Rachel's room. Right beside it, they planted pink rose bushes and white lilies that would give off a sweet and spicy aroma when in season.

With the help of her family, after Master Nathan, Richard, and the entire staff prayed over Locke Mansion and anointed each window from inside with oil, they could sense a new lightness throughout the mansion and even the grounds. It was surprising how much the atmosphere shifted after they'd finished cleaning out the house.

Now, here she was, months later, staring into the same fountain, but instead of people standing in it, floating on top of the pristine waters were hundreds of rose petals in various colors. Swirling her fingertips through them, they clumsily bumped into one another, creating distinct currents like a river.

Thinking of Richard and his new life, Rachel turned her head to the side with a gentle smile, glad he'd grown to deeply appreciate the beauty of God within himself, in others, and in nature. She adored watching how the simplest of things, from the sparkling mica in a stone down to the tiniest petal, left him awestruck. Since he gained the ability to clearly see God's kindness in every detail of life, he'd become a different person.

Once more, Rachel swirled the flower petals, daydreaming about her love, wondering how he and Master Nathan were managing on this glorious morning.

A loud bump to her right caught her off-guard, startling her. The staff was situating the preacher's pulpit on the other side of the fountain and had dropped it. She nodded their way kindly and stood to shift her focus back to her task, ensuring each area was set up for the wedding just as she envisioned. She appeared tranquil as her eyes roamed back and forth over the grounds while checking to be sure nothing was out of place.

The archway for the bride and groom to stand under that David built out of winding wisteria vines caught her attention. Erected about seven feet in front of the fountain, it would soon be covered in cut flowers and greenery. Looking at it from the guest's point of view after walking to the other side, she was confident that the rose garden beyond the fountain, still in full bloom with its stone archways and paths, would be the ideal backdrop for the ceremony.

Thrilled to see it all coming together, she meandered back onto the terrace with a grin. From any direction, every inch of Locke Mansion resembled an enchanted castle, and she inhaled deeply to absorb the scene.

Turning her glance skyward, she noticed that the exterior walls of the house and the archways surrounding the secondary double doors leading into the ballroom were adorned with cut flowers as well. They presented an excellent addition to the now, fall-colored, orange, and red ivy, that covered the mansion for years. Maroon, pink, yellow, orange, and white flowers, positioned sporadically throughout the vines as high as the servants could safely reach by ladder, spiced up the outside dining area nicely. But the archway around the center doors, which were adorned with white flowers only, offered the ideal focal point for the bride to make her grand appearance and start her procession down the path toward her groom.

When the orchestra started to practice on the terrace, Rachel slowly turned in a circle, once again in awe of her surroundings and God's goodness toward her. After spending months shopping and preparing for this day, she gazed up at the lights she'd carefully hand-selected to add ambiance to the evening. Lifting her face and arms high toward the heavens in praise to the Lord, she grinned wide and closed her eyes. She envisioned them lighting up the terrace dining area and the gardens nearest the back of the mansion after sunset. Having kept them a secret, she could not wait to see Richard's initial reaction to them.

Inside the ballroom, the tables were set with the most elaborate white dinnerware surrounded by a wreath of greenery. Highly polished silverware sparkled in the glow of the overhead ballroom lights. The cream-colored lace tablecloths, lightly sprinkled with random flower petals and fresh, brightly colored fall leaves, looked impressive when paired with the multi-colored floral centerpieces the staff created. They included tall, curly brown sticks, long-stemmed roses, and wildflowers arranged inside the Lockes' two-foot tall, etched glass vases that had been passed down for generations within the family. Rachel was amazed that these vases were so lovingly preserved and used during every Locke wedding for over a century. And it was an honor to use them again.

Her favorite display was deep inside the ballroom on the north wall opposite the terrace. Several long tables were set up just so and covered in ornate desserts. The treats that had been set up early looked almost too good to eat, displayed like artwork on top of maroon tablecloths and bright white dishes.

Rachel's tummy rumbled. She leaned forward and inhaled the scents of different fruits dipped in dark chocolate. The large variety of English desserts—chocolate truffles, jam rolls, Battenberg cake, Bakewell Pudding, cream puffs, and banana cream pie, which was Master Nathan's favorite—smelled divine. And since his family was from Scotland, they also had Scottish shortbread apple pie, chocolate and orange mousse, oatcakes, raspberry buns, and Scottish fruited gingerbread. It was a tempting spread indeed.

Strolling back to the south wall near the bottom of the staircase, Rachel circled the wedding cake. Baked by the finest confectioners in all of England, using Queen Victoria's cake as its inspiration, it stood an impressive six feet tall. Five round tiers, each a different flavor—strawberry, chocolate, vanilla, lemon, and raspberry—were carefully stacked with the largest at the bottom to the smallest.

Master Nathan wanted nothing but the best. This cake ended up like nothing Rachel had ever seen, so it was clear he had gotten his way. Detailed designs with white and cream-colored frosting made it a scrumptious masterpiece. Handmade buttercream lattice and icing flowers of lilies, roses, morning glory flowers and vines, daisies, and leaves, complimented each other perfectly.

For an added touch, Master Nathan also instructed the staff to add over seven pounds of real flowers. His chosen varieties included miniature roses of every color, pansies, forget-me-nots, and miniature daisies from the gardens and greenhouse. The highest layer, a work of art itself, had pillars wrapped in silk to hold up a lifelike gazebo topped with two white, sparkling, sugar-made turtle doves.

The head table, decorated like something out of a palace, had more colorful flower petals generously sprinkled over it to cover the cream-colored, satin tablecloth. Adjacent to the white and gold place settings, exquisite gold cutlery was exhibited instead of silverware. Several rows of smaller floral arrangements in low glass vases sat in the middle of the table so the guests could easily see the wedding party when seated during dinner.

As a backdrop for the head table, cut flowers and greenery had been hung on the staircase wall. Starting high up on the balcony, it dangled perfectly down to the floor. Since each section was only a few inches apart, it looked like a wall of live ivy and flowers, similar to the mansion's exterior.

Clusters of maroon, orange, pink, and yellow flowers mixed with white baby's breath and greenery, which resembled Christmas garland, wrapped down and around the entire length of both the right and left staircase railings, tumbling onto the floor near the bottom steps.

Matching flowers cascading out of tall flowerpots lined the exterior walls of the room on all sides, bringing the splendor of the gardens indoors to satisfy the eye at every turn.

Fixing a flower here and there, Rachel ascended the stairs toward her room to get ready for the ceremony. Although her hair had been done earlier, it was getting late, and she had little time to waste. Taking one last look at the ballroom, satisfied, she grinned, turned around, and ran down the hall.

Once she'd fixed her makeup, her attention then turned to her mother. She wondered how she was holding up. Knowing that Locke Mansion's vastness was new to Lydia and hoping she was not overwhelmed, Rachel planned to spend the rest of the morning with her and made her way to her mother's room.

Enjoying one another's company after a tender embrace, they reminisced over precious memories as they helped each other prepare for the blessed event. When Rachel carefully slipped into her dress, its details and beading appeared fit for a queen, and she marveled at its beauty. She and the staff then helped her mother with her dress, make-up, and hair. As Rachel complimented her mother repeatedly, Lydia blushed, yet she nervously accepted the attention.

While they waited, rather impatiently, they opened one of her mother's windows to absorb the warm sunshine. Rachel and Lydia noticed guests arriving dressed in their finest, making it difficult for them to remain calm. They both looked forward to seeing their friends, family, and church family, as well as meeting some of Master Nathan's factory staff, most of whom had worked for his father for years. Knowing there would also be members of his out-of-town family and friends from long ago, they grew more excited.

The sound of horses' hooves approaching filled the air when the mansion clocks chimed at two o'clock. Fancy coaches lined up in rows down the long carriageway after the drivers and coachmen dropped off their occupants. Even the horses looked their best, adorned with large feathers, flowers, and bells. Several had their manes braided with ribbons and bows for a special touch of style. Rachel and Lydia could not avoid feeling elated and fanned themselves to maintain their composure.

Once the guests were seated the music began to play, and as if it had been planned, the birds loudly chimed in to accompany them.

Master Nathan and Richard took their places beneath the archway on the right side, looking particularly handsome. Their gratitude was evident as they glanced at one another and then back upward toward the mansion with exaggerated smiles.

Richard inhaled deeply and puffed up his chest when he caught his first glimpse of Rachel. She looked stunning. His eyes filled with wonder as she progressed down the aisle with measured steps, a wild-flower bouquet in hand. Her dress was simply darling, flowing to the ground. With a partial up-do and a floral crown upon her head, most of her hair hung down, curly as ever. Smiling at Richard, she took her place across from him as he stood, beaming with pride.

Everyone rose as the music changed to play Master Nathan's favorite song. To his delight, Lydia emerged from the center double doors of the ballroom right on cue. She made the most beautiful bride. As she crossed the terrace, down the steps and along the path leading to the fountain, two young flower girls preceded her, throwing multicolored petals at her feet. Her joy, confidence, poise, and grace were evident as she took each step, arm in arm, with David.

They both looked splendid, but Lydia was a vision of purest elegance. Master Nathan could barely hold still as she made her way to his side. Fidgeting and grinning from ear to ear, he could not take his eyes off her.

Despite falling for Master Nathan within weeks of meeting him, Lydia had said nothing, unsure of his feelings toward her. She had been waiting, praying, and hoping they would someday end up together. And after spending months with him calling on her almost daily, she did not hesitate when he asked for her hand in marriage.

Smiling as she got closer, Lydia wondered what Master Nathan was thinking. He seemed so serious; it was hard for her to tell. She had grown to love him deeply, and her eyes lit up whenever she saw him. This day especially, her blue eyes sparkled in the sunlight, exciting Master Nathan's heart. When he began rocking back and forth on his toes and heels, she understood his stern face was simply due to nerves and gave him a comforting nod. The grin that grew on his face after he let out a long sigh made her feel much relieved.

Seeing Lydia in her dress made not only Master Nathan, but everyone, quite emotional. Its off-white satin had been thoroughly adorned with lace overlay. A fitted bodice, rich with appliques and beadwork, hugged her hourglass figure. The dress's hemline just touched her shoes in the front but spanned out long and wide behind her. Once buttoned into place the high neckline and pearl beading looked almost like a separate necklace. A fresh crown of flowers on her head identical to Rachel's, completed the ensemble. When a few loose curls of her blonde hair blew lightly in the breeze, she smiled up at Master Nathan, making him blush.

Ecstatic, Rachel looked over at Richard's beautiful face, and she could tell he was getting emotional, too, as he clenched his jaw tightly. Watching his strong jaw muscles flex and relax brought back memories of seeing him for the first time. Remembering when she'd first fallen in love with him so many nights ago in her dreams, she grinned with such pride that her eyes squinted nearly shut.

Even though Rachel knew she should be focused on enjoying her mother's wedding to her dear friend Master Nathan, it was difficult. Despite her best efforts, she could not stop her mind from wandering back to her own wedding day to Richard, which had taken place just the Christmas before. Her heart raced as she stood silently, reminiscing about their glorious celebration.

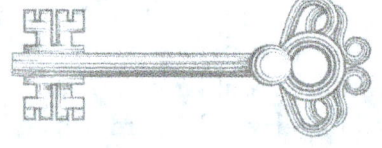

Chapter 21

On the morning of her wedding day, Rachel was roused from her slumber early. Sounds of icy raindrops pelting her windows confused her for a moment. Rolling over, she smiled at the thought of spending another day with Richard. Then her eyes popped open as she sat straight up in bed and gasped.

"Our wedding! It's today!" Rachel had waited several months for Richard to recover from his trauma before they chose a wedding date. It was essential to them both that he be fully confident and ready for the lifelong commitment of marriage. Early that September, once Richard, Master Nathan, Richard's new doctors, and his spiritual counselors all agreed that he was ready, she and Richard decided on having a small but elegant Christmas wedding.

Since Master Nathan loved surprises, he eagerly anticipated the surprise he had concocted about where their ceremony would be held. He enjoyed the opportunity to work with Lydia on the project while creating the most outstanding wedding celebration possible for their children, and he spared no expense.

The day Rachel and Richard had gotten engaged, he'd decided that he wanted to give them extraordinary gifts and knew exactly which would delight them the most. For several months, he managed to keep it a secret and finally revealed that he had rebuilt the chapel just for them. Having turned it into the most magnificent church for miles around, he hoped they would want to have their ceremony there.

Without losing its uniqueness and connection to the surrounding forest, he hired carpenters, masons, decorators, and more, to repair it with great care. They fixed the stone floors and the pillars to make them smooth. He sought out the best artists in England to restore the stained-glass windows and had them cleaned to perfection. The pews, reupholstered perfectly, were now padded and covered with soft, forest-green velvet. And every inch of the chapel had been cleaned spotless.

Other artisans designed a spectacular addition just for Rachel, with a powder room near the steps leading to the chapel, which included a secret side door. This way, the bride and bridesmaids could sneak into the chapel without being seen by the groom or guests. It had been fitted with several mirrors and makeup stations. Each station displayed the most expensive perfumes, makeup, brushes, and items for doing hair. On their wedding day, Master Nathan had filled it, practically everywhere you looked, with white, light green, and cream-colored roses, knowing how much Rachel adored them.

He also remembered that during Rachel's first visit to the chapel, she mentioned how much she loved the massive trees that hung over the damaged and missing roof. So, even though he removed the trees and shrubs growing wild within the chapel walls, he kept the splendor of the trees that grew over the roof alive. Despite it being a bit risky, he had them carefully trimmed and then instructed his builders to make the entire roof out of glass so the canopy could be visible year-round from the inside. Therefore, when evening came, everyone could view the trees by candlelight, accentuated by the moon in the twinkling night sky.

Inside the chapel, several flowerpots were overflowing with bouquets of fresh green cedar, mixed with dried blue thistles, white roses, and lilies he'd grown in the greenhouse to match her dress and crown. The twenty-three candles lit in each of the twelve, eight-foot-tall candelabras Master Nathan ordered from silversmiths in London, exclusively out of the purest silver, had an astounding effect on the room.

As another gift for Rachel and Richard, Master Nathan designed a pair of fourteen-foot-tall candelabras, also constructed from pure silver. They were adorned with life-like flowers of rose gold and real diamonds to resemble crab apple trees in full bloom. Knowing how his two darlings fell in love in the spring, he wanted them to remember how God brought newness of life to their home the spring that Rachel came to them. Master Nathan hoped they would use them in their wing of the mansion after the wedding, wanting the pieces to remain in the family for generations like the glass vases and jewels he'd saved.

To be sure that every detail of the event would work out perfectly, Master Nathan even had Sarah come down from the North house to help because, besides Austin, she was the most organized person he knew. He'd apologized for the way he treated her and gave her a promotion. Rachel was glad that they made amends. Sarah turned out to be most helpful, and her attitude had improved tremendously.

Hoping to combat the nervous flutters, she'd battled in her stomach for weeks, Rachel spent her morning in prayer to better prepare herself for the day. She knew full well how blessed she was to be marrying Richard and rejoiced with each passing moment.

Although she was still not used to getting dolled up to such a degree nor being the center of attention, Lydia and Jeanne ensured she was loved on, well-fed, pampered, and encouraged. Jeanne and Rachel were becoming the best of friends, and Jeanne adored spending time with her and her mother. So, for fun, with the staff's help, they spent hours doing Rachel's hair and makeup to be sure she was lovelier than any bride before her. When they were finished, she never felt more beautiful.

When evening approached, the bride and groom were brought to the chapel at separate times. Guests from the city, as well as guests from the church in town that Richard and Rachel had been attending, began to filter in while a string quartet played. Anticipation was in the air. While everyone filtered to their seats, the chapel's uniqueness astounded all. Master Nathan much enjoyed welcoming each guest individually, so he could listen to their comments as they marveled at the renovations.

In Master Nathan's most expensive carriage, Rachel rode from the mansion to the chapel with her mother and Jeanne seated across from her. She hoped that David might ask for Jeanne's hand in marriage one day so they could be sisters, but she wanted to let God handle their relationship, which had been developing since the day of the baptisms. Having learned the hard way not to interfere with God's plans, she knew that if it was meant to be, God would work it out in His own way and at His own pace.

While heading to the chapel, the girls each wore everyday clothing. Over the top, they wore thick, hooded wool capes that matched Rachel's to keep warm. Their fancy dresses were much too full to fit into the carriage with all three of them. Thankfully, the servants had each of their dresses for the wedding freshly pressed and waiting for them in the powder room. Lydia and Jeanne talked excitedly the entire way, but Rachel remained quiet.

She enjoyed observing the woods, the meadows, and the roads now covered in white snow that sparkled like crystals. And although the air was cold, Rachel stared out the window and pondered the warmth within her heart. Closing her eyes, she could not keep from smiling. Knowing she would soon be able to be alone with Richard as his wife in only a matter of hours, her heart fluttered, and she blushed.

The thought of holding him in her arms as her husband was almost more than she could stand. An expression of pure bliss came over her as she pictured his handsome face. She found herself praying the rest of the way, partly out of thankfulness and somewhat because her nerves seemed to be trying to get the better of her.

Once the carriage made it through the winding woodland roads to the chapel, the servants snuck Rachel and the girls through the side door directly into the powder room as Master Nathan planned. Keeping as quiet as mice, except for their giggles, the girls whispered amongst themselves while they slipped into their dresses. First, Jeanne and Lydia jumped into theirs as quickly as possible before they helped Rachel don hers.

"Oh, my goodness, my dear. You are a vision," Lydia told her once Rachel's dress was fully buttoned up.

She turned to face the looking glass that Master Nathan brought over from her bedroom, knowing how special it was to both her and Richard. Turning right and left, she watched the bottom of her dress swoosh back and forth around her ankles and began to quietly laugh at her reflection. Rachel never knew she could look so fancy.

To her, it was though her life was like a fairy tale that never ended. She smiled, pressed her palms together, rested her mouth on the tips of her fingers and praised God for her life once again.

Thanks to Master Nathan, she felt like a princess. Her dress was the most expensive bridal gown she; Master Nathan, Alfred, and her mother could create. It was made of the finest, pure-white satin. Every square inch of it appeared to be shimmering as she moved. The front had an exquisite, tiny pearl and diamond bead-encrusted design with flowers and ribbons of silk. It exhibited a fitted bodice and a delightful illusion waistline, with an extra full ballgown skirt and an exaggerated train, topped off with layers of tulle. Delicate beadwork and imitation diamond designs around the bottom captured her attention as they gleamed like real jewels.

Some of Rachel's hair was done up into a perfect bun with small braids and tiny white flowers intertwined. Still, most of her curls hung loosely around her waist, the way Richard liked it best. A veil of white tulle would soon lightly cover her face when the time was right.

When her mother put the wreath of white roses, blue thistles, and tiny pink and violet flowers with sprigs of cedar upon her head, Rachel swallowed down her tears. Her crown was just like she and Richard dreamed, and she sat, turning her head side to side to admire it.

She then stood tall as she remembered God's love for her. Feeling more like royalty than ever, she took a deep breath and lifted her chin. Her bouquet, matching her crown perfectly, had more of the same flowers, but extra-long sage greenery mixed in flowed freely downward over two feet.

Aware of how special each flower was to Rachel; Master Nathan had grown hundreds of flowers in the solarium for this day. He'd timed the cutting of each flower while in bloom to be hung upside down and dried to perfection for Richard and Rachel's wedding. Not only did Rachel's headdress of flowers match what she and Richard had dreamt, it represented the crown of Christ and what His beauty meant to her. She had no doubt, the miracle of her wedding to Richard would not have been possible without Him. Besides, she and Richard wanted to invite Jesus into their wedding and marriage as their Lord, Brother, and Friend.

The neckline of Rachel's dress bore gorgeous beadwork, and the arms were covered in detailed lace. It had also been sewn to leave a space in the center of her chest so she could show off Gloria's necklace. The cross hung precisely in the middle of her breastbone to comfort Richard during the wedding. Assuming he would very much be missing his mother and sisters this day, Rachel hoped that, if she wore the cross in Gloria's honor, Richard would feel his mother was somehow a part of their ceremony. She wished she had something from her father as well, but she tried not to think about it, not wanting to get too emotional.

The time was fast approaching for the ceremony to begin. Lovingly, Lydia placed her hand on Rachel's shoulder. "Darling, I have something for you," she said slowly, a graceful smile on her lips. Her hands trembling as she handed Rachel a scroll rolled up and tied with a steel-blue ribbon that matched the tiny flowers in her crown.

"Mother, what is this?" she asked. Lydia nodded to Jeanne to indicate that it was time to give Rachel a moment alone. Jeanne curtsied in reply, kissed Rachel, and quickly snuck out of the room with a grin.

Lydia turned back to her daughter, still shaking terribly, and said in an emotion-laden voice, "Rachel, my dear, this... this is a letter from your father."

Rachel gasped and covered her lips with one hand, in shock.

"Your father wrote this three days before his death. He asked that I save it for you until this very moment on your wedding day so that, in a way, he could be here with you when you needed him most. But he said you should probably wait until after the ceremony to read it so that you would not cry and mess up your makeup. He did not want you walking down the aisle with puffy, red eyes," Lydia explained.

Remembering her husband and his kind ways, Lydia chuckled. She then kissed her daughter on the cheek and shared, "I love you, darling. I am so grateful for you. You are radiant, and I've no doubt Richard will be thrilled. He is indeed a blessed man. I will give you a moment alone so you can decide to read this now or later, and if you need me, I will be right outside your door."

Dazed, Rachel held the scroll tightly, kissed her mother back, hugged her, and whispered, "Thank you so much. I love you, too, Mother."

Lydia embraced her daughter, told her she was proud of her, and gave her a soft smile one last time before leaving the room, shutting the door behind her.

Closing her eyes to think, but only for a second, Rachel sat in the chair placed in front of her looking glass, quickly untied the ribbon, and unrolled the scroll with quaking hands. It was now over four years old, so she handled it with extreme care. She swallowed hard and held her breath as she read:

My dearest Rachel,

I have a feeling you will not wait until after your ceremony to read this letter, and I am smiling now just thinking about you tearing it open without hesitation. Your passion for life and willingness to go after what you want are some of the reasons you have brought such joy to my soul.

God blessed me beyond measure when He chose me to be your father for the years I have had the pleasure of walking this Earth. I am so thankful to have been allowed to watch you grow into the amazing woman of God that you are. You have always been willing to go anywhere, say anything, and do anything the Lord asks. You amazed me as a little girl, and I am in awe of you still.

As I lay here now, knowing that my illness could soon bring me to meet my Savior, I am able to rejoice and praise Him, for He has given me the most startling glimpse into the future. Right now, I am picturing you as a vision of beauty in white on your wedding day. Your bridal gown is flowing, and your hair is stunning, with its curls gently framing your angelic face. The flowers wound into a crown,

placed delicately upon your head, proves your roy-
alty. Your eyes look like sparkling blue jewels as tears
well up while you sit reading this letter before you
take your vows.

If I were there, I would tell you how beautiful
you are in every way a woman can be, inside and
out. I would hold you in my arms to comfort you
and tell you how much I adore you.

By far, the proudest moment of my life was the
day of your birth when I held you in my arms for
the first time, and today, I would be prouder still
to see you as a bride. Although I cannot walk you
down the aisle, know I am with you in spirit, for
love never dies. Rest assured that as you carry this
letter you hold a piece of my heart.

There is no doubt in my mind that you will
make an incredible wife. You will be an encourage-
ment to your husband and a wife who is faithful,
loving, and kind. And one day, when you become a
mother, your children will be greatly blessed to have
someone so wise to guide them. I am deeply sorry
that I will miss meeting my grandchildren, so please
let them know how precious they are to me.

Sweet Rachel, do you remember when we talked
one evening by the light of the fire about how, some-
times, special events in our lives pass by too quickly,
and somehow, later, they become a blur? Well, today,
I will ask God to slow time for you during your wed-
ding so you can enjoy every moment. I am asking
Him that you will easily, with gratitude, recall each
detail of this day forevermore. I promise that I shall
pray for you without ceasing, that the Lord will bless
you richly, beyond what you can think or imagine,
and that He will make all your dreams come true.

I praise God for many things regarding you, but
I praise Him for this most of all: that you will remain

strong and faithful to the Lord in all things, even as you go through trials. Season after season, you have never been afraid to face the winds that blow your way head-on. I can rest in peace, knowing you will walk in the Light throughout your life according to His Word. I have faith that you will change the world according to Isaiah 61:1-11—with His love and His Holy Spirit who lives so evidently within you—because that is who you are.

On this most glorious day, do not lower your head in sorrow when you think of me, but keep your chin up, for I will be smiling down on you from Heaven above. So, please smile up at me in return. That way, as the father of the bride, my joy may be complete.

It is time to forget the past and press on to a bright future. Now, wipe away your tears and weep for me no more. Live your life to the fullest, for life itself is too short and precious, so you simply must. Cherish it as treasure and let it take your breath away as you run the race. Because it's a great day for the race... the human race.

Give my love to your husband, his family, David, and your dearest mother. And finally, my daughter, remember, you will never be alone. Let your entire being be filled with peace, knowing that God, your Heavenly Father, and His Holy Spirit are with you always. Cling to the truth that Jesus promised He would never leave you nor forsake you. Be joyful and walk down the aisle with confidence as you remember who you are, my little warrior princess.

Until we meet again,
Your Father Forever

Rachel's throat felt tight. Barely able to breathe, missing her father desperately, she choked back sobs that wanted to break free. A knock at the door startled her, making her shake as she inhaled, stood, and turned to face the doorway. With her letter in hand, mixed emotions, heart pounding, and tears flowing down her cheeks, she wiped them dry, forced a smile, and said, "Come... come in."

Master Nathan opened the door with excitement. "Rachel! Are you ready to—" He gasped. "You look sensational! I..." Suddenly noticing the sorrow on her face, he stopped talking, rushed to her side, and embraced her. "Oh, oh, dear. I see that you decided to read your father's letter before the ceremony." With his adorable grin, Master Nathan held her back a bit to observe her. "Why am I not surprised? Hmm, my dear?" Pulling a handkerchief out of his jacket pocket, he began to gently dab at her tears as he chuckled. "Oh, no, no, no. This will never do. Let us get you cleaned up, shall we?"

Rachel chuckled a bit, still half crying. "I know, I agree. I'm sorry."

He cocked his head to the side and stared at her with intention. "There is no need to apologize." Hugging her, he said, "Here. I have a surprise for you."

"Another one?"

"Yes. Another one." He reached for her bouquet, which was on the chair next to her.

"What is it? I am not so sure I can take any more surprises today."

"You'll see." Turning the bouquet upside down to inspect the handle, he pulled at the bottom of it, and said, "I made this myself especially for this moment."

The bouquet handle, wrapped in white satin, held a white wooden plug in the bottom of it. Master Nathan was able to pull the plug out to reveal a hollow compartment within the handle's center, below the stems. He showed her that it was empty and acted quite proud of himself because of it.

Rachel frowned, confused. "I don't understand," she shrugged. "It's empty."

Grinning, he said, "Allow me." He reached out his hand to take her father's letter. "Here. Hold this," he said, handing her the bouquet.

With a mysterious glance, he rolled up her father's letter and tied the ribbon back around the outside of it, so it appeared just as it had when her mother handed it to her. "May I?" he asked as he took back her flowers. He carefully held it up and placed her father's letter inside the handle. It fit perfectly. With her father's letter safely tucked away, Master Nathan replaced the plug and handed her bouquet back to her as a big, reassuring smile spread across his face.

Rachel covered first her mouth and then her heart with her hands. Overwhelmed and trembling, she smiled back and exhaled at his kind gesture. Upon realizing just how precious his gift was, a tear rolled down her cheek. "You are so thoughtful and so good to me. My dearest friend, I will love you forever, you know."

"Yes. I know," he stated casually. "I do not blame you. For I *am* Mr. Wonderful after all," he said sarcastically as he dabbed at her tears. "I love you, too. Now, young lady, you must stop crying. Richard is waiting."

She sniffled and shook her head. "Yes. Yes. You are right." Taking in another big breath, she borrowed the handkerchief from him, glanced at herself in the looking glass, and dabbed at the corners of her eyes. "All right, I promise; I am done crying," she said with a soft laugh. Fixing her crown, she smiled at her reflection before she asked him, "Now, how do I look?"

Master Nathan stood behind her and admired her reflection. Crossing his arms and putting one fist under his chin with his index finger covering his lips, he squinted and tilted his head to the right and left, acting as though he needed to think about it for a moment. "Um, well, you look fine."

She turned around and slapped his arm. "Fine? Really?"

"Ouch!" He teased, and then reached into his pocket to pull out a silver box. "Well, something is missing. That's all." Smiling, he handed it to her.

"What is this? she asked.

"Open it, silly."

Inside was a silver bracelet covered with diamonds that matched Gloria's necklace he had given her. "Oh, my! Did this belong to Gloria? It's incredible!"

"No. I designed this just for you. Turn it over and read the inscription."

Rachel already knew she adored it, no matter what was written on it. Placing a light kiss on his cheek, she said softly, "Thank you so much."

"You are welcome," he declared with a slight nod. His eyes then grew wide, and he moved his hands as if to hurry her along, getting impatient. "Now, read it."

Rachel read the back out loud while he watched her reaction. "My dearest friend Rachel, thank you for bringing my precious son, Richard, back to me. I will forever praise God for bringing you into our lives. Even though you drive me crazy, welcome to our family. Yours truly, Mr. Wonderful."

Slowly hitching it onto her wrist and wearing a proud grin, he replied, "I hope you enjoy it, my dear."

Laughing out loud, Rachel shook her head as she noticed the processional music beginning to play outside her door. She hugged Master Nathan, let him loose, and took a few big breaths to regain her composure. "You seriously need to stop giving me things and being so wonderful, or I will never stop crying," she said, trying to make a joke.

"Very well. I'm done," he proclaimed with a raised eyebrow and a sheepish grin, "for now."

"Good," she chuckled.

"One last thing," he said. Using both hands, he reached up over her head and behind her to bring her veil forward, covering her face. Rachel smiled, noticing what great care he took to remove each wrinkle from the sheer cloth as he whispered, "There you are, my dear."

She sighed, thankful for his friendship, and asked, "*Now*, do I look okay?"

He took both her hands, held them out, leaned back to see her better, and replied, "As always, Rachel, you look like an angel." He shook his head in amazement. "But with more poof," he commented, grabbing at her ruffles as she turned away.

"Oh, my goodness. Stop it!" she blurted out as she lovingly slapped his hand.

"Hey! Easy now," he joked as he walked to the door with a chuckle and opened it fully. Speaking with his usual sarcastic attitude to keep the mood light, he put on a stern face, held out his arm, and deepened his voice. "Shall we?"

Rachel, now all smiles, nodded with a new look of confidence. She maneuvered her dress out the door, readying herself to walk down the aisle. Holding her bouquet with her father's letter tucked safely inside, she was happy to walk with her dearest friend. "We shall," she declared, more ready to meet her love than ever.

Once Master Nathan took her arm, placing his other hand over hers, he spoke quietly, while staring straight ahead as though it was not easy for him to say what he was thinking. "Rachel, I am so proud of you. I know how much your father must have wanted to walk down the aisle with you on your wedding day. I am sorry he cannot be here. But I want you to know that it will be my greatest honor to escort you to meet my son today. He is a blessed man indeed."

While they stood around the corner, waiting for her reveal, Rachel looked at Master Nathan and noticed he was now holding back emotions. "Well, Mr. Wonderful, I am proud of you, too. I know special occasions and holidays are never easy for you. If it helps, I like to believe that my father is smiling down on us from Heaven right now. Perhaps if we picture God with the angels, Jesus, your brother, your parents, grandparents, my father, and your beloved family watching us, it might help us both. I am sure they love you dearly and are proud of how far you have come. So, good sir, it is an honor to walk with you as well," she said in a hushed tone as she curtsied to him, trying not to get worked up all over again.

"Agreed. Now, no more words. It is time," he stated, choking back tears, lifting his chin, unable to utter another sentence if he tried.

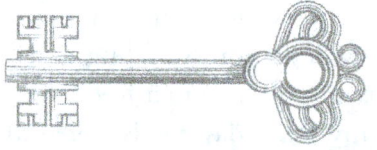

Chapter 22

The procession began with Jeanne as a bridesmaid. She walked down the aisle first while Lydia, Rachel's matron of honor, waited until Jeanne had taken her place at the front of the chapel. Jeanne and Lydia wore their hair in marvelous updos with white pearls and tiny silk roses placed throughout.

Their soft, light steel-blue velvet dresses were identical. Elegant embroidery and delicate beading accented the neckline and rows of beads in a floral design wrapped about their waists. The bodice was so tightly fitted, their feminine figures could not go unnoticed. Both of their full skirts were covered in the front with more extensive beadwork from the waist to the hemline. Long, white satin gloves kept them warm and matched their pearl necklaces, completing their flawless look.

When Master Nathan saw Lydia, it was their first interaction in days, and he froze. Somehow, he missed running into her in her dress thus far, and when their eyes met, there was no doubt he found her enchanting. He bowed toward her and looked dashing when doing so. She curtsied toward him, and her beauty made him blush.

Thinking that the flirtations between them were hysterical, Rachel raised her eyebrows at him. To her, it was adorable to see how the two of them acted toward one another, and she hoped that, someday, they would end up together. She wondered if her mother thought the same thing but didn't ask.

"What?" he whispered as Rachel snickered under her breath at them both.

Trying to look away, he could not hide how impressive Lydia was to him. She, too, blushed in return before walking down the aisle. The curtain then closed behind Lydia right in front of Master Nathan, which made him snap out of it. Rachel chuckled as he pursed his lips, pretending nothing was out of the ordinary.

Since Rachel missed her father dearly, she was glad to have Master Nathan by her side. She closed her eyes tightly to tell her father that she missed him and said a quick prayer, thanking God for the blessing of her friendship with Master Nathan, for the love of her family, and for the joy set before her.

She positioned herself directly behind the curtain and let every thought go, focusing her mind and heart on Richard. But she then began to tremble all over, knowing, at any second, she was going to see him for the first time that day and would soon become his wife.

While waiting for the music to change, out of nowhere, the light and airy sound of wind chimes in the distance comforted her. She recalled her mother's little wind chimes from home, and in a flash, her first dreams of Richard swept through her mind, exciting her.

Time seemed to move in slow motion, and Rachel stood at peace, thinking of how God had orchestrated their relationship before they'd even met. Thankful, she knew the faithful prayers her father stated in his letter were being answered and instantly realized she would be able to enjoy every second of this blessed event.

The soft light from the candles reflected off the stained-glass windows, drawing her gaze upward. She did not expect the newly remodeled chapel to be so magnificent. Seeing Master Nathan's surprise glass ceiling and renovations for the first time, Rachel gasped, making him extra thankful. He could tell she loved the changes he'd made to the chapel as she leaned forward and peered out the windows to glimpse the winter's evening woods. The blue hue surrounding the chapel outside due to the full moon above took her breath away.

As if it were a gift from God, the wet snow that had fallen that morning remained stuck to the branches of the trees above. Yet, heat from the chapel's stone fireplace caused the snow on the glass roof to melt completely, revealing the treetop's white canopy that knitted together overhead. Witnessing the stars twinkling just beyond them, lighting up the night sky, Rachel smiled Master Nathan's way, letting him know she was indeed impressed by it all. He did not look her way, but lifted his chin, and grinned proudly.

The boys' choir began to hum in unison, and David started to play the piano with the string quartet for the bride's grand entrance. Two servants pulled the curtains back gradually, revealing Rachel. The choir then burst into a resounding chorus so everyone would know it was time to stand.

Captivated, each guest gasped at the sight of Rachel in her dress. Hearing several of them whisper their thoughts on how lovely she looked, her face glowed, showing the depth of her joy.

Taking it all in, she slowed her mind to reflect. In her heart, Rachel knew that God had intervened to make this day possible. Astonished by the healing touch He so generously bestowed upon Richard, she honestly believed that, after so many years of torment and pain, his entire life was now going to be vastly different.

The sound of heavenly music echoed through the chapel, mesmerizing and warming the soul, as she and Master Nathan strode arm in arm, toward the front. When Rachel saw Richard desperately trying not to cry, she held back tears of her own, her breath catching in her throat. Master Nathan, knowing her so well, noticed and squeezed her arm a bit tighter to comfort her, which did help.

Fidgeting with his lapel briefly, Richard still appeared a little nervous. However, he stood strong and tall, just the way he'd done in her dreams, handsome beyond compare, like a prince. Rachel remembered the day in the garden when she taught him that, since he was a child of the King, he was indeed royalty. Yet, never had he appeared more regal than today: his wedding day.

When Rachel and Richard's gaze met, they both lit up, and their mutual love was evident. Never had either of them looked so happy as smiles spread wide across their faces.

Richard's chest lifted, and Rachel felt that he was praising God for his new life and his soon-to-be wife. His eyes welled, and Rachel caught a glimpse of the flecks of green and gold within them that she first witnessed in her dreams. *Oh, how darling this man is. I am astounded I will be able to call him my husband. God, you are so good to me.*

Excitement flooded Richard's heart as he looked into Rachel's blue eyes that glistened with the light of the candles. *I cannot believe I get to marry her.* Thankful to know the truth at last, Richard had grown to enjoy talking with Rachel about when Jesus would reunite with His Church, bride, and children, including Richard's own family.

Through his many Bible studies with her, he picked out a favorite verse that declared when Jesus returned for His people, it would resemble a wedding. Just thinking about the significance of what that meant, he had been looking forward to their wedding for months.

Once David finished playing, he rose to stand beside Master Nathan. Rachel and Richard's pastor, George, who'd counseled them for many months alongside David, greeted the guests.

"Dearly beloved, we are gathered here today to join this man with this woman. Who gives this woman to be with this man?"

David stepped forward and boldly declared, "Her mother and I." And then he stepped back into place beside Master Nathan, who was Richard's best man. Although some thought it strange that Rachel and Richard had chosen their parents to be their best man and matron of honor, they both felt that no one deserved the positions more.

Pastor George, with his head held high and in a loud voice, requested, "Let us pray. Dear heavenly Father, You are the giver of life and the worker of miracles. When Richard and his family had all but given up hope, You made a way where there was no way, and You brought Yourself, through Rachel, into Richard's world. Through Your grace, Richard not only recovered fully from his trauma and pain, but he is now more joyful and alive than ever. We are thankful for the many changes You have brought forth in this family and praise You for Your grace and commitment to them. We feel Your presence here and know that You are walking as one with these two as they two become one. From this day forth, may their adoration for You and one another shine brightly as a beacon of hope to all who feel hopeless. For Richard and Rachel are living proof that You can turn any situation around. We praise you, that through the power of prayer and patience, You can bring beauty from ashes. May their love endure, as Yours does for us, without limits, for all time. In Jesus' mighty name, amen."

The chapel was filled with a resounding "amen." Then, a few surprises for Rachel began. Months ago, Master Nathan retrieved the silver plate Richard's grandmother had commissioned for his wedding to Gloria and showed it to Rachel. He had secretly polished it back to its original, shiny state, so his children could use it to take communion during their ceremony on this joyous day. Rachel noticed and looked at Master Nathan with immense gratitude, making him grin.

As they partook of the bread and wine in remembrance of their Lord, she appeared dumbfounded. At Richard's request, a talented young man began skillfully playing the trumpet from the balcony at the back of the chapel. This was Richard's way to prove to himself, as well as Rachel and his father, that he had been completely set free from the events of the past.

The sound of the trumpet and what it represented was awe-inspiring as it echoed throughout the chapel. It bounced off the high glass ceiling and stained-glass windows and seemed to profoundly impact everyone. In each pew, attendees pulled out handkerchiefs and dabbed their eyes, overwhelmed by the moment's significance.

Knowing that Richard was truly okay upon hearing a trumpet play, Rachel and Master Nathan both tried not to cry, but they were so proud of him that it was nearly impossible not to.

Richard gave Rachel his handkerchief with a tender smile, and a nod of encouragement. She beamed back at him as if to say, "Thank you," and he winked to let her know everything was going to be all right.

The pastor then announced to all the vital importance of their marriage vows. "Richard and Rachel, as you stand here today before God and these witnesses, I would like to remind you of the serious nature of the relationship into which you are about to enter. Marriage is the voluntary and full commitment for a lifetime of two consenting adults to honor and love one another, above all, under

God. Do you both promise to be loyal and to stand firm in your defense of each other's hopes and dreams?"

Rachel bit her lip to hold back her enthusiasm after she and Richard looked at each other and answered simultaneously, "We do."

"You may now read aloud the vows you have prepared together," the pastor said, turning to Rachel.

Smiling sweetly up at Richard, she took in a long, calming breath. Having memorized her vows, she looked into his eyes and spoke to him directly.

"My dearest Richard, my father always taught me that there are two kinds of people in this world: there are givers, and there are takers. He encouraged me to be a giver and to choose wisely to whom I entrust my heart. He always hoped that, someday, I would be blessed enough to marry a giver like you."

She swallowed and continued, "I praise God that on this day, not only are my *father's* hopes for me coming true, but also, by marrying you, my dreams for myself are coming true. For only in my dreams did such an incredible man exist until I met you. I believe that your Christlike heart overflows with kindness and compassion and I adore you for it."

Although Richard seemed pleased, he began to shake. Yet, Rachel did not stop, "You are creative and wise beyond your years. You give your time, your heart, and your love so freely. You have shown great strength and courage through situations where the Devil tried to ruin you. You learned the truth about who you really are, rose above, stood strong, and overcame despite all odds. I could not have more respect for a man nor more love."

Feeling his nerves, she tried not to forget what she wanted to say, "I look forward to the time I get to spend with you, no matter how long or short that time may be. I promise to live each moment with you as if it were my last, for we both know that life is too short and so very precious. I promise never to take your love for granted and to tell you daily how much you mean to me."

To keep her voice from cracking with emotion, she raised it, speaking her favorite part of the vows, "My mother has always taught me that, in this troubled world, it takes great strength to be kind."

She flashed him a sweet smile. "Thank you for being so strong. I promise to love, honor, and cherish you always, and I will praise God all the days of my life for the gift of you."

Like ice cream on a summer's day, Richard's heart softened while he listened to his darling speak, astonished that she was going to be his forever. He put his shoulders back to boldly return the compliments she had just given with his own carefully memorized vows. His eyes twinkled, piercing into her soul, and she shivered with delight as he spoke with a powerful voice.

"Rachel, only in my dreams did I know a woman like you existed. For so long, I'd let go the dream of finding love and peace or having a normal life. Thankfully, my father never stopped praying for me. When we both had all but given up hope, the Lord blessed us tremendously when you came into our home. I honestly believe God Himself came to me through you to give me true love, renewed peace, inexpressible joy, and a new life."

As Rachel blushed, he went on, "My lady, you truly are the walking example of how to be His hands and feet. You sat with me in my brokenness and never judged me nor gave up on me. You came like a bright light into my dark world. Through you, God brought me much-needed healing as you faithfully read the Bible—His love letter—to me. You made it clear that Jesus' death on the cross did not reveal my sin nor shame but my value and worth to Him. You showed me that God bankrupted Heaven at the cross for my salvation."

Seeing tears now streaming down Rachel's face, one at a time, Richard did his best to stay focused, "You restored my faith when you shared that God reached down from His heavenly throne to rescue me so that I could be united with Him forever. Not because I deserved it but because of who He is. He is love. And from His willingness to surrender all for me and your willingness to share that truth, I am a changed man. In my loneliness, I lost my ability to see my way out of a most desperate situation, but still, you believed. You reestablished meaning in my life when you showed me that God had plans and a purpose for me. You taught me that He longs for me to prosper and be of good health. When I was afraid, you were the example of courage. Now, the good Lord has given me a spirit of boldness, not of fear. Perfect love casts out all fear, and His love for me is perfect, as is yours."

Inhaling, he ended his vows similar to Rachel's, "Rachel, each time I look at you, I see the Father's love shining brightly through your eyes—Love like no other, that is real, true, and precious. Thank you for being ever tender, kind, and wonderful. I promise to seek God first always as I lead our family. I promise to never put anyone or anything else before you besides Him. I vow to adore, honor, and cherish you always, and promise that I, too, will praise God daily for the gift of you."

Rachel's heart was so moved, she was unable to stop her tears as he poured out his devotion to her like sweet wine. He reached up and wiped one away with his finger reminding her of the kindness her father used to show her. She sighed with gratitude, thankful to be marrying someone so dear.

The pastor turned to Master Nathan and asked, "Do you have the rings?"

Master Nathan, smiling wide as he admired his darlings, acknowledged the pastor quickly. "Oh, yes," he said as he pulled them from his pocket and handed them to the pastor.

"Let us pray," Pastor George said, lowering his head.

Everyone bowed their heads and closed their eyes. Yet Richard, excited, could not help but sneak a peek at his bride and rocked back and forth on his toes.

Pastor George's loud voice echoed off the chapel walls, "Dear Lord, we ask for Your loving kindness upon Richard and Rachel. We ask that You bless these rings and anoint them with Your grace as a token of their vows one to another. In Jesus' name, amen."

"Amen," all agreed in unison.

To everyone's surprise, Master Nathan stepped to the side. He picked up his violin as Lydia made her way to the piano. When they began to play, Rachel smiled at Richard and readied herself to sing. She had written a special song just for him. He froze with an astonished look, stunned by her hauntingly beautiful voice and song.

"They say that love never dies.
Now, look into my eyes,
and know, for me, this is true:
I will ever love you.

Grow old, my sweet love, along with me,
as our joy is yet to be.
And I know, whatever fate may decree,
you will faithfully stand by me.

With all that I have, until the day I die,
I shall heed my soul's cry.
With all that I say and do, I shall ever adore you,
my beloved, through and through.

As the vine wraps 'round the stone,
I am grateful for how close we've grown.
You are the love of my life,
and I shall ever be proud to be your wife.

I gladly vow, before all,
to give you my heart until my life shall fall.
In my dreams, God revealed you to me.
And now, joined as one with you, I am finally free.

With all that I have until the day I die,
I shall heed my soul's cry.
With all that I say and do,
I shall ever adore you, my beloved, through and through.

So now, before the Father and the Son,
we two best friends, we join as one.
And the song has just begun.
The song has just begun."

Having no idea Rachel would surprise him with such a special gift, Richard swallowed back the lump building in his throat and squeezed her hands tight to thank her. She simply grinned with humility. Although there was not a dry eye in the chapel, Lydia and Master Nathan acted as though it was nothing and casually stepped back into place.

The pastor turned to Richard. "Richard, as you place this ring upon Rachel's finger, repeat after me," he said, handing Richard Rachel's ring. Richard repeated word-for-word the vows as instructed.

Rachel's face lit up when he stared at her looking exhilarated, showing no signs of hesitation. "My sweet bride, before God and these witnesses, I, Richard, take you, Rachel, to be my lawfully wedded wife. Please accept this ring as a token of my vow to love, honor, and cherish you to the best of my ability, forevermore."

The ring fit perfectly and matched the engagement ring that Richard gave her. It was extraordinary and detailed, with filigree and diamonds galore. Having kept it hidden for months, she was just now seeing it for the first time. He placed her engagement ring on after it, and the set together was magnificent. Her eyes beamed over their beauty and her smile showed she adored the pair. Rachel started trembling once more, just like she did during her first dreams of him, but she was thankful when her shaking stopped as quickly as it began.

The pastor handed Richard's ring to Rachel and asked her to repeat after him. "My beloved groom, before God and these witnesses, I, Rachel, take you, Richard, to be my lawfully wedded husband. Please accept this ring as a token of my vow to love, honor, and cherish you to the best of my ability, forevermore."

As she placed the ring on his finger, he was glowing and exhaled an exaggerated sigh of relief, causing Rachel to giggle quietly. It was evident they were overjoyed as they played with one another's hands.

The pastor boldly announced, "By the power of God vested in me, I now pronounce you husband and wife." He turned to Richard with a slight bow. "Richard, you may kiss your bride."

Richard stepped forward, and an emotional look took over his face, showing how much this moment meant to him. He lovingly lifted her veil, positioning it carefully behind her head. He took Rachel firmly into his arms and looked deep into her eyes. Ignoring the rest of the world, they kissed passionately, for they had not embraced each other since the day of Richard's *awakening*.

Master Nathan was the first to cheer, but he was immediately joined by the bridal party and congregation, but their cheers were a bit reserved since they had not yet stopped kissing.

"May I now introduce you to ..." The pastor waited for them to stop and laughed aloud as they turned to face the crowd. "...Mr. and Mrs. Richard Jonne Locke!"

The entire chapel then erupted with cries of delight as each instrument and voice in the room lifted with joyous song and applause.

Rachel and Richard, now smiling wide, grabbed hands, and marched out together—no longer two but one—heading out to the powder room, where they were joined by Master Nathan, Lydia, David, Jeanne, and Austin for a round of hugs and congratulations. Love was in the air, and their excitement was at its highest, but there was no time to waste. Putting on their overcoat and cape, the joyful couple slipped out the side door and rushed off.

Before Richard helped Rachel into their carriage, they both noticed Master Nathan must have asked the staff to decorate it to the nines. It was covered in white, light green, and blue, dried roses, mixed with white bows and ribbons, which blew in the wind as they left for the mansion. Their family and friends, waving and throwing rice their way, quickly followed along behind in carriages of their own to join them for a magnificent Christmas-themed reception.

Inside the carriage, Rachel and Richard kissed, laughed out loud, and fully embraced one another several times. Briefly discussing how lovely the chapel and ceremony were, showing tremendous gratitude, Rachel was surprised when Richard began to cry.

Deeply worried, she placed her hand on his leg and asked with a concerned tone and squinted eyebrows, "My love? What is it?"

Richard sniffled, then chuckled, and replied with a mix of smiles and tears. "I," he paused and swallowed hard. "I-I just had forgotten what it was like to feel so happy."

Relieved, Rachel shook her head and sighed. But now, she too was crying tears of joy, and placed one hand on her chest. "No one in the world deserves happiness more than you, my sweet. I love you so."

He nodded, took her hand, and kissed it firmly, saying, "During our wedding, when I vowed, I will forever praise God for the gift of you; never have truer words been spoken. I will love and cherish you forever." He inhaled sharply before wiping his wet cheeks.

The rest of the trip, they shared their strong feelings for one another and openly praised the Lord for bringing them together. Also, deeply grateful for all their parents had done to make their day special, they looked forward to what lay ahead.

For weeks on end, prior to their wedding, Master Nathan, Lydia, and Austin, would not allow Rachel and Richard anywhere near the ballroom, planning yet another surprise for them. Knowing their parents were up to something, they suspected the decorations would be grandiose and grew antsy with anticipation.

More importantly, they were glad Master Nathan had decided to decorate the house at all. Since the accident, he had not allowed a single decoration or Christmas tree to be put up, saying, holidays brought back too many memories he was trying hard to forget. In fact, he had forbidden embellishments in any room, no matter the holiday. This year, however, feeling healed, to show his excitement for his darlings and express his new zest for life, he went all out. Weeks before the wedding, he instructed the staff to get busy decorating every room in the house, each in a different color scheme. Everywhere you looked, there were tastefully crafted pine boughs, ribbons, dried flowers, berries, twisted twigs, and more. Yet, the ballroom was his primary focus. He'd searched far and wide to find the tallest, fullest, and most beautiful Christmas trees in all the land. Once they'd been delivered, he had them installed on the outside edges of the ballroom's interior walls precisely every twelve feet. This way they sat in between each set of double doors just in front of the mirrors and directly across from one another on the opposite side of the room. These hunter-green, live, massive trees stood erect, topping off at least twenty-feet-tall, and were safely contained within four-foot high and wide, round pots. He planned to have these trees carefully planted in the gardens after spring thaw to create what he wanted to call his R & R garden. This new garden would be just for Rachel and Richard to enjoy resting in, when so inclined. Regarding the trees, the biggest surprise of all, was the fact that he had pre-ordered some of the very first strings of Christmas lights to ever be sold. Edward Johnson, a friend of Thomas Edison's, was responsible for this innovative design. He had created them with Christmas trees in mind a few years prior, but 1890 was the first year they had become available for purchase. Naturally, Master Nathan bought thousands upon thousands of these glorious lights, months in advance, just for this festive occasion. Tree after tree was decorated with a mixture of blue bows, small fans made from blue satin cloth with white lace, silver balls, white ribbons, glass crystals, dried white baby's breath, blue silk flowers, and hundreds of white lights. Even though he loved his chandeliers, he only had a few of them lit in the room, to be sure the tiny Christmas lights on the trees would reflect like fireflies off the mirrors and windows to provide the most captivating ambiance.

The round cake table, placed in front of the staircase, held a delicious looking, circular, three-foot-tall, layered, white cake with sprigs of pine and sage sitting on top of a shimmery silver tablecloth. This cake, covered in sparkling edible diamonds, had lovingly been surrounded by a wreath of brown, twisted wisteria vines, fresh baby's breath, and thick white and light-green, silk rose blossoms. Treats of all colors fully covered two rectangular tables, one on each side of the cake. The cake itself looked lovely, yet up high, just behind it, Christmas garland made from pine boughs with long needles, wrapped its way around and down the staircase railings from top to bottom, landing on the floor in swirls. Blue bows, and dried white flowers, had been woven into the garland, but the addition of more white lights and blue ribbons intertwined within the pine, made the staircase railings exceptionally pleasing to the eye.

From outside, when walking across the terrace to reach the ballroom's entrance through the center double doors, one would encounter several tall pear trees. They had been placed to make a path that curved to and fro along the terrace underneath an enchanting archway. Each leafless tree had been fully decorated in white ribbons and snowflakes made from crystals that blew lightly in the cool breeze, sounding like tiny wind chimes. Stepping just inside, each guest marveled at the ballroom's beauty. Never had anyone seen anything like it, and Master Nathan, similar to the reactions from the chapel renovations, loved receiving unlimited amounts of praise.

While waiting for the bride and groom, sounds of joyful chatter over the stringed quartet tickled the ears. Due to the visually stunning trimmings blending with scents of sweet forest pine, excitement filled the air. The crowd stood behind their seats and hushed to a dull murmur when Rachel and Richard finally arrived.

As they were announced, all were honored to witness the bride and grooms' reaction to the whole affair upon their grand entrance. Rachel almost shouted with glee. Instead, a wave of shock enveloped her due to the glorious sights and sounds of the room, rendering her speechless. Holding back tears, she covered her mouth with the back of her fingers to hide her nervous laughter and placed her hand over her heart while the crowd cheered with delight. Squeezing Richard's arm with her other hand, she curtsied slowly toward Lydia and Master Nathan (who were all smiles) to show her appreciation for their hard work. Dumbfounded, she observed the trees and white lights, and thought, *Oh my! How incredible. This is amazing. Thank you, God. You are so good to me.* Glancing up at Richard, she could tell that he, too, was awestruck. Kissing her lightly on the cheek, he looked into her eyes filled with wonder, and said in his deep tone, "Welcome home, my lady." Escorting Rachel to her seat at the head table on the north wall, she nodded and smiled gracefully toward each guest that bowed her way as though she were a princess. When she found her seat, she admired her table setting and ran her fingers over the pale blue satin cloth. The shiny, white china, and silverware, set on top of a circular, white placemat braided from quarter-inch thick cotton, attracted her eye. These place settings were meticulously encircled by a low wreath of tiny royal blue, white, and pale blue dried flowers. Above the dishes, white candles, and several clear glasses in a variety of sizes made from the finest crystal, glistened in the light. In the center of every plate, she noticed stark white napkins had been folded into the shape of swans, making her chuckle. Looking about the room, she observed that the center of the guest tables included amazingly tall floral arrangement, held within the glass, etched vases. Around each vase sat large baskets. Woven from vines, overflowing with pine, cedar, blue thistles, dried white roses, and tall, white, curly sticks, they resembled the flowers in her crown. Inside these baskets were encouraging messages and Bible verses for friends and family to take home, written with great care by Master Nathan himself. He and Lydia had rolled them up and tied them with blue ribbons so they would resemble the letter Rachel had received from her father.

Wiping a tear from her eye, she placed her bouquet on the table in front of her and acknowledged the crowd once more with a curtsy. She kissed Richard after he pulled out a seat for her and thanked him for making her feel like royalty. Although she sat low in her seat; her spirits were higher than ever.

Once the formal introductions were finished and the guests were seated in the ballroom, Master Nathan raised his glass for a toast. With gratitude, he announced, "Before we begin this evening's festivities, I would like to thank you all for coming. I could not be more pleased with the wife my son has chosen, and I would very much like to be the first to congratulate them publicly. There will be many more toasts made throughout this evening, but first, I would like to give them one more gift."

Master Nathan, turning to face the newlyweds said, "Rachel and Richard, I know that this is not something you expected, but in your name, I have purchased and recently reconstructed a large building outfitted to be an orphanage for you to own and care for as a way for our family to give back to the community. It sits on over fifty acres, and I have had it fully furnished with nothing but the best bed-ding. We have installed indoor plumbing, electricity, a playground, a library with mountains of books, a school room, a crafting room filled with supplies, a theatre, an outdoor swimming pool, horses, a barn, and many horseback riding trails for the children to enjoy. I know it is your heart's greatest desire to serve those in need, and so you shall." He raised his glass. "To Rachel and Richard and the Locke Orphanage Project. May your marriage and life be as fantastic as you are. May the Lord give unto you sweetly, without holding back, just as you give of yourselves to all you meet."

The room erupted with glee as Rachel's jaw dropped, and she covered her mouth, squeezing her cheeks with her fingertips. She looked at Richard, who was also in shock; his eyes lit up with amazement. Rachel then jumped up and ran over to Master Nathan with Richard following close behind, to properly thank his father for his kind gesture.

"This is unbelievable. What a special gift. Thank you so much!" They blurted out many thanks simultaneously, unable to contain their enthusiasm.

Master Nathan explained that he heard them talking about wanting to start an orphanage together. After he'd overheard them discussing hiring as many widows as possible to help with the children, to give them a sense of belonging and pride, he just knew he had to intervene. Having learned that many widows in town felt alone and needed income desperately, he could not help himself.

Shortly after that, he visited town to meet some of these widows. He said, these delightful women each shared that they enjoyed children immensely and told him how much they missed their families. One widow affected him greatly and solidified his decision the instant she spoke. He could see that she was on her deathbed. When she shared that her only regret in life was that she had never taken the time to visit an orphanage to read stories to the children, it broke his heart. That day, he purchased the building and surrounding lands to give the orphaned children the room to play and explore the outdoors. He knew that eventually, he would be on his deathbed, too, and he wanted no regrets.

Rachel previously taught Richard the importance of serving others to help the mind and soul heal, and she hoped being charitable in this way would be restorative for him. She was delighted to think of working with her dearest to make their orphanage the best place in the world for needy children and hugged Master Nathan and Richard once more.

In an instant, after Master Nathan gave another elaborate and heart-warming toast, he put his hand in the air, snapped his fingers, and the music and festivities began.

During their first dance as husband and wife, Richard and Rachel appeared enraptured while gazing into one another's eyes. They held each other tightly for the rest of the night, vowing never to let go. The love they shared made Rachel extremely thankful for her father's answered prayers that she be richly blessed. She acknowledged Richard was a blessing to her beyond what she could have hoped for or imagined.

She remembered how Richard floated across the floor in her dream like a ghost, and even though at the time it seemed strange, now it made perfect sense as they floated around the ballroom.

Still reminiscing, Rachel was sure that she would cherish the precious memories of their wedding for an entire lifetime. Much relieved that he was happy for them, she treasured Master Nathan's prideful expressions and his many gifts, especially her bouquet. She would forever adore her father's surprise letter and her endearing family standing by her side.

Smiling, Rachel recalled the mesmerizing music, the glorious candlelit chapel canopied by its glistening, snow-covered trees, and the elaborate celebration afterward at the mansion with a marvelous dinner and dancing that lasted long into the night.

Her favorite part was the confidence, love, and light she witnessed in Richard's eyes compared to how he used to be. *He was lost, and now he is found. He was dead, and now he lives. Truly lives.*

Thankful that her dreams about Richard had not been just random dreams but a prophecy given directly to her by the Lord, she recalled how he'd smelled like Christmas in her first dreams about him. Since they married at Christmas time, she marveled at God's ability to reveal the future for His beloved children through prophecy, even while they slept.

When a crisp fall breeze blew across her face, she smiled, and inhaled deeply. Pastor Aaron's loud preaching made Rachel jump to attention, bringing her back from her trip down memory lane. He had mentored Rachel's father and was a dear friend of Lydia's, also counseling Lydia and Master Nathan for months leading up to now. Although he was quite advanced in age, he was one of the loudest preachers Rachel ever heard. Despite that, she revered the advice their family had gained from him over the years. His words of wisdom and Bible teachings helped them tremendously through their grief.

Chapter 23

Letting out a sigh, feeling honored as she stood by her mother, Rachel put her hand on her stomach. Elated to be witnessing the two people she loved dearly getting married, she smiled for a different reason altogether. She and Richard were now expecting Master Nathan and Lydia's first grandchild, due to arrive in the spring. They were greatly anticipating hearing the pitter-patter of little feet again. She was pleased to see them both at peace, cheery, and so in love, knowing how much they'd suffered, but was even more thrilled to bring them a new bundle of joy.

Rachel jumped again, but this time, it was not the pastor's voice that startled her. She flashed a big grin in Richard's direction when she felt the baby kick inside her belly for the first time, not once, not twice, but three times. Because she was standing up in front of the guests and it was the middle of the ceremony, she tried to contain herself, but it was not easy.

With each passing moment, the baby seemed to grow more active. It reminded her of the story in the Bible of John, who leaped excitedly inside his mother's womb when Mary, carrying baby Jesus at the time, entered the room. Rachel was overjoyed and swallowed back her emotions. Thinking about all the gifts God had given them after so many years of trial, Rachel wondered if the baby was excited, too.

As her mother's matron of honor, Rachel wore a satin, sage green dress that hung just off her shoulders. The skirt's cream lace and ruffles flowing down toward the hem made her worry that she might look extremely pregnant, but her empire waistline covered her belly nicely, and she looked adorable. A crown of lavender, white baby's breath, and miniature sunflowers adorned her head. She was positively glowing and looked lovelier than ever.

Richard wore a dapper black dress coat with long tails to match his father, as his best man. Both incredibly charming, everyone noticed that they appeared to be on cloud nine as they stood next to one another, grinning from ear to ear.

It was emotional for all in attendance to watch Rachel and Richard be at their parents' wedding. The story of their lives, their loss, and all they had overcome was no longer a secret. Those who attended church in town started praying for the family well over a year ago once they learned the truth about the trials that had taken place within the walls of Locke Mansion. It meant a great deal to Rachel and her family for everyone who had been praying for them to be a part of their special day.

Since Master Nathan and Richard's baptisms, the day after their engagement, their church grew to be like family to them. Some in high society snubbed them for mixing classes, but they were unaffected and paid no attention to the gossip. One thing that Rachel learned from Master Nathan during her interview was that what others thought of her was none of her business. The Lockes ignored others' opinions of them, and they were much happier for it.

Rachel noticed that the entire staff was dressed in their best and paused their work to witness the special occasion. Even Miss Sarah made her way back down from the North house; per Master Nathan's request. She had moved up North permanently, but He did not want anyone he knew to miss the joyful day.

Jeanne stood as a bridesmaid beside Rachel in a gown that matched hers. She had been such a help to them throughout the many months of Richard's recovery, and everyone adored her for it.

David proudly walked his mother down the aisle and stood next to Richard. His smile showed that he was not only glad for his mother, but the glances he flashed Jeanne's way made it clear that he had fallen in love with everything about her. He was thankful she was being treated like family, and he hoped to muster up the courage to ask for her hand in marriage soon.

Austin read a few lines from the Bible first. But then, per Lydia's request, David had prepared a scripture to share during the ceremony. He stood nervously, praying that he would not fumble over his words. Richard nodded in David's direction to calm him. They had grown close and did their best to support each other when needed. David was teaching Richard how to hunt and fish, and Richard was teaching him about engineering. Early each morning, they enjoyed fishing together, for Richard had learned to love the great outdoors even more than in the days of his youth. He said being in the woods made him feel alive and free, and he had become noticeably more vibrant with every passing day.

Thankfully, Austin held it together when he quoted the scripture from Song of Songs that Master Nathan had never heard until the Lord spoke to his heart in his drunken stupor the day he and Richard were reunited. "Set me as a seal upon your heart, as a seal upon your arm; for love is as strong as death, jealousy as demanding as the grave. Many waters cannot quench this love." Soon after he spoke, Austin appeared choked up when, to everyone's surprise, Richard sat down to play the cello with Rachel accompanying him on the piano.

While communion was served, they performed a piece they had composed, a special gift to their parents. It was an impressive duet about their story, filled with scripture and poetry. The way their voices blended was riveting. The beauty and deep love of God the lyrics expressed were especially touching. After the ceremony, several guests complimented them. Some even said they felt the love of the Lord flowing in the winds and throughout the gardens as they sang.

With heightened emotion, most in attendance shed a tear when it came time for Master Nathan and Lydia to say their vows. Having personally written them, just as Richard and Rachel had done, their sincerity was unmistakable. Lydia went first as Master Nathan flashed his irresistible grin her way, making it difficult for her to concentrate.

"My dearest Nathan, the first moment I met you, I knew God was working a miracle in our family. I had nearly lost hope when a severe illness almost took me from this earth. But then, God brought you into our lives in the nick of time. Without you, I would not be standing here on this glorious fall day."

She smiled and continued, "When you took a chance on my daughter and hired her, God saved me through you. Your help not only brought me back to life, but you brought me happiness. I never dreamed that I could ever love again. I never imagined that I could meet someone so kind, wise, compassionate, fun, and wonderful as you. You have brought much-needed laughter back into our lives after our loss. I am deeply grateful for who you are. I pray that I will be as much of a gift to you as you are to me each day, and I will forever praise God for giving you to me."

Rachel realized she forgot her handkerchief and needed to dry her tears. Not wanting to wipe her wet fingers off onto her dress, she started panicking. Thankfully, Richard noticed her rapid breathing and discreetly snuck his handkerchief to her so no one would see. *He is such a gentleman*, she thought as she wiped her tears, feeling the baby kick once more.

Master Nathan choked up but, of course, pretended he was fine so he could begin the vows he had written for Lydia. His tempting, chocolate gaze stared into her baby blues. They sparkled in the sunlight, distracting him. He jumped to attention when he realized he had been silent for too long. All eyes fell upon him, waiting for him to speak. Even the birds and winds seemed to hush and listen in.

Clearing his throat, he took a deep breath and held it for a bit as though trying to cherish every drop of the moment. He then began his vows, speaking slowly and directly to his bride, almost too quiet for the crowd to hear, but he did not care.

"Lydia, I, too, had all but given up hope in my life. But the kind of love that only comes from Heaven above, that you sweetly instilled into your daughter, met me just when I needed it most. You and her father taught her how to love God so strongly that she was able to teach me about God's true character. Now, I know how He loved me and wanted to help my beloved son, Richard, whether I believed in His ability to do so or not. I praise God that He took pity upon me when He brought Rachel, David, and you into our lives. After many years of grief and loneliness, I never expected to love or be happy again. I have learned that God's ways are not our ways, that His timing is not our timing, and that He loves me for who I am, proving that He truly has a sense of humor."

Everyone chuckled, yet he continued. "But more importantly, I now know that He genuinely cares about me and is filled with mercy, or He would have never given you to me. You, Lydia—the most elegant, caring, patient, graceful, and precious gift you are—astound me. I know I do not deserve you, but I promise to forever cherish every second with you. And I will praise God each day for giving you to me," he finished.

All in attendance could tell Master Nathan desperately wanted to kiss Lydia right then as he moved his lips close to hers. Once he realized he was supposed to wait for the pastor to direct the timing, he quickly backed away to wait for the right moment. Making a comical face of regret, he looked at Aaron, embarrassed. "Sorry," he whispered, while laughter rippled throughout the seated area.

As they exchanged rings, Lydia and Master Nathan, both grinning, took their time, passing flirtatious glances back and forth while the anticipation mounted. Immediately following the exchanging of rings, their family and some of their closest staff and friends stood and gathered around them to lay hands on them and bless their marriage. Lydia could not help but feel grateful and nodded at each one after they were done. Master Nathan's friend, Lauren—who played the viola—and Lydia's dear friend, Gordon—who played the hammered dulcimer—accompanied by two women from church, Linda and Nancy, on the violin, played an airy song during the prayer. It was a spirit-filled moment to remember.

David then read Lydia's favorite scripture as those who had prayed returned to their seats. "1 Corinthians 13: 4-8: 'Love is patient, love is kind. It does not envy, it does not boast, it is not proud. It does not dishonor others, it is not self-seeking, it is not easily angered, it keeps no record of wrongs. Love does not delight in evil but rejoices with the truth. It always protects, always trusts, always hopes for the best, always perseveres. Love never fails'"

The ceremony ended with the pastor praying loudly, "Dear heavenly Father, today, You are joining together two people who would have never met if it were not for Your divine hand. As family and friends, we are grateful to be witnessing this truly blessed event here today, which, I must say, seems to be happening a lot in this home of late."

He paused, letting the guests express their amusement, then said, "We are thankful to be a part of it and are amazed by Your favor. We feel the warmth of Your love shining upon these two families that have joined as one. We declare Your heavenly blessings upon Lydia and Nathan on this joyous day and for many years to come. We praise You for the gift of life, peace that passes all understanding, and true love. In Jesus' mighty name, amen."

Raising his head and voice even more, he declared, "By the power of God vested in me, I now pronounce you husband and wife." He acknowledged Master Nathan with a slight bow. "*Now*, you may kiss the bride."

Master Nathan took Lydia in his arms and surprised her, as well as everyone else. Dipping her backwards and extremely low, she needed to hold onto her crown since he kept her down in a "dipped" position, kissing her for longer than anyone expected. Finally, bringing her up while the guests clapped with glee, he gave her a look that showed he hoped she knew what she was getting herself into, making her laugh.

Standing as husband and wife, with big smiles, they turned to face the cheering crowd. In an instant, the winds swirled, and leaves seemed to dance around them both as if God wanted to show His approval and hug the happy couple Himself. Master Nathan did not even seem surprised and simply watched the leaves rise into the sky, like he knew just what God was saying. He smiled and bowed to his bride before they joined arms. "Are you ready, Mrs. Locke?"

Just then, Rachel's other surprise which she'd kept from Master Nathan, delighted all. From the back of the aisle, bagpipes began to play. Lydia smiled back at her new husband and his eyes lit up, before they ran off, hand-in-hand, toward the mansion. Due to their excitement, they hurried up the path, across the terrace and into the ballroom like children at play. Austin accompanied Rachel, Richard, David, and Jeanne as they all followed along behind.

The family made their way up the ballroom's grand staircase, out of the hall, and into the receiving room for privacy. Austin then closed the balcony's double doors at the top of the stairs leading to the hall and turned around. Although he said little, it was evident that he, like Rachel, was thankful for the changes that had taken place within Locke Mansion. An unusually big grin planted itself firmly on his face, as he stood at attention facing the ballroom with his back to the double doors. His expression made his heart appear full and his lifted chin made him look proud to be of assistance to the family he held so dear.

He observed from the balcony while the guests entered, and Miss Sarah helped organize the staff. The servants assisted everyone with finding their tables so that Austin could re-open the doors at the right time for the wedding party's grand entrance down the stairs to the ballroom.

The orchestra resumed playing to entertain the guests, who slowly moved from their seats on the lawn, onto the terrace and into the ballroom for dinner and dancing. Those who had never set foot inside Locke Mansion were awestruck.

Upstairs, the wedding party waited for Austin to direct them. Talking excitedly, they marveled at the extravagantly decorated room. The many vases of flowers and hundreds of gifts for the new couple looked amazing.

Packages of every shape and size, covered in brightly colored wrapping and large bows arrived all week and were set up on display. This way, everyone could come up to view them at some point during the reception at their leisure, as it was customary for guests to admire one another's gifts.

Enjoying a few moments of hugs and merriment, the wedding party stepped out into the hall to talk, giving their parents some time alone in the room. Closing the door, Richard first snuck a peek at his father, who was kissing his new bride, and he grinned, pleased to see his father in love and full of joy.

Once the door was shut, Richard turned and grinned upward toward God in approval of all He had done. *Thank you, God.* Unexpectedly, a feeling washed over him that his mother was happy for his father. Whether it was his imagination or not, it brought Richard great comfort to think of her that way.

"Wasn't that simply wonderful?" Rachel asked with enthusiasm, kissing Richard firmly on the lips.

"It was indeed!" he replied. "How I love to see my father acting like himself again."

"Oh, I agree!" Rachel said as they discussed the beauty of the ceremony. "But more importantly, my dearest Richard, I love to see *you* back to the joyful, loving man that God created you to be. I'm amazed by you each day and am overwhelmed to think we are now married and having our first child. Thank you, my love. Thank you for who you are. I pray our child acts just like you. For if they inherit only a tenth of your heart, they will be incredible in every way," she said, choking up.

"And if they act anything like you—oh my—the two of you would certainly keep me on my toes," he joked, making Rachel laugh. He then proceeded to shower her with compliments as they lovingly embraced and encouraged one another.

Holding her face gently, he softened her heart with his glance when their eyes locked, "Rachel, I hope you know that it was because of your sweet love, my yearning for life has returned. I would have been lost in an endless sea of pain for eternity without you, but now I praise God that even hints of sorrow elude me. I can honestly say that nothing but joy fills my heart each time I hear your voice or touch you. And if I ever start to feel low, all I have to do is think about you, and everything changes. You, our child, and God, are my life now, and I could not be more pleased. So, no, thank *you*, my lady." Bowing low, he kissed her tummy as she placed her other hand on her heart.

After a while, Master Nathan and Lydia opened the doors to the gift room and returned to their wedding party in the hall to prepare themselves to enter the ballroom as Mr. and Mrs. Locke. It was then that the family enjoyed showering the cheery couple with praise and proper congratulations.

Richard hugged his father tightly. "Congratulations, you handsome groom, you." He chuckled.

"Why, thank you, best man," Master Nathan replied with a serious tone, acting quite silly before he hugged Richard back. They joked around a bit and proudly patted one another on the back.

Turning to Lydia, Richard stated, "You are lovely, and I am overjoyed for you both…" he bowed and kissed Lydia's hand respectfully. "…Mrs. Locke."

"Thank you, Richard," she replied sweetly with a curtsy.

They continued talking amongst themselves to give Rachel and Master Nathan a moment alone.

Rachel glanced at Master Nathan and shook her head. "Look at you. A groom. Smiling. Handsome and wonderful as ever."

He chuckled but did not reply.

"What's so funny?" Rachel asked with furrowed eyebrows.

"Oh, nothing. I was just pondering something," he said with a sly grin.

"Oh? Do I dare ask what?"

"I was thinking, 'I am now a husband.' I feel like a normal father once more, and soon, I will be a grandfather. A grandfather! I am simply astounded," he blurted out enthusiastically, shaking his head.

Continuing in jest, he put his ear to her belly to listen to the baby for a moment, then spoke loudly, "Hello, baby! You know, I cannot wait to meet you, young man." Laughing aloud, he stood tall, acting unusually stern, although she knew better, and then he looked up to the side, feigning innocence.

Rachel asked him with a chuckle, "And how do you know it's a boy, may I ask?"

"Oh, I don't know. I just think so, but you know I will be happy either way. Especially if you have at least seven more children after this one. In fact, I would like to put my order in now, if I may? I request eight grandchildren: four boys and four girls, please. And if you could have two of the boys be a set of twins, that would be splendid," he said with one raised eyebrow.

"I see. Is that all?" she questioned with a chuckle, shaking her head.

Changing the subject, he said, "Rachel, you have been calling me 'Master Nathan' for far too long. It's better than 'sir,' but I no longer want you to call me that."

Austin interrupted and informed them that the guests were ready and the doors were about to open, so they quickly took their places to walk down the grand ballroom steps. David and Jeanne stood arm in arm first in line, with Rachel and Richard to follow and be seated in advance of the bride and groom's introduction.

"What am I supposed to call you then?" Rachel asked, taking her place in line and whispering back to Master Nathan, now standing directly behind her.

The doors flung open wide, revealing David and Jeanne to a room full of people. As they were introduced and headed down the stairs, Master Nathan leaned forward, making sure no one could see him as he whispered into Rachel's ear, "How about..." He wiggled his eyebrows. "... 'Dad'?"

Taken aback, she laughed out loud, and Master Nathan stepped back, pleased with himself. He loved teasing Rachel and knew his timing had been impeccable.

But she learned early on how to hold her own and give it right back to him, so in front of everyone, she shot back, "Or how about, 'Gramps'?" Lifting her chin, she put on a poised air as she and Richard waited to hear their names.

Taking his bride's arm, Master Nathan snickered at Rachel's comment, amused by her wit. Lydia just shook her head, smiling at the two of them.

When Austin announced them, Rachel was astonished by the fullness of the room. "May I introduce Mr. and Mrs. Richard Jonne Locke." As they headed down the stairs, the crowd erupted in applause.

Making her way with Richard, step by step, toward the ballroom's floor, Rachel smiled at the thought of calling Master Nathan "Gramps." She sure did love him, though, and thought, *Well, why not call him 'Gramps'?* For a moment, she thought back to their time spent together. *Oh, my goodness. I am glad we never kissed. That would have made our relationship awkward for life. Phew!* She chuckled, and shifted her focus back to Richard while they continued down the last steps.

Remembering how he had captivated her soul, months ago in this very ballroom by the light of the moon, she glanced his way. Enthralled by how majestic he looked, Rachel appraised him thoroughly.

Reaching her seat, she faced the crowd. Richard kissed her hand and bowed to her. "I look forward to having a dance with you this evening, my lady."

"Just one?" she asked, with a smirk.

"Oh, no, no. I will take as many dances with the most beautiful woman in the room as I can get," he stated enthusiastically.

"Indeed, my love," she replied with a curtsy, as he kissed her hand once more. He gave her a wink and moved to his seat beside David.

Austin announced loudly for everyone to stand, and after the room settled, he spoke in a formal and bold tone, "It is now my greatest pleasure to introduce to you, for the first time ever, Master Nathan Harrison Locke and Mrs. Lydia Gabrielle Dawn Locke!"

The guests clapped and cheered louder as Master Nathan and Lydia slowly descended the steps. They were as elegant and handsome as a couple could ever be.

Weeks in advance, Master Nathan had made it clear to the orchestra that it was important to him they dance as husband and wife prior to being seated. So, to everyone's delight, Master Nathan and Lydia walked right past their seats and directly to the center of the ballroom.

He bowed low, kissed Lydia's hand, and sweetly asked her, "May I have this dance, Mrs. Locke?"

When the orchestra began to play just the way he had requested, he lifted his chin and stepped into position to receive his new wife.

Lydia blushed and curtsied to her new husband. "Of course, Mr. Locke. It would be my pleasure."

The lights dimmed, and the guests sat to admire the lovely couple's grace as they began to move about the room. From that moment on, everyone could feel the spirit of light and joy fill the atmosphere.

Chapter 24

Once the delightful meal and drinks were served and many dances had taken place, Austin instructed the orchestra's conductor to stop the music. Richard tapped his fork firmly against his glass to get everyone's attention for his toast. Rachel put her palm over her heart, thrilled that he was now confident enough to speak in front of such a large and attentive crowd without showing any signs of fear.

"May I have your attention, please?" Richard said as his voice, deep and robust, lifted above the noise whirling throughout the room. It did not take long before the guests grew silent, and all eyes turned to him. He stood tall to address them, "I would like to sincerely thank you for coming. We appreciate your presence with us here today. And now, I would like to give a toast to the bride and groom."

He turned to Master Nathan and Lydia with glass in hand. "Mrs. Locke, I want you to know there are two reasons I am thankful to God for you: One, you gave birth to my lovely bride—which, by the way, we would like to announce tonight, that we…" he paused for effect. "We are expecting our first baby soon!" The crowd erupted with applause. "Thank you. Thank you," he said, bowing twice before he turned back to Lydia.

"Mrs. Locke, your daughter, Rachel, is the most caring, compassionate, and godly woman I know, which reveals a great deal about your character. She changed me by teaching me lessons you and her father instilled within her since she was a child. You should be proud of how you raised her." Richard nodded toward Lydia.

"Rachel has taught me that no matter how deep the pit of our failures or despair, God's loving arms are always long enough to reach down and retrieve us."

He glanced in Rachel's direction. "Through the lessons you have taught your children, I now know the vital importance of renewing the mind. I have learned to keep my mind steadfast on the truth of His undying love as opposed to following my feelings. There is a vast difference between a true believer and someone who merely lives by how they feel, tossed to and fro by circumstances. Feelings will rise and fall like the waves of the sea, but now, no matter what circumstances may come, Jesus will be the solid Rock on which I stand."

Looking back at Lydia, he went on, "You are a shining example of a Christlike mother and woman of God, and it is a privilege to call you family."

Lydia started to tear up but simply sat, poised as ever.

"Reason number two I am so thankful for you is this: I am delighted that you have been able to put the spark back into my father's eyes, bring joy into our home and love into his heart. He is my inspiration, the bravest man I know, and my truest friend. And yes, he jests constantly; however, we all know it is due to how sensitive and caring he is deep down."

With a sheepish grin, Master Nathan seemed embarrassed and lowered his gaze to the floor. He glanced up again with just his eyes as Richard said, "I could not be more thankful. He has been an amazing father. He was patient with me and faithfully prayed for me during many long and difficult years. And well, I am better, so clearly, it worked."

The crowd whispered amongst themselves, wearing friendly smiles, as Richard finished his toast. "Jesus never glorifies the storms in our lives, but He will bless us *through* them. My father has been an encouragement to me each day through the storms of my own life, and I will never forget his love and support for me. May the good Lord now bless you both richly. May you find comfort and lasting happiness in one another's arms as you discover the pleasure of growing closer together. And may you find peace in the Father's arms as He holds you both unto Himself."

Raising his glass, Richard boldly stated, "Let us all toast to two of the most remarkable people I know."

The guests raised glasses of their own and waited as Richard said, "To Mr. and Mrs. Nathan Harrison Locke! Cheers!"

The ringing of goblets commenced, and everyone drank enthusiastically before the sound of chatter permeated the room.

After several minutes, Master Nathan stood. He banged his fork on his glass. "May *I* now have your attention, please?"

The room grew only somewhat quiet.

"Shh, shh, shh," he said, getting the guests to hush after a bit of coaxing. "If you would indulge me, I, too, would like to make a toast. Three toasts to three people, to be exact, so don't touch glasses yet," he announced with a wink toward the crowd before he began. "Well, it doesn't happen very often, but it seems as though I have been proven wrong," he joked with a bow.

Those who knew him well chuckled before he became serious. "Which just goes to show God truly can work miracles and turn any life around." Smiling her way he said, "My darling Lydia, you have brought me more love and joy than I ever thought possible. But more importantly, you have brought back meaning into my life. I look forward to growing old with you while we enjoy getting to know one another more in the years to come. Thank you for putting up with my foolishness and wild ways. Thank you for being such a sweet and strong woman of God and for loving me more than I deserve." He bowed low toward her, then stood tall. "To Lydia, my endearing bride. I love you dearly, and I will do my best to prove it to you every day of my life.

"I would also like to toast Richard. I wholeheartedly agree with Rachel. He is truly the most Christlike, caring, sensitive, and charitable man I know. In fact, he is so incredible that I hope to be just like him someday when I grow up."

The guests chuckled as he turned toward his son and proceeded. "Richard, you will never know how deeply thankful I am that the Lord brought you back to me. I love you beyond words, and I am so proud of you. Rachel always says that you are such a giver, and she is right. In getting to know you as my new brother in Christ, you have helped me to see how deeply God loves me. To think that God let His only Son die in my stead, well, it is a good thing I am not God, for I know I could have never sacrificed such a treasure. To my beautiful son, Richard, I will praise God for who you are, every moment, for the rest of my life." Master Nathan bowed and flashed an affectionate grin Richard's way.

"And finally, to Mrs. Rachel Elizabeth Locke. She took months to plan and prepare this entire event for us, and she has done a 'fine' job, I must say," he teased.

She rolled her eyes at him for using the word "fine," but he continued, "Rachel has not only given me and Lydia an enchanting wedding; she has given me back my life by bringing me back to a right relationship with God and my son. She worked with him daily, praying with him and *for* him. When I saw no way out, she lived out Hebrews 11:1 and showed awe-inspiring faith to believe in things hoped for and unseen. She proved to me that God truly does bring beauty from ashes."

Cocking his head to the side, he said, "She has taught us the importance of obeying the Word that says to rejoice always, pray without ceasing, and give thanks. For years, I doubted God's love and ability to forgive me. Yet now, I can honestly say that I have a renewed sense of purpose in my life. And if He can put someone like me on the road to recovery, He can help anybody."

Rounds of laughter and applause broke out before Master Nathan finished, so he raised his voice, "Through Lydia, Rachel, and Richard, I have learned that faith does not ignore the trial nor the tragedy or simply say to *think positive*, but it knows that, despite the things we face, God's heart is always *for us*. You see, faith is profound, for it acknowledges His desire to turn our situation around for our good and for His glory, no matter how grim things might appear."

His smile was genuine as he said, "From now on, in our family, when we have a problem, we will look at it through the eyes of faith instead of giving fear a voice. We will renew our minds until the impossible seems logical. We will give thanks for everything as we trust in the One who gave us everything to begin with. We will dance on disappointment and learn to overcome the most difficult of days by dancing with God, even in the rain."

Suddenly distracted, he lifted his hand and said, "And can I just add that I am so looking forward to Rachel and my son's new baby," he bowed, "coming soon to a mansion near you." Turing toward Richard and then to Rachel, he said, "If it's a boy, I hope they name him Nathan!"

Everyone chuckled as he flashed an infectious smile around the room, picked up his glass of water from the table, and cleared his throat. "To get serious now, earlier this evening, I joked with Rachel that I wanted her to call me 'dad,' yet trust me, I have missed both of my daughters terribly..." He turned back toward Rachel with a slight bow, "But it truly is an honor, Rachel, to call you my daughter. And Lydia, what a joy to be able to call you my wife." With tears in his eyes, he raised his glass and shouted, "To Rachel, Richard, and my beloved new bride, Lydia! Cheers!"

Most of the room, in unison, replied with a "Here, here," touched their glasses together and drank once more. Then merriment and the clinking of silverware resumed.

Holding back her emotions over Master Nathan's kind words, Rachel inhaled. Deep down, even though she understood he could never replace her father, she was incredibly thankful for their friendship and the ability to call someone like him "dad." She thought about how he acted wild at times, but she knew that was, by far, her favorite part of his character.

Several couples took to the dance floor as the Locke family gathered around. Master Nathan showed everyone his affection, but he hugged Rachel last. She shot him a sideways glance. "Fine? Really? I did a 'fine' job?"

"What? Oh, come now. You know I was only trying to get under your skin, silly," he said in a playful tone.

Her mother hugged her next. "Ignore him, darling. Of course, we are both immeasurably grateful and could not be more delighted with all your hard work. Every detail of this wedding has been exceptional. We are very pleased, and so appreciate you. In fact, we have one last gift for you this evening."

Rachel lowered her chin and peered upward with her eyes as though admonishing them, "Another one? You two really must stop."

"We saved the best for last," Lydia whispered.

As the guests danced nearby, Master Nathan nodded to Austin, who was standing against the wall holding a neatly wrapped box. He made his way through the moving crowd toward Rachel and bowed before her. With Austin and her family sharing secretive glances, Rachel's curiosity grew.

After Austin handed the box to her, she thanked him and kissed his cheek, making him blush. "This, my dear, is a gift, not from your family nor me, but directly from God. Yet, I shall take the kiss, nonetheless," he said, bowing low and giving her a bashful smile.

As David and Jeanne joined Rachel, she opened the gift quickly.

"Be careful, my dear," Lydia stated.

"But hurry!" Master Nathan spoke up, acting impatient, moving in for a closer look.

She glanced up suspiciously. Opening the box, it revealed a Bible, worn and tattered.

"Remember this?" Master Nathan asked, with a bright twinkle in his eyes. "It's the Bible from the chapel that you read to me the first time I took you there."

"Oh, how splendid!" Rachel exclaimed with glee.

Lydia turned and touched Rachel's forearm to grab her attention. "No, my dear, you do not understand."

"What is it?" Rachel inquired tentatively.

Speaking slowly, Lydia explained, "Sweetheart, this Bible belonged to your father."

Flabbergasted and confused, Rachel's eyebrows narrowed, and she fumbled her words, "What? I do... I do not understand."

Reaching between Lydia and Rachel, Master Nathan leaned forward and opened the front cover. "I put this Bible back into the pulpit before I left the chapel that day. But when we started construction on the chapel's roof to rebuild it, I inspected the Bible more closely and found this. Here: read the inscription."

As Rachel covered her mouth with one hand, she read the most heartwarming letter from Lydia to her father that revealed him as the book's original owner. Seeing Rachel's shock, Richard stepped behind her and put his arms around her in case she grew faint. Instead, speechless, she hugged the Bible to her chest, and leaned against her mother for support.

Lydia explained further, "This Bible was my gift to your father. I gave it to him as an anniversary present a few weeks before he preached at the chapel one Sunday as a guest. That day, after service, he'd forgotten it inside the pulpit but planned to get it the following weekend. That week, when he heard Master Nathan locked up the chapel and bought it to tear it down, he was devastated because he could not retrieve it. But upon praying about it, the Lord told him the importance of leaving it exactly where he'd left it. Being the man of faith that he was, he obeyed."

This story brought Rachel to tears, yet she was more astounded than sad. They *all* were. Knowing how God had intervened in their lives so far in advance, she and the entire Locke family were deeply touched. They knew they would eternally be affected by His grace. She held her father's Bible tight then hugged each family member, one at a time, thanking them for saving it for her.

"Rachel, we are all blessed more than we could ever have dreamed or imagined. But I am blessed beyond measure to have you for a daughter. I love you, sweetie. Thank you for everything. You have sown into all of our lives. Returning your father's Bible to you is the least we could do," Lydia said softly.

Still so glad to have her mother in her life after how sick she'd been, Rachel squeezed her in return, hugging her tightly.

Master Nathan agreed with Lydia, "She's right. You have done an outstanding job, but not just with the wedding. With the Lord's help, you have saved both our families. And we will always be grateful." Beaming, he put his hand on her shoulder as they bantered back and forth.

Trying to lighten the mood, Rachel slapped the side of his arm. "You'd better be!"

"Ouch! Hey! That time, it actually hurt!" Master Nathan said, acting as though he was in pain, rubbing his arm where she'd slapped him.

"It did? Really?" Rachel asked excitedly.

"Ah. No. No, it didn't," he teased, making a funny face.

Richard shook his head and chuckled as he turned and bowed to Lydia. "May I have this dance, Mrs. Locke?"

Lydia curtsied and acted honored as she and Richard headed out to the middle of the ballroom floor.

Master Nathan bowed low to Rachel, "Shall we?" With a sideways nod toward the dancing guests, he asked her to join him for a waltz as he had many times in the past.

"I would love to, Gramps," she said, quickly raising one eyebrow.

"Oh. Hmm. Well…" he cleared his throat, "I am not a grandfather yet." He gave her a grimacing face as though he was feeling rather stiff. "Getting old is not for the faint of heart, you know? And I do believe I will need some time to process that title, my dear."

"That's fine," Rachel stated facetiously.

Master Nathan chuckled with satisfaction, knowing his sarcasm was rubbing off on her.

"Here, David, I trust you will take good care of this," Rachel said, carefully handing her father's Bible to her brother.

"I shall indeed, sister," he said with confidence.

"And here. I trust you will take good care of this, too," Master Nathan said, giving David the key to the chapel. "As you know, the church folks in town have needed a bigger building since I closed the chapel doors. I have recently been informed that Pastor George is retiring and that the church leaders have already vetted and commissioned you to be their new preacher. Well, my good man, if you want it, I am sure you will be perfect for the job. So, the chapel is yours now."

Rachel and Jeanne both gasped, amazed by Master Nathan's elaborate gesture. David was speechless but attempted to remain dignified as he took the key. He bowed and stood with tears in his eyes, holding the key close to his heart and smiling wide. "Good sir. I shall take care of the chapel as if I had built it with my own two hands. You can count on me."

After a firm handshake, Master Nathan grabbed David's arm and gave him a trusting glance. "I know you will."

David and Jeanne then hugged Master Nathan and Rachel again before heading off to dance, their eyes bright with hope.

Smirking in Rachel's direction, Master Nathan reached for her hand as she laughed, not at him but with him, thankful for his generosity toward her brother.

He grinned, knowing just what she was thinking and stated, "You're welcome."

She shook her head, amused by the fact he seemed to still be able to read her mind, but before she knew it, he pulled her onto the dance floor, and they were off together twirling around in a rush. Richard and Lydia, David and Jeanne, and many guests passed by them in a blur as they danced around the ballroom in unison.

To Rachel's surprise, even Austin and Miss Sarah joined in the fun. She was glad to see, for the first time, that Sarah appeared to be cheerful.

Master Nathan then gave Rachel an affirming bow and said, "I shall love you always, my friend."

Rachel replied sarcastically, "I know, Gramps." She grinned, but then curtsied respectfully and expressed in a genuine tone, "And I shall love you always, too, my friend." After a sweet embrace, Master Nathan winked at Richard and passed Rachel off to his son before rejoining Lydia.

To envision a more pleasant evening was unfathomable. The dancing continued to the accompaniment of the orchestra for hours. Everyone ate a marvelous meal and delectable desserts that never seemed to end. They enjoyed a great deal of cake, walked in the gardens, swung on the swing, and danced even more on the terrace underneath the glorious lights Rachel had installed.

The delightful weather the Lord provided ended up picture-perfect. There was not a soul that wanted the celebration to end, for, in a way, the splendor of the reception at Locke Mansion was like a little slice of Heaven on Earth.

Sounds of amusement swirled in the air as several guests, who were planning to spend the night, had a little too much to drink. But as for Master Nathan, he had not consumed a drop since the day of his baptism. Rachel's prayers for him about overcoming addiction had been answered and everyone praised God, because they knew it was truly a miracle when Master Nathan never craved it again.

While Master Nathan danced with his new bride, moments of his life flashed across his memory: when Rachel arrived and taught him truths he so desperately needed to hear, when Richard miraculously came back to him, when he met Rachel's family, the day before he had gotten baptized, and today, his wedding day with Lydia. And there was no doubt in his mind that each of these events had wholly changed him.

Despite his newfound joy, he could not help but miss his family. He would never forget his wife and daughters, but he knew Lydia would not want him to. They would be a part of him forever, just as her husband, Christopher James, would always remain an important part of her. Master Nathan understood that her husband, as well as the grief she endured after losing him, shaped her into the strong woman she had become. He treasured Lydia for keeping her husband's memory alive. And he adored the fact that she wanted him to do the same for his family, knowing that, for each of them, it was the healthy thing to do.

Watching his beautiful son Richard, who led the celebration long into the night, was like observing yet another miracle unfold as he energetically interacted with each guest. Since Master Nathan and Richard had grown closer than ever, being able to witness every glimpse of shyness, sorrow, and confusion vanish from his son's life meant a great deal.

For ten painful years, his son's soul's cry was to be set free from the bondage of shame, and now, by the grace of God, he was free, indeed. Having learned that the key to unlocking joy in this life lies in seeking the beauty of God like treasure, Richard's incredible spirit and shining light had returned. Now, all that remained was the outstanding, kindhearted, and fun-loving man, his son was born to be.

Glancing around at the jolly faces in the ballroom, Master Nathan realized just how right Rachel had been. Her lessons about trusting in God to work all things out for our good, turned out to be true.

Upon recalling the many nights, he had spent at Locke Mansion alone and in despair, he inhaled and soaked up the buzz of happiness that swirled around him. He felt confident that the satisfied smile he now wore, due to feeling forgiven and free, was there to stay.

Rachel, staring into Richard's eyes, was lost in his embrace. Grinning happily, she sighed while entertaining a mix of emotions. Unsure if she was feeling the exhilaration of God's favor, immense gratitude, or pure love, she cherished each one. Astounded that the Lord had chosen to bless her beyond what she ever expected, she was exceedingly grateful.

She'd always believed God was generous in pouring out blessings, but she never imagined so many in one season. Overflowing with joy, she whirled to the music. Dancing with her sweet Richard, knowing his precious child was nestled safely inside her, she was reminded of her first dance with him in this very spot.

To her delight, he spoke. The powerful vibrations of his deep voice moved her heart as he smiled down at her, his eyes flashing flecks of green and gold. "Rachel, thank you for not giving up on me and for pursuing me like God does His beloved children. With each passing moment, the depth of my affection for you grows deeper still. I shall love you, always, my lady."

Her face flushed red upon remembering the day of his *awakening* in the tower and when he'd first called her, my lady. Inhaling his sweet sent, Rachel responded kindly, "And you, dear husband, will never know how much I love you. Although, I promise daily to express how I adore you, I know there are no words, even for me."

Resting her head on his chest that he had lifted high when she shared her feelings towards him, she thought, *Glory be to God*. In an instant, the vision the Lord had given Rachel that evening long ago, of the ballroom filled with dancing wedding guests, came to pass right before her eyes. The same dress-skirts, pantsuits, and shoes while they stepped to the rhythm of the music, as well as the decorations, and colors she had seen, flashed before her eyes. But this time it was real!

Praising her heavenly Father for it all, she joked with God: *Now it appears You are simply showing off, but I would not have it any other way.* She looked up and noticed Richard closing his eyes out of pure enjoyment. Lifting her gaze further toward her favorite chandelier, feeling closer to God than ever before, she thanked Him with a wink and a smile.

The merriment that could be felt, seen, and heard at Locke Mansion on this festive occasion was unmistakable. Lifelong wishes had come true, and many prayers had been answered. Since Rachel's arrival, breakthroughs and transformations had taken place within each life, and the miracles of love, meaning, and connection, were abundant at every turn.

The biggest miracle of all, however, was that just over a year and a half before this grand day, the Lockes had not yet even met. They each were grieving in their own way and seemed lost in despair. Now, due to God's grace, people of vastly different backgrounds and upbringings were able to dance the night away as a happy family, proving how our Heavenly Father loves to surprise His children and radically change their lives, often when least expected.

Throughout the evening, there was endless talk of the upcoming addition to their home. Rachel's winsome smile while rubbing her tummy, further warmed Richard, and her entire family's hearts. They excitedly discussed how they planned to change the world together by being good stewards of the favor the Lord had bestowed upon them.

As a result of Rachel and Richard's orphanage project and the children they planned to adopt, they hoped to help many. Through Richard's inventions, their families mills and factories, along with their investments overseas, they were excited to share their many financial blessings. They knew that sharing and serving those in need was sure to bring tremendous reward, trusting in the truth that it is always better to give than to receive.

Circling the dance floor as if in a dream, their hearts swelled with bliss, and they looked forward to spending the rest of their days enjoying the gift of life together. Although things hadn't been easy, the Locke family had learned that, despite great trials, one can still triumph. For even when our situation seems hopeless, in *His* timing, with Christ, all things are possible.

Thank you for purchasing this book from Lia Jaye!

Please sign up to periodically receive:

Free eBooks

Updates

New Releases

Bonus Chapters

& Announcements on Giveaways, Book Signings,

Or Speaking Engagements

At: liajayebooks@gmail.com

And visit our website at: liajayebooks.com

Acknowledgements

Even though this book is dedicated to my parents, George, and Gloria, I would like to acknowledge the many people listed below, who in one way or another, have also blessed me with their example of how to live life to the fullest, with meaning. Your presence, love, wisdom and never give up attitude you show the world, is priceless.

First, to God, the Father, His Son Jesus Christ, and the Holy Spirit for saving a wretch like me. I once was so lost, but You found me just in the nick of time. Without You, who knows what would have happened to this rebellious preacher's kid. I thank you with all that I am and will forever be grateful.

To my husband, David, my real-life Mr. Wonderful. You have supported me, encouraged me, brought unlimited joy into my life, and taken care of me through the worst of times. As I stated in my wedding vows to you over thirty-three years ago, I will forever praise God for giving you to me. You truly are a gift and the best husband, father, and Bumpa, in the entire world. Thank you for loving me, just as I am. I don't deserve you. I love you beyond words, even for a writer. Yours forever.

To my sons, Alex and Aaron. You are my inspiration for this book. As a mother who has seen the brink of death too many times, when all I could think of was you, it brings me comfort to know this book, alongside God's Word, will be here for you as needed. Thank you for loving me despite my flaws, for loving each other well, and for following Him. Your laughter is infectious. Your courage gives me strength. Your heart makes me want to be a better person when I grow up one day. Your handsome faces, and beautiful eyes, melt my soul. You have been my greatest joy and make me proud every day.

I miss you terribly when we are apart but am so thankful to see you living your dreams. I will like, love, and cherish you always.

To Laura and Hayley. Thank you for loving my sons so well. The beauty of your selfless hearts, your kindness, and dedication to the Lord as women of God, brings a smile to my face. May you find Jesus in my son's and your children's eyes with each glance. I love you for who you are. Thank you from the bottom of my heart.

To Lori P., Gabrielle P., Gloria P., Jonne T., Hayley D., Cheryl A., Laura B., Gisella F., Carole E., Faith D., Ladonna D., Joyce H., Sidney W., Loralai R., Linda T., and my many other beta-readers and editors. I cannot thank you enough. Your work to pick apart and edit this book has helped shape it into the love letter to humanity that it is today. Your insight, encouragement and corrections were priceless to me. May you be richly blessed beyond measure for your work and time selflessly helping me in my weakness. I will forever be grateful for your advice and feedback. Reading this book before it was cut down was a grand undertaking and I applaud you for it. You were a huge help. Thank you so much for your dedication. ...Lori, you rock!

To the many preachers, teachers, musicians, authors, thought leaders, clients, influencers, and all-around amazing humans that have helped shape and mold me over the years through your advice, sermons, lessons, selfless random acts of kindness and more. Although you may not all be perfect or agree with each other, and although some might not agree with your lessons or lifestyle, your life-long dedication to sharing your story, advice, humor, kindness, or the Gospel itself- is legendary. I could write a list a mile long, but you know who you are. Thank you!

To Olivia H., for being my model for Rachel. Your sweet spirit is ingrained into her character. May God bless you always.

To my friends, Brenda B., and Maribeth P., and all the moms and dads out there who have lost a child. I wrote this book with you on my mind. To all the children, young and old, who have lost parents, you are not alone, and you are not an orphan. The Father is always with you. To the friends, siblings, cousins, nieces, nephews, Aunties and Uncles, who no longer have their best friends by their side, you will forever be in my thoughts and prayers.

To Gold Star families, active and retired military, and veteran's, you mean the world to me, and I will forever be grateful for your service. I can sleep at night because of your sacrifice.

To my readers. When I write about how important and deeply loved you are, I mean every word. I hope to meet you one day.

Finally, to Jack and any future grandkids. I love you to the moon. You are such a gift and a constant reminder of the goodness of God. Thank you for making me laugh with your humor and for melting my heart with your adorable face and sweet voice. May your life be filled with adventure and wonder always. I will love you forever and ever. Mimi.

About the Author

Dedicated to the Lord since the age of eighteen, Lia Jaye strives to be His hands and feet by sharing His love with a world in need. Committed to serving her family, friends, church, clients, and readers, she is a constant source of light and encouragement. Her ability to overcome many obstacles in this life, with a "never quit" attitude, has made her the strong woman of faith she is today. Although still learning, she has been as an example for us all on how to triumph despite trial.

Lia is an empathetic public speaker, researcher, nutritionist, personal trainer, corporate wellness coordinator, a coach in health, detox, weight loss, and life, as well as a specialist in corrective exercise and behavioral change. Her expertise in the field of wellness has allowed her to help improve countless lives over the last 30 years and her books are an inspiration.

For more information about the author, to inquire about hiring her for speaking engagements, to learn more about the Unlocked series, or to follow us on social media, please visit: liajayebooks.com

For details about the various charities and foundations Lia Jaye and her team will be donating a percentage of profits to from each book sale, or to sign up for our newsletter, potential give aways and competitions, go to: liajayebooks.com and enter your contact information. (We will never sell your information and take your privacy very seriously.)

Soul's Cry Press
soulscrypress.com

www.ingramcontent.com/pod-product-compliance
Lightning Source LLC
Chambersburg PA
CBHW070918260626
47162CB00007B/2714